Dear Reader,

As you may know, Harlequin Books is a longtime supporter of women's causes. We are proud to continue this tradition through the Harlequin More Than Words program. Established in 2004 as our main philanthropic initiative, the More Than Words program remains dedicated to celebrating and rewarding women who make extraordinary contributions to their community. Each year we solicit nominations from our readers and the general public and each year we find five very deserving women to honor.

We are pleased to present our current More Than Words honorees to you in this, our fifth *More Than Words* anthology. These individuals are real-life heroines who have each made a tremendous contribution to the charities they serve. Whether their initial motivation was based on a personal experience or on their need to intervene on behalf of others, each one's story gives proof of the overwhelming and far-reaching effect that a single act of kindness or a steadfast determination can have. These women have already been an inspiration to many, and we believe through sharing their stories they will inspire you, as well. Once again we have enlisted some of our most acclaimed authors— Heather Graham, Candace Camp, Stephanie Bond, Brenda Jackson and Tara Taylor Quinn—to write wonderful stories inspired by these recipients. These authors have generously donated their time and creativity to this project, and all proceeds will be reinvested in the Harlequin More Than Words program, further supporting causes that are of concern to women.

It is my pleasure to present *More Than Words, Volume 5*. I'm sure you will enjoy this book and will be as inspired by it as we are.

Please visit www.HarlequinMoreThanWords.com for more information, or to submit a nomination for next year's awards.

Sincerely,

Donna Hayes
Publisher and CEO
Harlequin Enterprises Ltd.

More Than Words

VOLUME 5

HEATHER GRAHAM

CANDACE CAMP

STEPHANIE BOND

BRENDA JACKSON

TARA TAYLOR QUINN

HARLEQUIN®

TORONTO • NEW YORK • LONDON
AMSTERDAM • PARIS • SYDNEY • HAMBURG
STOCKHOLM • ATHENS • TOKYO • MILAN • MADRID
PRAGUE • WARSAW • BUDAPEST • AUCKLAND

ISBN-13: 978-0-373-83669-7
ISBN-10:   0-373-83669-4

MORE THAN WORDS

Heather Graham Pozzessere is acknowledged as the author of
   If I Were Queen of the World.
Candace Camp is acknowledged as the author of *Breaking Line*.
Stephanie Hauck is acknowledged as the author of *It's Not About the Dress*.
Brenda Streater Jackson is acknowledged as the author of *Whispers of the Heart*.
Tara Taylor Quinn is acknowledged as the author of *The Mechanics of Love*.

This edition published by arrangement with Harlequin Books S.A.

www.eHarlequin.com

Printed in U.S.A.

CONTENTS

ERIN PUCK

∾ Toys . Calm ∾

Looking at her, you would never think Erin Puck, a vivacious, energetic twenty-one-year-old senior in college, has ever taken a sick day in her life. But when she was just twelve years old, doctors gave her parents terrifying news. Erin had a malignant brain tumor at the base of her cerebellum that would require surgery, six weeks of radiation therapy and thirty-six weeks of chemotherapy.

No child at any age should have to endure these procedures or spend weeks at the hospital, but as an early adolescent, Erin had a particularly tough time dealing with the treatment. Like many twelve-year-olds, she found her body changing, she was becoming interested in boys and she missed her friends—but was too embarrassed to let them see her looking pale and bald.

"I was a bad patient," she says now, laughing. "I hated the hospital and kept asking when I could go home. That was my constant question."

Erin also hated the noise of other children crying. When she mentioned this to one of the social workers there, the woman told her the hospital was running out of toys for the little kids to play with. They were scared, tired and bored.

Then came a moment that changed Erin's life. After going through a medical procedure, she arrived back in her hospital room to find a toy left on her bed. A family had donated it and left a note that said simply, "We care about you."

"I remember feeling so good, thinking that people besides my family knew I was having a hard time being sick by myself," she says.

Right then, Erin knew what she wanted to do: start a fundraiser and donate toys to the pediatric floor of the hospital.

In her small town of Little Silver, New Jersey, Erin was already a household name. Kids at school and at church knew about her condition. The local pizza restaurant sent deliveries to Erin to fatten her up. What she couldn't eat, her big brother, Ryan, took care of, deftly stepping in to help with the task. Other families dropped off food and gave Ryan rides to school so their parents, Laura and Bill, could focus on Erin and meeting work demands.

Knowing she had the town's support—and in the middle of her own treatment—Erin tacked up posters and set up boxes at school, the pizza place and her church to collect donations of new toys. Soon, a local reporter wrote an article about Erin's plight, and checks began rolling in.

"My dad was a banker, so he started to flip out," says Erin. "He was worried we'd get into trouble."

Toys.Calm, Erin's charity, was born.

Today, with the help of her family and a few volunteers, Toys.Calm has delivered over 200,000 toys, from stuffed animals to board games, Lego sets, books and video games, to area hospitals such as Robert Wood Johnson, Jersey Shore Medical and Monmouth Medical. Other donations make their way to the Children's Hospital of Philadelphia and New York Presbyterian Hospital. Toys.Calm has also raised money for larger items such as air-hockey tables and over a hundred computers.

The laptop program, also known as KID CONNECTIONS, is one of Erin's favorites. She remembers wishing she could have stayed in contact with her friends while in the hospital without having to wait for a computer to become available down the hall. Having a laptop loan program means kids can e-mail or instant message friends without needing to leave the bed, ensuring they still have their comfort, privacy and dignity.

Erin says she remembers the first toy she ever gave a child after her first shipment of donations came in. A toddler had just gotten a needle and her mother couldn't comfort her. Erin asked the mother what the little girl liked.

"Winnie-the-Pooh," the woman replied.

Erin wandered to the storage room where the toys were kept at the clinic and found a Pooh Bear puppet.

"As soon as I gave it to the little girl, the tears just stopped and there was a smile. I turned to my mom and said, 'This stuff really works. Toys really do calm!'" she says now.

Toys must be new, so as not to further compromise sick children's immune systems, and they're distributed by nurses and social workers the children already know. Erin says she rarely visits the children herself, since she remembers all too well the panic she felt every time the hospital doors opened, knowing she was in for some bad news or a needle. And even when their hearts are in the right place, when strangers make a visit with a gift, the children are often too sick or weak to pretend to be happy. Toys.Calm prefers a "No Thanks Required" policy instead.

Although Erin rarely gets to see where the toys end up, being the founder does have its perks—particularly when it comes time to buy them.

"It's so much fun going to Toys 'R' Us and having little kids look at me with my three big carts overflowing with toys. They can't believe I'm getting that much stuff. They think I'm buying it all for me!" she says.

These days Erin's mom and Toys.Calm president, Laura (at thirteen, Erin was too young to be declared president herself), handles much of the day-to-day work of writing thank-you notes, shipping toys and handling phone calls. Laura also mentors other parents with children who are facing frightening diagnoses. Meanwhile, Erin, healthy and vibrant for nine years running, is busy working toward a degree in political science at Villanova University in Pennsylvania, and is toying with the idea of going to law school. She's not completely committed to the idea yet, but says she knows what career she will definitely *not* pursue.

"I think it's funny that people keep asking me, 'Do you want to be a doctor?' No. I never want to be in a hospital again if I can help it," she says. "I'm a needlephobe. I see one on TV and I cringe."

For more information, visit www.toyscalm or write to Toys.Calm, P.O. Box 153, Little Silver, NJ, 07739.

HEATHER GRAHAM
~ IF I WERE QUEEN OF THE WORLD ~

HEATHER GRAHAM

❧—HEATHER GRAHAM—❧

New York Times and *USA TODAY* bestselling author Heather Graham majored in theater arts at the University of South Florida. After a stint of several years in dinner theater and backup vocals, Heather began to write following the birth of her third child. Since then, she has written more than one hundred novels and novellas in varied genres, including series romance, suspense, historical romance, vampire fiction, time travel and the occult. She has also been published in approximately twenty languages and has 60 million books in print. The recipient of many awards, Heather has had books selected for the Doubleday Book Club and the Literary Guild, and has made guest appearances on many television programs, including *Today* and *Entertainment Tonight*. She loves travel and anything that has to do with the water, and is a certified scuba diver. Married since high school graduation and the mother of five, she believes her career has been an incredible gift. Her greatest love in life remains her family, but she also is grateful every day to be doing for a living something she loves so very much.

❧ PROLOGUE ❧

T he sun was out, and it was a beautiful day. Spring had come
to the mountains and valleys of Pittsburgh, Pennsylvania,
and it did so with a dazzling display of greens and pastels.
Laurie closed her eyes, feeling the warmth on her face. When
she opened them again, *he* was there. Right there, not ten feet
away, on the balcony of Care for the Children Hospital.

For a moment, she forgot that she was rail-thin and wearing a
brightly colored scarf her mother had purchased for her and tied
about her bald head with forced cheer and enthusiasm, and that
she wasn't certain there would be many more days, beautiful or
otherwise, left for her.

He was tall and well-built, probably a few years older than she was, and absolutely gorgeous. He had both hands on the rail and was looking out over the mountains, but not really seeing them. She knew that because she could see his eyes. They were deep and dark, but the expression in them was distant. Tormented, she thought.

He had sable-dark hair to go with those hypnotic eyes, and strong features.

He noticed her before she had a chance to even think about hiding. She wasn't sure that, even if she looked *normal,* she would ever be in his league, and now, thanks to the cancer, she looked anything but.

"Hello," he said. He had a great voice. And then he smiled. She definitely felt very much alive at that moment. Her heart fluttered with the speed of hummingbird wings.

"Hello," she replied. She realized that his smile, like his gaze, was sad.

He came over to the patio table where she was sitting, and drew up a chair across from her. "It's a beautiful day, huh?" he asked her. "I think spring has finally come."

"Yeah, feel that sun. And check out the flowers." She smiled and tried to keep the conversation going, all the while wondering if she could be any more inane.

He stared at her very seriously, then offered her a rueful smile. "You're being treated here."

"Yes," she said dryly. "I'm what they call a 'frequent flyer.' I almost think of this place as home, I've been here so much the last few years."

"I'm sorry," he told her earnestly.

"Don't be," she answered. She really wished she had hair; she would have loved to flip it dismissively over her shoulder. "It's all right, really. The doctors here are great. This is as good a home away from home as you're ever going to get."

She wasn't sure why she was trying to convince him that the hospital was all right. Before he had walked out on the balcony, she had been feeling depressed, torn between hope and fear. Hope that the treatments she was receiving really were working as well as her doctors said.

Fear that each day in the sun could be one of a dwindling few.

He leaned back, his smile becoming more rueful. "A frequent flyer, huh? So how do you spend your time when you're here?"

She laughed. "Well, I do my best to keep up with school."

A slight frown creased his brow. "How old are you?"

She knew that most people had a hard time guessing her age, what with the chemo-caused baldness. "Seventeen," she told him. "I'm hoping to graduate with my class in June. How about you?"

"Twenty-one," he said. "And if I managed to graduate, so can you. I was pretty wild back then."

Looking at him now, she couldn't imagine him being anything less than serious.

"What else do you do, besides schoolwork?" he asked.

"I love books," she confessed. "I read a lot."

"Aha."

"And I play a game."

"A game?" he asked.

She looked down, for once not noticing how pale her skin was, how she could see the veins in her hands, because she was wondering why she had spoken. If she actually told him the truth, she was going to sound awfully immature.

"What game?" he persisted.

She looked back up at him and saw real kindness in his eyes. Not pity. Just empathy.

"All right," she said. "Just don't go sharing this with anyone, huh? I have a few friends here, and we like to play something called If I Were Queen of the World. Or King," she added lightly, "as the case may be. It takes our mind off things."

"Let's play," he suggested.

She opened her mouth, surprised, and a little afraid. Drop-dead gorgeous, *healthy* guys didn't usually go in for games that belonged to dreamers who didn't know if they would see another birthday.

"You don't have to entertain me, you know." She offered him what she hoped was a mature smile.

"*You'll* be entertaining *me*," he told her. "Please."

"Okay..." She looked away. "All right, if I were queen of the world, no child would ever contract a horrible disease."

"If I were king of the world," he said, "no child would ever be born with a congenital disease."

She nodded at him, smiling. "Very good. If I were queen of the world, no country would ever go to war against another."

"If I were king of the world," he countered, "there would be no need for countries to go to war. There would be no hunger or poverty, and everyone would have a safe place to live and a job they enjoyed."

She laughed. "You do know how to take things a step further, don't you? Why don't you start this time?"

"Um, okay." He was thoughtful for a moment. "If I were king of the world...there would be no such thing as pain."

She hesitated, silent. "I like the concept. But pain is important. It lets us know when something is seriously wrong."

"But what happens when it's wrong and there's nothing that can be done?"

She saw again the torment in his eyes. She wished so badly that she could alleviate that pain.

"If I were queen of the world," she said, "I would make it so that anytime there was pain, it was for a reason. And it would never last long, and what came after would always be beautiful."

"From your lips to God's ears," he said fervently.

"If I were queen of the world," she added quickly, wanting so much to see him smile again, "this would be a ski resort. And we'd

23

be on top of the mountain, ready to ski down and then have hot chocolate by the fire."

"And if I were king of the world, it would be the most wonderful hot chocolate ever served, with little marshmallows and whipped cream on top."

"And if I were queen of the world, there would be something to go with the hot chocolate. Maybe shortbread, or pound cake."

He laughed. "I'm a chocolate kind of guy. If I were king of the world, we would have fudge brownies with nuts to go with our hot chocolate."

"Perfect. And the fire would be hot but not too hot, and the couches would be all puffy and super comfortable. Plus there'd be music, but not too loud," she added.

"And there would be all kinds of books, so when we wanted, we could sit and read, and then tell each other about what we were reading," he said.

"Nice," she murmured. "If I were queen of the world, I'd have back the book my grandmother gave me that I lost when we moved once, and I'd read it again and be very careful with it this time."

"What book?" he asked her, a smile returning to his face at last.

"A twenty-fifth anniversary illustrated edition of *Little Women*— and don't you dare laugh. I've always loved the story, plus it was a present, and when my grandmother passed away recently, I felt awful all over again about losing it. Anyway, I guarantee you, if I were queen of the world, I'd find that book. And then I'd make the world perfect."

He laughed. "That would be an accomplishment, finding that exact book. But finding that same edition...well, that might be possible."

"I don't know. My grandmother bought it when an antique bookstore went out of business. I don't think it would be easy to find. It's a nice idea, though, and I'm going to hang on to it."

He grinned, but then grew somber, studying her eyes. He offered her his hand suddenly. "I'm Brian Thompson, and you've helped make today easier for me. I appreciate all the time you've given me."

She shook her head. "No, not at all. You're very nice. Thank you for *your* time."

"And you are?" he asked her, the teasing light in his eyes deepening.

"Laurie," she said. "Laurie Mayberry."

He rose. "I have to go back in. But I enjoyed your game. Very much."

She laughed. "I love to dream about big things, but the little things can make a difference, too. And who knows? Little things can always create a greater good."

"I'm sure you're right. *You* definitely improved *my* day."

"I'm glad. Bye."

"Bye."

Then he was gone. She stared at the door to the patient lounge and wished he would come back. She thought about how, for the few minutes he had been with her, she hadn't felt ugly or frail. And she hadn't been afraid.

He didn't come back, of course. But a few minutes later, her mother came out. And there were tears in her eyes.

Laurie's heart sank. She knew she was about to get bad news.

"Laurie!" her mom cried, dropping to her knees by her chair. "Laurie, your blood count is normal. *Normal!* You can come home in a few days. We'll have to keep a close check on things, but…" She started crying in earnest, unable to talk anymore.

Her father came out then, looking like a man who had just won the lottery.

"Baby, did you hear?" he asked. And then he started to cry, too.

Laurie was simultaneously incredibly happy and afraid to believe the good news as she hugged her parents and cried with them, with the sun shining down like a good omen.

She found herself thinking about Brian Thompson. Maybe, in a way, he *had* been the king of the world. He had talked to her, and magic had happened.

A FEW DAYS LATER, Laurie was packing her things and listening to the long list of instructions the nurse was giving her, when Sabrina Ewell, one of the young volunteers from the college, stepped into the room, carrying a package. "This came for you," she said.

"What is it?" Laurie asked.

"I don't know. I guess you'll just have to open it," she teased.

Laurie did so. There was no card, nothing to identify who the package had come from.

But she knew.

Inside the plain brown wrapping was a book. A twenty-fifth anniversary illustrated edition of Louisa May Alcott's *Little Women*. Laurie stared at it incredulously, then turned to Sabrina. "Where did it come from?"

"It was left for you at the nurses' station. Don't you know who sent it?"

"It must be from the guy I met a few days ago," Laurie said.

"What guy?" Sabrina asked with a smile.

"His name was Brian Thompson."

"Oh," the nurse said knowingly.

"Oh?" Laurie repeated. "What does that mean?"

"Nothing bad—I mean, nothing bad about Brian. He lost a cousin the other morning. She had been sick for a very long time, and she'd been unconscious for weeks, but even so..." The nurse smiled quickly, trying not to cloud Laurie's departure. "He's a nice young man. His grandfather was the lieutenant governor, and he grew up with a strong sense of responsibility. Both his parents are gone, but he was always there for his cousin. You must have said something that made him feel better, for him to get you a present like that." She squared her shoulders and turned deliberately cheerful. "And now, young lady, *you* are going home."

The nurse went back to her list of instructions, but Laurie didn't hear a thing. She was too busy staring at the book, amazed. He hadn't just been gorgeous. He'd been kind. In the midst of his own pain, he had cared about her, a girl he had never met before and would probably never see again.

Her parents arrived then, her mother nervous, with the energy of a hyper Yorkie. She noticed the book right away. "Oh, goodness! Where did you get that? It looks almost like the one Nana gave you."

"A friend found it for me," Laurie told her. "And, yes, it is almost like the one from Nana."

Before they left, she wrote a note for Brian and left it at the nurses' station. She didn't think he'd be back to get it, though. His cousin was gone; arrangements had been made. This was a good hospital, a good place to be if you were a sick child.

But few people came back.

She certainly hoped that *she* wouldn't be back. Ever.

CHAPTER
~ ONE ~

Five years later

"**M**ayberry!"

Craig Wilson didn't talk. He barked.

Somewhere in his life, he had probably been told that the editor of a major newspaper was required to be brusque and sound as if he was growling all the time. He wasn't a bad guy; Laurie was thrilled to be working for him, even if she usually drew the most mundane assignments. When she walked into the office that morning, Craig was striding through the rows of desks and computer screens as if he was running from a fire. But that was his way. Underneath the gruffness, he was a nice man. Maybe he was afraid that if people suspected he was too nice, he wouldn't be respected as a top-notch journalist.

"I'm here," Laurie said. She glanced quickly at her watch. She wasn't late. She'd worked at the *Valley News* for almost a year, and she hadn't been late a single day yet. It was also surprising to see Craig anxious to see *her*. She wasn't one of his ace reporters; she was more bottom of the totem pole. She was young, and she was new.

"Sybil Chaney is getting married up in St. Marys."

"St. Marys," Laurie repeated, looking at him blankly.

"St. Marys, Pennsylvania. Just a few hours north of home. You need to head up there. Since she's big local money and we're a local paper, we'll do a major piece, covering the lead-up and the wedding itself, which will be Saturday night. Which means you need to get up there ASAP," Craig said.

She stared at him, not at all sure why he was so gung ho to give her an assignment about a socialite's wedding.

"Wedding. Great," she said.

"Don't be a wiseass, young lady," he admonished.

"I said great," she protested.

"Do your homework. It's Sybil Chaney. She was engaged to the Braff Steel heir and threw him over for an artist. It's a great human-interest story. Sal will follow you up in time to take pictures of the place and the ceremony. You can go home now and pack, so you can leave this afternoon."

"Wait!" Laurie called. He had already started for his office. She ran after him, and he spun around and stared until she felt her cheeks redden. "I can't go until Thursday morning."

"Why? Have I given you an assignment I don't remember?" he asked her.

"No."

"Then...?"

"I have to go to the hospital tomorrow night," she said.

His brow furrowed. "Are you ill?"

"No, I'm fine. I go every other Wednesday night. You know that. You're the one who allows me to canvas the office for toys, books and electronics for the kids."

"It's that important to you? You can't miss one night?"

"Will it make any difference if I go now or Thursday morning?"

He stared at her a moment longer. "I have a solution. Go to the hospital tonight. And be in St. Marys by noon tomorrow. You have an actual appointment to talk with the bride at one. And I've finagled an invitation to the wedding itself. You should be thanking me for this one, not making excuses to get out of it."

"Of course. A wedding for a woman I don't know. I'll be all teary-eyed. Craig, I'm not sure if I can switch nights at the hospital. They have very strict rules about people coming in to work with the children," she told him.

Then she hesitated. *Sybil Chaney.* Maybe she *did* know the woman. A girl named Sybil had been a fellow patient at Care for the Children Hospital, and now that Laurie thought about it, she recalled her last name *had* been Chaney or something similar. Like Laurie, she had beaten cancer. At the hospital, though, all the children had been the same. Laurie had never associated the local heiress with the girl she had known five years ago.

"I'll take care of it."

"What?" she asked, deep in her memories of the lowest time of her life.

"The hospital."

"Craig—"

"Just pack up your goodie bags and head over tonight. And be ready to drive up to St. Marys tomorrow."

She was silent, still not certain he had any sway with the children's hospital.

She let out a sigh as he disappeared into his office. Maybe he *could* arrange for her to go in this evening. She had done the Wednesday night routine for so long, she wasn't sure herself what the current rules were. At least he hadn't suggested that her job was more important, and if she wanted to keep it, she had to cancel. To many people, her time there might be no big deal, but those Wednesday nights back at the hospital were important to her. Laurie had sworn to herself that as long as she lived she would never forget what it was like to be a kid in a hospital, and she had wanted to help others who found themselves in a situation she knew all too well. Then, just a year ago, she had heard about Toys.Calm, an incredible organization started by someone just like her, a young woman who had been a cancer patient at the age of thirteen and had received an anonymous gift that had made a world of difference to her. Laurie simply loved the name of the Web site—Toys.Calm. Because toys and books really did provide comfort and a sense of calm in the midst of the chaos and stress of a long and depressing hospital stay.

She still valued her book, her illustrated edition of *Little Women*. The book that Brian Thompson had brought for her. Little things could make so much of a difference for a child in the hospital.

"A SOCIETY WEDDING. WOW," Jack Mason teased as she sat down in her cubicle. Jack, who had the cube next to her, was good-looking in a tawny-haired beach boy way, and he was a flirt. He had been with the paper a year longer and was a thousand times more cutthroat than she was. She was pretty sure he would trample his own mother to get a story.

She liked to think that she got more of a story by being a good listener. Of course, it didn't matter all that much how well you listened when the topic was a dog show or the newest diet craze.

"Yeah, thanks," she replied, then turned her attention to her work. There was nothing wrong with human-interest pieces, she told herself.

She was deep in an obit when she felt a presence at her shoulder. Looking up, she saw Craig standing over her.

"You're on for tonight."

"Really?"

"And tomorrow, bright and early, St. Marys," he said gruffly, then nodded curtly and moved away.

A few minutes later she looked up and saw that Jack had wheeled his chair over and was right behind her.

"What's on for tonight?" he whispered, looking from side to side to make sure he wasn't being overheard. "What are you and the boss cooking up?"

Good God, the man thought she had something going with Craig, she realized after a moment's puzzlement. And he was jealous, afraid that she would start getting the better stories.

She almost laughed out loud. "Pardon?"

"Tonight. What's the secret mission?" Jack asked.

"It wouldn't be a secret if I told you."

"Come on, what's going on? I'm an investigative reporter, so you know I'll just hound you until I find out the truth."

"Jack," she said firmly, "my life is none of your business."

He arched a brow, indicating the entire office. "It might be *our* business," he said knowingly.

It would have been amusing to play him for a while, but she didn't want to take a chance on any repercussions. "Jack, I'm going to the hospital tonight. I was supposed to go tomorrow, but I'm going tonight instead, so I can leave tomorrow to cover the wedding."

"You're going to the hospital? Why? Are you sick?"

She let out a long sigh, thinking, *No, not anymore. I'm one of the lucky ones. I'm cancer free, and I have been for five years. But I'll never forget what it was like to be a kid with cancer and how one brightened moment can mean everything.*

"No. I drop off toys and books and things for kids who are sick, remember?" she told him.

"Oh, yeah." He studied her face for a long time, as if making sure she was telling the truth, and once he decided that she was, he lost interest and wheeled his chair back to his own desk."

SABRINA EWELL WAS NOW a resident in pediatric oncology, but tonight she was the one to greet Laurie, instead of the community relations director, Tim Wadell.

"Hey there," Sabrina said, hurrying over to help her get things out of her minivan.

"Hey," Laurie replied. "Thanks for letting me come in tonight."

"It's not a problem. You know Tim. He's completely anal, but he has the kids' welfare at heart. And speaking of the kids, a couple of the younger ones can't wait for you to read another chapter from *Dragon-Spy.* So what have you got?" Sabrina asked, looking into the back of the van.

"Tons of video games, and—you're not going to believe this—two almost new computers. My next-door neighbor has a small business and just upgraded, so she gave me two of their old computers. She said this way she gets a tax cut."

"That's wonderful. Come on, I'll give you a hand."

Sabrina helped her on and off the elevator, and then toward the glass-walled playroom. As they approached, Laurie was surprised to see that there was already a large crowd of children, some in chairs, some on the floor, sitting around the small stage, where some kind of performance seemed to be under way.

"Sabrina, what's going on in there?"

"Oh, it's just Brian. He always comes on Tuesdays."

Laurie frowned and asked slowly, "Brian...Thompson?"

Sabrina was momentarily startled, and frowned at her. "Oh, right, you know him, don't you?"

"I don't really know him. I met him that one time when his cousin died. I had no idea he still came here."

"Yes. I can't believe I never thought to mention it. He's been coming for the last few years with stuff for the kids. He brought in a Wii a few months ago, and he's donated several portable DVD players for the kids who are bedbound." She smiled. "You know, come to think of it, he told me once that he'd been inspired by Toys.Calm, too. Amazing, the way one person's charitable dream can inspire others, isn't it? I love it. Anyway, Brian is just finishing up."

"No problem," Laurie said, looking through the window again. He was reading—and directing two kids in their early teens, who were laughing and acting out whatever Brian was telling them to do. The performance seemed to be ending just then, because suddenly all the kids stood up, clapping and laughing.

Laurie smiled as she looked at their happy faces, but she felt her heart squeeze, as well. It was so easy to remember when she had been one of the children in that room. Like several of the ones there tonight, she had often gone everywhere with an IV attachment following her. And yet the human spirit was amazing. No matter what misfortunes had entered their lives, these children were clearly determined to enjoy every moment.

"Let's go on in," Sabrina said.

As she walked beside the other woman, Laurie felt her heart start pounding, so loudly that it seemed to echo in her ears. Brian was a few years older, but her reaction to him hadn't changed at all.

He was still gorgeous, with that dark hair and those deep dark eyes. His face was less boyish now, his features more sculpted, and he was taller, with a man's physique. And he had the kind of confidence that didn't seem to need applause or recognition, though she could see on his face how much he enjoyed being there, surrounded by the children.

He looked across the room at Sabrina and Laurie, and smiled. "I heard the kids were getting a double treat tonight," he said, and glanced at his watch. "I finished on time, right?"

"Exactly," Sabrina said.

"It wouldn't have mattered," Laurie stated. "They were having a great time."

He laughed. "Thanks, but Mary-Katherine over there warned me that the story lady was coming, so I'd better hurry up. How do you do? I'm Brian Thompson."

She blushed, feeling foolish. He hadn't recognized her. Well, of course he hadn't. She gained twenty pounds and turned into a grown woman with a head of long blond hair. She accepted his hand. "Actually, we've met."

"Oh?" He looked at her curiously, then suddenly seemed to recognize her. "There is something about your eyes." He laughed. "That sounds like a line, doesn't it?"

"You met me here about five years ago. I was a patient."

"Oh." He studied her, and his grin deepened. *Little Women.*

She nodded. "Thank you so much. I left you a note, but they didn't know if you were coming back."

"After my cousin died," he said, "it was a very long time before I came back."

"I heard. I'm very sorry."

He nodded, looking away, then returning his gaze to her. "Well, it's wonderful to see you again. I'll leave you to your dragon story. The children are waiting for it."

"Thanks, Brian," Sabrina told him.

"Always a pleasure," he replied.

He started out of the room, but then he looked back, his expression a little unsure. Laurie felt that thumping in her chest once again. "You know," he said softly, "you really made things better for me. You were so sick, but at the same time, you were still so full of hope and life. And when you told me about the book...I don't know. I found it for you, and after that I thought about sending things now and then, but later read about Toys.Calm and started making a habit of it."

"Me, too!" she said, smiling.

"They were my model, my inspiration, but it was because of you that I knew I really could do it."

"Thank you. I still have the book," she told him. "And I cherish it."

He nodded, looking delightfully awkward once again. "Well, good night."

"Good night."

"That's amazing," Sabrina said after he'd left. "I can't believe he remembered you after so many kids and so many years."

"Five years. Not exactly decades," Laurie reminded her dryly.

"Yes, but still...you know, he's a huge lawyer now."

"Tall, and well-built, but I wouldn't say huge," Laurie said lightly.

Sabrina looked at her with exasperation. "Very funny. But I mean it. There's talk that he'll run for mayor in a few years, and then...well, he's got the right connections for a major political career."

"He's also a really nice guy, whether he gets into politics or not," Laurie said, not at all certain why she was so averse to the idea of Brian Thompson being *huge*.

Was it because she was afraid that "huge" meant out of her league?

"Laurie! Laurie!"

A little hand was tugging at her skirt. It was Mary-Katherine, smiling up at her. A brightly colored bandanna was tied around the child's head, to hide the hair loss from chemotherapy treatments. Laurie remembered how important the choice of bandanna could be.

"Hey, you. You look great. Your eyes are so bright and pretty tonight," Laurie said.

"I can't wait to hear more about the dragon."

Laurie laughed. "Okay, I'm ready. I've got my book all set to go."

"Everybody sit down!" Mary-Katherine shouted. "It's time for the dragon story."

Sabrina smiled and gave Laurie a wave, then started out of the playroom. Two volunteer monitors were there, though. The children were never left without hospital supervision.

Laurie sat down where Brian Thompson had been just minutes earlier.

"Hi, everybody," she said.

They called out to her in greeting, and then settled in to hear more of the book.

She read a couple of chapters, then talked with the kids about the characters. One of the older boys had some suggestions for changing things, but Mary-Katherine told him indignantly to write his own story.

"You were here once, right, Laurie?" Mary-Katherine asked.

"Yes, I was."

"And now you're a writer," the boy with the suggestions said.

"I work for the paper and I write news stories," Laurie explained. "One day, though, I'm going to write fiction. Fun stories—about dragons."

"For children?" Mary-Katherine asked. "Like us?"

"For children just like you," Laurie assured her.

"You and Brian should come together sometime," a teenage boy told her. He'd been one of the actors in Brian's play. "That would be cool."

Laurie's heart made another annoying leap.

"Sure. I'd love to come when Brian is here sometime. We could work out some kind of a story together," she said, and smiled.

A little while later she told them all good-night, promising that she would be back.

Some of the kids would have gone home by then, she knew. But some of them were frequent flyers, just as she had been.

"You can't come tomorrow night?" Mary-Katherine asked her.

"No, I'm so sorry. I have to work," Laurie said. "That's why I was here tonight." Tomorrow night she would be writing about a rich girl about to have a beautiful wedding.

And what was wrong with that? she chided herself. Just because Sybil Chaney was rich, that didn't mean she didn't deserve the wedding of her dreams.

It just seemed…

Well, it was hardly the kind of story that was going to change the world.

It wasn't fulfilling, exciting, like making a difference in these children's lives, or even like those few seconds when she had seen Brian Thompson, when her heart had started to race….

She waved and hurried out, suddenly anxious to get home.

CHAPTER
~TWO~

L aurie was surprised to discover that there was a great
deal to enjoy in tiny St. Marys, Pennsylvania.

The drive up was beautiful, with the Alleghenies
rising high and displaying the onset of spring in all its brilliant
colors.

The massive Chaney family lodge, where Sybil had chosen to
live, was just outside the town limits. The property itself wasn't
fenced, but there was a wire perimeter closer to the house, so
artfully camouflaged by the landscaping that it was difficult to
see. There was also a gate across the drive before Laurie reached
the house, and she had to roll down the window and press a
button on a call box to get through. She saw several strategically
positioned security guards, along with several cameras. Laurie

hadn't met Sybil yet, but already had the feeling that the woman loved the forest and its wildlife—and that rich did not equate to stupid.

Laurie studied the two-story house. It was beautiful in a rustic style, rising from the ground as naturally as the trees and following the contours of a gently sloping hill.

As she was getting out of her car, she was greeted by a tall man in a flannel shirt who strode from the house.

"Morning. I'm guessing you're the reporter we've been expecting?"

"Yes, I'm Laurie Mayberry."

"I'm Danny Turo."

"Hi," she said, surprised, as she took his hand. She'd guessed he was the caretaker, but Danny Turo was the groom-to-be.

"Welcome," he told her.

"Thanks, and congratulations," she replied warmly.

"I'm a very lucky man," he said. "Come on in. Sybil is just inside. We've been expecting you."

The interior of the house was as charming as the exterior, not ostentatious, with leather and wood furnishings, Native American art and a pair of huge, tail-wagging mongrels.

The bride-to-be came over as Laurie hunkered down to pet the dogs.

"Sybil," Laurie said happily. "It *is* you."

"Of course it's me. I asked for you, you know." They exchanged a huge hug.

"You're well?" Laurie asked.

Sybil nodded, the glow in her eyes one only survivors could share. "And you?"

"I'm great, but I feel like an idiot. I never put two and two together and realized that you were *the* Sybil Chaney until yesterday."

"You don't mind being here, do you? Covering a wedding instead of real news?" Sybil asked.

"I can honestly say that I'm delighted to be here," Laurie told her, and realized that she was. It was great to see the girl who had once been so sick looking so well and happy. Laurie thought back to being in the hospital and all the dreams they'd had, and how they'd known those dreams wouldn't matter at all if they didn't beat the cancer.

"My photographer will be up this afternoon," Laurie said. "His name is Sal Pacheco, and he's really good. You'll like him."

"I'm sure I will," Sybil declared. "Come on. Danny and I can show you the place, and we'll catch up."

After a little while Danny slipped away, and Laurie knew he was giving the two of them a chance to visit.

They sat outside, on one of the garden benches. Sybil talked about how she had almost married the kind of man she was expected to marry, until she remembered that life came with no guarantees. She wanted to be happy, not dutiful, and she was happy with Danny. "And you?"

"Journalism school," Laurie told her.

"You always wanted that. Whenever we played Queen of the World, that was part of your dream."

"We were both dreamers."

"And we're getting to live our dreams," Sybil said, and they hugged again, then cried a little, remembering the past.

"So, Ms. Almost-married woman," Laurie said, "what's most important in a relationship?"

"Are you asking as a friend or a reporter?" Sybil asked.

"Both," she admitted ruefully.

"Love, passion and trust," Sybil stated. "Trust is one of the most important elements in any relationship. Danny and I trust each other with everything."

Just then Danny himself appeared, along with Sal, who had just arrived. Sal was gruff and nearing retirement, but he was an award-winning photographer. He took pictures of the happy couple in the house, out by the pool, and looking at the brochure for their honeymoon cruise to the Caribbean. Afterward, Sybil invited him to join them for dinner, adding that a few friends would be coming, as well.

After that people suddenly materialized to show them where they would be staying. Sue-Lynn, Sybil's assistant, and Bertram, the head of security, were gracious and efficient.

The "guest cottage" was larger than most people's houses and was set up like a small motel, with a common area and eight bedrooms, each with a private entrance, either on the ground level or via a stairway. Laurie and Sal were assigned ground-floor rooms that opened onto small porches. After they had unpacked, they met again outside Sal's room.

"So you two were friends when you were kids?" he asked.

"Yes," Laurie said. "I hadn't seen her for years. I didn't even recognize the name at first. We met when we were both being treated for cancer."

"Maybe that's why she's so nice," Sal said thoughtfully. "Most people have a tendency to take things for granted. Maybe we all need to pause a moment to appreciate life."

Laurie hugged him impulsively. When he looked at her as if she'd lost her mind, she chuckled. "Sorry, I didn't mean to go all mushy."

He smiled. "Listen, I'd love to get some pictures of the woods, the flowers on the hill. Come with me. My photos will be a lot more interesting with someone in them."

TEN MINUTES LATER, they were off. She had changed into a casual skirt and even heels at Sal's request. They kept sinking into the dirt as they headed toward a grove of aspens shimmering gently in the breeze, a profusion of wildflowers growing around them.

He had her lie back among the flowers and close her eyes.

She heard a rustling and opened them again, expecting to see Sal. But, to her amazement, she found herself staring up into dark eyes. Her heart immediately started that annoying racing again.

She was looking up at Brian Thompson, who was kneeling at her side, grinning, twirling a daisy between his fingers.

"I'm sorry," he said. "I didn't mean to startle you." His grin deepened. "You were just too tempting, lying there. And then your photographer saw me and waved me into the picture." Brian stood, and reached down to help her to her feet. As she dusted grass from her skirt, he bent to help, then drew back, as if thinking it might be too intimate a gesture.

Laurie introduced the two men, and then Brian turned back to her.

"So your day job is modeling?" he asked.

She flushed. "No, I'm a reporter."

"Here to cover the wedding?" he asked her.

"Yes."

"Sybil says you're an old friend. Your paths crossed at the hospital, I take it?"

"Yes," Laurie said again, desperately wishing that she could come up with something witty to say. Something charming. Even something semi-intelligent.

"Well, we're housemates then."

"You're staying for the wedding?" she asked, then wanted to kick herself. Of course he was. Naturally, he and Sybil were friends. They were both from money and had probably moved in the same circles all their lives.

"Sybil and I go way back," he told her, confirming her guess.

"My family has a place not far from here, but Sybil wanted friends around for tonight's dinner, the bachelor and bachelorette parties tomorrow night and the wedding day, so even though I have a place down the street, so to speak, I'm staying in the guest house."

"Oh," Laurie said lamely.

Brian glanced at his watch. "Hey, I think it's about time for dinner."

She looked quickly at her own watch, then started brushing at her clothes again. "Maybe I should change…"

"You look fine. Just one or two twigs here, so if you don't mind…" He reached out, plucked the offending objects from her hair, then smoothed it down. "Honestly, you look lovely."

"Do I look lovely, too?" Sal teased. "I'm going to go put away my equipment. See you at dinner."

"So you're a reporter, huh?" Brian asked, as they headed for the house.

She nodded. "Sort of. Dog shows, Renaissance festivals, chili cook-offs… I'm not exactly covering the important stuff yet."

"Rome wasn't built in a day," he reminded her.

"No," she agreed, and looked up at him. "So what about you? I'm told politics run in your family."

She was surprised when the comment made him wince. "I hear that all the time. I shouldn't mind, I suppose. But going into politics should be a choice. You have to study the issues, then weigh what other people are doing against what you think you can do, and maybe even make a few compromises. One thing I'd like to fight for if I *do* go into politics, however, is better pay for teachers. They hold the future in their hands. They create the citizens who will inherit the world." He stopped speaking and stared at her ruefully. "Sorry. That's one of my causes, I guess you could say."

"No, it's fine. I agree. Teachers should definitely make more money."

"If I were king of the world," he told her, grinning, "they would."

She grinned back. "And let's not forget the nurses. I'm not denying the brilliance of many doctors, but nurses are with patients around the clock. They deal with so much of the hard work!"

"You're right. My mother told me I was delivered by a nurse. Then the doctor came in ten minutes later and took all the credit."

"There you go. If I were queen of the world, nurses would definitely receive much more acclaim. And better paychecks, too," she added.

He slipped an arm around her shoulder as if it was the most natural thing in the world, and led her into the house.

THE GROUP THAT GATHERED for dinner that evening was somehow bigger than Laurie had expected. Sybil's only two cousins were there, along with her college roommate. Danny's best friend, a rock musician named Hal Perry, and his brother, Joshua, rounded out the guest list.

Sybil sent Sal back for his camera, and told Laurie to be sure to mention Hal Perry—and the Allegheny Atoms—in her story.

Dinner was a friendly affair, with lots of joking and laughter. Naturally, given that a wedding was only a few days away, the talk turned to romance.

Sal told them he was married, and hadn't dated since 1975.

"I guess I'm dating my job," Laurie admitted when it was her turn. "I'm the new man—well, woman—on the paper, and sometimes it seems like I'm always working."

"Well, thank God, you're working here, then," Sybil told her. "At least you'll get to have some fun."

"She isn't always working," Brian said, studying her from his end of the table. "Laurie volunteers at the children's hospital. She brings books and reads to the kids, and she collects donations of toys and electronics, too."

"That's wonderful!" Sybil said, and Laurie found herself blushing.

Dinner ended a little while later, and while some of the guests opted for an after-dinner drink, Laurie excused herself. She wanted to start writing notes for her story. She was surprised when Brian told Sybil good-night, as well.

"I'm over twenty-five, you know," he said with a grin that always made Laurie's heart beat faster. "I want to be able to stay awake tomorrow night at the bachelor party. Laurie, I'll walk you out."

They left together, stepping into the soft air of a spring night.

"I hope you're having a good time," he said. "You clearly spend a lot of time at work, and you're volunteering when you aren't working, so you *do* deserve to have some fun."

"I have fun when I volunteer, believe me. I love what I do at the hospital," she exclaimed.

"Just one of the things I like about you," he told her.

She couldn't help wondering what the other things were, and warned her thundering heart to take care. She had fallen a little bit in love with him the first time she had seen him, when she hadn't dreamed that he would ever speak to her.

Before she had known he was the kind of gorgeous that really mattered: gorgeous on the inside.

"Thanks." She forced herself to speak lightly.

"You're so passionate about your world," he said.

"I have reason to be. As you know."

"I do. And I feel the same way." He linked his arm through hers as they neared the guest house. "I think we should combine our efforts one night a month and come up with something extra special for the kids. What do you say?"

"I say that sounds wonderful." And it did, she thought, not the least because it would mean getting to spend time with him.

He talked about his desire to write skits for the children to perform, and manuals for other volunteers around the country to use in planning programs to help sick kids. As she listened, she could hear the thumping of her heart the whole time, and wondered how he could miss it. When they reached the guest cottage, he walked her to her door. "It's really great to see you again. I never forgot you, you know. You were waiting that day, weren't you? For results. You had to have been miserable, terrified, wondering what you were going to hear, but still you sat there, making me feel better."

"And you sent me a wonderful thank-you gift. How you managed to find that book so quickly is beyond me."

"It was nothing compared to what you did for me. Anyway, good night."

"Good night," she repeated.

Then he kissed her.

It wasn't a passionate kiss, like in the movies. It wasn't even on the lips. He just drew her close, so close that she could smell the scent of his aftershave and feel the heat of his body, and planted his lips gently on her forehead.

Thankfully, she did nothing foolish. She didn't pass out, she didn't stagger. She even managed a pleasant smile and another "Good night."

But when she was in her room, she sank to the mattress and fell backward, staring at the ceiling.

God help her, could she be falling in love?

CHAPTER
❧ THREE ❧

The following day was the bachelorette party, which was both fun and extremely low-key. Sybil was given the usual lingerie and silly gifts, and then they set off for what turned out to be a local medieval show with a few risqué jokes. Afterward they went to a club and ran into the bachelor party, none of whom had imbibed any more heavily, or behaved any more outrageously, than the women had.

Laurie found herself cherishing every minute with Brian. And the more she was with him, the more she admired him. His intelligence came through in everything he said, he had nothing bad to say about anyone, and he was impassioned but rational even when discussing politics. After the party he walked her back to her room again and, despite the presence of a number of other guests, kissed her once more.

This time on the lips, and without hesitation. It was a "public" kiss, nothing wildly passionate, but it seemed to burn with a sweet heat from the moment it was delivered to the moment she finally fell asleep.

SHE DIDN'T SEE BRIAN at all on Friday and tried to lose herself in her writing so she wouldn't feel disappointed that he was busy with his duties as a groomsman, and then with the rehearsal dinner. The morning of the wedding, she sat down to look over what she'd written, and was amazed to realize how good it was. Yes, it was a human-interest piece, but Sybil came across as a real person, both beautiful and down-to-earth, not some stereotypical rich girl. Sure, Laurie had all the stats on the gown, the guests and the venue, but the real focus was on the life Sybil led, giving to so many causes, and the life she meant to lead as a wife and mother.

The wedding itself was beautiful. Brian looked impeccable in his tux, standing with other members of the wedding party. Laurie listened with tears in her eyes as the couple exchanged vows they had written themselves.

She was happy to find herself seated next to Brian at the reception that followed at the country club. He invited her to slow dance, and once they took to the floor, he asked her when she was leaving.

"Right after the reception. My article has to be finished up by tomorrow, so my editor can go over it and it can run next weekend. How about you? What's up next on your social calendar?"

"Social calendar?" he echoed with amusement. "I have several days in court ahead of me. I'm filing suit right now on behalf of a miner who was injured during a cave-in."

"Really? That doesn't sound like the kind of case your firm would take on," she said.

"We do a lot of pro bono work. I enjoy it. But here's my real question. What are you doing next Friday night? We could get together and start tossing out some ideas for working with the kids. You can help me decide what to write."

"I'm sure you know how to write—you're a lawyer."

"I can write what I need for a courtroom, yes, but I want to do things that are fun. Kids are kids no matter what kind of a battle they're facing. Childhood is a time of imagination and dreaming. Just because a child is sick, that shouldn't stop. So I'd like to learn about fiction."

"Hey," she protested. "I may be on the social beat, but I'm not writing fiction for a living, you know."

"No insult intended," he told her, laughing. "But you know more about fiction than I do, and I could really use your help. So, what do you say? Next Friday night?"

"Sounds like a great idea."

They were still in one another's arms, even though the music had ended and the groom was about to throw the garter.

Suddenly embarrassed, they broke apart. Brian went to stand with the single men as the band started playing a stripper theme.

Laurie found herself imagining a romance-movie moment, with Brian catching the garter, then turning to look at her with a knowing smile.

He didn't catch the garter.

Nor, a few minutes later, did she catch the bouquet.

After that Brian's attention was captured by his groomsman's duties. Sal came over to tell her goodbye, and she decided it was the natural moment for her to casually make her escape, as well.

She realized she was actually afraid to see Brian again. Afraid to jinx something.

"So how was the wedding?" Jack said in greeting the next morning.

"It was fine. Thanks for asking."

"You're supposed to ask me how my political thing went," he told her.

"How did your political thing go, Jack?"

"Brilliantly! I got an interview with our mayor and possible soon-to-be governor," he said proudly. "And don't worry. The next opportunity I get, I'll drag you along."

Craig came breezing toward them just then.

"Took him long enough," Jack said, hooking his thumbs in his pockets. "The boss is coming by to congratulate me." His expression when Craig turned to Laurie, instead, was almost comical.

"Laurie, great work. It's going to be a wonderful piece. What with you and Sybil being friends, you got the story from an inside angle not many people could have managed."

"Thanks, Craig," she said.

"Did you like my piece, Craig?" Jack asked, looking poleaxed.

"Of course. Top-notch," he said, then kept walking.

Jack looked absolutely deflated. Laurie almost felt sorry for him, but knew that his ego would find a way to survive without damage.

"You're friends with Sybil?" he asked her, puzzled.

"I knew her a long time ago. We hadn't seen each other in years," Laurie told him honestly.

"You must have been rubbing elbows with some really big money," he said.

"I don't know. I didn't ask about everyone's financial status. I was reporting on Sybil's wedding, not her bank account."

"Maybe I should have been at that wedding," Jack muttered.

"And miss your political thing? You must be joking," Laurie said.

He shrugged. "Of course."

But he didn't look as if he'd been joking.

MONDAY, SHE WORKED. Tuesday, she worked. Wednesday...

She waited and waited. Brian didn't call. She began to feel sorry for herself. Maybe he had started regretting his suggestion and had changed his mind.

She had been crazy to dream that something might be happening between them. They shared an empathy with and understanding of children who were seriously ill, who needed diversions to keep up their spirits just as badly as they needed medications for their bodies. She and Brian might make a good working team, but that was clearly the most they would ever be. Luckily, she had parents who loved her, good friends and a great job. She was a very busy person.

So busy that, in truth, she had no life.

But that was all right, she told herself. Because she did have life itself, and she knew how precious that was.

"Hey, line four, some guy," Jack told her, just before five o'clock.

She picked up and was more excited than she wanted to admit to hear Brian's voice. "So are we still on for Friday?" he asked.

She swallowed. "Sure." Had she sounded casual enough? she wondered.

"Should I pick you up at your office?" he asked.

Her heart fluttered a little. This was just friendship, she told herself. She wasn't supposed to go home, shower, change into something nice.

"Oh, wait. I was thinking of trying out Green Street, that new place down by the bridge. It's pretty fancy. Do you think you'll be too tired to head home and dress up a bit? I can pick you up at your place instead."

She was trembling. She had to hang up quickly before she embarrassed herself. This was absurd. She was an adult, too old for such a nerve-racking crush.

"I don't mind at all. What time should I be ready?"

"Is seven-thirty too early?"

"No, that's fine. I'll see you then. Bye now."

"Wait."

"What?"

"I don't know where you live."

"Oh. Sorry." She gave him her address, then said another quick goodbye and hung up.

To her horror, she could tell by the heat that her cheeks were bloodred. And worse, Jack was staring at her with a knowing grin. "Looks like you have a thing for the guy on line four. Who is he?"

"Just an old friend."

"Don't forget," he reminded her. "I *am* an investigative reporter."

"There's nothing to investigate. I'm going to dinner with an old friend. We both work with the kids at the hospital, that's all."

"Okay, so you don't want to share with your best friend in the world," he said, shaking his head.

"Jack, you're not my best friend in the world," she told him.

"Hey, who do you spend the majority of your time with?" he asked her. "Me, that's who. Day after day, I'm your closest human contact," he said, trying to sound hurt.

"Okay, my closest human contact," she said, "I'm having dinner with an old friend. We're putting together some special events for the children's hospital. That's it, that's the truth, I swear."

He looked at her skeptically and swung back to his desk.

Laurie didn't care. On Friday, she was going to see Brian again.

BECAUSE IT WAS A LOCAL paper—and because Craig had been impressed with Sal's pictures, as well as Laurie's prose—they'd added a teaser piece to run in advance of the main article. On Friday morning they printed one of Sal's photos on the front page of the news and entertainment section, with a caption describing Sybil as a newly married philanthropist, who had overcome childhood challenges. Laurie knew that, like herself, Sybil had learned to appreciate just waking up in the morning. No one, regardless of their circumstances, was granted any guarantees. Sybil had been given the opportunity to give back, and that was what she did.

"Nice piece," Jack told Laurie when he saw it.

"Thanks."

"So I take it your old friend was at the wedding, too?"

"Yes."

He put the paper down suddenly. "It's Brian Thompson, isn't it?" he asked excitedly.

She froze.

"Aha! It *is* Brian Thompson," Jack said triumphantly. "Hey, can you get me an exclusive with him? He's a real hotshot, you know. Kind of a tree-hugger, but not radical about it or anything. Of course, you know that. He's your old friend, after all. No one's ever gotten a really good interview with him, though. For a politician, he can be very private."

"He's not actually a politician, he's a lawyer," she explained. "And if he has political ambitions, I don't know what they are. Why don't you hold off a little, huh? I'm not seeing him as a reporter. He's a friend."

Jack let out a sigh. "Think you can help me out somewhere along the line?" he asked. "Seeing as you have a personal in with the guy."

"Sure, if I can. But I told you, there's nothing personal about it. We're just working together to help out some sick kids."

"Still holding out on me, huh?"

"No, just telling it like it is," she said.

If only there *were* more to tell, she thought. She'd be such a happy woman she'd probably be willing to tell total strangers all about it.

CHAPTER
~FOUR~

O n Friday, Laurie couldn't wait for five o'clock to roll around. When it did, she raced home as quickly as possible, unable to believe how nervous she was. She showered quickly, then started figuring out what to wear.

She was trying on her third outfit when the doorbell rang. In a panic, she snagged her panty hose with her nail. She grabbed a new pair and raced to the door to look through the peephole, afraid that Brian was going to catch her dithering over her outfit. But it was just Cindy, her next-door neighbor. "Help!" Laurie pleaded, letting her in.

"Help?" Cindy asked. "Oh, my God! You've got a date."

Hurrying back toward her bedroom, Laurie insisted, "It's not a date. Not really. It's just dinner with a friend."

"You don't get that dolled up to go with me," she teased.

Laurie shimmied into a flower-print halter dress and stepped into the hallway. "This one? Or something with sleeves?"

"Boy, and here I was going to see if you wanted to catch that new Julia Roberts movie," Cindy said.

"Oh, I'm sorry," Laurie told her. "I'd love to see it with you."

"Are you kidding? We can do a matinee tomorrow. Tonight… you have a date."

"It's not a date."

Her friend laughed. "No one stresses over what they're wearing when it's not a date. Who's the guy?"

Cindy was young and genuinely gorgeous and could have had a date every night of the week, but she seldom went out. She said she was looking for a dream, and that when the dream came along, she would know it.

"His name is Brian Thompson. We're working on some events for the children's hospital."

Cindy was quiet for a minute, then asked, "*The* Brian Thompson?"

"I don't know what you mean, *the* Brian Thompson. I met him when I was a kid. When I was in the hospital," she told Cindy. "Then I ran into him again at the hospital last week, and at the wedding I was covering last weekend."

"Where's he taking you?"

"That new restaurant. Green Street."

"Then let's not go summer floral. Night black will be better. You have the perfect thing, the black silk you wore to that fundraiser."

Just then the doorbell rang again, and Laurie jumped. Cindy rushed her back into the bedroom and went to answer the door.

Laurie slid into the spaghetti-strapped black silk, glad she hadn't worn it at the wedding. She hoped she didn't look too sexy. They were just going out as friends, and she didn't want to be presumptuous.

But he *had* kissed her. Admittedly, the first kiss had been nothing more than friendly, but not the second.

She looked at herself in the mirror. How could she still appear so young and wide-eyed? At least she was taller now, and she had plenty of hair that curled and waved down her back. She didn't look the least bit chic or sophisticated, though.

Especially next to Cindy. Laurie wasn't a jealous person; she seldom thought about Cindy's exquisite beauty. But now she was getting palpitations because her gorgeous friend was opening the door.

Laurie hurried toward the hall, then paused. She couldn't appear to be too anxious. And she *wouldn't* suddenly be jealous of a good friend. She was an adult, and she wasn't going to fall prey to adolescent angst.

Oh, hell, she was getting out there as fast as she could.

When she reached the living room, Brian was standing by the door, speaking politely with Cindy.

He didn't seem to be flirting, she thought. That was a very good thing.

In fact, his eyes lit up and a smile curved his lips when he saw her.

"Hi," she told him.

"Hey," he replied. "You look stunning."

"Thanks, so do you," she answered. It was the simple truth. He was one of those men who could wear a suit with a casual James Bond elegance.

Cindy looked at her with an expression that plainly said, *See? I told you I knew the right thing to wear.*

"Well, guys," her neighbor said, "go off, be good, solve the problems of the world and drive safely."

"Thanks. We can catch that movie tomorrow if you want," Laurie told her.

"Did I mess up your plans?" Brian asked.

"No, because we didn't have any plans," Cindy told him. "But we'll probably go to a matinee tomorrow. Want to come? It's a chick flick."

He laughed. "I guess, if you're going to a chick flick, it's good to go with a few gorgeous chicks. Maybe I'll take you up on that."

Brian told Cindy good-night, then helped Laurie into her light wrap, took her arm and escorted her out to his car. She hadn't known what to expect; he was a big-deal lawyer, or so she kept hearing. But his car was a modest Saturn SUV, clean and shiny but very average-American, and she found herself glad. It added to the impression that Brian was down-to-earth, and that seemed important somehow.

"I saw the teaser for your piece on Sybil," he told her, as he drove out of her lot. "I'm looking forward to reading the whole thing."

"Thanks," she said.

"Sybil came across as someone anybody would like, who just happens to be rich," he commented, smiling.

"Thanks," she said again. "I wrote what I saw. I think it's wonderful that someone who has the resources she has wants to give so much. It makes my efforts look like a drop in the bucket."

He glanced over at her. "Our efforts may be a drop in the bucket," he said, "but they count. Yes, Sybil can do great things. She can donate enough money to build a whole hospital wing if she wants to. What we do…well, it's kind of like taxes."

"Taxes?" Laurie repeated dryly.

"Yes, and not in a bad way. I mean, could you or I build a bridge, a highway or a new airport? Hell no. Maybe Sybil could," he admitted with a laugh, "but seriously, who builds what we need in this country? We do, the American people. Maybe we don't always agree where our tax money should go, but the point is, a lot of people put in a little bit each, and in the end you build a highway. Those drops in the bucket count."

"I have a feeling that you give a lot more than I do. I bet your drops would fill the bucket a lot more quickly than mine."

"You're missing the point," he told her, but he was smiling. "First of all, my family is comfortable, but politicians aren't all filthy rich. I make a decent income, but I'm also paying back college loans—there really was no silver spoon when I was born. And we don't need silver spoons. We need to figure out what we want to do in life, how to make a living doing something that makes us happy. Then we all put our little drops into the bucket and build that highway. Or a bridge. The drops in a bucket are just as important as the deluges."

"I'm glad to hear it," Laurie said.

"Drops in a bucket do more, too," he said. "They can create smiles, and smiles are one of the best rewards we'll ever get in life."

"I definitely agree with you there," she told him.

GREEN STREET WAS AS elegant as its reputation. They were led to a booth upholstered in soft leather, and though it was spring, a fire was burning in a giant hearth decorated with copperware. Brian might be paying back student loans, but he was good with a wine list and ordered a delicious merlot. He suggested one of the beef entrées for two, and Laurie was happy to go with his choices.

He asked about her family as they ate their appetizers, and she told him that her folks were doing great and were down in Florida until the summer heat sent them back north. She knew he had no family left, so she asked about his career plans instead.

"Everyone tells me you're being groomed for the governor's seat," she said. "Is that true?"

"I don't know," he told her. "I've worked on campaigns when I agreed with the candidates' positions, but I don't know if I really want to go into politics myself. I guess it would depend on whether I thought I could make some real changes for the better."

Over dessert Laurie asked him, "So where do you want to start?"

"Start?"

She laughed. "With our project for the hospital."

"Ah. Well, like I told you, I want to write skits for the kids to act out, even the kids in wheelchairs. We could jot down some ideas, I guess."

"If you like, we could go back to my place," Laurie told him. "My computer is always at the ready."

"That sounds good to me," he agreed.

He slipped her wrap around her shoulders as they left the restaurant. His featherlight touch was like a breath of air that warmed and chilled in one, and seemed to reach right into her. She tried to act normally as they walked to his car, and she tried not to wear her heart on her sleeve. Of course, technically, she wasn't wearing sleeves. She was afraid of how much she felt for him so quickly, and was well aware she needed to keep her defenses up.

But something inside her was begging her to let her feelings grow. Telling her not to destroy what might be simply because she cared so much.

When they reached her apartment, they went into her office and sat down side by side in front of her computer.

"So all that stuff you brought in when I saw you at the hospital, the computers and things, they're not from...?"

"From...?" She looked at him, puzzled.

"I'm sorry. I should have asked you this before. Not someone with whom you're in a relationship, right? I mean, I know you said you were dating your work, that night at dinner, but honestly, if I had been involved with someone, I doubt *I* would have admitted it in that group, either," he said.

She shook her head. "I'm not in a relationship. I wasn't lying," she assured him, hoping she wasn't blushing at what she could only believe was his interest. She had to change the subject—and fast. "Let's do this. Where do you want to start?"

"Medieval. Kids love knights. And maybe there should be a superhero. An underdog who turns out to be a superhero," he amended.

"Let's start by giving the hero a name," Laurie suggested.

"All right. Max. The hero will be Max. Max is a…farm boy, who's longing to be a great knight. He lives in the kingdom of…Pittsatalia. The kingdom is being threatened by…"

"By a race of giants who have conquered the nearby country of West Gettyson. The king is actually a good guy, but he has a daughter and no sons, so he's decreed that all the knights in the kingdom will be given a chance to fight for the right to lead his army and win the hand of his daughter, who is of course the heroine," Laurie declared.

"And her name is…?"

"Sarah," she said after thinking for a moment. "Princess Sarah. And she's no shrinking violet herself. Princess Sarah wants to lead her own army against the giants."

"There has to be a narrator," Brian said, "because that way the kids can take on the roles and act out what the narrator describes, so they won't have to memorize any lines."

They went on that way, writing and rewriting, and completely losing track of time. Finally they reached the point where Princess Sarah and Max had cleverly bested their enemy and declared their love.

Just after Laurie typed "The End," Brian leaned over and kissed her.

Not on the forehead.

Not a public kiss on the lips.

It was a kiss that began with wild excitement and deepened

into sweet, wet, tongue-dueling, mouths-locked passion. She drove her fingers into his hair, felt the power and strength of his hands on her, and the full searing heat of his body. The kiss seemed to go on forever, but finally, starved for breath, they broke apart.

She was dazzled, afraid to speak, breathless with longing.

Brian stood up quickly. "I'll see you at the movies," he told her.

She was aware that he left. Aware that she had to rise and lock the door. And then she fell into bed, her fingers against her lips. She had to be careful. She had to be *very* careful. It would be foolish to fall in love so quickly.

Too late. She already had—years and years ago.

CHAPTER
❧ FIVE ❧

"He must be crazy about you," Cindy told Laurie. "He's seeing a chick flick just for you."

"Well, we'll see if he shows up," Laurie said.

They were sitting in her apartment. She had slept late—having stayed wide awake for hours, just staring at her ceiling, the night before—and was thoroughly enjoying her first cup of coffee. Cindy was across the table, reading the morning paper.

"Whoa!" Cindy exclaimed suddenly.

"What?" Laurie asked.

"Look at this shot Sal got of you." Her friend thrust the paper toward her.

Laurie stared. Beneath the article on the wedding, where she was given credit, Craig had posted one of the pictures Sal had taken of her—one with Brian in it.

"Fairy-tale wedding, fairy-tale times," the caption read. "Reporter Laurie Mayberry takes a few minutes to enjoy the beauty of our state with fellow guest Brian Thompson."

Laurie stared, saying nothing.

"What's the matter?" Cindy asked.

"Brian is in it."

"So?"

"He'll be upset. It makes it look like we're…you know. Together."

"Don't be ridiculous!" Cindy said. "He's not going to be upset. He's a good guy. And he likes you."

"Let's see how he feels after he sees this. Whether he shows up at the movies. Or calls back. Ever," Laurie muttered.

"You're underestimating the guy. He must have known Sal was taking pictures," Cindy reasoned. "Your piece on Sybil is wonderful, by the way."

"You should let me do a piece on you. You work hard, and you're always giving me things for the kids," Laurie said.

"No thanks. I like my anonymity. I know you appreciate what I do, and I know the kids do, too, and that's all I need. You keep my name out of things, right?"

"I do," Laurie assured her. "That's why you, of all people, should understand why I'm afraid this might really upset Brian."

"Brian is a politician," Laurie told her. "It's the American way—politicians are fair game."

"He's not a politician, he's a lawyer. He doesn't even know if he wants to go into politics yet," Laurie told her.

"He'll be fine," Cindy assured her. "Now you'd better make tracks, or we won't know if he's at the movies or not, because we'll be so late we'll miss it ourselves."

BRIAN *WAS* AT THE MOVIES. He had the tickets, and he was waiting for them outside the theater. He was in sunglasses, jeans and a polo shirt. Totally casual, totally down-to-earth.

"Hey," he said in greeting, giving Cindy a kiss on the cheek and Laurie a lingering kiss on the lips.

"Hey, you two. Get a room," Cindy teased.

"We're seeing a romance, right? I'm just gearing up," he replied.

"Just don't make me jealous from the get-go, huh?" Cindy said easily.

Laurie felt her heart skip. It was as if they really were a couple.

As they purchased popcorn and sodas, he complimented her on her article. "Great picture of the two of us, huh?" he asked.

Cindy nudged her in the ribs.

"I thought Sal was only taking those shots for artistic reasons," Laurie said. "I didn't expect the paper to run one of them."

Brian shrugged. "It worked for me. Hey, when the movie's over, why don't we grab some dinner, then try out our skit on Cindy? If you don't mind?" he added, turning to her.

"I'd love to see what you're doing," she said.

So after the movie—which even Brian enjoyed—they settled on sushi for dinner. Afterward, they headed to Laurie's house, where she took the role of narrator and Brian single-handedly played all the parts. Cindy was on the floor with laughter.

After he left, Laurie asked Cindy wistfully, "He'll call again, right?"

"Of course. I told you, he's crazy about you," her friend said.

Laurie wished fervently that she *were* queen of the world, because then Brian would definitely call.

THE NEXT DAY SHE SPENT most of the morning in a cleaning frenzy, waiting for her phone to ring.

When it did, her heart jumped.

But it wasn't Brian.

It was just her mom, checking in.

On Monday, Laurie threw herself into her work.

Then, on Tuesday, Brian called.

"I know this isn't your usual night, but I just heard from Tim. There will be extra children tonight because Pitt Med Center is having a plumbing problem, so we got some of their kids, and I thought you might be able to come help me out. Do you mind?

Are you ready for our opening night? We can share narrating duties."

She buried her disappointment that he wasn't calling to ask her out, and said, "Sure. I can meet you there."

"That would be great. I have a ton of electronics to bring, so the car is pretty packed."

"What time? Six?"

"Six is fine. See you tonight."

When she hung up, her heart was racing, and she wondered if she would actually survive this falling in love business.

WHEN SHE ARRIVED AT the hospital, she was carrying a box of books Cindy had donated, mostly ones required by the state school system.

Sabrina met her as one of the nurse's aides came out to take the books up to the library. "It's been an impossibly busy week," Sabrina told Laurie. "Every bed in the place is taken, and we've even had to claim a few spaces in the E.R. I'm so glad you and Brian are here tonight. With this many kids, we really need help keeping them occupied."

"I'm happy to do it," Laurie told her. "So is Brian here already?"

"He's in the playroom. Go on. The place is packed to the gills."

When Laurie got there, she was sorry to see that little Mary-Katherine was still in the hospital, sitting cross-legged on the floor right in front of Brian. Laurie recognized some of the older teens, as well. Girls in bright bandannas, boys dragging their IVs along with them. But they were smiling, and as they talked and laughed, they had the glint of life in their eyes.

Brian saw her as soon as she opened the door, and his smile seemed to ignite something inside her. She tried not to act like an adolescent herself as she walked toward him through the crowd, greeting kids along the way.

"This play requires involvement from all of you," Brian said, as soon as they were ready to get started.

"We need a princess," Laurie informed them.

"You be the princess," Mary-Katherine said.

Laurie laughed easily. "No, Brian and I are the narrators. Why don't *you* be the princess?" she suggested.

Mary-Katherine was thrilled. The princess, of course, had friends, ladies in waiting, requiring more volunteers from the crowd. Next they cast Max, and then a dragon, and before long, all the roles were filled. One of the quietest kids took on the part of the evil giant king and had everyone laughing as he lost himself in his performance. The kids followed directions and ad-libbed where they were meant to, and overall it was an amazing night. By the time they finished, there was a lineup of parents out in the hallway, all applauding.

Laurie and Brian left together, flushed, exuberant.

"Think we can do it again?" he asked, hugging her in the parking lot.

"I'd be heartbroken if we didn't," she said with a smile.

"Heartbroken?" he teased.

"Heartbroken," she assured him.

"Can you get away this weekend?" he asked her, still holding her in those strong arms.

The breath seemed to rush from her lungs. "I— Yes."

"Great. Pack what you need, and I'll pick you up from work on Friday. We're just going over to Philly, taking our show on the road for the kids there."

She was going away with him for the weekend.

A car horn beeped; someone needed to get by. They broke away from one another. "Friday, then," Brian called to her.

"Friday," she agreed.

ON FRIDAY SHE FINISHED up the obituary she was working on, e-filed the piece to Craig right at five o'clock, then hurried out of the building.

Brian was already there, leaning against his car, looking as if he'd stepped out of a spread on weekend fashion from *GQ.* He saw her coming, and smiled.

Her heart literally skipped a beat.

She made herself walk calmly over to him, and he gave her a quick kiss, then ushered her into the passenger seat. In a moment he was sitting next to her and they were on their way.

Heading out of town for the weekend.

Together.

CHAPTER
∽ SIX ∽

They stayed at a hotel on the edge of the historic area of the city. She'd been curious—and maybe even hopeful— to find out how many rooms he had reserved.

She didn't know if she was relieved or disappointed that the answer was two. She was delighted to discover, however, that they connected.

It was almost midnight when they arrived, having stopped for dinner near Hershey. During the meal, he had told her about his connection with the hospital in Philadelphia. A corporate friend was on the board and had arranged for their stay, and a local restaurateur had invited them to enjoy a meal the next day; he had a son who was frequently in and out of the hospital with cystic fibrosis.

When they reached the hotel, they were both exhausted. Laurie thought Brian might follow her into her room, but he didn't. She thought he might open the connecting door.

He didn't do that, either.

She was actually so tired that she fell asleep quickly, despite her niggling fear that maybe there was nothing personal about this trip, after all.

The next morning he knocked on her door, and they hurried down to the restaurant for coffee and a croissant before heading for the hospital.

Though Laurie had never been there before, she was greeted by the staff as if she was a long lost friend. And though neither she nor Brian knew any of the children, it didn't matter. Children were children wherever you went, young enough to be full of hope, and more than willing to play and be entertained.

They were thrilled with the presents Brian had brought, and Laurie herself marveled at the bounty he had managed to acquire. But the crowning achievement of the morning was the skit and the children's eager participation. The play ended with tons of laughter, and Brian promised that they would come back again with a new story to perform.

When they left, they both felt energized and excited. Since it was still early, Brian suggested that they do the Freedom Trail, so they visited Independence Hall, the Liberty Bell and Ben Franklin's burial place. They left pennies on the famous man's grave, though Brian did point out that Franklin had suggested people not waste their pennies. "Back to the whole bucket concept," he told her.

"Oh?"

"I've read that there are about three billion dollars' worth of pennies sitting in jars, on the ground, between sofa cushions…all over the place. If you put them all together, you could build a lot of bridges," he told her.

When they finished their tour, they went for their complimentary dinner, then strolled back to the hotel.

And up to their separate rooms.

Brian saw her to her door.

She leaned against it, looking up at him. "Thank you," she said.

He set a hand against the door, leaning toward her. "Thank *you*," he said softly.

"It was incredible, wasn't it?" she whispered.

He nodded slowly. "*You* were incredible."

"It was your idea," she pointed out.

"I couldn't have done it alone."

His face was barely an inch away from hers. She studied the darkness of his eyes, the texture of his skin, the generous quality of his mouth. He was gorgeous, inside and out.

She smiled ruefully, not knowing what to say.

She didn't need to speak. He leaned forward and kissed her.

Laurie thought that she could quite happily die in Brian's arms.

His mouth covered hers with a firm power. The kiss was deeper and more intimate than any she had ever known, sending heat streaking through her, making her blood sizzle with pure electricity. She slipped her arms around his neck and kissed him back with all her heart, leaning into him as if she could somehow merge their two bodies into one.

At last he drew away, his eyes meeting hers, and shifted her hair from her face. He touched her lips briefly once again, then stepped back.

"Good night, and thank you," he said softly, then turned and walked to his own door.

Feeling adrift, filled with longing and confusion, Laurie hurried inside, then closed her door and leaned against it, her heart racing.

She believed—really believed at last—that he did care for her, but the signals were so mixed... She shook her head and mechanically began getting ready for bed.

She showered, then brushed her teeth, finally stopping when she realized she was in danger of removing every speck of enamel. She decided to brush her hair instead, then was afraid that she might make herself bald again if she continued.

She set the brush down, plumped the pillows, turned on the television and crawled into bed, then realized a few minutes later that she hadn't seen or heard a single thing from the show she'd randomly chosen.

Finally she stood up and went to the connecting doors, drew a long breath, opened her own door and tapped on his.

A second later, he opened it.

He'd showered, as well. His rich dark hair was damp, and he smelled of soap. He was wearing a terry robe he had evidently just thrown on, and boxers. He looked at her with surprise and concern.

"Is everything all right?" he asked quickly.

"Yes...no," she said, pushing her way into the room and taking a seat on the foot of his bed. "You tell me. What's wrong with me?"

"With you? Nothing. You're a dream. You're perfect. You're beautiful, intelligent...the most empathetic human being I've ever met." He walked over and knelt in front of her, taking her hands. "What is this, Laurie? Why did you ask me that?"

"So you think I'm attractive?" she asked, ignoring his question.

He laughed. "Only a blind man could miss the fact that you aren't just attractive. Laurie, you're stunning. Your face...hair... lips..." He swallowed hard. "Lips," he said again, grinning. "And even a blind man would say your voice is beautiful. I think you're the most beautiful creature in existence."

She looked at him. "You really *are* a politician," she stated gravely.

"Lawyer," he corrected.

"You will be a politician," she insisted, amused. "You excel at speeches."

He frowned. "That wasn't a speech."

"Whatever." She drew a deep breath and asked, "Why don't you ever make a move on me?"

He stared back at her, then smiled, looking downward for a moment.

"You mean too much to me."

"Too much how? As a friend? Brian, I know people change. If we tried something and it didn't work out, I'd still be your friend. I'd never forget the kids or the hospital. I'd still be your... partner in this."

He shook his head, his eyes flashing. "I know that. Did you think I was only interested in you because of the hospital?"

"No. Yes. I don't know."

"Oh, Laurie. That's not it at all. I want things to be right between us. I want to be sure you feel the way I do. I die a little every time I walk away from you. And I don't want to casually use the most important words in the world as if they mean nothing. I'm falling in love with you. Quite frankly, I set up this morning's hospital visit *after* I asked you to go away with me. I wanted time with you."

And when he kissed her then, she knew he wasn't going to walk away.

IN THE MORNING, THEY lingered in bed for a long time, and before they finally left the hotel room, Brian pulled her into his arms again and kissed her.

When he lifted his lips at last, she smiled up at him. "Think you might be free to spend next weekend with me?" she asked him.

"If I weren't, I'd be heartbroken," he told her seriously.

"Heartbroken?" she asked.

"Heartbroken," he assured her.

CHAPTER
~SEVEN~

Laurie didn't think it was possible to be any happier. Every week she worked hard from Monday to Friday, then spent the weekend with Brian. Sometimes they managed an evening together during the week, and he shifted his schedule so every other Wednesday they went to the hospital together to see the children.

They laughed a lot, thinking of new ways to entertain the kids. They both brought whatever gifts they could, inspired by the work of Toys.Calm and others who had learned that when everyone gave a little, the bucket got filled, then refilled again and again every time it was depleted.

Laurie's euphoria lasted for almost two months, with nothing to mar the utopia in which they both seemed to be living. She attended a business dinner with Brian and met his coworkers, and she went to charity events with him to raise funds for the different projects he was involved in.

He came to the paper's Memorial Day picnic, and though Jack was a little bit of a jerk, Brian laughed about it and even said that if he hadn't had the dubious pleasure of meeting him, he might have been jealous, since Jack wasn't a bad-looking guy, and he did sit next to her day after day after day.

Then, on a Monday morning soon after the Memorial Day party, Laurie was called into Craig's office. She drew up a chair in front of his desk, feeling inexplicably wary. Sybil and Danny were having a party that weekend, and she hoped Craig wasn't about to ask her to cover it. She and Brian were going—together—as guests, and she would feel uncomfortable if she also had to write about it.

"I need an article on Brian," he said without preamble.

"What?"

"He's defending Justin Murano over the Groverton Hotel incident."

"So?" she asked carefully. She knew a little about the case. Justin Murano was a guitarist with a group called Weeping Willow, and was accused of property destruction to the tune of several hundred thousand dollars. She also knew that Murano was being accused because the hotel owner refused to acknowledge that his daughter was at fault, having admitted a score of her friends into Murano's suite, young people who carried out the destruction while the musician was on stage.

"Why? It isn't a major case," she protested.

"Trust me, in this city, it is. The conservatives see it as youth run amok. The prosecution is painting the daughter out to be an angel seduced by the sleazy out-of-town musician. The local teen population sees it as the establishment trying to trample what they don't understand. Everyone's jumping on it. Even the national media are picking it up. We need to cover it, too. Look, I really like Brian, Laurie. If anyone is going to write anything about him, it should be you."

"Like the readers won't see it as biased," she argued.

"You can write it, or I can give it to Jack. Your choice," Craig warned her.

She stood. "Can I think about this?"

"No. I'm sorry, but I need this now or we're going to get scooped."

"I'll write it, then. I'm not letting Jack sharpen his skills—or his knives—on Brian," she said, hoping the anger she felt over being blindsided didn't show.

When she returned to her desk, she sat down, logged on to her computer and started pulling up everything that had already been written on the case—and on Brian. She was jotting down notes when her cell phone rang. It was Brian.

"I have to back out on dinner tonight," he told her apologetically.

"Oh, no," she said. "I really need to talk to you."

"I'm sorry. I have witnesses coming in and I need to interview them. How about later? I'll come by."

"Okay, but please, please, make sure you do."

HE HAD A KEY, AND by the time he let himself in, she was sleeping. When she awoke, she was in his arms.

They ended up making love, then drifting off to sleep. Laurie's last thought was that she could talk to him about the article in the morning. But when she woke up, he was already gone.

As soon as she got to the office, she walked in on Craig, determined.

"What?" he asked her irritably.

"You should do a different piece."

"What are you talking about?" he demanded.

"You said that everyone will be doing a story on Brian and the Murano case, so we should do something different."

"I'm listening," he said warily.

"Let's do a human-interest story on Brian, on the man behind the lawyer in the courtroom. Let me do a piece that explains why he's determined to defend the underdog, not just in this case but as often as he can."

Craig was thoughtful a moment, then pointed his finger at her. She smiled inwardly, though she was still wary, because that meant she had won. Yet there was going to be a "but."

"It better be good," he said.

"It will be great," she promised.

She felt relieved when she left his office. Back at her desk, she started writing about the day she had first met Brian, and the way he had been there for his cousin until her death. Laurie wrote about meeting him again just a few months ago, and how he had been inspired by Toys.Calm and his own experiences to start working with the kids at the hospital.

As she worked, she found herself pleased to be writing a human-interest piece that was coming from the heart, one much better than a standard article about a court case. There was always so much information a lawyer wasn't at liberty to share, and she had to be *investigating,* not just reporting.

In telling the story of the man, she was explaining why he believed in others, why he believed in justice, and why he was willing to go out on a limb for someone who needed help. She wrote about everything he did for the children and explained the bucket principle.

BRIAN WAS SO BUSY with the case she wasn't able to see him that week, but even so, she was happy, convinced that she had come up with an approach he would really like.

He picked her up late Friday night and they headed up to Sybil's St. Marys estate, with Laurie sleeping in the car most of the way. They spent the next day by the pool, so it wasn't until late that afternoon that they really had a chance to talk.

"Guess what?" she began enthusiastically. "I'm doing a piece on you."

He paused as he was going through his luggage, and stared at her, perplexed. "What?"

"Craig wanted a story on the Murano case, but I thought that would cause all kinds of problems. There are too many things you aren't allowed to tell me, and too many things I'd have to investigate, try to dredge up. But I think I came up with the perfect solution."

"Oh?"

"I'm focusing on you as a human being," she told him. "I'm writing about the work you do at the hospital."

"What I do at the hospital?"

It surprised her to see that he didn't seem to be happy about that.

"Brian, what's wrong?"

"I don't know, exactly. I think I would rather have you do a piece on the trial."

"But—"

"Forget it," he said impatiently. "I'm sure it will be fine."

"Is there something about you I don't know?" she asked him.

He shook his head. "As far as I'm concerned, you know everything there is to know about me."

"Then what's the problem? I've written a good article, I promise."

"Written? It's already done?"

"It's going to run Monday."

He looked away, the expression in his eyes distant, cold.

"Brian?" she said.

He shook his head. "I'm sorry, I'm sure it's a wonderful article."

He walked toward her then, the distance, the coldness, disappearing as if there had been a spring thaw. She laughed as he lifted her up, and she slid down against him, happy to be in his arms.

That evening, as Sybil and Laurie carried the dinner dishes into the kitchen, Laurie mentioned the article and was surprised by her friend's concern.

"You didn't mention Marty Breslin, did you?" Sybil asked.

"His boss? Why would I?"

Sybil shook her head, then shrugged. "Marty had a little brother who died of cancer, and now he's the one behind all the expensive donations Brian brings to the hospital. But he doesn't want his name out there. There was actually some legal trouble over it a year or so ago, though I can't remember all the details."

"I don't know a thing about that, so I never mentioned it. And it's fine with me if Marty wants his privacy," Laurie said. "I had no idea he was involved."

ON THE DRIVE BACK TO the city the next day, it was as if that small moment of awkwardness had never existed. Laurie and Brian spent the time working on another skit, a mystery with a host of eccentric characters for the kids to play, searching for a missing object that could be strategically hidden beforehand.

He said good-night to her outside her apartment, because he had to be in court at seven, and he still had briefs to go over before he went to bed.

They clung together for a long and lingering kiss before he left, and when he pulled away, he was smiling.

"I'm sure the article will be fine," he told her. "I'd trust you with my life, you know."

And then, with a final kiss, he was gone.

The following morning Laurie picked up the paper and was about to turn to her story when the phone rang.

It was Brian, and he was furious.

CHAPTER
~EIGHT~

"What the hell did you do to me?" Brian demanded when she picked up the phone.

"What?"

"Skewer me as an attorney, if you have to. Say whatever the hell you want about *me*. But how dare you betray the people who matter to me? What you've done has caused irreparable damage. And I don't even know how you found out. Oh, wait, yes, I do. You were talking to Sybil last night in the kitchen. You must have been up all night rewriting before the paper went to press. I can't believe I trusted you. Laurie, what you've done... You can never imagine the harm. I would have expected so much more from you, so much more."

95

And then the line went dead.

It was barely seven, but a moment later she heard someone tapping at her door.

Cindy was standing there with the newspaper. "What were you thinking?" she asked.

"What on earth is the problem? What did I supposedly say that has everyone so upset?"

Laurie took the paper and started skimming, and within seconds had found the problem. Someone had added a paragraph about an incident in which the hospital had been accused of receiving stolen goods. Brian had wound up in contempt of court for refusing to name the donor, though he had produced bills of sale, but with the name blacked out. Whoever had embellished her article had uncovered the fact that the donor was Marty Breslin, however, a man who'd lost his own brother to childhood cancer.

She winced, sinking into a chair at the breakfast table. "I don't know what happened. Craig must have found all this out and changed it. I didn't even know about any of this myself until Saturday night. And even if I'd known, I never would have written about it. This is awful! It looks like he betrayed his boss. No wonder he's so angry."

"You need to tell him the truth," Cindy stated firmly.

"I didn't even know what he was talking about when he called," Laurie said. "He must know I wouldn't have done this. But it or so long. So I   d do, either, changing my

, huh?"

lid it! You went   dy reminded her.

              nake up stories, and we

happened to dis-

             old her.

ing to help you.   happened."

with indignation.   de straight to Craig's

er phone, hoping   ory?" she demanded.

hew it.   are you talking about?

s of courage and   xactly as you gave it to

hed ahead.

didn't even know   , booted up her com-

              reen in disbelief.

nputer, and found   he paper—was right

u must have done   n't even look up.

re quite an amaz-   hard hitting. Bring-

me, but you don't   ed his role to stay

he truth. I didn't

e your holier-than-   rd is out. I saw him

shine!"   sn't know why he

was so determined to keep his charity a secret
guess it's a good thing someone spilled the beans

She stared at Jack in sudden realization. "You
into my computer and changed my story!"

He smiled broadly. "I did you a favor. I just
cover that tidbit, and I gave *you* the credit."

"Oh, Jack, that was so wrong!"

He looked hurt and angry. "Laurie, I was try
Give your story some depth."

He stood and walked away, his shoulders rigid

WHEN SHE GOT HOME that night, she stared at h
it would ring. But it wasn't going to, and she k

At last she summoned up her own reserve
called Brian. The minute he answered, she rus

"Brian, I didn't write what you think I did. I
about Marty Breslin until Saturday night."

"Laurie, I called Craig. He checked the con
you'd amended your copy Sunday morning. Yo
it while I was in the shower. Good job. You'
ing reporter."

She let her rage fly. "You said you trusted
want to listen to me when I'm telling you
write a single word about Marty Breslin. So tak
thou attitude and stuff it where the sun don't

Then she hung up.

And burst into tears.

She supposed she should have told him that Jack had gone into her computer to "help" her, but what was the point? Brian would probably have called her a liar.

It was over. Sybil had told her that trust was the most important thing after love and passion, and Laurie had thought it was something she and Brian had shared.

But she'd been wrong.

A WEEK AND A HALF LATER, on a Wednesday, she and Cindy were sitting in a restaurant, having coffee. Cindy was watching the closed-captioned TV over Laurie's shoulder while they waited for their order, when she suddenly said, "He won!"

Laurie swiveled to look at the screen and asked confusedly, "Who won what?"

"Brian. He won the case."

"Good for him," Laurie said coldly, and turned away from the TV.

"You don't care, huh?" her friend asked.

"No, I don't care. Brian didn't trust me."

"Well," Cindy reminded her, "your name was on the byline, and you didn't tell him what Jack had done."

"He should have known I would never do anything to hurt him," she protested.

"It seems a terrible shame that you two are going to fall apart because of this."

"It's been nearly two weeks. He hasn't tried to call me back."

"He *has* been pretty wrapped up in that trial," Cindy noted.

Laurie wished her friend would stop. She was going to start crying in public, something she had vowed never to do.

"I have to go. Are you coming to help me at the hospital tonight or not?" she demanded.

"Of course I am," Cindy told her.

"Good. Then we need to go."

"And what are we doing?"

Laurie sighed. "Just follow my lead. I wrote a story for the kids to act out."

"Lord, help us," Cindy said. "It's not about a princess throwing a prince off the turret or something like that, is it?"

"No," she replied. "It's about a prince thinking he was betrayed by a princess, then finding out that he wasn't."

WHEN THEY REACHED the hospital, Laurie got out of the car, but Cindy didn't move. "What's the matter?" Laurie asked her.

"I'm scared," she said.

"What?"

Cindy stared at her. "What if the kids don't like me?"

"They're going to love you. Now hurry up, because there are forms you have to sign before you work with the kids."

Cindy climbed out of the car, and they both grabbed boxes of books she'd brought, and headed for the elevator. A couple of aides took the books on to the library, while Sabrina arranged for Cindy to sign the proper forms.

"They're so excited to see you tonight," Sabrina told Laurie. "Poor little Mary-Katherine is back for another round of chemo, and she's been talking about you all day."

"Thanks," Laurie told her.

"Laurie!"

Mary-Katherine ran to hug her when she stepped into the room. She hugged the child back, then introduced Cindy to the kids.

"Hi, guys. This is my friend Cindy. She's going to help me tonight."

Cindy was ashen, but she waved. One of the older boys whistled, and Cindy turned a bright shade of red. "I don't think I can do this," she whispered.

"Of course you can."

"Can she be the princess?" another boy asked.

"Sure," Laurie said.

"No!" Cindy protested.

"All right, Cindy will help me tell the story. Mary-Katherine, you can be the princess."

"No, you be the princess tonight. Please?" Mary-Katherine asked.

"All right. Cindy, you'll have to read the story," Laurie said.

And then they began.

Laurie chose children to play goblins and elves and the king, who was pretending to be cruel so the invaders would stay out of his kingdom, but was really good underneath—a situation the princess, who was engaged to the prince, had apparently revealed. Finally Laurie said, "I need a prince."

"Right here."

She turned around and froze.

She hadn't even heard Brian come into the room.

She swiveled and stared at Cindy, who stared back meaningfully, then returned to her script and started reading. "The prince believed that the princess had betrayed him and his father by revealing the secret of the king's true nature. And he was very angry with her."

"The elves did it, not the princess!" Mary-Katherine cried.

"The elves did it?" Brian asked, and he strode through the rows of seated children, pausing to stare at them one by one. "Are you an elf? Are you the elf who did this thing to my father, the great king? Because I alone knew my father's secret. That means that I was asked never, ever to tell. When the secret came out, and I was supposed to be the only one who knew, it looked very bad for me."

"Did they take his allowance away?" one of the boys asked.

"I bet they took his cell phone," a little girl suggested.

"Did they have cell phones then?" another child said doubtfully.

"The thing is," Laurie stated firmly, stepping out of character, "the princess didn't do it. But the prince never even asked her."

"The prince was only human. He felt betrayed, and he was too hurt to think logically about what had happened, because he loved the princess very much," Brian said.

Laurie stared at him across the room. His eyes were on hers as he smiled slowly, ruefully. "He should have known that a princess—the right princess for any prince—comes along only once in a lifetime. Even if the prince still doesn't know which elf did it or why, he knows he behaved very badly, and that if the princess said she didn't do it, then she didn't."

"Then he needs to tell her so," said one girl.

"And he needs to spank the elf," said another.

"He needs to get on his knees and beg the princess for forgiveness," Mary-Katherine said very seriously.

"It would be a good idea," Cindy said, as if reciting her lines from the script.

"No, no…" Laurie started, backing away.

But Brian caught up to her and went down on his knees in front of her, taking hold of her hands.

"My princess," he said, "I humbly beg your forgiveness. A true prince should never jump to conclusions. He should trust in the honesty and goodness of his princess."

"That's right," Mary-Katherine said emphatically.

Brian struggled not to laugh as he continued gazing up at Laurie. "The prince didn't have faith when he needed to. And so he has to find a way to convince the princess that from now on he will *always* have faith. When the prince was younger and first met the princess, she taught him a game called If I Were King of the World. And if I were king of the world right now, I would go back in time and show the princess how much I trusted her. But I can't go back, so now I have to beg her for forgiveness."

"Princess, you have to forgive him!" a little girl cried, and it quickly became a chant.

"Forgive him, forgive him, forgive him...."

"Wait!" Laurie said. The room fell silent. "You have to understand. The princess fell in love with the prince when she barely knew him, and she thought he was falling in love with her, too, which made her the happiest princess in the whole world. When the prince got so mad at her, it broke her heart, and now she's afraid to let herself love him again."

Brian rose slowly. "What if the prince promised before the entire kingdom—and even the elves and the goblins—that he would love her and trust her for the rest of his life, and he would never, ever lose faith in her?" he asked quietly.

She stared at him, and then she could actually hear her heart start to race.

"The prince loves her with all his heart. And he believes that she loves him, too. And that together they can make the kingdom the best one in the world," Brian added, his eyes on hers, dark and deep.

He sank to his knees again. "The prince begs the princess to accept his hand in marriage. His kingdom is hers, along with his heart."

Laurie was stunned. Was this part of the play? Or was he really asking her to marry him?

"Oh, for God's sake, say yes and let the poor man off his knees!" Cindy exclaimed.

"Say yes, say yes, say yes!" the kids chanted.

"Brian, get up," Laurie pleaded.

He looked at her solemnly. "Not until you say yes."

"Brian, get up," she repeated, embarrassed.

"Say yes," he whispered. "Please?"

"Yes, yes, you're forgiven, get up—er, rise. All is well, the prince is forgiven," Laurie said.

"You need to kiss her," Mary-Katherine ordered. "That's how they do it in the movies."

"Don't go getting carried away! This is a children's hospital," Cindy teased.

Brian took Laurie gently into his arms and looked into her eyes. And then kissed her.

It was a quick, soft kiss.

And yet...

It was a kiss that touched her soul. That burned all through her. That spoke of love and passion with more eloquence than any words ever could.

He pulled back, looking down at her, his expression somber.

The children broke into applause. Cindy stood. "And they all lived happily ever after," she said. "Except for the poor narrator, of course, who is still looking for a prince."

"I'm right here!" said the boy who had whistled at her earlier.

"Down, boy," Cindy said. "The narrator is looking for a prince who can vote."

Then she thanked the children for being such a good audience, said goodbye and left the room.

Embarrassed and still a bit unsure as to what had happened, Laurie quickly said her own goodbyes and fled. She headed straight to the parking garage, then stood still.

The car was gone.

They had come in Cindy's car, and her friend had left her.

"Laurie."

It was Brian. She turned and looked at him.

"You can't lie in front of kids, you know. You said that you forgave me," he reminded her.

She shook her head. "Brian, I… You didn't phone," she said. "You wouldn't listen to me."

"Wait a minute. The last time we talked, *you* hung up on *me,* you might recall. And you had some pretty choice words for me, too."

"You deserved them," she said.

"I got a lot of flack because of that article," he told her.

"But I didn't do it," she insisted.

"I know. Have you figured out what happened?" he asked her.

She nodded. "Yes. Jack did it. He thought he was doing me a favor."

"What? Why didn't you tell me?"

"You didn't trust me. You didn't give me a chance."

"I am so sorry, but...I realized you hadn't done it."

"How?" she asked him. "What changed?"

"I thought about it. And I just...*knew* that you wouldn't have done it. After my initial idiocy, I knew you wouldn't lie to me."

A car went by, beeping. They both ignored it.

"Jack should be shot, or fired at the very least," Brian said.

She shook her head. "I forgave him. He thought he was helping me, making it a better story."

"Still..."

"He'll never do it again."

"Can I at least punch him?" Brian asked hopefully.

"No. You can't go around punching people," she told him.

"Well, he's not coming to the wedding."

"What wedding?" she asked, trying to hide the jolt of excitement that went zinging through her.

Brian walked toward her, and she didn't back away—a good thing, since a large sedan came barreling around the corner just then.

"You did just agree to marry me," he reminded her.

"But…we were doing a skit for the children."

He shook his head and smiled. "The children were there, yes, but the proposal was real. I'm praying that the answer was, too." He suddenly dropped to his knees again, startling her. "If I were king of the world," he said softly, "you would definitely say yes."

She was even more startled when he reached into his pocket and produced a ring box, then opened it and showed her a diamond. It wasn't ostentatious, it wasn't ridiculously small.

It was just right, and beautifully set in entwining gold leaves.

"Laurie, I'm asking you to be my wife. I've never asked anyone before. I've never said 'I love you' to anyone before. My past isn't pure as the driven snow, but that is the truth. I have never loved anyone before, certainly not the way I love you. Please say you'll marry me."

"Brian, get up!"

"Laurie, please, answer me. And quickly. I think a Hummer is coming around the corner."

"Yes, yes, I'll marry you!" she said, and practically dragged him to his feet. But there was nothing coming, after all. She laughed, then realized that tears were streaming down her cheeks at the same time. "Yes, yes, I will marry you," she said again.

And he slipped the ring on her finger.

～EPILOGUE～

S ome might have considered it a strange venue for a wedding, but since Laurie wanted to keep things small, it was perfect.

Sybil was happy to come, having known the playroom well enough herself at one time, and Sabrina was comfortable there, as well.

Laurie's parents understood, and Brian's boss didn't mind.

The children were all assembled, and the minister was waiting. Mary-Katherine and all the little girls were flower children, while the boys were ushers.

Brian looked beyond handsome in his tux.

When Laurie, wearing a medieval-style dress, walked in on her father's arm, she heard friends playing the wedding march on guitars, and could see her mother shedding happy tears. Then Cindy started sniffling, and even Craig cleared his throat several times.

It came time to exchange their vows. Brian went first. He spoke so eloquently and earnestly in his rich tenor voice that Laurie was afraid she was going to start crying herself. He promised her faith and trust eternally, and a home where hope would be ever present and love would be the virtue that bound all the rest together. He promised to love her until his dying day.

Then it was her turn.

She slipped his wedding ring on his finger and met his dark eyes. "If I were queen of the world...I could wish for no more for myself than this." She had planned to say more, but the words wouldn't come.

It didn't matter. They had become one long before making their vows. Where she left off, he began.

"You *are* the queen of my world," he told her.

And then he kissed her tenderly.

The children applauded, her mother kept weeping, her father stepped forward and embraced Brian.

It was wonderful.

There were presents for all the children, courtesy of Marty Breslin. He and Cindy seemed to have bonded over their shared penchant for anonymous donations and the fact that they had both been inspired by Toys.Calm, two discoveries that seemed to be like glue, welding them together. The two of them seemed dazzled and a little bit lost, but, as Brian whispered to Laurie, they looked good together and certainly seemed to be enjoying one another's company.

At last it was time to leave. They were going out to Sybil's for a full-scale reception before honeymooning in Fiji, and the children threw confetti as they headed for the door.

As they left the room, Mary-Katherine yelled after them, "That was the best skit ever!"

Laurie and Brian looked at one another and laughed. "We're going to have to work hard to outdo this one," he said.

"We'll manage," she promised. "After all, we *are* king and queen of the world."

* * * * *

Dear Reader,

I didn't exactly plan it, but I ended up the mother of five. And as I stumbled into motherhood, I also stumbled onto an amazing realization: there is nothing like a child. Children are the future; they are our hopes and dreams. And there is nothing so horrible and terrifying as sitting in a hospital when your child is sick.

Unless, of course, you *are* that child.

I was honored to have the opportunity to write this story. Toys.Calm is an amazing organization. It was created by Erin Puck, who knows what it is like to be that child, and what every little bit of kindness, every additional moment of life, means.

As I found out what my part in *More Than Words* would be, I was planning—along with a group of fellow writers who, like me, are also performers—to head to a children's hospital to put on a skit. The day came, and I was amazed by the courage and resilience of those children. They had suffered so much and had so much to be afraid of, and yet they never forgot that life is a gift, each moment precious, something to be cherished. Toys.Calm provides hospital-bound children with toys and books and entertainment to lighten the load of the IVs so many have to drag around, to make an hour, even an hour spent in a wheelchair, more fun. Those children are strong and magical; they fight to live. Toys.Calm fights to bring humor and love, along with gifts, to enrich their lives. Please join that fight, in whatever way most moves you, and visit www.toyscalm.org to learn more about this wonderful organization.

This story is dedicated to C.J. Lyons, Harley Jane Kozak, Connie Perry, Dave Simms, Chynna Pozzessere and Lance Taubold, with thanks for sharing their time. And it's dedicated to the staff, children and volunteers of the Children's Hospital of Pittsburgh, for all that they do.

Mostly, of course, it's dedicated to Erin Puck, the brilliant founder of Toys.Calm, the incredible woman who inspired the story and who has touched my heart in ways she will never know.

Sincerely,

Heather Graham

JOHANNA KANDEL

⌒ The Alliance for Eating ⌒
Disorders Awareness

A few years ago Johanna Kandel, founder of The Alliance for Eating Disorders Awareness in West Palm Beach, Florida, sat down across from a reporter from the local college newspaper and began to tell her story. As the young journalist taped the interview and asked questions, Johanna tried to paint a picture of what it was like living with anorexia, a lethal psychiatric illness that had robbed her of love, laughter and self-esteem as a teen and young adult. She explained how even years after recovering, she still suffers from osteoporosis and doubts she'll be able to have children.

After the interview, the young woman holding the tape recorder turned it off and began to cry. She suffered from an eating disorder, too, and until she opened up to Johanna, only her mother knew the truth.

"Will you help me?" she asked.

Johanna did, providing one-on-one mentoring, group support sessions and hooking her up with a psychologist and nutritionist. Slowly the young woman not only recovered, but three years later, graduated college and landed her dream job in broadcast journalism. Last year when The Alliance hosted its annual healthy body image fashion show, Johanna's new friend got up to speak to the audience.

"If it wasn't for Johanna, I wouldn't be the person I am today," she said.

"I started bawling," says Johanna now. "That's the stuff you put away in your heart's little bank and you carry it around for the rest of your life."

The Alliance for Eating Disorders Awareness started as a grassroots effort in 2000 to help spread awareness about eating disorders and the positive effects of healthy body image. It also hands out educational material to parents and caregivers about the warning signs, dangers and consequences of anorexia, bulimia and unhealthy fixations on exercise. Since its inception eight years ago, when Johanna was twenty-one—and had graduated magna cum laude with a major in psychology and a minor in women's studies—over 70,000 children, teens, parents and health professionals across the U.S. have listened to her tell her story and messages about positive body image.

"There are a lot of days that go by when it seems like you're hitting your head against a wall and you feel like you're not getting anywhere. Then you get an e-mail or phone call from someone who says, 'I heard you speak. For the first time in my life I realize I have a problem,'" she explains. "It's so gratifying to make a difference in someone else's life."

Johanna's own struggle with anorexia started when she was twelve years old and on her way to becoming a professional ballet dancer. She calls herself a "textbook case" anorexic now: growing up in a loving family, straight-A student, type-A personality and a perfectionist. When a dance instructor told the class they would need to lose weight before trying out for the next *Nutcracker,* Johanna says she remembers thinking, *I am going to show them. I am going to be the thinnest in the class and for sure they will want to cast me.*

But soon, Johanna's need to be the best imploded. She developed an unhealthy fear of fat, and it didn't help that as she became thinner and thinner, dance teachers, friends and family told her how good she looked. Little did they realize that Johanna was sinking into a quagmire of deprivation and self-hate.

"When I was struggling, I didn't laugh. I didn't love. I didn't have a life. Your eating disorder is all-consuming. It's the first thing you think about when you wake up every morning, it's the last thing you think about at night, and it's every other thought in between," she says.

It wasn't until her mother saw her body as Johanna undressed that things began to change. Not that Johanna was ready for the help. As her parents dragged her from specialist to specialist, she told them everything was all right, or tried to say what they wanted to hear. Eventually she quit dance, hoping that by taking away the triggers, her eating disorder would evaporate. It didn't. It only got worse.

When she went to college and started volunteering at an eating disorder organization, she finally hit the wall. She called her parents and told them she was sick and tired of being sick and tired. She was ready to heal and recover in an outpatient setting with the help of a psychologist, psychiatrist and nutritionist. The road was wavy and full of potholes, but she made it.

As she neared graduation she started to consider grad school, but then a thought hit her.

"I'd made a pact with myself that if I ever did get better, I would do everything in my power to help other people overcome this problem, too—and know they are not alone," she says. So Johanna put the brakes on grad school, took out a student loan to pay for legal and corporate fees, and started her own nonprofit organization. Her parents gave her a year to get it off the ground, and if it didn't succeed, wanted her to go to grad school.

Luckily, it did succeed, despite the organization's difficulty in securing funding. In fact, funding and recognition are still a challenge today, despite the fact that ten million women and one million men in the U.S. suffer from the illness. Johanna admits people are still not ready to talk about eating disorders, and many more think victims choose to suffer. Yet studies are beginning to show the disorders are partially influenced by genetic factors, as well as societal pressure. Then there's the shame. Johanna says she sees it in action every time she buys an information booth at a health fair.

"A lot of times, nobody will come up to my booth. I used to take it personally. I thought, *Oh, my gosh, do I have something in my teeth?* But people don't want to be seen walking up to my table. They worry other people will think they have an eating disorder. There's still that stigma attached to it."

Johanna hopes her talks will help erase the stigma, especially with the elementary schoolchildren she now visits. When she visits schools, she talks about how people come in all shapes and sizes. She tells them everyone is beautiful, and helps kids develop better self-esteem. Johanna admits she worries that eating disorders are emerging earlier in children, but that means her wisdom, humor and stories are needed now more than ever.

"I'm going to keep using my voice. I spent ten years keeping silent, so now I'm just going to keep on talking to anybody who will listen," she says.

For more information, visit www.eatingdisorderinfo.org or write to The Alliance for Eating Disorders Awareness, 1016 North Dixie Highway, West Palm Beach, FL, 33401.

CANDACE CAMP
∽ BREAKING LINE ∽

ഹ—CANDACE CAMP—ഹ

Candace Camp is the bestselling author of more than forty contemporary and historical novels. She grew up in Texas in a newspaper family, which explains her love of writing, but she earned a law degree and practiced law before making the decision to write full-time. She has received several writing awards, including a *Romantic Times BOOKreviews* Lifetime Achievement Award for Western Romances. You can contact Candace or find out more about her books at www.candace-camp.com.

CHAPTER
~❧—ONE—❧~

Nicole pulled her hair up into a ponytail, then swept it around into a tight knot and pinned it, her moves smooth and unconscious from years of practice. She wore her hair long, as did the other dancers. She had worn it that way all her life. Indeed, she could not quite imagine what it would be like to have short hair, to not feel the weight of her thick, dark brown hair upon her head. She remembered that one summer her mother had wanted to cut her hair short, and Nicole and her aunt had protested in horror.

Her mother, her own hair styled in a smooth chin-length bob, had just shaken her head and smiled. Nicole and Aunt Cyn had shared a glance——*what could be expected from a woman who had quit the ballet to get married and raise children?* Nicole's mother had a job. But ballet was a way of life. And in ballet, one wore one's hair long and wrapped it up in a knot.

Nicole smiled a little at the memory. She understood her mother's viewpoint better now. More than once when she took her hair down and felt the relaxation spread across her scalp, or when she rinsed her hair for minutes at a time every afternoon as she showered, she had wondered what it would be like to be free of the weight and routine. And now and then when she happened to see some new chopped-off trendy style on a popular actress, she couldn't help but wonder what it would be like to try a new hairdo. To do something different, even a little crazy.

But different and crazy were not her, of course. Nicole understood tradition. Indeed, she had always embraced it. The tradition of the ballet was part of what she had fallen in love with all those years ago—the waifs in their white poufed dresses in a Degas painting, arms and necks bent gracefully, frozen in a timeless world.

The reality, of course, was not quite so delicate. Nicole picked up her backpack and set it in her locker beside her shoes. She glanced around the room at the other dancers changing into their rehearsal clothes, and, as so often happened, a perfect opportunity for a picture caught her eye—one of the girls, dressed in leotard and tights, sitting on a bench, headphones on her ears and her eyes on a magazine as she stretched down over her straightened leg.

Nicole reached into her backpack and withdrew her camera,

quickly taking several pictures. The dancer, Kate, looked up and made a face at her, sticking out her tongue and crossing her eyes. Nicole laughed and took another shot before she turned off her camera and put it away.

"What are you going to do with all those photos, anyway?" Kate asked now, removing her headphones and stowing them and the magazine away in her locker. "Blackmail?"

Nicole laughed, her large, expressive gray eyes lighting with warmth. "I can't imagine who'd pay to suppress these."

She had enjoyed taking pictures ever since her mother bought her a camera for her fifteenth birthday. She had plagued everyone for a year afterwards, snapping photographs of everyone and everything she could. The hobby had fallen to the wayside for a few years after that. She had been accepted into the ballet academy, and ballet had become even more her life than it had been before.

But in the past three years, after she'd joined the Grayson Ballet Company and moved to Austin, Texas, she had rediscovered the joys of photography. There was something supremely satisfying to her in finding a subject and framing it just so. And, unlike a number of other things, taking pictures worked in well with her career. It was easy enough to carry a camera with her wherever she went, and images of hard work, beauty, weariness and delight were all around her. The other dancers were accustomed to her snapping photos of them at work and rest.

"I keep telling her she ought to frame them and sell them," another voice said, and Nicole turned to see that her friend and roommate, Sarah Duncan, had come up behind them.

"Hi," Nicole greeted her. "I didn't see you this morning. You must have left early."

Usually the two of them drove to practice together to save on parking fees. Like the much larger and better known Ballet Austin, the Grayson was quartered in the old warehouse district—though not in such elegant new headquarters—on the edge of downtown, where parking was at a premium.

"I decided to go for a run early, so I just caught the bus." Sarah stripped off her sweatpants and loose T-shirt as she talked. Underneath she was already clad in tights and leotard. Stowing her backpack, she sat down on the bench and pulled on her ballet slippers.

The three young women moved toward the far doors, where the rest of the dance troupe was congregating, slowly passing through.

"What's the deal?" Kate asked, and Nicole shrugged.

When they stepped inside the rehearsal room, it was immediately clear why a traffic jam had developed at the door. A scale had been set up a few feet inside the room, and the dancers were lining up before it.

"Oh, no..." a girl in front of them groaned.

Beside Nicole, Sarah put her hand to her stomach. Nicole glanced at her and saw that her friend's face had gone stark white.

"I knew I shouldn't have had breakfast," Sarah murmured.

Nicole sighed. Very few ballet companies still engaged in the random and public weighing-in of the dancers. But Adele Grayson, the executive director of the company, was a law unto herself, a rigid traditionalist and a former dancer and choreographer of such skill and renown that dancers flocked to her tryouts, more than willing to accept her unbending strictures.

"Ballet," Ms. Grayson was fond of saying, "is the art of discipline. Without one, there is no other."

"Don't worry," Nicole assured Sarah. "You'll do fine."

"Do you think so?" she asked, her face knotted with worry.

No one liked the weigh-ins, including Nicole. They were, frankly, humiliating, as if a dancer were a side of beef to be weighed and measured. But she had always been a petite person, blessed with a good metabolism. She had to watch what she ate, of course, even with the large amount of exercise she got in rehearsal and performance, but she had never had to really struggle to maintain the low weight required in ballet.

Sarah, on the other hand, was taller and big-framed. Entering ballet classes as a girl, she had not been much larger than any of the other girls her age. But in her teens, she had spurted upward until she was five feet eight inches tall, larger than anyone in her class. Ever since then, she had had to work at maintaining the same level of weight as the other, shorter dancers. Nicole knew that Sarah dreaded the weigh-ins, fearful of the wrath of both the revered Ms. Grayson and the acid-tongued artistic director of the company, Joff Harlow.

Joff himself was the one weighing the dancers, calling out the numbers to his assistant, Pris, who sat at a table several feet away. Nicole felt a familiar spurt of dislike. It was bad enough that they forced everyone to be weighed like this. But they could have at least set the table closer to the scales, so that everyone's weight was not trumpeted across the room.

Nicole smiled reassuringly at Sarah. "I'm sure you haven't gained any weight. You're thin."

"Really?"

Nicole looked closely at her friend, realizing as she did so that Sarah did indeed appear as thin as she had ever seen her. If anything, she thought, Sarah was even slimmer than she had been a couple of months ago when they had had their last public weigh-in.

"Yes," Nicole answered honestly.

Ahead of them, Kate stepped on the scales. Joff moved the weight up one careful pound after another, stopping and checking the balance each time. Nicole noticed that a pink line touched Kate's cheeks, brightening with each added pound. It was scarcely fair, Nicole thought, given that the girl who'd been on the scale before Kate was the smallest in the corps.

Joff finally read Kate's weight off to his assistant, adding sharply, "You need to lose ten pounds, Miss Cummings. One can hardly expect your partner to lift you if you're going to eat like a lumberjack."

Kate's face was now fiery red, and she hurried away from the scales, going to a spot on the barre at some distance from anyone else. Nicole stepped up onto the scale, thinking of a number of less than complimentary comments she could make regarding Joff's appearance. But, of course, she kept her face blank, as she had learned to long ago whenever she or one of the other dancers fell under the wrath of an instructor or ballet master.

She stepped away from the scales and waited for Sarah. Joff read out her roommate's weight with a note of surprise, adding, "Excellent, Miss Duncan. I'm glad to see that there are some who make an effort to restrain themselves at the table. Now, Miss Wilson."

Nicole turned to Sarah, shocked at the figure Joff had called out. She could not remember what Sarah had weighed last time, but was certain it had been quite a few pounds more than this. It was a good bit less than what Nicole herself weighed, and she was five inches shorter than Sarah.

But, noting Sarah's bright face, Nicole bit back the worried words that rose to her lips, and smiled. "See? I told you you'd do fine."

She reached out her hand and curled it in a friendly way around Sarah's arm. She felt a small, queasy shift in her stomach at how thin that arm was, how little flesh lay between skin and bone.

"I know. I just have to keep at it," Sarah agreed, heading for the barre.

Nicole followed, her uneasiness growing. She cast a critical eye over her roommate. How had she not noticed how much weight Sarah had lost? Surely she was far too thin.

However, Nicole didn't know what she could say or do. Sarah was obviously pleased with her weight loss, and Nicole wasn't about to prick that balloon of happiness. Besides, it wasn't really any of her business, was it?

She sighed, aware of a lingering sense of disquiet, and raised her leg to the barre to begin her stretches. Before long, as she went through the familiar stretches and exercises, the worries she had felt slipped away. Once again she gave herself up to the order and beauty of ballet. *The art of discipline.*

REHEARSAL WAS INTERRUPTED midafternoon for a round of costume fittings. This did not mean, of course, that rehearsal was skipped. Practice, after all, was never ignored. Rather, it meant that they would come in this evening to finish.

Given a couple of free hours, many of the girls went home or shopping or, like Sarah, decided to take a run along the hike and bike trail. It was a beautiful spot, and Nicole often went for a run or walk herself on the trail that ran along the edge of Lady Bird Lake, the name given to the stretch of the Colorado River that ran through downtown Austin.

However, today Nicole decided to walk over a few blocks to one of her favorite galleries. Bryce Gallery, in the upscale area of condos and stores that clustered in the old warehouse district around Second Street, was a smart gallery with a perfect blend of style and casual ease that suited Austin. Nicole had found it a few months ago on one of her rambles through the area near the ballet company, and she had immediately fallen in love with it.

Bryce carried several different kinds of artwork, but its specialty was photographic art, a fact that had immediately lured Nicole. She remembered there had been a sign announcing a new show starting this week, and now seemed like a perfect opportunity to drop in.

She was greeted with a smile by the young woman behind the ultramodern desk near the door. Nicole was enough of a regular that she felt sure the clerk recognized her, though on a dancer's salary, she rarely had enough money to make a purchase.

The new showing dominated the center wall, and Nicole strolled along it, quickly lost in the stark, intriguing black-and-white images. One, of storm clouds boiling up behind the low skyline of a small West Texas town, was particularly compelling.

"Grabs you, doesn't it?" said a low masculine voice behind her.

Startled, Nicole jumped and turned to the speaker.

"I'm sorry," he said, a smile curving his lips. "I didn't mean to scare you."

"It's all right. You didn't scare me," Nicole assured him.

The truth was, few women would feel anything but delight to have this man speak to them. A little taller than average, he had the slender build of a man who stayed in shape without devoting himself to bulking up. Thick black hair framed a strong square face, and there was an indentation in the center of his chin that just invited the touch of her finger. His eyes, under straight slashes of dark brows, were a dark and compelling blue. His hands were well-shaped, with a slender, supple strength, and devoid of any sort of jewelry, including rings... Now, why, Nicole thought, had she noticed that?

"I'm Gregory Bryce," he told her.

"Oh. You mean, as in Bryce Gallery?"

He nodded, smiling again. "Yeah. For better or worse, it's all mine."

"It's a wonderful place," Nicole exclaimed.

"Thank you. I'm glad you like it." He paused, then added with a grin, "You know, here is where you tell me *your* name."

"Oh! I'm sorry." Nicole felt a blush forming on her cheeks. Why was she acting like a social klutz? You would think a man had never come over to talk to her before.

Of course, she had to admit, she wasn't sure if a man who looked as gorgeous as this one ever had.

"I'm Nicole McCasland," she said, holding out her hand in a businesslike way.

He took her hand, engulfing it in the warmth and solidity of his own. He held it for a moment, his eyes gazing directly into hers, and Nicole found herself unable to look away. Then he smiled and released her. She felt suddenly awkward, and stuck her hands in her pockets.

"I've noticed you in here before," he stated.

Embarrassed, she wondered if he had spoken to her for a purpose. Perhaps he had noted how she came to browse and never buy. Her blush deepened.

"I love to look. You have such beautiful things," she told him honestly. "Unfortunately, most of them are out of my reach."

His smile never wavered. "Sorry. Was I coming on like a salesman? I didn't mean to. I'm just happy to have people come back."

"Oh, I'll definitely do that."

"You like Atchley's work?" He gestured toward the photo of storm clouds.

"Very much."

"Let me show you my favorite." He guided her toward the back of the gallery and up a set of circular metal steps.

At the top of the stairs was a small loft overlooking the gallery. Tucked into the back corner was an office. Bryce opened the door and ushered her inside. It was a large room and utterly utilitarian except for an enormous photograph that hung behind the desk.

Unlike the pictures downstairs, this blowup was in vibrant, compelling color, though just as stark in its own way. A dusty flat landscape, dotted with prickly pear and yucca, stretched to a blazing sunset in the distance. The sun was a huge, almost blood-red orb, just beginning to sink, and above the horizon, the sky was streaked with glorious reds, golds, pinks and purples, a stunning blend of colors that seemed almost too vivid to be real.

Nicole let out a gasp of pure pleasure. "Oh, my…this is beautiful! It's wonderful…" She moved closer, drawn to the photograph. "Words are utterly inadequate."

He smiled. "I never even offered this one for sale. As soon as Jason pulled it out, I bought it. For just that spot."

"I can see why." Nicole turned and smiled at him. "It must be difficult, I suppose, to keep from buying all your own merchandise."

He returned the grin. "With some people more than others. Atchley's one of them. I have three more of his works at home. I have to remind myself sometimes that if I don't sell some of his photographs, I won't be able to buy the ones I have to have. Actually, I think the reason I got into the business in the first place is because I realized that while I could never buy all the art I wanted—I wouldn't have enough wall space, if nothing else—I could have it and admire much more of it if I set up a gallery. This way, I can look at it for days or weeks at a time."

"Do you ever show things you don't like?" Nicole asked as they turned and made their way back down the stairs.

"Not really. Sometimes I have carried an artist because I knew he had a good clientele, even though I was not personally very drawn to his work. But I don't think I could be certain that what I show is good if it was something that didn't appeal to me."

They strolled through the gallery below, with Bryce pointing out this work or that, adding little tidbits about the artist. Nicole entered into the conversation animatedly, unaware of the way her cheeks flushed and her eyes sparkled, as they talked about such things as clarity, perception, depth and contrast.

She could not recall when she had talked with someone like this. Ever since she could remember, all her conversations had centered on ballet—either in a broad way of trends, personalities and history, or in particular ways about companies, rehearsals, steps and practices. In school and now in a company, she spent the vast majority of her time involved in dance, and all the people she worked with and even lived with were equally involved. What conversations did not revolve around ballet were generally about the people she knew in the field.

It was, she realized, delightful to have something new and different to discuss. It was like stepping into a whole new world... and it did not escape her notice that she was plunging into this most enjoyable new sensation with an exceptionally attractive and charming man.

In fact, it was so delightful that not until some subtle shift in the traffic noise on the street made her turn and glance outside did she notice how late it had become. The traffic was no longer the bumper-to-bumper crush of rush hour, and the sun was definitely slanting more acutely from the west.

Nicole made a low noise and looked at her watch. She let out a soft cry. "Oh, no! I'm late!"

Rehearsals started again in only fifteen minutes, and she needed to change back into her practice clothes.

"I'm sorry." She flashed a smile at Gregory Bryce, already backing up as she did so. "I have to leave. I'm sorry. It was very kind of you to show me around."

"But—Nicole—" He took a step after her.

She whirled and was already hurrying toward the front door as he spoke. He hesitated, then started after her. But by the time he reached the door, she had slipped out and was running down the street.

CHAPTER
~ TWO ~

"**W**here have you been?" Sarah whispered as Nicole slipped into place beside her at the barre. "Another minute, and you'd have been late."

"I know," she panted, still winded from her sprint to the ballet studio and up the stairs to the practice room. She had whipped off her clothes in record time, slipping into leotard, tights and slippers, and zipping into the room just before Megan Crawford, the ballet master, came across to close the door.

Any later, and Nicole would have had to open the door to enter, and Crawford's gaze, chilly now, would have been positively wintry. Joff could be biting, but Crawford was stricter than anyone. One could never slack off a bit when she was at rehearsal, and she was an absolute martinet about tardiness and poor form.

Nicole stretched, breathing in and out in full, deep breaths, more to focus her concentration and calm herself than from any need of air.

"Where did you go?" Sarah murmured again.

"A gallery," Nicole whispered back.

Sarah rolled her eyes. The idea of risking Crawford's ire to look at a bunch of pictures was beyond her.

"I met a man," Nicole added, knowing that this fact would be of much more interest to her roommate than photographs.

Sarah's eyes widened, and she turned to look at her. "A man? Really?"

"Miss Duncan. Miss McCasland. Perhaps you would like to continue your conversation outside. I feel sure the company would all be happy to wait for you."

The two young women chorused their apologies and settled down in silence to stretch.

It was not until much later that they were able to continue their conversation—after rehearsal, when they had driven home and were digging into the refrigerator for something to eat.

"So who was this guy?" Sarah asked, pulling out a package of shredded lettuce and opening it, then carefully measuring out four cupfuls.

"Gregory Bryce. He owns the gallery. And he's absolutely gorgeous."

Sarah's eyebrows rose questioningly. "And is he the reason you were late?"

Nicole shrugged. "Yeah, I guess. In a way. He came over and introduced himself, and we started talking about all the pictures. He specializes in photographic art, and he had the most amazing collection of——"

Sarah made a winding motion with her hand, as if to speed Nicole along. "I know, I know. Great art, et cetera. What about the *guy?*"

"Black hair, nice build. Absolutely riveting blue eyes," Nicole reported in staccato fashion. "And a smile to die for."

"Plus, rich," Sarah added.

"How do you know that?"

"Well, he owns a gallery. Stands to reason."

"Or maybe he's in debt up to his eyeballs," Nicole countered, sitting down with her plate across the small table from her roommate.

She glanced over at her friend's plate. It was piled with lettuce and topped by a few sprigs of broccoli, and Sarah was squeezing half a lemon over it. Nicole watched as she dug in. "Is that all you're eating?"

Sarah nodded. "Yeah. I always eat lightly at night. So I won't gain weight, you know."

Nicole nodded in turn. It was an argument she had heard

many times. Personally, she was always so hungry after rehearsal that she had to have a good meal.

"Yeah, but… haven't you lost enough weight?" Nicole asked. "I mean, the scales this morning…"

Sarah smiled. "I know. But I can't let up just because I've lost some weight. You know how I am. As soon as I stop dieting, I go right back up."

That, Nicole knew, was probably true, and the reason was that, given her height, Sarah should weigh a good deal more than she did.

"So, are you really interested in this guy?" Sarah asked, shoving the conversation back to the original topic.

Nicole smiled faintly, then shook her head. "No. Not really. He was cute, but I doubt I'll see him again." She was faintly surprised at the tug of dismay she felt at her own words.

Sarah nodded once again and sighed. "Yeah… As Ms. Ethridge used to say…" she assumed the tight-lipped expression and stilted tone of one of her former instructors "'…you can date or you can dance.'"

Nicole chuckled, but she knew that the words were all too true. Ballet was a full-time occupation that left little room for romance and dating. It was not something from which one could take a break. A dancer needed to retain her conditioning, strength and agility, which meant daily stretches and exercises. She had to work at improving her form, as well as rehearse for whatever performance was coming up next. And when one was performing, it was a nightly grind. It was, as every ballet instructor had drilled into her head since she was a child, a passion to which one devoted one's life.

"Of course, she was right," Sarah said now with a melancholy sigh, echoing Nicole's thought. "A boyfriend is death for your career."

"Harsh," Nicole commented.

Sarah quirked a brow. "But true. I mean, look, he takes you out to dinner, and you know how many calories are in restaurant food. So you either eat twice as many calories as you can afford to and then you have to work them off somehow, or you just pick at your food and he gets offended because he spent all that money on you and you're wasting it. Then he wants to take you out when you have to work."

"And you're in love, so you want to go out with him instead of working," Nicole chimed in.

Sarah dipped her head emphatically. "And your discipline starts to slip. Either that, or he stops dating you because you don't ever have the time to hang out with him."

"Plus, he can't understand why you're so obsessed with your career. Other women have jobs and don't spend their whole lives on them."

"Exactly," Sarah agreed. "Then, if you do make it through a few months of dating him without getting dumped, you decide you're in love, and you want to marry him and have a family. Only how can you take off a couple of years here and there during the time you're in your prime? Provided, of course, you can even get the job back after you've had the baby and worked yourself into shape again."

"I know."

There were always hundreds of young girls waiting in the wings, coming out of the academies, eager to get into a professional company. Unless you were a principal, a star, it was incredibly hard to get a job back once you walked away from it—and even then it depended on whether or not the company regarded you as a traitor for leaving in the first place.

Nicole sighed and stood, picking up her plate and carrying it to the sink. "Oh, well…I know nothing's going to come of it. But it was kind of nice to flirt, just a little bit."

"Wish I could remember what that felt like," Sarah joked.

She wouldn't go back to Bryce Gallery, Nicole thought, at least not for a while. She didn't want to give Gregory the idea that she was interested in him. And, she admitted silently, she didn't want to give herself an opportunity to get even more interested in him.

Over the course of the next week, the pace of rehearsals began to pick up. The company was drawing closer and closer to opening night, which meant an increase in the number of rehearsals, as well as their duration. And, of course, it also meant more visits from Ms. Grayson herself, as well as photographs and stories for publicity and fittings and refittings for costumes.

As a result, Nicole's spare time grew less and less. She had a two-hour break on Tuesday between exercises and rehearsal, so she grabbed her purse and camera and headed out to take some pictures. It was the best way she knew of burning off some of the stress that an approaching performance always brought on.

She was dawdling along Second Street when a little gust of wind sent dust and trash flying upward in a miniature tornado just as a bicycle messenger went speeding past. Nicole managed to click off several shots of the humorous image that resulted, a juxtaposition that appeared as if the cyclist's speed had whipped up the eddy of wind. Her eye was caught by the slant of sun on the sidewalk and building, the almost perfectly round shadows of umbrellas in front of a coffee shop, and she raised her camera again, framing possibilities.

"Nicole! Ms. McCasland!"

Nicole turned, glancing around her, surprised at hearing her name. She saw Gregory Bryce walking toward her, smiling.

She could not keep from smiling back. "Gregory."

The last few days she had convinced herself that Gregory Bryce was not as devastatingly attractive as she remembered. But, with the little leap her heart made when she saw him, she knew that, if anything, she had underestimated his good looks.

Nicole strolled forward to meet him. "How are you?"

"Excellent, now that I've seen you," he replied. "When you left so fast the other day, I was afraid that I might not see you again."

"I'm sorry. I realized I was terribly late. I had to run. As it was, I just barely made it in time."

"Well, I'm glad it wasn't something I said."

"No, of course not."

He glanced down at her hand, still holding the camera. "So you're a photographer?"

"Oh." Nicole looked embarrassed as she raised her camera and turned it off, tucking it back into her purse. "No. Not professionally. It's just a hobby. I was taking a break."

Someone passed them, and they stepped out of the way. Gregory glanced down the street toward the coffee shop's brightly striped umbrellas.

"Why don't you take your break with me?" he suggested. "I'll buy you coffee. Or lunch, if you haven't eaten."

"Oh, no, I had lunch, thanks." Nicole told herself she should decline the invitation altogether, but instead found herself saying, "But coffee would be nice, thank you."

"Sure." He turned, and they walked back down the block to the coffeehouse.

Nicole glanced up at him as they walked. The sun glinted on his thick hair, as black as a crow's wing, and she was aware of a stirring sensation deep inside her. This would not do, she told herself. There wasn't any room for handsome men in her life.

But another part of her could not help but wonder why there wasn't. It was only natural, after all. Surely devotion to one's career shouldn't take up all one's time and interest. If a person was careful and didn't let herself get swept away....

"If photography isn't your profession..." Gregory said as they stopped outside the coffeehouse and he politely pulled out her chair.

She smiled at him. "Ballet. I'm a dancer."

"Really? I don't think I've ever met a ballerina before. I suppose I should have guessed, though."

"Because I walk like a duck?" she teased.

"No. Because you are so graceful, of course."

She felt herself blushing a little at the compliment.

"Was that where you went rushing off to the other day?" he asked, and she was grateful to him for covering her sudden awkwardness. "A performance?"

"A rehearsal. But the ballet master is an absolute dragon. She makes you feel like a second-year student again."

He grinned. "Sounds like something out of a movie."

"Oh, she is. Crawford prides herself on it. She's very old school."

"Is there old school and new school in ballet? I didn't realize."

"Well, the whole system is very tradition oriented, of course. But there are variations. Grayson Ballet Company is traditional. Very traditional. And controlling—they hate tattoos, and you have to get permission to color or cut your hair."

He stared at her. "You're kidding."

She shook her head. "No. I mean, there's a basis for it. The major aspect of the corps——" When he looked questioningly at her, she explained, "The line of dancers behind the principals, like the chorus line in a musical. Anyway, the corps should all look alike. It's part of the whole performance. They dress exactly the same, wear their hair the same. Their steps match perfectly. It's part of the beauty. It's usually not too much of a problem with heights, as dancers tend to be small. And one can hardly manage to have a whole group of women with the same hair color. But if everyone else has their hair up in a bun, then the one girl with short hair stands out, you see. And bright green hair, for instance, would be glaring."

"Mmm. I can see that. A big ole snake tattoo up your arm might not look ballerina-like, I imagine."

Nicole smiled. "No. It wouldn't." But she couldn't hold back a sigh. "Still…it can get a little repressive."

"I understand." He nodded sympathetically.

"Sometimes I think it would be wonderful to cut my hair—or put a permanent in it or dye it."

"No, don't dye it," he protested quickly. "It's much too beautiful as it is."

Warmth blossomed in Nicole's abdomen, and she quickly looked away to keep the pleasure from showing in her face. "You're very kind."

"Just honest. I'm sure you've had more than one guy tell you that."

She smiled a little, but didn't answer. "My mother was in ballet, but she gave it up. I once asked her how she could have given up her life as a dancer, and she told me that ballet wasn't her life. That my dad and I were her life. At the time I thought it was the lamest answer." Nicole shrugged. "But lately I've wondered more and more if it's really so bad to want to live a normal life."

She looked away, surprised at how candid she had just been. Such a thought about her lifelong love seemed traitorous, and she would not normally have spoken about it to anyone. How bizarre that her thoughts had slipped out so easily with this complete stranger.

"I'm sorry," she said quickly. "I don't know why I said that. It isn't as if I would ever give up ballet. Or even want to."

"No? It doesn't sound that odd to wish you could look the way you really want to. Not many people have to sacrifice something like that for their career."

"It's more than a career," Nicole answered automatically. "Ballet is something you devote yourself to. It sounds corny, I'm sure, but it's a…a life choice, I guess you'd say. There are other areas where you choose to live with such restrictions. The military, say—uniforms and short haircuts, rules and regulations. Or nuns and monks."

"But that's a religion."

Nicole chuckled. "Trust me, to a great many people, so is ballet."

"And do you love it that much?"

"Of course," Nicole answered automatically. "I've loved it since I was a child. It was the only thing I ever wanted to do. I couldn't believe my mother had given it up—though obviously I can't help but be grateful that she did, since I wouldn't be here otherwise. But I thought she was wrong. It was my aunt whom I admired. Cyn stayed in ballet, and when she got too old to dance, she taught. She was my teacher when I was growing up, and I thought she was absolutely perfect. Aunt Cyn was sophisticated, she was beautiful. She didn't cook or clean or do anything mundane. Her life was all about art and beauty. She and I had a bond that was different from what I felt with my mother. Better in some ways. I mean, your mother is your mother, and I love mine. But Aunt Cyn and I were alike. We belonged to a sort of sisterhood."

Nicole rolled her eyes comically. "Now you must think I am a perfect dork."

"No. Not at all. I'm drawn to people who have a passion for things. It's why I own a gallery. I never had the talent myself to create beauty. I wanted to. I tried. But all the art lessons and photography lessons in the world can't give you the eye of an artist, the mind of a creative person. That comes from within. And part of it is a passion for what you do. I enjoy that passion, that dedication. Devotion, as you say."

"But it's terrible when you lose it," Nicole told him, her voice suddenly tinged with sadness.

He looked at her carefully. "Have you lost it? Your passion for ballet?"

"No, oh, no. Of course not. I mean, it's natural to have doubts sometimes, isn't it? To wish that things were a little different."

"Of course." But still his deep blue eyes were watchful on her face.

Nicole found herself breaking their hold.

"Sometimes, I wish I could do more things," she admitted, not even realizing what she was going to say until it came out of her mouth. What was it about this man that made it so easy to talk to him? What made her deepest secrets just pop out, as if she were commenting on the weather?

"What things?"

"Oh, like photography, for instance. I really enjoy it. It's such a great feeling when something just clicks, when you know it's a great picture. The light, the timing, the angle—everything's perfect. And it's wonderful."

Nicole smiled, unaware of how her face lit up.

"If that's how you feel, then you should spend more time taking pictures, I'd say."

Nicole gave him a wry grin. "Easier said than done, I'm afraid. But here I am, blabbing on and on, and you haven't said anything about you. Where are you from? How did you get into the gallery business?"

"Nothing terribly exciting about me, I'm afraid," he told her. "I'm a native of Austin—strange, I know, but true. So, of course, when I was young, while everyone else was rushing to move here, I was rushing to get out. I went to college back East."

"Let me guess...Ivy League?"

He let out a groan. "Does it show?"

"Hardly at all," she assured him.

"Then law school. Big law firm in Dallas. And a couple of years ago, I decided I just couldn't do it anymore."

"You got tired of law?"

He shrugged. "I don't know how much I was ever *into* law, really. It's one of those things that was kind of...I don't know, the sort of route you think you should take. I knew I wasn't cut out to work for a corporation. I wasn't an academic kind of guy. And all the artistic things I liked—well, I knew I wasn't good enough at any of them to even consider them. So if you make good grades, and you have a certain facility with words, well, law seems like it's the spot for you. Only there I was, after not wanting to work for a corporation, slogging away in a firm with three hundred lawyers. And I wondered, *how did I wind up here?* So I quit that and went into private practice, which was better. At least I didn't have to answer to other people. My life was...okay. Everybody told me I was crazy to want something else. I had good money. A nice house. An expensive car."

"What else could you want?" Nicole asked, with a smile that mocked her words.

"Maybe to wake up in the morning and not dread the rest of my day. Then, as luck would have it, I went to a showing at a gallery in Dallas and got to talking to the guy who owned it. It turned out his friend owned a gallery here and was looking to sell, and suddenly, I realized that this was what I wanted." He grinned, his blue eyes glinting. "See, some of us don't figure out what we want to do until we're thirty-three."

"In ballet, that would be a little late," Nicole pointed out. She sighed and glanced at her watch. "And, speaking of late, I'd better go if I don't want to earn another black mark from Crawford."

"Can't have that." He stood up with her, and his face turned serious as he put his hand on her arm, saying, "But I don't want this to end. I'd like to see you again."

Nicole felt the warmth of his palm travel through her, and her heart began to hammer. He was asking her out, and she felt confused, excited and distressed all at once. She didn't want to have to face this decision. "Gregory…"

"Let me take you out to dinner. You name the time and place. I know you have a schedule you have to work around."

"I would like that. I really would."

"Then say yes."

He would never know how much she wanted to, Nicole thought. And it was possible, of course. She could find a few hours here or there to go out and eat with him or to take in a movie. A date or two was not the problem, and if she had liked him a little less, she might have said yes. But she knew that it was in the long run that problems loomed. A few dates didn't matter. Falling in love did.

And this was a man whom she knew she could all too easily fall in love with.

That was why, with a sigh, she replied, "But I can't. I'm sorry, Gregory. I really am. But it's best we don't go any further."

CHAPTER
~ THREE ~

With opening night barreling down upon them, Nicole had little time to spend in regrets over turning Gregory down. Every day was crammed with activity, and when she wasn't doing something, she was struggling with performance nerves. Even though she had been dancing in public for twenty years now, one way or another, the anxiety of opening night never completely went away. She still woke, sweating, from dreams of being late onto the stage or forgetting her steps while everyone whirled around her. She still worried over each difficult passage, rehearsing in her mind when she was not actually dancing.

She was not the only one. Tempers were short and nerves frayed all through the company, from wardrobe assistants to stage managers to the primary dancers themselves. Something or other was always going wrong. A spotlight was not the right color or a set wasn't in the proper place. A headpiece fell apart; a skirt was too tight, too loose, too short.

But that, of course, was simply business as usual. Even though she still had pre-opening night jitters, at least over the years she had learned to deal with them. She expanded her nightly yoga sessions. She sneaked every spare moment she could to go off by herself to Zilker Park and the hike and bike trail along the lake and the Garden Center, snapping pictures. She reminded herself that it would all come off right; it had before. And never once had she tripped or fallen or otherwise made a complete fool of herself, even if she had once or twice blanked out completely on her steps for an instant.

Sarah, Nicole noticed, was apparently dealing with her jitters by tightening up even more on her eating. She seemed to exist these days almost entirely on green salads and hard-boiled eggs, and even those were consumed rarely.

Ever since the day of the weigh-in, Nicole had been paying more attention to Sarah's eating habits, and what she had noticed alarmed her. She had not once seen Sarah consume a dairy product. She rarely ate fruits, and carbohydrates seemed to have been banned from her diet altogether. Nicole tried to remember an occasion when she had seen Sarah eat a pasta of any variety, but she could not. Steamed green vegetables, salads without dress-

ing, half of a broiled skinless chicken breast, carefully weighed
and cut down to two ounces exactly—those were the stuff of her
meals.

Sarah had a number of odd rituals and habits centering around
food and mealtimes. It amazed Nicole that she had never really
thought about them before. She had noticed some of them, of
course, but she had shrugged them off as the sort of odd quirks
that everyone had about something. But now she began to realize that the majority of Sarah's quirks had to do with food.

She noticed, too, the way Sarah dressed. When she was out of
costume or not practicing, her clothes were uniformly baggy. She
wore sweatpants and long sweatshirts or T-shirts. Once, as she
was dressing, Nicole watched her yank the drawstrings of her
loose pants as far as she could and tied them tightly. But the waist
was still loose on her. The sweatpants were positively billowing
around her legs. Sarah was always cold and wore layers of clothing. Although it was April, and the last few days had been warm
almost to the point of a summerlike heat, she kept on a sweatshirt over her other clothes. Even in practice, Sarah bundled up
in leg warmers and long-sleeved leotards.

Sarah needed the extra clothing because she was so often
colder than everyone else, Nicole knew, but she also suspected
that the bagginess and layers served another purpose—to hide
Sarah's now stick-thin arms and legs.

Guiltily, Nicole felt like a terrible friend and roommate to have not seen the extent of Sarah's obsession with thinness and food. She tried a time or two to bring up the matter of her constant dieting, but Sarah, she discovered, was a master at sliding out of this sort of conversation, diverting it to some other topic or shutting down into silence or flaring into anger or tears.

Nicole was not the only one who had begun to notice the drop in Sarah's weight. One of the male dancers, Mike Lawton, joined Nicole as she trotted down the stairs to the break room in the basement on the night of the last dress rehearsal, and bluntly asked, "What's up with Sarah?"

If it had been someone else, Nicole would have stonewalled, joining Sarah's silence in the solidarity of friendship. But Mike had been their friend from the first, joining the company at the same time that Nicole and Sarah had. He had been their roommate for a year, as well, until he had moved in with his new boyfriend a few months ago. Nicole knew that his question came only from concern, not a desire to gossip.

"I don't know," Nicole answered honestly. "Is it that obvious?"

Mike cast her a sardonic look. "Girl, are you serious? She's looking like Olive Oyl. I heard Pris tell Joff that she's lost seven pounds since her last weigh-in, and that girl didn't have seven pounds to lose, I'll tell you that. 'Course, you know Joff, he just said, 'Good. Now if only she could cut off three inches, too.'"

"Yeah, Joff's all heart."

They rounded the stairs and went into the break room halfway down the hall. The space, usually half-empty, was almost full this evening. The final rehearsal was always the toughest and ran the longest. They had only thirty minutes for eating before they had to return to the theater, and most people opted to eat in the break room.

Sarah was there, too, a rather limp-looking salad and a package of carrot sticks on the table before her. Nicole bought a micro-wavable soup and a yogurt from the vending machine and joined her. Mike followed, carrying two of the questionable machine sandwiches and a small energy drink.

"Sarah! Sweet-pie!" Mike bent to kiss the top of her head.

"Hi, Mike." Sarah smiled up at him. "We never see you any-more."

"I know. I know. I got no time to hang out. Every minute I'm not here—Barry complains if I don't spend it with him. You know how that goes."

Mike nodded toward Sarah's salad as he dropped into his chair and began to open his shrinkwrapped sandwiches. "That disgust-ing looking lettuce all you eating?"

"At least I won't get salmonella," Sarah retorted with a wary glance at his meal.

Nicole dug her spoon into her yogurt. She had the feeling Mike was going to bring up the forbidden topic and all hell was about to break loose. She could only hope that Sarah would be less defensive with Mike's questions.

It was a vain hope.

"How you gonna dance tonight, eating nothing but that?" Mike pressed.

"I'll manage," Sarah replied shortly.

Nicole glanced at Mike. He shrugged and took a bite of his sandwich. They ate in silence for a moment. But Mike was apparently only contemplating his plan of action, not dropping the subject, because after a few minutes, he began again. "Sarah...don't you think you've lost enough weight already? When you going to stop this dieting thing?"

"I don't ever stop."

"That's my point. You can't diet forever. You'll waste away to nothing. You already are."

Sarah shot Nicole a dirty look. "Did you put him up to this?"

Nicole raised her hands in a gesture of surrender. "I didn't say anything to him. I swear."

"She didn't have to say anything to me," Mike pointed out. "Anybody with two eyes can see you're looking like a skeleton these days."

"Gee, thanks."

"Well, it's the truth. You need to face reality, girl, or you're going to do yourself harm."

Sarah set her jaw, shoving the plastic bowl of lettuce away from her and crossing her arms defensively over her chest. "You're the one who isn't facing reality. I can't eat whatever I want and dance. I'm not a guy. I don't have the same kind of superme-tabolism you do. And I'm not a dainty little girl like you." She turned her wrathful face toward Nicole. "I have to diet."

"Sarah, you don't have to diet this much," Nicole told her pleadingly. There must be some way, she thought, to make her see reason.

"You're skin and bones," Mike said bluntly.

"I have to be!" Sarah cried. "Don't you see? It's so easy for you two! You don't have to diet to stay thin. You can eat anything you want."

Nicole knew that this was not true. She watched what she ate, only rarely treating herself to sweets or high-fat foods. But, wisely, she decided to stay silent.

"I don't know why you all are harassing me!" Sarah continued, her voice near tears. "You know how important ballet is to me."

"I know, Sarah. Believe me, I know." Nicole reached out to pat her arm.

Sarah jerked away, but not before Nicole realized sickly how very thin it was.

"You don't know. You can't. My mother loved the ballet. It was— She used to brag about me all the time to everybody. How graceful I was. How she had always wanted to take ballet lessons when she was a child, but her parents couldn't afford it. She came to every recital I was ever in, and she always took pictures."

Sarah's eyes filled with tears, and Nicole could feel herself tear-ing up in sympathy. Sarah had told her about her mother's death when Sarah was still a teen, and Nicole knew how very hard it had been on her friend.

"Even Daddy used to call me his 'little ballerina.' And after Mom died, he always told me she was watching me dance from heaven. When I got accepted to Grayson, he was so proud of me! He said Mom would have been so happy, so proud of all my hard work and dedication."

"I'm sure she would have been," Nicole told her earnestly. "I know how important she was to you, and I can see how that makes ballet even more special to you. But do you really think she would want you to starve yourself? You're thin enough, Sarah. You don't need to be any thinner."

"We both know I barely made it in here. I've always barely made it in—every school, every summer ballet program. Ever since I was fourteen, I've seen it in the judges' eyes when they look at me—I'm too big. I'll look like a giant in the corps. My partner won't be able to lift me high enough. It'd be different if I were un-believably talented, but I'm not. I've never been good enough. I just worked harder than everybody else. I never quit. I just always practiced more and knew my steps better. I never made a mistake."

"That's not true!" Nicole gasped, aghast. "Sarah, you're plenty good enough. You're just as talented as anybody in the company." She had never before realized that her friend felt this sort of inadequacy.

"Don't patronize me!" Sarah snapped. "You know and I know that I have to work harder to stay in. That's the way things are. And I'm not going to quit ballet just because I have to diet!"

"But—"

Before Nicole could say anything else, Sarah jumped to her feet, grabbing up her half-eaten salad. "Stop it! Just stop it! I'm not doing anything wrong!"

She swung away and rushed from the room, dropping her lunch in the trash as she left. With a sigh, Nicole settled back in her chair. "Well, that went well."

Mike shrugged. "We had to try. She's going to wind up in the hospital if she keeps this up." He shook his head. "I hate having to dance with one of the anorexic girls. I'm always scared I'm going to break one of her bones when I pick her up. They're like birds or something."

Nicole looked at him, her heart swelling with sadness. "Is she that bad? Do you really think she's anorexic?"

Mike leveled his cool dark gaze on her. "What do you think?"

Nicole nodded, and they finished their meal in silence.

That night after the final run-through, the air was chilly between Nicole and Sarah as they drove home and went into their apartment. Nicole hated to have her friend mad at her, and she started to apologize, but she could not think of any way to apologize for being concerned about Sarah's health without sounding resentful.

So she said nothing, hopeful that Sarah's silent treatment would eventually grow tiresome to her, too.

Sarah went straight to her bedroom when they got home. Nicole grabbed a snack and puttered around in the living room, trying to unwind. It was always like this after dress rehearsals and performances—she felt both weary and somehow jazzed up, still too full of adrenaline to sleep, yet too tired to do anything.

She sat down on the couch and leaned her head back, staring at the poster across from her without really seeing it. It would be nice to have someone to talk to. Suddenly, with an ache that surprised her, she wished that Gregory Bryce was here with her.

She missed him, Nicole realized, startled. It seemed silly; she had, after all, only known the man a few days, had spoken with him only twice. But ever since she had turned him down, she had found herself thinking of him at various points during the day. She would see something and think that she would like to tell Gregory about it, or she would wonder what he was doing at that moment. Sometimes she found herself daydreaming about him, remembering his smile or the vivid blue of his eyes.

Nicole sighed. So not seeing him was not as easy as she had assumed it would be, but that didn't mean she was wrong. Indeed, it proved she had acted just as she should have. If he was this hard to get out of her mind after being around him a couple of times, imagine how difficult it would be after dating him! With some men, she could risk dating, not really caring if it worked out, knowing she was not going to get into a conflict between ballet and a man. But Gregory Bryce was different. She had the sneaking suspicion that any time spent around him would only make her want to see him more. Gregory was someone who would be all too easy to fall in love with.

And that was a conflict she was not prepared to face. To have to give up the man she loved in order to do the only thing she had ever wanted to do—no, that would just be too awful. Even harder to face would be the opposite—what if she fell for him so hard that she chose him over ballet?

Nicole picked up the remote, switching on the television. She was *not* going to sit around second-guessing the decision she had made. She had made up her mind not to see Gregory anymore, and that was that. In a few more days she wouldn't even think about him.

Idly, she thumbed through the channels; it was late enough that the choices were mostly infomercials, syndicated TV shows and old movies. She hit a news station and was about to click past it when the word *anorexia* caught her attention, and she stopped.

The television host, an older woman with champagne-blond hair, was quoting statistics, "Anorexia is primarily a women's disease. Ninety to ninety-five percent of anorexia sufferers are females. According to the National Institute of Mental Health, one in five women today struggle with an eating disorder. Wow! That is hard to imagine." She gave the camera a wide-eyed look, then went on. "Even worse are the numbers that indicate that very young girls—nine- and ten-year-old girls!—are caught up in the vicious cycle of dieting. Fifty-one percent of them feel better about themselves if they are on a diet. And, most frightening of all, a girl with anorexia is twelve times more likely to die than other girls her age."

The blonde shook her head. "Some pretty scary statistics. Here with me today to discuss some of these issues is the founder and executive director of The Alliance for Eating Disorders Awareness, Johanna Kandel."

The camera pulled back to show the other woman sitting in a chair facing the host's. Nicole was surprised to see that she was young, probably no older than Nicole herself.

"Now, Johanna, why don't you tell us a little bit about yourself? You were a ballet dancer, were you not, when you first began to struggle with this disease?"

Nicole leaned forward, even more interested, as Johanna began to describe her years-long battle with anorexia, talking of the time when she was twelve and was among a group of young ballet students eager to get a chance to be in a production of the *Nutcracker*. Told that all the girls would need to lose weight before the auditions, Johanna had plunged into dieting with all her might.

Nicole listened, fascinated, as the young woman described the years that had followed, the strict adherence to calorie-counting and exercise, the initial praise she had received from friends and acquaintances, as well as ballet instructors, for how much weight she had lost. It was only later that everyone around her began to notice the extremes to which her weight had fallen, and friends, family and teachers began to confront her about her problem.

Johanna spoke of the battle with the eating disorder that she had fought all through high school, and her decision finally to seek therapy and help others with the same problem. Even more amazingly, at the age of only twenty-one, she had decided to create an organization to bring awareness of eating disorders to public attention.

The show cut to commercials, and when it came back on, an author of a book about anorexia and bulimia and a psychiatrist specializing in eating disorders had been added to the group. The television host turned to the author and asked, "You've heard Johanna's story. Is ballet the only culprit in this disease?"

"No, of course not. Any of the industries in which appearance is important—movies, fashion, et cetera—are constantly pressuring the young women involved to be unnaturally thin. Young women of normal size, even ones the majority of people would characterize as thin, are being told by teachers, agents, directors, clothing designers that they should weigh less. And fashion and movies, of course, have tremendous influence on all young women."

"Absolutely," the psychiatrist chimed in. "Pick up a women's magazine or a teen magazine, and you may very well find an article decrying anorexia or bulimia, but just turn the page, and there will be a four-page fashion spread featuring abnormally underweight young women. Which do you think has more impact on the young reader?"

"I find it appalling," the author added, "that when a horse breaks its legs at the Kentucky Derby and has to be put down, there is this huge outrage, but when a twenty-two-year-old model steps off the runway and collapses and dies of complications caused by anorexia, hardly anyone even hears of it."

The panel began to discuss the warning signs that a friend or loved one was grappling with the disease of anorexia. Nicole listened with a sinking heart; they might have been describing Sarah.

Even worse was the listing of medical complications that could result from anorexia, running all the way from fatigue and dehydration through fainting, muscle loss and heart problems to death.

Tears sprang into Nicole's eyes. She could not let Sarah do this to herself. She jumped up and grabbed her purse, digging around in it until she found a pen and a scrap of paper. Then she jotted down the name of Ms. Kandel and her foundation. Awful as it was to hear the grim information, for the first time since she had noticed Sarah's weight loss, Nicole felt a little better. She had been floundering, not knowing what to do to help her friend. But now, at least, she had some hope.

CHAPTER
~ FOUR ~

The following morning, Nicole called the telephone number she had written down the night before. A pleasant woman assured her that the organization would send her a packet of information, including the names of several professionals in the Austin area who specialized in the treatment of eating disorders.

When she hung up, Nicole felt much better. She decided to wait until she received the information before talking with Sarah again. Opening night was not a good time to talk to anyone about anything, much less to discuss a topic that would annoy her friend. In any case, Nicole would feel more confident after she had gone through the information The Alliance was sending.

The rest of the day was spent in the usual state of nerves that preceded an opening, and the time crept by. But then, at last, the curtain went up, and there was the familiar rush of excitement, the beauty and pleasure of performing, the wonderful sense of concentration in the flawless execution of the steps. This was the magic, the essence of ballet. The reason she had practiced and performed and sacrificed since childhood. It did not matter that the lights poured their heat down upon her or that the costume itched or that her stage makeup felt like a mask. What mattered was the precise curve of her arm, the extension of her leg, the perfect line her body formed.

It was all worth it on opening night. There were no questions, no regrets, no stirrings of rebellion. There was only the dance.

And when it was at last over, so, too, were all the nerves, all the harsh words, all the resentments and arguments. Everyone smiled at everyone else and kisses were spread around with the same lavish abandon as words of praise. Mike and Sarah hugged each other and Nicole, and Sarah and Nicole chattered animatedly as they removed their makeup and changed back into their jeans and T-shirts.

There was a party, it seemed, at Kelly Swarthmore's apartment— for ensemble dancers only, of course, not the sophisticated affair that Adele Grayson held at her home after opening night, where sponsors came to rub elbows with the principal dancers and slather praise upon Adele and Joff. Sarah, floating high with adrenaline, was going to Kelly's, as were Mike and most of the others. Nicole smiled and agreed to go, but without the measure of enthusiasm which her friends felt.

It wasn't that she wasn't happy or excited. It wasn't that she didn't feel like celebrating, or didn't want to go over the dance in endless detail. It was just…there seemed to be something missing. She didn't know what it was until she was walking out the side door into the parking lot with all the other dancers and saw Gregory Bryce standing there, leaning up against a car, waiting for her.

A smile burst across her face, and she hurried toward him. "Gregory!"

He straightened, smiling back, and started across the parking lot toward her. Nicole thought that she had never seen anyone quite as handsome or as effortlessly sophisticated as he was in his elegant dark suit and gray-and-silver tie.

Gregory reached out his hands to her, and the next thing she knew she was throwing her arms around his neck and he was lifting her up and holding her close against him.

"You came!" she exclaimed softly.

"Of course." He set her back on the ground and stood looking down at her, his hands now holding both of hers. His eyes were midnight-blue in the dim light, but the expression in them was clear, and it warmed her inside. "How could I not see you dance?"

She smiled and gave a little shrug. "I thought perhaps…after the last time we talked…"

The rest of the dancers and crew were straggling out the door and walking past them, turning their heads curiously to watch the couple. Nicole knew that she normally would have been embarrassed. But right now she was too full of surprise and delight to care what anyone else thought.

Gregory chuckled. "I think you'll find that I'm somewhat more tenacious than that. Besides, even if you never want to see me again, I couldn't not come to see you perform."

Nicole felt herself blushing. "It wasn't that I didn't want to see you again. Not at all."

"Good. I'm glad I wasn't entirely lying to myself." He paused, then added, "So there's a chance you'll let me drive you home?"

"I have my car," Nicole said, and instantly regretted her words. She glanced over at her vehicle, where Sarah and Mike were standing, waiting for her and watching the scene before them with unabashed interest. "But, um…just a minute. I'll be right back."

She hurried over and Sarah and Mike immediately closed ranks around her.

"What gives?" Mike asked, eyes alight. "Who is the hunk?"

"Is that Gallery Guy?" Sarah asked, her doubts about Nicole getting involved with Gregory obviously shelved in the greater cause of friendly gossip.

"Yes, that's Gallery Guy," Nicole admitted. "Listen, would you like to take my car to Kelly's party?"

Sarah's eyes grew wider. "You're not going to the party? Why don't you bring him?"

Nicole shook her head. The thought of Kelly's party had little appeal compared with a quiet evening alone with Gregory. "He's going to take me home."

"Well, you be careful," Sarah told her, frowning and casting a suspicious glance toward Gregory. "You tell him we have his license number, so he better not try anything."

Nicole laughed. "I will. You two have fun."

"No need to tell *you* that," Mike commented dryly.

Nicole grimaced and handed her keys to Sarah. When she turned and strolled back to Gregory, his grin widened. He straightened and walked around the car to open her door for her.

"Where to?" he asked as they settled into the car. "Straight home or would you be amenable to a celebratory drink first?"

Nicole smiled. "Actually, a drink sounds nice."

They went to one of the bars on Fourth Street, a long, narrow room, dimly lit and furnished with plush booths and chairs with high backs. Right after work, it was always packed with office workers, but this late at night, it was much quieter and, fortunately, lacking in the loud music that permeated most Austin bars. It was possible to settle down in a quiet corner and actually talk as they sipped their drinks.

"So how did you like *Sleeping Beauty?*" Nicole asked.

"It was lovely. *You* were lovely."

She chuckled. "Did you even know which one I was?"

"Of course I did!" He looked offended, then grinned. "I brought my opera glasses so I could be sure to find you. But, in any case, I was close enough to recognize you on my own."

"You came on a good night. No major mishaps. No pratfalls."

"Does that ever happen?"

"Oh, yes." Nicole rolled her eyes comically. "It has—though not to me, thank goodness. At least, not in front of an audience."

"Dancing must be very fulfilling," he hazarded. "Exciting."

She nodded. "Yes, it is."

He leaned in a little, scrutinizing her. "I sense a *but* here."

Nicole laughed. "It's thrilling opening night—to know that you're dancing well, to hear the applause. It's a feeling that's hard to describe—pride, excitement, joy. But it just isn't the same feeling it used to be. When I was at the academy, whenever we performed, it was…absolutely grand. I've never felt so alive. But now—I don't know. I don't feel quite the same high as I used to. I guess I'm growing accustomed to it."

"Did you go to school here, too?"

"No. I'm from California originally. Los Angeles. That's where I trained. Grayson doesn't have an academy. Ballet Austin does, of course—a rather large academy—but they're much differ-ent from us. They're the, I don't know, I guess 'official' ballet of Austin. We're a private company. Much smaller…and with a much smaller budget. Adele, Ms. Grayson, is concerned only with professional dance. She isn't into 'training children.'"

"That sounds like a direct quote."

"It is. Ms. Grayson is...well, dedicated to the ballet. Everyone's intimidated by her—even Joff, I think, at least a little."

"If she's so scary, why do people want to work for her?" Gregory asked reasonably.

"Her reputation, of course. Ballet's always had intimidating directors. But when you are as talented as she was, when you've danced for Balanchine, well, people want to dance for you, no matter what."

They continued to talk about the performance for a few more minutes, and from there fell into talking about Austin and from there moved on to bicycling, then running, then a host of other topics, skipping from one thing to another, laughing and enjoying themselves so thoroughly that before they knew it, the bartender was announcing last call.

Gregory drove her home to her apartment and walked her to the door. She hesitated. It was late; she should say good-night.

Instead she found herself saying, "Would you like to come in? I could fix us a cup of coffee."

He smiled. "That would be nice. Thank you."

She unlocked the door and led him in, hoping that the place would not prove to be too messy. Housekeeping was one of the many things that got ignored when opening night drew near. Of course, the good thing was that they were usually not home enough at that time to make a mess.

Nicole gestured him toward the couch in the living room, casting a quick glance around the room—*not too bad*—then headed into the kitchen to start the coffee. When she returned, she found Gregory standing in front of the couch, studying the framed photographs on the wall.

"I like your pictures," he said. "Whose are they?"

"Well, actually…they're mine. I took them."

"Really?" He shot her an intrigued look. "When you said photography was your hobby, I didn't realize you meant…such a professional hobby."

Nicole felt her cheeks pinkening. "Thank you, but I'm afraid they aren't professional at all. I just take pictures of things I like."

"Very good pictures. And trust me, I can see the professionalism. The framing, the composition, the use of light and dark—if you just picked this up on your own, you're very talented."

Nicole's blush deepened. She felt both pleased and embarrassed by his words. "Thank you. I—I better check on the coffee."

It had barely started to drip, of course, so she was soon back in the living room with Gregory, who now asked to see some of her other photos. Before long, she was hauling out her favorite albums to show him. He moved through the pages of the albums, studying the pictures intently, barely noticing when Nicole got up to pour their coffee and returned with the cups. Absently, he sipped the coffee, and continued to peruse the photos.

"These are great," he said, turning to her, his eyes bright with enthusiasm. "You should work up a show. We could have one at the gallery."

"A show?" Nicole stared at him. "Oh, no, no, really. I mean, I wouldn't know what to do. I've never——"

"Ah, but I *do* know what to do. So no problem there. You'll just need to go through your photos, pick out the best ones, see how much you'd need to add, explore what themes you have and how you'd like to add to them. I'll take care of the spacing, the arranging, the publicity—all that kind of stuff. That's what I do."

"But I'm not a photographer!" Nicole protested. "I'm a dancer."

"Can't you be both?" he countered. "I'm not saying you need to quit the company. You could do it in your spare time."

Nicole let out a little laugh. "I don't have spare time. No, really, not enough for a project like this. A person can't be a member of a company part-time. Ballet…ballet takes up your life." She didn't add that if she dated him—something she was realizing more and more that she really wanted to do—she would have no spare time at all.

"Well, think about it, okay? Maybe for the future?"

She smiled. "I'll think about it. But, really, it's not a possibility."

He sighed. "Then I suppose I'll have to be content with having broken through your dating barrier."

Gregory reached out and took her hand, and Nicole felt the heat all through her. She didn't know how a mere touch could stir her so, but she realized that she felt flustered and overheated and even a little giddy, all at once. She looked into his eyes, and the feelings intensified.

He leaned forward, stopping just inches from her face. He was about to kiss her, she knew, and she realized that he had paused to give her the option of retreating if she wished. But Nicole had no desire to retreat. Instead she leaned forward.

And then his mouth was on hers, soft at first, then more heated and searching. His arms went around her, pulling her to him, and Nicole melted against him, returning his kisses eagerly. It was a long time before he drew away, and his voice was a trifle shaky as he said, "I should go."

Nicole was aware of a treacherous urge to tell him he didn't need to go, but she refrained. She could not rush into this heedlessly. With an inner sigh, she said, "Okay," and walked him to the door.

But as she stood in her doorway, watching him walk down the stairs and out of sight, she knew that this was one man whom she was not willing to push aside for the sake of ballet.

NICOLE AND GREGORY WENT out the following Monday evening, the one night each week when there was no performance, and after that she managed to fit in a little time with him wherever she could, whether it was a coffee after her morning run or a late dinner after a performance or a quick meal between workouts and the evening show.

She was aware that she was not exactly proceeding slowly with Gregory, but she could not seem to stop herself. She wanted to see him more and more every time she was around him, and she found herself thinking about him whenever he wasn't there. If she didn't watch it, she told herself, she was going to find she was in love with him. The only problem was, she couldn't work up any dread of falling in love with Gregory.

He continued to urge her to devote more time to her photography, to let him put together a show of her work, but she laughingly held him off.

She received the information The Alliance for Eating Disorders Awareness had promised to send her, and she went through the personal stories of those with eating disorders, as well as the pamphlets about anorexia, bulimia and binge eating. It was eye-opening, to say the least, and Nicole quickly realized that the way she had approached Sarah had been wrong. It had been a mistake, she saw now, to talk to her about it with Mike, especially sitting in the midst of their fellow dancers. And she had to guard against getting sucked into a conversation about calories or weight or food with Sarah.

The Alliance had included, as well, the names and phone numbers of several therapists in the Austin area who dealt with eating disorders. Doing her best to follow the guidelines, to be supportive without confronting or being overly involved in her friend's problem, she handed Sarah some of the personal stories and a brochure about anorexia.

"I want you to know I'm here for you, Sarah, but I'm not going to bug you about what you choose to do."

"Good." Sarah gave her a wary look as she took the papers, and Nicole noted with some disappointment that she immediately stuck them in a drawer.

"They sent some names of counselors, too," Nicole said. "You could call one of them and talk."

"I don't need a counselor," Sarah told her tightly.

"It's your choice," Nicole reiterated. "I just want you to know they're available, and I'll help you however I can."

After that conversation, Nicole refrained from talking to Sarah about anything touching on weight, but the atmosphere continued to be strained between them.

The last week of the performances, Gregory and Nicole planned to spend the entire Monday off together. He came over to her apartment early in the afternoon, and they discussed plans to see a movie.

"Maybe you'd like to come with us," Nicole invited Sarah. Perhaps doing something enjoyable together might help ease the tension between the two of them.

Sarah hesitated, then shook her head. "I thought I'd go over to the studio and practice a little."

"But we aren't even performing tonight."

"I know. But I thought I was a little bit ragged last night. You know how it is—you get careless after a while and make mistakes. I need to make sure I'm sharp."

"Well, we could wait for you. Or you could practice this evening."

"Yeah, but I haven't done my weight training," Sarah explained. "Today's a good time to get it in."

Nicole refrained from pointing out that Sarah did not need to fill every spare moment of the day with another method of burning off calories or improving her skills. Arguing would do nothing but drive her further away.

"Okay," Nicole replied evenly. She turned toward Gregory. "Hang on a sec. Let me get my purse."

Sarah jumped to her feet, starting toward her bedroom. Nicole had the distinct feeling she was eager for them to leave so that she could start on her routine without any interference.

As Nicole watched her walk out, Sarah wobbled. Her face drained of all color, and she raised her hand toward her head. Then she crumpled to the floor.

CHAPTER
⌂ FIVE ⌂

"Sarah!" Nicole ran to her friend, followed closely by Gregory.

"What happened?" he asked, kneeling down beside them.

"She fainted, I think. It's happened before." Anger pushed into Nicole's voice. "She probably hasn't eaten anything today, and when she stood up, she became light-headed. Sarah." She leaned in closer to her friend, saying her name again. "Sarah. Are you okay? Sarah?"

Sarah's eyes opened and for an instant she gazed blankly at Nicole. Then she blinked and sighed. "I'm sorry. I don't know what happened."

"I think you fainted." Nicole struggled to keep the anger out of her voice. *How could Sarah continue to do this to herself?* "You're probably feeling weak."

"No. I'm okay." Sarah started to sit up, pushing up with the arm that lay beneath her. She let out a sharp cry and fell back, her face even whiter than before. Her eyes were huge and panicky, filled with tears. "My arm. Oh, Nicky, I think I hurt my arm."

"Here, turn over on your back." Gently, Nicole rolled her friend off her arm, reached out her hand.

"No! Don't touch it!"

"Okay. Okay, I won't." Nicole looked up at Gregory.

"I'll call an ambulance," he said, replying to her silent plea.

"No," Sarah cried. "Oh, no, don't. Please."

"Sarah, you have to go to the emergency room. What if your arm's broken?"

"It's not. It couldn't be. I just fainted, that's all. It's not like I fell down a flight of stairs. I probably sprained it."

Nicole fixed her with a disbelieving look. "Sarah, you and I have both sprained a lot of things over the years. I don't think a sprain is going to make you shriek like that."

"I didn't shriek," Sarah protested, but she cast a fearful glance at her arm that belied her words. "Okay, I'll go to the hospital. But can't I just go in the car? You could drive me."

"And move your arm? I don't think so. You need to have it immobilized."

Sarah tried to lift her arm and bit back another cry of pain. Sweat popped out on her forehead. "Okay," she whispered.

Gregory dialed 911, and Nicole sat down beside Sarah to wait for the ambulance, holding her friend's uninjured hand. Sarah's fingers felt fragile in hers, as though the slightest pressure could break them. It would be no surprise, Nicole thought, if Sarah *had* broken her arm. Her bones felt like bird bones these days, with no padding to cushion a fall.

Sarah was crying, tears streaming down her face, and Nicole's heart broke for her. She suspected that it was not just the pain that was causing her tears. It was also the fear of what this meant for her position in the company. Sarah would be unable to dance—not just for the few performances left in this run, but also for the daily round of exercises and rehearsals for the next show.

A pulled muscle or tendon was bad enough, but at least with those, you could use ice and the whirlpool and megadoses of ibuprofen, and you could manage to dance even if you weren't at full strength. They had all been there and done that. But a broken bone—there was no way to make it heal faster, or to use it before it did heal. No, a break removed you from dancing entirely.

Maybe it wasn't a break. Maybe it was just a very painful bruise or an injured tendon or…

Nicole looked at her friend's face and knew she was just lying to herself. Like athletes, dancers recognized pain and injury; they dealt with it all the time and worked through it and around it. Sarah's anguish proved that this was serious.

The E.M.T.s arrived and immobilized Sarah's arm, then took her down to the ambulance. Nicole picked up Sarah's purse, knowing that she would need it at the hospital, and she and Gregory followed the ambulance in his car. When they got inside, they found that Sarah had already been wheeled off to get an X-ray of her arm, and they sat down to wait for her.

"She'll be all right," Gregory assured Nicole, looping his arm around her comfortingly.

"I know. It's just—she can't dance. You'd think an arm wouldn't be that important, but it is. Nobody wants to see one of the ballerinas out there with a big cast on her arm. Besides, it affects your balance, and your arm movements are just as much a part of the dance as the footwork."

"But surely there are understudies or something."

"Oh, the show will go on," Nicole assured him, her voice heavy with sarcasm. "There's no worry about that. But they won't be pleased with her. And depending on how serious it is, she could be out for weeks. It will put her out for the next production, too, because she won't be able to rehearse."

At that moment, Sarah was wheeled back into view and placed in a cubicle in the emergency room. Nicole slipped into the space with her and sat down in the chair beside the bed.

Sarah gave her a wan smile. Her face was pasty, and she looked terrible. Nicole smiled at her, doing her best to hide her thoughts.

A middle-aged man in a white coat came in. He stuck a couple of X-rays up and lit them, revealing the bones of Sarah's forearm.

"Ms. Duncan." He turned and looked at her. "I'm afraid you've had a nasty break." He went back to the X-rays for a moment, studying them, then cut off the light and came over to stand beside the bed. "It's going to require surgery. We need to insert a pin to make your arm stable."

Tears filled Sarah's eyes and spilled over. "No. Oh, no. I can't."

"I'm afraid you have to. Your bones are exceedingly fragile." He paused, then went on. "I'm not a psychiatrist or a therapist. So I'm just going to speak to you as a blunt old country doctor. Looking at your X-rays, looking at you, I would guess that you are anorexic. Am I right?"

He glanced from Sarah to Nicole. Neither of the women could hold his gaze, which was apparently answer enough for the man.

"As I suspected. You have the bones of a sixty-year-old woman, Ms. Duncan. What are you?" He glanced at her chart. "Twenty-four?" He sighed. "Your eating habits are robbing your body of calcium. Anorexics lose bone density and suffer from osteoporosis. If you continue in this manner, I can assure you that this is only the first in a series of this kind of incident."

"It was an accident," Sarah protested weakly.

"I'm sure it was," he replied. "You told the admitting nurse that you fainted, I see. Another common symptom of anorexia nervosa. Trust me, this is not the first X-ray I've seen like this, and you are not the first patient. I get a lot of young girls with brittle bones. Unfortunately, all I can do is put them back together as best I can. I can't do anything to correct the damage you are doing to your internal organs, including your heart. I can't stop the memory loss or the fatigue, the dehydration, the muscle weakness and loss. Most of all, I cannot stop you from doing what you are doing to yourself. But I can assure you that if you do not change, your health is only going to deteriorate further."

He fixed his stern gaze on her for a long moment, then swung his head to look at Nicole. "And, you, young lady, if you value your friend's life, I suggest you do something to get through to her."

Sarah began to cry, and Nicole squeezed her hand, angry with the doctor for being so hard on her friend, and angry with herself for not having helped her.

The man sighed and his face softened. "I don't want to upset you, young lady. But you need to wake up to what you're doing. As for your arm, it's a serious break. We're going to have to operate. Insert a pin. A nurse is going to come in and take you to your room. She'll also give you something for the pain. We'll keep it immobilized, and tomorrow morning we'll repair it."

Sarah nodded, looking numb. When the doctor left, she turned to Nicole. Nicole wasn't sure what she thought Sarah was about to say, perhaps something about her fear of the surgery or her dislike of the blunt doctor, or even, perhaps, the grip anorexia had on her.

But what she said was, "Don't tell Joff I broke my arm!"

"What?"

"Please, Nicole," she begged. "Please don't tell them."

"Sarah…" Nicole studied her with a mingling of exasperation and sympathy. After the doctor's harsh warning of all the damage she was doing to herself, this was what Sarah was worried about? "Your arm is broken. Joff is going to notice."

"I can dance, though," Sarah argued. "It's not my leg. I can still—"

"Sarah, be realistic," Nicole told her as gently as she could. "You can't hide a broken arm. And you can't perform with one."

"Joff is going to kill me," Sarah wailed. "Nicky, what if they drop me from the company?"

"They won't drop you," she replied with more confidence than she felt. "I'm sure they'll grumble, but…"

"I'm always on the edge. You know that."

"No, I don't, and neither do you," Nicole told her. "Don't worry about it. You just get a good night's rest, and tomorrow the doctor will fix your arm and then everything will seem a lot better. It really will."

Sarah let out a snort of disbelief.

"Listen, shouldn't I call your dad and tell him about this? I mean, surgery… He might want to come down." Sarah's father lived in Dallas, only a two or three hour drive away.

"Oh, no. No. Don't tell him. It's not that big a deal," Sarah replied quickly.

Nicole glanced at her curiously. She knew how much Sarah loved and admired her father. He had been both father and mother to her after the death of her mom, and Sarah always spoke of him with great admiration and affection. Nicole had seen him several times, especially when Sarah was first with the company.

As she looked at Sarah now, it struck Nicole that it had been several months since Gary Duncan had been to Austin to see his daughter. Another moment's thought dredged up the fact that Sarah had not gone to see her father in Dallas, either. That was not that unusual, of course; the company took up most of their time. But surely it wasn't that hard for Mr. Duncan to drive to Austin for a weekend.

"Sarah, don't you want to see your father?" she asked, watching her shrewdly.

"Of course. Don't be silly." Sarah turned her face away. "It's just...oh, you know, he fusses so."

Nicole was suddenly certain that Sarah had been avoiding her father. Now that she thought about it, she realized she'd heard her on the phone a couple of months ago, assuring him that that particular weekend would not be a good time for him to visit. On how many other occasions had she done the same thing?

Nicole felt equally certain that she knew why Sarah was avoiding Mr. Duncan. Sarah didn't want her father to see her. She didn't want him to realize how thin she had become. Along with that came the subsequent realization—Mr. Duncan did not know what his daughter was doing to herself.

The nurse popped back in, smiling, with a little pill cup in her hand, and asked Nicole to step outside while she and the doctor made sure that Sarah's arm was properly stabilized. "I'm going to settle our patient in her room. So why don't you just take an hour or two to relax? Then you can come back and visit with Ms. Duncan."

Nicole looked at Sarah. She seemed so small and vulnerable lying there on the examination table. "I'll be back," she assured her, and Sarah nodded in a way that left Nicole in no doubt that her friend did not relish the idea of spending the rest of this day and evening alone.

She turned and walked out into the waiting area, smiling when she saw Gregory, sitting there patiently. She walked over and sank down into the chair beside him. "I'm sorry. I guess our day is kind of ruined."

"Not your fault." He shrugged. "Nobody's fault, really. How is Sarah doing?"

She told him what the doctor had said about her arm and the surgery, adding the rest of his blunt assessment of Sarah's illness.

"Wow. He didn't pull any punches, did he?"

"No. I don't know. It was harsh, but maybe she needs something like that. At least she wasn't able to use any of her excuses and evasions with the doctor." Nicole sat for a moment more, thinking. "The thing is, when I was talking to her afterward...I don't think her father knows what she's been doing."

"Really?"

"Yeah. It occurred to me that he hasn't come to visit her much lately, not as much as he used to. I just put it down to her being away from home for the first time, and so the first year or two he came more often. But now I wonder if she hasn't been avoiding him, so he wouldn't see what she looks like. When you're living with someone, it's not as easy to notice the changes. But when you see someone after several months, it's obvious if they've lost a lot of weight."

"Do you think that if he knew, he might be able to help?" Gregory asked. "That he could convince her to stop?"

"I don't know. She's very close to him. Her mother died when she was fourteen, and he raised her." Nicole paused, then continued, "She didn't want me to call him and tell him about her breaking her arm."

"I see. So you're wondering if you would be a bad friend if you ignored her wishes and told her father about the break and about her anorexia."

"Yeah. I mean, you respect your friend's wishes. Normally I'd never get involved with something between one of my friends and her parents. I think I'd feel as if I was snitching or butting in where I don't belong. But with this...well..."

"You might be saving her life," Gregory finished for her.

Nicole nodded. "In the brochures The Alliance sent me, one of the things they said that you should *not* do is agree to keep her anorexia a secret. I can't help but think in this instance—isn't not telling Sarah's dad about all this helping her keep it a secret?"

Gregory gazed at Nicole levelly. "What do you think you should do?"

She returned his gaze for a long moment. Then she picked up Sarah's purse and pulled out her cell phone. She flicked through the numbers until she found the one she wanted, and tapped it out. A man answered the phone on the other end.

"Hello? Mr. Duncan? This is Nicole, Sarah's roommate. No, she'll be okay. But there's something I need to tell you...."

CHAPTER
᨞ SIX ᨞

Nicole sat in Sarah's hospital room, idly flipping through the pages of a magazine. Sarah was dozing again, as she had been on and off all through the evening. After Nicole talked to Sarah's father, Gregory had driven her back to her apartment, where she had picked up some toiletries and clothes for Sarah, then returned by herself to the hospital.

Sarah had been groggy but awake, and had seemed so grateful to see her that Nicole felt she could not leave even after her friend fell back asleep. She thought of Gregory sitting in his condo alone, going over some paperwork and half waiting for her to drop by when she left the hospital, and she released a wistful little sigh. It would be better, she thought, when the present run was over and the company returned to a regular rehearsal schedule, leaving most of her evenings free. Then she and Gregory would be able to spend more time together, and she wouldn't always feel as if she was having to carve out little bits and pieces of her days to be with him.

Sarah had been right about the danger of dating him, Nicole thought—but it wasn't for the reasons she had assumed, that dating him would impinge upon ballet. No, the danger with Gregory was exactly the opposite, she found herself resenting ballet because it impinged on her time with Gregory.

The door opened cautiously, and a middle-aged man stuck his head inside. When he saw Nicole, he smiled. "Nicole?"

"Mr. Duncan!" She jumped to her feet.

He pushed the door all the way open and stepped inside, and his eyes went to the bed where Sarah lay. He stopped and stared at the sleeping woman, the blood draining from his face.

"Oh, my God. Sarah."

He could not seem to move. He hung there just inside the doorway, gazing at his daughter. Nicole could only imagine how Sarah must look to him. At least she had been with Sarah, had become accustomed to the changes in her gradually. But Sarah's father had not seen her in several months, and she knew this first glimpse of her must be devastating.

Mr. Duncan moved into the room finally, letting the door shut behind him. Sarah's eyes fluttered open at the sound of his footsteps and she gazed at him in confusion for a moment.

"Daddy?" Delight, then anxiety chased across her face. She struggled to sit up, hampered by the contraption on her arm that held it in place. "What are you doing here?"

She swung her head to look at Nicole, her eyes suddenly fierce. "Did you call him? I told you not to."

"I'm sorry, Sarah," Nicole said evenly. "I had to. I knew he would want to know."

"Of course I did." Mr. Duncan came to her bedside. "Sarah, honey, what's happened to you?"

"It was nothing, just a fall, that's all." She summoned up a smile. "Don't worry. It's only a break. I'll be fine in no time."

"No. I didn't mean that. I meant..." He waved his hand vaguely, as if encompassing her entire body. "Sarah, what have you done to yourself? You're...you're skin and bones."

He reached out for the hand on her uninjured arm, then hesitated, and Nicole knew that he was fearful he would hurt her just by touching her.

"I'm fine, Dad," Sarah lied valiantly, forcing a smile. "You just haven't seen me in a while. You know how it is with ballet—we have to be small."

"Surely you don't have to be emaciated," Mr. Duncan retorted.

"I just need to have an edge," she explained, and started to reel off the same arguments she had used with Nicole and Mike when they had tried to talk to her about her problem.

But when she finished the catalog of reasons why she needed

193

to be thinner in order to be better, her father did not nod in understanding, but simply said, "Then perhaps you ought to quit."

Sarah gaped at him. "What?"

"If this is what ballet demands of you, I think you would be better off without it."

"No! What are you saying? I love ballet—it's all I want. All I've ever wanted to do. I can't quit ballet."

"I know how much you love it, and I see no reason why you can't eat just because you're a dancer," her father pointed out reasonably. "But you say that you can't. So the only thing left is for you to stop dancing."

She stared at him, then said in a whisper, "But I've always wanted to be a dancer. I—it's what Mama wanted. She loved to see me dance. You told me—you told me how proud you were, how proud she would have been of me."

"Of course I'm proud of you. And your mother would have been, too. She loved to see you dance. But she loved *you* far, far more than she loved your dancing. So do I. Honey…" This time he did reach down and curl his hand around his daughter's. "Your mother would not have wanted this for you. She would never have chosen ballet over your life. And neither would I. Please, Sarah, I don't want you to die."

Tears welled in his eyes, and Sarah, staring up at him, suddenly began to cry, her skeletal body shaking as sobs racked her. "I don't want to die, either, Daddy!"

He leaned down and wrapped his arm around her shoulders, holding her to him, his head bent to hers. Nicole, watching them, felt her own eyes flood with tears. She turned and slipped out the door, leaving the two of them alone.

NICOLE SAT DOWN IN the waiting room, not sure what to do. She thought of leaving and going home. With Sarah's father there, her friend really did not need her company any longer, and hopefully, Sarah and Mr. Duncan would have a good long talk. Still, Nicole felt a little odd about leaving without saying goodbye, and, more importantly, when she left the room, she hadn't thought to take her purse with her. She would have to go back into Sarah's room, so she decided to wait for a while to give them some privacy.

She was thumbing through a celebrity gossip magazine, wondering who a third of the people in it were, when Mr. Duncan stepped into the room. He smiled at her wearily.

"Hi. Sorry. You didn't have to leave."

"I thought you needed some privacy."

"We had a nice talk. A good talk." He blinked and looked away. "I never would have believed it if I hadn't seen her with my own eyes."

"I'm sorry. Maybe I should have told you earlier."

"I understand. I know you felt you would be disloyal to Sarah. She's—" He shook his head. "I can't even begin to understand it.

I know it's not just ballet. There's something wrong—something she needs to work out in herself."

"No, it's not just ballet." Nicole paused. "Though I'm not sure…well, I mean, I don't know if she can work it out while she's in that environment."

"She'll have to stay away from it for a few weeks while she heals. Maybe that will help her come to grips with it. Will you… She'd like to talk to you. Would you come back in and see her for a few minutes?"

"Of course."

Mr. Duncan walked with her to the room and held the door open in a demonstration of old-fashioned courtesy, but he stayed in the hall, murmuring, "I think she wants to see you alone."

Nicole stepped over to the bed. Sarah's eyes were closed, but they opened at her approach. For an instant, Nicole was afraid that her friend was going to berate her for calling her father, but Sarah only gave her a wobbly smile.

"Hi. I—I'm sorry I've been so…" Sarah's eyes filled with tears again.

"No, don't apologize. You don't need to do that. I just—I want you to get better."

"I want to, too…I think," Sarah added with wry honesty. "I don't know, Nicky. I'm scared."

"I know you are." Nicole reached for her hand. "I'll help you. I'll help you any way I can."

"I'm going to go see one of those counselors you told me about. I promised Dad." She let out a sigh. "And I know I need to."

"Good. That's a good first step."

Sarah nodded. "Will you—would you go with me? I don't want to have to go alone."

"Sure."

"Do you think…will I have to give up ballet?"

"I don't know," Nicole answered honestly. "I—I guess it would mostly depend on whether you could continue ballet without going back to doing all the same things."

"I can't remember far enough back to when I didn't go to ballet class."

"I know. Me, neither." It seemed as if it had always been there, just part of her life. What would life be like without it?

"Will you tell Joff tomorrow morning? About what happened?" Sarah asked.

"Sure."

"I should have called him this afternoon, but I couldn't. I know I shouldn't make you face him, but…"

"It's okay. I'll manage." Nicole had been the recipient of Joff's temper or icy sarcasm on more than one occasion, but she was not terrified of him as some of the other dancers were. "Do you want me to be here for your surgery tomorrow?"

"Oh, no. No. You'll have to go to the studio. Joff would probably have a coronary if you missed the morning rehearsal."

"It's okay. If you need me, I can do it."

Sarah shook her head. "No. Dad's here. I'll be okay."

"Good. Well, I think I'll take off now." Nicole walked over to the chair, where she had set her purse.

"Yeah. Thanks."

"I'll come by to see you tomorrow."

Sarah nodded. "Nicole?"

Nicole turned back to her friend, her hand on the doorknob.

"Do you think I'll be able to do it? Can I conquer this thing?" She looked very small and fragile lying there in the hospital bed.

"I know you can," Nicole assured her.

NICOLE PULLED INTO ONE of the visitors slots at Gregory's condo and took the elevator up to his floor. It was early enough that he would still be up, and she wanted to see him, at least for a little while. She had had to buzz him from the lobby to be admitted, so he was waiting for her at his door, smiling and relaxed in jeans and a green T-shirt, his feet bare.

For some reason, the sight of his bare feet below the faded jeans struck her as incredibly sexy, and when he bent to kiss her in greeting, she wrapped her arms around his neck and clung to him, deepening the kiss.

"Whoa." He smiled and took a step back into the condo, pulling her with him. "Now that's a hello."

Nicole chuckled and leaned against him, her arms around his waist, her head resting on his chest. The steady thud of his heart beneath her ear, the warmth of his body, the strength of his arm encircling her, soothed and reassured her. And somehow, at the same time, aroused her.

She was dangerously close to falling in love with him, she knew—or had she already slipped over the edge?

"Come in," he told her, drawing her farther into the large brick loft. "Let me get you a glass of wine. You've had a tough day."

"That would be heavenly," Nicole agreed.

He went into the kitchen, and she strolled over to the bank of windows that looked out over the city.

"How is Sarah?" Gregory asked, coming up beside her and handing her a glass of wine.

"Better. Much better, I think." She sat down on his couch, curling her feet up under her, and took a sip. "Mmm. This is wonderful."

Gregory sat down beside her, sliding his arm around her shoulders, and she leaned against him, letting out a little sigh of pleasure.

"Her father came in this evening," Nicole said, and told him of the emotional scene that had ensued and Sarah's decision to seek counseling for her anorexia.

"Do you think she can break free of it?" Gregory asked.

"I told her I was sure she could. But I don't know if I'm as confident as I sounded. I think it will be very hard. But I'll help her all I can. I promised her I would go with her. She's worried about having to leave ballet. I think it will be very hard for her to succeed with this disease if she doesn't."

"I would think it's like a drug addict needing to stay away from the old places and people that were part of his addiction."

Nicole nodded. "But she's scared of life without ballet."

"It would be hard not to be scared when that's what you've always known," Gregory agreed.

Nicole arched an eyebrow. "I'm sensing a significant look here. Are we talking about me now?"

He laughed. "Just saying that it's hard to leave what you've done for so long…even when it's not what you want for yourself anymore."

"But I do want it. It's my life."

"That's fine…if that's really true. But I see you doing all the things you've done to help Sarah, to pull her out of the pit she's in. And I wonder why you're not willing to do the same for yourself."

"But I'm not in a pit," Nicole protested. "I love ballet. I always have."

"Do you still? I've watched you talk about photography. Your face lights up, and you bubble with excitement and joy. I've seen the concentration on your face when you're taking a picture, the intensity and the—that thing that's inside an artist when he's creating. I don't even know a word for it because it goes beyond pleasure or happiness—it's some kind of deep connection to beauty. That's a rare thing, something to be treasured. And it shines out of you when you're creating your pictures."

Nicole smiled. "I do love it. I wish I could spend more time on it."

"That's what I mean. Why aren't you spending more time on something you love? You know, I've seen you when you talk about ballet, too, and the same joy isn't in your face."

"Well, it's not new," Nicole said, with a shrug. "It's not exciting anymore. I've become accustomed to it."

"I saw you when you came out that door after your performance the other night," he added. "You were happy. You looked pleased. But your face didn't shine the way the other dancers' faces did. You even told me that opening night didn't feel the way it once had."

Something soft and sad was centered in Nicole's chest, like a deep bruise of the spirit. She shook her head, feeling tears gathering. "I can't just walk away from it."

"Sweetheart, I wouldn't ask you to. Not if it's what you want." He took her hand and raised it to his lips, kissing her knuckles softly. "I want you to be happy, that's all. I want you to look at your life and be able to say, 'This is what makes me happy.'"

Nicole wanted to say the words, to assure him that what she was doing was what made her happy, but the words somehow stuck in her throat.

"I don't know," she whispered, realizing with some amazement that it was true. Doubts had been creeping up on her for months, and she had refused to acknowledge them. For the first time in her life, she was no longer sure what she wanted.

"Don't worry," he said, and kissed the top of her head tenderly. "It'll come to you."

Nicole pulled back and looked up at him, and her heart melted within her. "You're such a good man."

He chuckled. "I'm sure there are a few people who wouldn't say that. But I'm very glad you think so."

"You don't push."

"I don't want to push you into anything. Nicole, don't you get it? I want you to be happy. What you do is up to you. I just want to be with you while you're doing it. I love you."

She gazed at him, surprised and suddenly aware of everything shifting and turning inside her. It was so easy, so simple, like everything about Gregory. And this, she realized, this one thing was just as easy for her.

"I love you, too," she answered, and stretched up to kiss him.

NICOLE REALIZED SHE WAS humming as she walked into the ballet studio the next morning. She had awakened late and had had to rush like mad to get here, but she couldn't find it in her to be anxious about it.

She went first to the office area to tell Joff the news about Sarah, but neither Joff nor his assistant was there. She turned and trotted up to the rehearsal room, pausing outside the door to slip off her street shoes.

Joff was standing across the room, deep in conversation with Adele Grayson. Ms. Grayson was no longer involved in the day-to-day running of the company, but she frequently stopped by to watch and critique. It was her values, her ideas, that formed the backbone of the company.

At one time a prima ballerina of some note, Adele was, at sixty-five, still as slender as a reed, her long hair, unnaturally coal-black, pulled up into a tight knot atop her head. She turned as Nicole approached them, her dark eyes sweeping down the length of Nicole's body, taking in her clothes, and her mouth tightened a fraction in disapproval.

Nicole hesitated a few feet from them, not wanting to inter-rupt. However, Adele raised her eyebrows questioningly and said, "Yes?"

"I need to tell Joff that Sarah Duncan will not be here today. She fell yesterday and broke her arm. I had to take her to the hospital. She's having surgery on it this morning."

"What?" Joff's voice rose. "She broke her arm? But we have three performances left!"

"What was she doing?" Adele asked, irritated. "That careless girl! Why didn't she think?"

Nicole stared at them, stunned. She wasn't sure what reaction she had expected. Not an outpouring of sympathy, for Joff was not known for his warmth, but she had not expected this com-plete lack of concern for Sarah.

"She didn't do it on purpose," Nicole snapped, facing the other two squarely. "It was an accident. She fainted and fell down."

"Fainted?" Adele raised an eyebrow, looking as though she found fainting a weakness of character. She sighed. "Well, there's nothing that can be done about it." She started to turn away, then glanced dismissively at Nicole. "Thank you, Ms. McCasland."

Adele and Joff began to discuss what was to be done for this evening's performance, given Sarah's absence. Nicole stood for a moment, staring at them.

"I can't believe it," she said finally, taking a step closer to the two.

Ms. Grayson and Joff swung to look at her, their eyebrows rising in identical looks of surprise at finding themselves so addressed by a member of the corps.

"Excuse me?" Adele asked, her voice frosty.

"You haven't asked one thing about Sarah," Nicole pointed out. "Not a single, 'Is she all right?' All you can think of is the performance! Don't you care anything about Sarah?"

"I *care,* Ms. McCasland, about my art," Adele Grayson said firmly.

"Well, I care about Sarah's life! Do you not have any interest in why she fainted? Do you not care that she's been starving herself to the point of making herself ill—all for the sake of staying in this company?"

"Ms. Duncan's mental problems are not my business," the other woman retorted. "This company, ballet—those are the things I care about. If she cannot control her weight without falling into some sort of unhealthy obsession, then I'm not sure that she belongs at Grayson."

Nicole stared at the other woman for a long moment, then turned on her heel and strode away. As she headed toward the outer doors, Joff called after her, "Wait! Where are you going?" He pointed in the direction of the dressing rooms. "You need to get ready. We're about to start."

Nicole turned. "I'm leaving."

She had the satisfaction of seeing almost comical expressions of shock on Joff's and Adele's features.

"What? What do you mean? What are you going to do?"

Nicole felt suddenly light, as if something was bubbling up inside her. She smiled. "I'm not sure. I think I might cut my hair. Or dye it red. Or maybe get a tattoo." She paused. "I'm going…to get a life."

She turned and walked out the door, leaving them staring after her.

⊷ EPILOGUE ⊷

I t was opening night, and Nicole's stomach was a knot of nerves. She had spent the last three months preparing for this moment, and now that it was here, she felt so torn between excitement and fear that she could scarcely breathe.

Slowly, she pivoted, letting her eyes drift over the gallery walls where her photographs now hung. *Would her first show be the success Gregory was certain it would be? Or was she making an utter fool of herself?*

A door opened in the loft, and a moment later Gregory clattered down the stairs. He smiled and started across the room toward her, as elegant and handsome as ever in a black silk suit.

"How you feeling? A little scared?"

"Terrified," Nicole replied.

He took her hand and squeezed it. "I know it's useless to say so, but don't worry. You're going to do great."

She smiled and leaned in for a kiss. "Thanks. However it turns out...thanks."

"No regrets?"

Nicole chuckled. "Amazingly enough, I haven't missed the sore muscles and fatigue a bit."

In fact, the past three months had been the happiest of her life. She had awakened every day eager to get started, and however many problems with the show had cropped up along the way, it had been deeply satisfying to work them out.

There was a knock on the locked door, and she turned to see Sarah standing outside. Nicole waved and walked over to open the door.

"Good. You got here early." She hugged her friend.

"Yeah. I came straight from work. I wanted to see you before the crowd came."

Nicole stepped back, smiling. "You look great."

Sarah had obviously gained several pounds, though Nicole was careful not to ask her how much weight she had put on. She had accompanied her to her first therapy session, shoring up her courage, and since then had done her utmost to be supportive without pressing Sarah for information about any of it.

She knew dealing with anorexia had been a struggle for her friend, but Nicole had also seen Sarah giving up many of her rituals and obsessions with food, and she believed she was truly on her way to recovery.

"I'm doing great," Sarah replied, and Nicole noticed there was a new sparkle in her eyes.

"What? You've got some good news, I can tell."

Sarah nodded. "Yes. I've got a new job."

With her broken arm, there had been no possibility of her returning to Grayson when she got out of the hospital, and early in her therapy, Sarah realized that she would have a better chance of succeeding away from the world of the ballet company. Nicole knew how much the decision had pained her. While Nicole had found that it rarely cost her a pang to no longer dance professionally, Sarah had been saddened by her decision, and more than once, Nicole had found her turning the pages of her scrapbook, looking at pictures and reviews of performances. Sarah had gotten a temporary job in a clothing store, but it had never been more than a stopgap situation, something to pay the bills while she tried to find what she wanted to do.

"What?" Nicole asked, delighted that Sarah seemed so pleased.

"I'm going to work at Come On and Dance."

"Where?"

Sarah grinned from ear to ear. "It's a children's dance academy.

There's one in Westlake and one in north Austin. Can you believe it? I'm going to teach little kids to dance."

"Sarah, that's great!" Nicole hugged her friend again.

She nodded. "I know. I can't believe how excited I am. I never thought I'd wind up in the suburbs, teaching dance to six-year-olds. But you know what? I think it's going to fun. I mean, it's not the same, obviously. But I know I can't go back to that. I like kids, and it'll be nice being around dance again. And there won't be the competition, you know. I won't be performing or trying to impress anyone. It's not serious dance, just fun. I can just…enjoy it."

"It sounds wonderful," Nicole assured her. "I am so happy for you."

"I'm going to be okay," Sarah said, growing serious again. "You know? I'm going to come out all right."

"You are. I know you are."

"And so are you." Sarah smiled and pivoted to scan the room of photographs. "Wow. I guess I never realized how talented you are. I'm going to go check them all out before everybody comes."

She started off across the room to the far wall and began making her way back slowly. As Nicole watched her, Gregory came up once again beside her.

"First critic, huh?" he asked, nodding toward Sarah.

"Yeah. But I think I can count on a positive review," Nicole joked back.

"I wanted to say something to you before everybody got here," Gregory said.

She looked at him, a little surprised. "What?"

"Well, ask you, actually."

He looked suddenly tentative, and Nicole frowned, wondering what could be on his mind.

"I've been thinking...well, what I wanted to say was that I know your show is going to be a tremendous success, and I'm very happy that I've gotten to be a part of that. But...I want something more. I want another kind of partnership with you."

He reached into his pocket and pulled out a small box. "What I'm trying to say in my own very inarticulate way is this. Nicole, will you marry me?"

He snapped open the box and extended it to her. Nicole stared at the sparkling diamond solitaire nestled inside.

"Oh. Oh."

"Don't you like it? They said I could bring it back and exchange it if you didn't."

"No! No, it's not that. It's beautiful. I just—" Nicole looked up at him, her eyes glittering with tears. "Oh, Gregory, it's perfect. I love you."

"Then your answer is yes?"

"Yes! Yes, I'll marry you." Nicole threw her arms around him, laughing, and he picked her up and swung her around.

Finally he set her down and kissed her thoroughly. "Now." He grinned. "Let's go open that door and start selling you to the world."

Taking his hand, Nicole smiled and walked forward to unlock the door.

* * * * *

Dear Reader,

I have always written books to entertain, but for "Breaking Line," I also had a chance to inform readers about one of the serious problems affecting young women today: eating disorders. I had a chance to talk to Johanna Kandel, the young founder of The Alliance for Eating Disorders Awareness, and hear her awe-inspiring personal story. She was a pleasure to work with, and the materials she provided me were an enormous help. Even more, she inspired me, as I hope this story will inspire you, to help causes as worthy as this one. Please take the time to visit www.eatingdisorderinfo.org to learn how you can help.

I would also like to thank my daughter, Anastasia Hopcus, for her involvement in this book, taking the time out from working on her own young adult novel to help me on this story. Her research and ideas were invaluable, as were her own personal experiences in the acting world, another profession in which great pressures are placed on young women to conform to an unrealistic ideal of feminine body weight and shape.

But for all the valuable understanding that I hope can be found in the words of this novella, it is still, above all, a fictional story. There is no ballet company such as the one depicted herein, any more than this ballet director or these dancers actually exist. I hope that you will find in my book an opportunity to laugh, to cry and to lose yourself for a while in another world.

Sincerely,

Candace Camp

JOAN CLAYTON & INA ANDRE

∽— Windfall Clothing Service —∽

There's something about stepping into a brand-new skirt or throwing on a new jacket that makes a person feel like a million dollars. Yet for many of those struck by poverty and hardship, new clothing, and the upbeat feeling that accompanies it, is a luxury they're unlikely to enjoy.

In 1991 Joan Clayton and Ina Andre, two friends from Toronto, Ontario, decided to change that after walking through a local store one day and asking themselves a simple question: what happens to all the stylish clothing that doesn't sell?

After conducting some research, they arrived at the heartbreaking answer. Many of the brand-new garments ended up in a Dumpster, eventually making their way to a landfill site.

"If there's surplus out there that nobody wants, you might as well put it to good use," says Joan today.

The concept was really that simple. Ask clothing manufacturers and retailers to donate clothes they didn't want or couldn't sell, and Ina and Joan would distribute them to people who could use them.

Fortunately, it was a tried-and-true concept that had already put their first nonprofit on the map. Six years before, in 1985, Ina and Joan launched Second Harvest to address the growing problem of hunger in Toronto. They took perfectly edible food from restaurants and small grocery stores, which would otherwise be going to waste, and reclaimed it to provide thousands of tasty meals to a number of social services across the city.

At first the clothing venture was small, merely a tangential component of their work at Second Harvest. Ina and Joan drove the clothing around in a station wagon and used their dining rooms as storage space. But while making a dropoff at a shelter for homeless men, they heard a staff member remark, "If you give a man clean underwear, he'll go take a shower." The comment struck home and galvanized Ina and Joan to secure start-up funding, gain support from the city's mayor and the media, and incorporate their new charitable organization as Windfall Clothing Service—all in less than two months.

Soon, fashion heavyweights from Levi Strauss & Co. Canada to Gap Inc. started to give new clothes and funding to Windfall.

At one point, two tractor-trailers jampacked with the previous season's athletic shoes showed up ready to unload.

"We found out really early in the game that running shoes get thrown out in the garbage because their style changes so rapidly," says Joan.

"It was incredible. Just amazing," agrees Ina.

The organization's growth has been just as astounding. Employing a small but supremely dedicated staff, this past year Windfall ran like a well-oiled sewing machine and processed over 250,000 pieces of clothing, valued at more than ten million dollars retail. A local trucking distribution company donates shipping, so clothing can shoot around the city and into the hands of the people who need it within forty-eight hours. The timing makes it easier for ninety-six social service agencies to distribute the clothing to those caught in the cycle of poverty. Between Second Harvest and Windfall Clothing Service, Joan and Ina's work and vision, not to mention thousands of hours of volunteer time, have touched the lives of over one million people in Toronto.

"When we had our two hatchback cars and the dining-room table, did we ever think this would be the kind of operation it is now? Of course not," says Ina.

They have much to be proud of—and much to lament.

"I'm amazed that the need is still so terribly strong. The level of poverty in this very wealthy city has deepened. The people at

Second Harvest and Windfall are able to make just a tiny dent," she explains.

The fact that Windfall gives out new clothes is important, Joan and Ina know. The growing numbers of people living in poverty are used to receiving others' castoffs and hand-me-downs, but a new item of clothing is difficult to come by.

"But for women going out for a job interview who have never really had anything new and stylish, it's very special," Ina declares. "It really boosts self-esteem."

It also means people who thought they couldn't even afford to go to job interviews are now agreeing to meet employers in person—and, wearing new clothes to school themselves, their children get an ego boost, too. In fact, Windfall Clothing Service is always searching for new children's clothes and accessories, to deal with the swelling number of financially deprived kids who simply want a pair of jeans that fit, a winter jacket that looks new, or a backpack to carry books and their homework in.

Joan and Ina, now in their late seventies, generally stay at arm's length from day-to-day activities, but say they're amazed by the expertise and enthusiasm of Helen Harakas, their executive director, who recently added Windfall's KIDPACKS to their Clothes for Kids program. With the help of volunteers and media, last year Windfall distributed twelve hundred backpacks filled with school supplies, so fewer children would have to carry schoolbooks home in plastic bags.

"This way they're like all the other kids," states Ina, who lets slip that Joan was elbow deep in pencils and rulers the day they stuffed the bags.

Joan *does* seem to have endless supplies of energy. She moved heavy boxes around warehouse floors into her sixties, and today volunteers with the Labyrinth Community Network, which created and maintains one of the first labyrinths in a Canadian public park in downtown Toronto. Anyone can use a labyrinth for reflection and meditation. In 2004 Joan was awarded the Order of Canada and an honorary Doctor of Civil Law from the University of King's College in Halifax, Nova Scotia.

As for Ina, she recently retired as a student liaison at a theater school and is going to continue her work with Second Harvest in a public relations capacity. She is also hunting for another charity that speaks to her need to help people and add dignity, grace and independence to their lives.

"I'm still looking for an organization that will capture my imagination and need my support," she says, "but not my arms or my back!"

For more information, visit www.windfallclothing.ca or write to Windfall Clothing Service, 29 Connell Court, Unit 3, Toronto, ON, M8Z 5T7, Canada.

STEPHANIE BOND
⤛ It's Not About the Dress ⤜

CHAPTER
～ ONE ～

C hloe Parker looked in the mirror and her eyes welled with tears. "It's absolutely perfect."

Melinda, the owner of Melinda's Bridal Shop, handed her a tissue and grabbed one for herself. "All the consultations, all the fittings, all the phone calls, all the times I wanted to fire you as a client—it was all worth it. You look like a fairy princess."

Chloe dabbed at her eyes and sighed at the reflection of the wedding gown that had been customized under her close supervision. Featuring a fitted bodice with delicate boning, a sweetheart neckline, short puff sleeves and a ballerina skirt with a six-foot-long train, the stunning garment had been fashioned from the finest Italian silk in a shade of white chosen specifically to complement her skin tone and dark hair. Clear Austrian crystals, each hand set and applied, sparkled from the full skirt, as well as the airy veil and matching silk mules.

It was the wedding dress that Chloe had dreamed of since she was a little girl—magical. The kind of dress that would set the mood for the wedding and for her marriage. How could any woman not be deliriously happy to walk down the aisle in this fanciful dress?

"I wish I could wear it every day until the wedding," she said with a sigh.

"What you do in your own apartment is your business," Melinda said slyly.

"No." Chloe shook her head. "I've waited this long, I can wait another twenty-one days."

Melinda picked up Chloe's left hand to study the sizable cluster of diamonds on her ring finger. "You're a lucky woman—the perfect dress *and* the perfect groom."

Chloe nodded in agreement. Dr. Ted Snyder was a sought-after cosmetic dentist, young and handsome, with impeccable manners and good breeding—not to mention amazing teeth. The engagement ring he'd had made for her still had tongues wagging in Toronto social circles—especially gratifying to Chloe, who had grown up outside of the "in" crowd.

"Everyone says your wedding is going to be the event of the year."

"That's my plan," Chloe said with a grin. From her bag her cell phone rang. She lifted the skirt of her dress and tiptoed over, leaning carefully so as not to wrinkle the silk, then pulled out her phone. "Chloe Parker Events Planning."

"Hi—this is Ann Conway."

Chloe glanced at her watch. "Hi, Ann. I'll be there in twenty minutes to double-check all the decorations for the birthday party and to meet the caterer. Is everything okay?"

"Actually, no. The magician just called to cancel."

Chloe frowned, but managed to inject a carefree tone into her voice. "I'm sure it's a mix-up of some kind, Ann. Just relax and I'll take care of everything." She disconnected the call, then consulted her day planner and punched in the phone number for Morton Green, aka Morton the Magnificent.

"Hello?"

"Hello, Morton, it's Chloe Parker."

"Chloe," he said, his voice squeaking nervously. "About the Conway boy's birthday party—"

"Morton, I told you never to cancel with a client directly."

"I'm sorry. I was afraid you'd be mad at me."

She could picture the middle-aged man cringing. "Wrong, Morton. I'm not mad because you're *not* canceling. I'll be at the Conways' house in twenty minutes, and you'd better have your magic butt there, too."

"Chloe, my assistant is sick—I can't go on without her."

"Then find someone else."

"Who am I going to find on such short notice?"

"That's your problem. I've never not delivered a talent act for a party, and I'm not going to start today. My reputation is like gold to me."

"What size do you wear?" Morton asked.

"I beg your pardon?"

"If you can fit into the assistant's size-eight outfit, you can do the show with me."

"I don't think so."

"It's up to you," Morton said in a singsongy voice. "How far are you willing to go to preserve that fourteen-karat reputation of yours?"

Chloe screwed up her mouth, then rolled her eyes. "I draw the line at being sawed in half."

"See you there."

She disconnected, then sighed. It wasn't the first time she'd gone above and beyond the call of duty to preserve her standing as one of the top events planners in Toronto, and it probably wouldn't be the last. She took a last wistful look at herself in the glorious dress. "Melinda, will you unzip me? I have to run."

"At least this time you get to take the gown with you," the woman said.

"I know. I'm so excited just to be able to look at it whenever I want."

Melinda lowered the long back zipper. "You're not going to show it to Ted, are you?"

"I don't know. Maybe."

"You can't let the groom see the wedding gown before the wedding! It's bad luck."

Chloe gave a little laugh as Melinda eased the silk from her shoulders. "I'm not superstitious...but apparently I do believe in magic."

"Hmm?"

"Never mind. I have to go save a birthday party."

"That's why you're in demand," Melinda said, helping her step out of the garment. "I'll bag the dress, veil and shoes, and write up your final receipt."

Chloe couldn't help but notice that the woman was a little giddy, and nursed a fleeting pang of remorse for all the hoops she'd made Melinda jump through in this quest for the perfect dress. She suspected the woman would be glad to see her *and* the gown on their merry way.

After quickly dressing, Chloe emerged from the changing room and went to the counter to pay the final installment. The gown's hefty price tag reflected the time and effort put into the exquisite creation.

Melinda happily handed over Chloe's credit card, and the receipt to sign, then jogged around the counter and took the bag down from the hook. "Allow me to carry it to your car."

"That's okay, I got it," Chloe said, slipping her finger through the hanger and holding it up high. "I'll miss seeing you, Melinda."

The seamstress pasted on a wide smile. "Good luck with your wedding."

Chloe strode to her van and hung the dress inside, feeling philosophical and unapologetic for the fuss she'd caused. Her wedding would be the feather in her cap, the best advertisement for her growing events coordinating business, an example of everything she could do for a client—from finding the most unique floral arrangements to the finest videographer to the most perfectly trained white doves to exit the church on cue. Her wedding would be proof that she would do almost anything to ensure a client's happiness.

She glanced at her watch, frustrated that she was going to be late. A delivery truck sat in front of her with its right signal on, waiting to turn. When the traffic light changed to green and the truck still didn't move, Chloe muttered, "Come on," and honked her horn loudly several times.

A long arm emerged from the driver's side, waving her around. She pulled up alongside the truck, which read Windfall Clothing Service, as the driver emerged from the cab to jump down and inspect a flat tire. Chloe felt a pang of regret for honking at his misfortune. He looked up as she drove slowly past, and she locked gazes with him.

Her stomach tingled as if she knew him, but there was nothing about his blond hair or rugged features that seemed recognizable. She didn't know anyone who drove a delivery truck, but maybe she'd seen him before on one of her jobs, transporting tables or chairs or a thousand other things. He smiled and gave her a friendly little wave. Odd, considering he had a flat in heavy Saturday traffic and would probably be late at his destination himself.

The car behind Chloe honked, jarring her out of her reverie. She continued on around the truck and made the turn. A few minutes later she pulled up to the Conways' house and saw that Morton the Magnificent was waiting for her, wearing a long black cape and a top hat. He grinned and held up a short, sequined outfit. Chloe heaved a resigned sigh. When she moved into Ted's house and into a bigger home office, she could hire her own assistant to do the tedious stuff. Meanwhile…

"Abracadabra," she murmured, then conjured up a bright smile and climbed out of her van.

THE CONWAY BOY'S birthday party was a raging success, but ran longer than planned, so she was late meeting Ted for dinner. When she arrived at her apartment, he was sitting on the couch waiting for her, wearing neat chino pants, a long-sleeved dress shirt and a decided frown that deepened when he saw her sequined outfit. "What on earth are you wearing?"

"Long story," she said, tossing her purse and briefcase on the desk that took up most of the living room. She bent down for a quick kiss as she rushed by, carrying the bagged wedding gown. "Let me change. I'll be right out."

He glanced at his watch sourly. "Okay, but try to hurry. I didn't have lunch and I'm starving."

Once in her bedroom she hung the dress on her closet door. Ted had been impatient lately with her long hours at work and her preoccupation with the wedding details. Saturdays were usually more hectic, and sometimes she had back-to-back events. She told herself to make a special attempt to be more attentive during dinner, lest he start feeling neglected.

All would be forgiven the day of the wedding, though, when the most incredible production that Toronto had ever seen would unfold in front of five hundred lucky guests. Photographers from a bridal magazine and the *Toronto Star* would be in attendance to capture pictures of the twelve bridesmaids dressed in discriminating butter-yellow dresses, the tiny ballerinas who would spread flower petals as they danced and twirled down the aisle, and the white-and-gold horse-drawn carriage that would carry her and Ted away to the elaborately decorated reception hall for a sitdown seafood dinner and dancing to a string quartet.

Chloe smiled to herself. Ted would thank her for making their day so special.

She glanced at the bagged wedding gown and bit her lip. Why

not give him a preview? When Melinda's warning of bad luck flitted through her head, Chloe dismissed it as nonsense. All the phone calls, all the consultations, all the arrangements she'd made probably seemed abstract to Ted because she didn't have anything concrete to show him.

But the wedding dress—*that* he could understand.

She quickly changed into the gown, contorting to close the long back zipper and hook up the extensive train to form a bustle. She slid her feet into the matching shoes, and attached the veil to her hair. Then, with heart pounding, she swept into the living room and waited for his reaction.

When he glanced up, he did a double take, his eyes wide, his mouth open. "Wh-what's this?"

"It's my dress, silly," she said with a laugh, turning in a circle for effect. "I picked it up today—what do you think? Isn't it amazing?"

He stood and nodded, his Adam's apple bouncing. Chloe was filled with feminine satisfaction that she'd managed to render him speechless.

"I thought I wasn't supposed to see it until the day of the wedding."

She gave a dismissive wave. "An old wives' tale. Won't it look wonderful with the yellow bridesmaids' dresses?" she asked, her excitement building. "And the charcoal-gray tuxedos? And the yellow lilies—"

"Chloe," he interrupted, his face pale. "I…I've changed my mind."

"About the dark gray tuxedos? Because we can still go with dove-gray if you want." She retrieved her cell phone from her purse and began punching in numbers. "I'll change it right now."

Ted snapped her phone closed. "I'm not talking about tuxedos, I'm talking about the wedding."

She frowned, then laughed. "What do you mean?"

"I mean the *wedding,* Chloe. I've changed my mind."

She shook her head. "I still don't understand. You've changed your mind about what?"

His jaw hardened. "I've changed my mind about marrying you. The wedding is off."

Chloe stood there, her mouth opening and closing. By the time Ted's words had sunk in, he was gone.

CHAPTER
∽ TWO ∽

Chloe stood in the silent vacuum created by Ted leaving. He'd changed his mind about marrying her? Just like that?

She ran after him, but her feet moved in slow motion because she was weighted down by the heavy dress. "Ted!" she yelled. "Wait! Ted!"

It was a struggle to fit through the door. She raced out onto the balcony of her second-floor apartment and searched for him in the parking lot below. He stood with his car door open, looking up at her. Some of her neighbors who happened to be outside walking pets and unloading groceries gaped at her, too.

"Ted, come back!" she called. "We can talk about this!"

But he only shook his head. "It's over, Chloe. I'm sorry." Then he climbed into his car and drove away.

Chloe stood there until she realized she was freezing in the spring chill and her neighbors were still staring up at her. What a sight she must make, standing there in a wedding gown, shouting after a man screeching away in his car.

She trudged back inside her apartment, hindered by the bulky dress and all that it symbolized. She closed the door and leaned against it, taking deep breaths, trying to make sense of what had just happened.

Ted had been distracted lately—irritable, even—but she'd attributed it to both of them being busy. Not once had she suspected he was having second thoughts about their marriage. Her heart squeezed painfully when the enormity of his rejection washed over her like a cold wave. She realized her cheeks were wet with tears, and hastily wiped at them before they fell and stained the gown.

As if it mattered. She looked down at the dress that she had so painstakingly selected and had tailored, the fairy-tale gown that was to be the centerpiece of her perfect showcase wedding and set the tone for her marriage. Suddenly, the hundreds of hand-set Austrian crystals mocked her. The yards of Italian silk suffocated her.

She couldn't get it off fast enough.

Of course the zipper stuck. Chloe yelled in frustration, twisting around and giving it a hard yank before it finally gave way. She tore off the dress and tossed it on her bed, then kicked the silk shoes across the room. How could Ted do this to her?

Her panic ballooned as the arrangements that would have to be canceled whirled through her mind—the church, the minister, the harpist, the soloist, the photographer, the videographer, the media, the dancers, the florist, the reception hall, the caterer, the string quartet, the limousine service, the hotel rooms, the gift registries, the horse-drawn carriage.

And the Hawaiian honeymoon… She choked on a sob. After slaving over the details of the wedding for months, she had so been looking forward to two weeks of fun and sun to relax.

She drew a few shaky breaths, and her mind kicked into practical mode. There would be dozens of people to call—the brides-maids, guests, her mother…

Her mother, who had raised Chloe by herself on few resources. Her mom, who was so proud of Chloe's successes, and so happy that she was marrying well.

A new wave of tears swept over her. How would she tell her mother that she'd been dumped?

And she didn't even know why.

Sudden anger sparked in her belly, fanning to a flame. Chloe yanked up her cell phone and punched in Ted's number. After three years of dating and a year-long engagement, the very least he owed her was an explanation of why he would call off their wedding. How dare he humiliate her like this?

His phone rang and rang, and when it rolled over to his voice mail, she hung up and redialed. After five futile attempts, she threw down the phone and shouted in frustration. Incensed, she removed her engagement ring and bounced it off the wall, leaving a dent. She didn't see where the ring landed, didn't care. She paced, restless, overcome with the need to *do* something.

Chloe glanced at the clock. It was five-thirty on a Saturday afternoon. Most offices and retail stores would be closing soon; the calls to cancel the numerous arrangments for the wedding would have to wait until Monday.

When her gaze landed on the dress piled in a heap on the bed, she was overwhelmed with sadness. Her magical dress. She couldn't stand to look at it.

And if she hurried, she could return it before the bridal shop closed.

It was the one thread she could begin to unravel now, one proactive step to begin undoing all that she had put together over the past several months. One thing that would make her feel less helpless.

Resolved, Chloe stuffed the wedding gown, veil and shoes into the bag and raced to her van. She was numb on the short drive to the bridal shop, single-mindedly focused on getting the garment out of her sight.

Melinda was turning the Closed sign on her door when Chloe ran up, carrying the dress. The woman's eyes went wide and she tried to pretend she didn't see her, but Chloe pounded on the door until she relented and let her in.

"I'm returning the dress," Chloe said flatly. "The wedding is off."

Melinda looked incredulous. "What happened?"

She didn't want to admit that she should've heeded the warning about the groom seeing the bridal finery before the wedding. "Just take it," Chloe said tearfully. "And get rid of it."

"But, Chloe, this is a custom gown. I can only give you back ten percent of what you paid for it."

"That's fine," she said, thinking something was better than nothing. She'd already be losing a fortune in deposits all over the city. She swallowed against the lump in her throat.

"I'm so sorry," Melinda said when she handed over the refund.

"Thanks," Chloe mumbled, her face flaming with embarrassment— a feeling she was going to have to get used to when word got out that Ted had dumped her.

She left the store and walked slowly to her van. Maybe Ted had decided he didn't want to marry someone who didn't have the pedigree of most of the people he hung out with. Or maybe he'd met someone else. Chloe climbed into the vehicle and sat with her hands on the steering wheel for several minutes, dreading the thought of going back to her apartment. Her empty stomach rumbled, reminding her of the dinner with Ted she was supposed to be having. Across the street, the sign of an ice cream shop beckoned.

She'd been watching her weight for the sake of looking good in that darn dress, which now was a moot point, so why not?

Chloe parked the van, then went inside and ordered a carton of strawberry chocolate cheesecake ice cream. When the worker extended napkins, as well as a tiny wooden spoon, across the counter, Chloe shook her head. "I'm going to need a bigger spoon."

The guy's eyebrows furrowed but he obliged, handing over what looked like a wooden paddle.

She was digging in before she drove away. The chocolate, caffeine, sugars and fats hit her system like a drug, the ultimate in self-medication. She moaned in contentment and noted that Ben & Jerry's was missing out on an I Was Dumped Devil's Food flavor of ice cream.

By the time she got home, the container was empty, her stomach hurt and her heart ached. All around her apartment were pictures of her and Ted, reminders of the life they'd planned together. How had things gone so wrong so quickly? And why hadn't she seen it coming?

Then a terrifying thought sent alarm spiraling through her: how many people had Ted already told? Had he called her mother? His family? His friends? *Her* friends? The notion sent her running to the bathroom, where she emptied the contents of her upset stomach into the commode. She emerged somewhat calmer, reasoning that if he'd told people, they would've called her, and her cell phone remained silent.

But she wouldn't be able to wait much longer before she started making the calls.

She tried to think of someone to phone for support, but just wasn't ready to bare her soul. Humiliation coursed through her like a toxin, burning her from the inside out.

After slowly lowering herself to the floor in front of the couch, she hugged her knees, seized by the irrational thought that if she remained very still, perhaps time would, as well. But as she sat in the silence reliving the surreal one-sided conversation that had left her a jilted bride, evening shadows fell across her living room, across her arms and legs. Evening turned into night and when she dragged herself up to go to bed, her limbs were stiff. The sharp pain of Ted's rebuff had turned into a constant ache. Her eyes and throat were swollen and raw. Her head pounded. Her stomach was leaden.

She fell onto her bed, hoping for the quick release of sleep, but no such luck. She tossed and turned as she played out what would happen in the coming days…weeks…months…years. Dismantling the wedding would be a Herculean effort, but it was nothing compared with this feeling of having her heart ripped out and stomped on. She'd had glimpses of Ted's casual dismissal of certain things and even some people, but she'd never dreamed that she would be on the receiving end of his alienation.

He'd said he loved her. Wanted to spend the rest of his life with her…

Chloe turned over, looking for a cool spot on her damp pillow. Would she be considered damaged goods? Many of her customers were wealthy acquaintances of Ted's; she relied on their referrals to keep her business afloat. Would they withdraw their support when they found out that one of their own had tossed her aside?

And the word *why?* kept hammering away in her head.

Somewhere toward dawn, she began to tell herself all the practical things she'd heard on talk shows. It was better to find out before the wedding versus afterward. You couldn't make someone love you. If Ted didn't recognize what a catch she was, then it was his loss.

But the platitudes did little to assuage the abject mortification of being so heartlessly discarded.

As light began to filter into her bedroom, Chloe finally dozed, but was jarred awake what seemed like only minutes later by a piercing sound. She sat straight up, disoriented, before realizing that her cell phone alarm was going off. As she searched for it groggily, the events of the previous evening came crashing back— along with a splintering headache. When she found the phone, she pushed her hair out of her eyes to read the display.

REMINDER: SHALE BRUNCH AT 10.

Chloe groaned. She'd forgotten about Mindy Shale's bridal-shower brunch. Of all days to have to coordinate a wedding-related event, and to top it off, Mindy Shale was a friend of Ted's sister, Jenna.

Chloe put her hand to her throbbing head and wondered if they knew yet about Ted dumping her. She could beg off with a phone call, say she wasn't feeling well. Check in with the hotel banquet director and the caterer via phone to make sure everything was in place.

Then she gave herself a mental shake. She'd never skipped out on an event that she'd coordinated, and she didn't plan to start now. If Ted's friends were inclined to take their patronage elsewhere, it was even more important that she give this party her best shot and attract new clients.

But she almost changed her mind about going when she saw her reflection in the mirror. She hadn't bothered to remove her makeup the night before, and it was smeared and streaked from tears and sleep. Her dark hair was a rat's nest from tossing and turning. And her eyes were nearly swollen shut. If Ted could see her now, he'd be thanking his lucky stars that he'd backed out of the wedding.

That almost made her smile—which was the first glimmer of hope she'd had that she might get through this ordeal intact. So she downed a couple of aspirin for the headache, took a bracing cold shower to rejuvenate, and spent twice her usual time applying makeup to camouflage the effects of an all-night crying jag.

The result wasn't half-bad, she acknowledged. She put on a bright floral dress and pink shoes and made it to the hotel forty-five minutes before the start of the shower. After smoothing out a couple of problems, tweaking the table decorations and test-tasting items on the menu, she took photos to add to her scrapbook and was ready to greet Mindy Shale and friends when they arrived.

Mindy was blond and perky and reeked of money, as did all of her friends. They were the same age as Chloe, but they seemed so much more worldly, she thought with envy. Most of them had traveled abroad and gone to prestigious universities. Their parents were physicians or attorneys or politicians. She felt a bit like a servant hovering on the periphery, answering questions and fetching things for Mindy, but it took her mind off Ted.

Until his sister arrived.

Chloe and Jenna's relationship had always been amiable, but at times Chloe thought she detected a faint air of disapproval from Jenna, as if she wanted Chloe to know that even if she married Ted, she wouldn't truly belong to their social circle. When the young woman said hello, Chloe tried to act natural, but could feel her face warming. Did Jenna know? She and Ted were close, so it seemed reasonable that he would've told her he'd called off the wedding.

But Jenna's expression remained cool and impassive, as always. Whatever secrets she knew about her brother, she wasn't revealing them. Chloe put on her best professional face and went about handling details of the brunch while trying to hide her ringless left hand. The only time she came close to losing her cool was when she thought of her own shower brunch, which was supposed to take place in one week at this very hotel.

Yet another set of phone calls to make.

She blinked back the threat of tears and somehow made it through the event with her smile intact. Mindy seemed pleased with the outcome and especially with the party favors, blown-glass perfume bottles that Chloe had found at an exclusive boutique.

"I'll recommend you to all my friends," the bride-to-be gushed.

Chloe thanked her, and as she walked to her van, muttered under her breath that she hoped the woman felt the same after she discovered Chloe had been dumped by Ted. And everyone would know soon because she intended to start making those dreaded phone calls when she got back to her place.

"Hello, Chloe."

She looked up and almost stumbled to see Ted leaning against her van, his hands in his pockets.

"What are you doing here?" she asked, her pulse thumping.

"I came to see you," he said simply. "I remembered you were coordinating Mindy's shower, and when Jenna mentioned she was attending…well, I thought this would be a neutral place to talk."

Chloe crossed her arms. "To talk about what?"

He looked sheepish. "To talk about what an idiot I am."

Hope fluttered in her chest, but the anger still lingered. "I'm listening."

He pushed himself from the van and lifted his hands in the air. "When I saw you wearing the wedding dress, I just panicked. I guess I got cold feet, and I didn't handle it well. I want to marry you, Chloe."

She wavered, near tears and exhausted from a sleepless night. A tiny part of her asked how, if he loved her, he could put her through something so ghastly. But another part of her whispered that it was her fault for springing the wedding dress on him un-expectedly when he was already in a bad mood. It had blindsided him, spooked him.

"Can you forgive me?" he asked.

They'd lost less than twenty-four hours—a minuscule lapse compared to the rest of their life together. Chloe smiled. "Yes." Then she went into his arms for a makeup kiss. She closed her eyes and squeezed him, telling herself that eventually the hurt would subside and everything would feel perfect again.

He clasped her hand. "Where's your ring?"

"At my apartment," she said, reluctant to tell him that she'd bounced it off her bedroom wall. "I'll put it on as soon as I get home."

"Good. Did you tell anyone about my stupidity?"

She shook her head. "I guess I was hoping you'd change your mind."

Ted smiled. "I'm just glad I came to my senses before you pulled the plug on the entire wedding."

The dress. Chloe winced, wishing she hadn't acted so impulsively in returning it. The bridal shop was closed Sundays, but no matter, she thought happily—she'd get it first thing tomorrow morning. Melinda would be relieved.

"THE DRESS ISN'T HERE, Chloe."

Chloe leaned forward on the counter. "Melinda, how can the dress not be here? I brought it back Saturday as you were closing, and now you're just reopening."

Melinda turned pale and wrung her hands. "You told me to get rid of it."

A finger of alarm tickled Chloe's spine. "Melinda, where *is* my wedding dress?"

"I gave it to a charity, along with a truckload of other gowns."

Chloe's throat convulsed. "You gave away my wedding gown?" She grabbed the lapels on the woman's jacket. "I'm getting married in less than three weeks—I have to have that dress!"

Melinda cringed. "I'm sorry, Chloe. A couple of times a year I give leftover stock to an organization that distributes clothing to the needy." She rummaged behind the counter and came up with a brochure, which she extended to Chloe with a shaking hand.

Shell-shocked, Chloe took the brochure and read the name of the organization, Windfall Clothing Service. The words strummed a memory chord and she had to think for a few seconds before she recalled the delivery truck with the flat tire. And the handsome driver. What a strange coincidence.

"When was the dress picked up?" Chloe asked.

"Saturday evening after I closed."

So chances were good that it was still sitting in a truck somewhere, perhaps at the organization's office, or in a warehouse. She glanced at the address on the brochure and headed toward the door.

"Chloe, where are you going?" Melinda called.

"To find my wedding dress!" she shouted.

CHAPTER
∽ THREE ∽

C hloe lifted her gaze from the brochure and stared at the entrance to the Windfall Clothing Service office. The organization had been founded by two women who recognized the opportunity to redirect clothes and other basic-need items that manufacturers and retailers wanted to clear out. Agencies would then distribute them to the homeless, those displaced by natural disasters, and refugees from other countries, among others.

Guilt plucked at her heartstrings. This organization was doing wonderful things for many people, marrying resources to need. She felt embarrassed to go in and admit she was there to take back an expensive wedding dress that had been inadvertently donated after her fiancé had called off the wedding, which was now back on. Her problem seemed petty in light of the work that Windfall was doing.

Although…perhaps she could make a donation to offset the time and trouble it would take to locate her dress. Feeling better, Chloe climbed out of her van and entered the office.

An attractive brunette standing next to a file cabinet smiled at her. "Welcome to Windfall. I'm Terri. How can I help you?"

Through a large window behind the desk Chloe caught a glimpse of a vast warehouse bustling with workers and filled with pallet after pallet of clothing and other items. The sheer magnitude of merchandise that the organization dealt with began to dawn on Chloe, making her dilemma seem even smaller in comparison.

She manufactured a smile. "My name is Chloe Parker. I heard about your organization through a retail store owner who donates clothing."

The woman nodded. "We have so many wonderful retail contributors. Which one?"

"Melinda's Bridal Shop on Queen Street?"

"Oh, yes, of course. It sounds strange, I know, donating gowns and formal wear to the needy, but there are people out there who are grateful for the chance to celebrate happy events with a special dress they couldn't otherwise afford."

Chloe swallowed miserably. "How nice."

"What can I do for you?" Terri asked cheerfully.

"I…" Feeling trapped by her own selfishness and looking for a way out, Chloe glanced around the office, her gaze landing on a sign that read, We Always Need Volunteers. Her mind raced furiously. There was nothing she wouldn't do to satisfy a client, and right now, she was her own client. If she volunteered to work for the organization, maybe she could secretly look for her gown. It was probably somewhere in that warehouse, waiting to be sorted and distributed locally.

She just needed to buy a little time until she could find it. And if she volunteered, she wouldn't feel so bad about what she was doing. Everybody won.

"I'd like to volunteer my time to Windfall," Chloe said impulsively.

"Oh, wonderful! We can't have enough volunteers." Terri gestured for her to sit, and pulled out a form. Dropping into the chair behind the desk, she began filling in Chloe's background, references and contact information. "Do you have any special skills you'd like to share?"

"I run an events-planning company, so I'm very organized." She withdrew a business card and extended it across the desk.

Terri took it, nodding. "Great. We can always use help here in the office and in the warehouse. Routing the clothes to the proper outlets takes a lot of coordination, especially in peak times, such as emergencies."

"Sounds perfect for me," Chloe said, nodding in turn.

"How many hours a week would you like to volunteer?"

"I was thinking a couple of hours a day for now."

"Would it be possible to work mornings?"

"Actually, early mornings are best for me," Chloe said, relieved that she wouldn't have to juggle her regular work schedule. "From seven to nine?"

"Great. The office will already be unlocked, although there might not be very many people here at that time."

All the better, Chloe thought.

"I see you have our brochure." Terri nodded to the paper sticking out of Chloe's purse. "There's more information on our Web site, too, if you'd like to know the full spectrum of what we do here at Windfall."

"I'll check it out," she promised.

"Good. Then I just have one more question," the woman said with a grin. "When can you start?"

"How about tomorrow morning?"

"Perfect. Would you like a tour?"

"Sure." The sooner she learned the logistics of the business, the better.

When the door to the warehouse opened, Chloe looked up and blinked in surprise to see the blond man who'd been driving the truck with the flat. He walked in studying a piece of paper, which he laid on the corner of Terri's desk, some sort of list. When he looked up, he glanced over at her and tilted his head, as if trying to place her.

Chloe squirmed, hoping he didn't remember she'd been the driver blasting her horn.

"Hi, Andy," Terri said. "Meet Chloe Parker—she's a new volunteer."

"Hello," he said, giving her a friendly smile. "I'm Andy Shearer."

She smiled back, a little dismayed at the way her pulse accelerated. He was a big guy, with broad shoulders and an earthy appearance that made her think of hiking and camping, things she hadn't done since she was a child. "Nice to meet you," she murmured.

The phone rang and Terri excused herself. After a few seconds, she covered the mouthpiece. "Sorry, I need to take this. Andy, I was about to give Chloe a tour. Would you mind showing her around?"

"Not at all," he said smoothly, opening the door and sweeping his arm in front of him. "After you, Chloe."

She walked past him and a shiver of awareness traveled over her shoulders. He had deep blue eyes, pale lashes and freckles on his tanned cheeks. His dark blond hair was short and thick, glinting with golden highlights from the sun. His shirtsleeves were rolled up past brown, muscular forearms. His faded jeans were low-slung and molded powerful thighs. His work boots were scuffed and worn. He was…what was the word?

Hot.

"Are you okay?" he asked, flashing white teeth.

"I'm fine," she said, picking up the pace and chiding herself for observing the man's physical assets. Considerable as they were, it wasn't like her to notice other men. She was engaged, after all, mere weeks away from tying the knot. And she was here on a mission—to find her wedding gown. Not to ogle the help.

He was squinting at her. "Have we met before?"

Chloe's stomach did a little flip. "I don't think so."

"You seem familiar to me for some reason."

"I m-must have one of those faces," she stammered.

"One of those nice ones," he said, nodding.

Her cheeks warmed with a blush. "Thank you." She averted her gaze, trying to focus on the matter at hand rather than the disconcerting man next to her.

"This, as you can tell," he said, gesturing to the noisy scene in front of them, "is the warehouse. Donors either deliver items to us, or we pick them up. Everything comes here to be sorted and bundled for distribution to agencies and shelters all over Toronto."

The warehouse was as big as a football field, and every section of it bustled with activity. Chloe looked at the mountains of clothing and boxes that workers were picking through, and her stomach sank. Her dress could be anywhere. It would be like looking for a needle in a haystack.

Granted, a white, sparkly needle, but still...

"It's a little overwhelming," she said, surveying the goings-on.

"So is the need," Andy remarked. "This organization has grown from a small operation to a vital source of aid in our community."

"I had no idea," Chloe murmured, feeling humbled.

"So what brings you to Windfall?"

She pulled a half-truth from thin air. "I…heard about the organization…and wanted to…help." Maybe she should just come clean and admit why she was there and ask for their help in finding the dress.

"I'm sure Terri is thrilled to have an extra body."

His gaze traveled down her legs, and the chilly warehouse suddenly seemed overheated. It occurred to Chloe that he was flirting with her…and she was enjoying it. She looked everywhere but at him.

Andy cleared his throat. "And what do you do when you aren't volunteering, Chloe?"

"I own an events-coordinating business."

His eyebrows went up. "You plan parties?"

Chloe bristled. Why did it sound frivolous when he said it? "Yes. And other…events."

"Sounds interesting," he said, his eyes dancing. "And a nice way to spend your days—making people happy."

She smiled. "That's the general idea."

"You have a nice smile. You should use it more often."

She held his gaze for a few seconds until an alarm sounded in her head. *This man is dangerous to your peace of mind.* Instead of responding, she glanced away and resumed walking. But she was ultra aware of him walking beside her.

They toured all around the warehouse, with Andy pointing out steps of the operation along the way. Chloe scanned every pile of clothing for a flash of white, sparkly fabric, not sure what she would do if she spotted something. But as it turned out, she didn't see anything resembling her dress. The air was full of dust and lint. Part of their job, he pointed out, was opening packages and removing labels from the clothing before it went out to various agencies.

"Cutting out the labels protects the donors," he said, "so no one can return the items to a store for a refund."

"How long does it take for the items to be processed, from pickup to delivery?"

He shrugged. "Depending on the demand, as little as a few hours to maybe a week or two."

"Depending on the demand?"

"Coats in winter, kids' clothes and backpacks when school starts, that kind of thing. We try to be as responsive as possible, given our constraints."

Chloe nodded. Andy had a pleasing, natural way of speaking and carrying himself. He was, she decided, a good ambassador for the organization. But he unnerved her with the way he looked at her—as if he was trying to figure her out. And she felt as if her ulterior motive for being here was written all over her face. To her relief, they were soon back where they'd started.

"Thank you for the tour," she said, edging toward the office door, eager to put distance between her and his perceptive blue eyes.

Andy nodded, then put his hands on his hips. "Look, I'm not one for beating around the bush. Are you single, Chloe Parker?"

She was so taken aback by his forthrightness that for a few seconds she lost her voice…and her memory. Then she recalled the reason she was here. "Actually, I'm engaged to be married," she said finally.

He looked at her left hand. "Sorry, I didn't see a ring."

"It's at home," she said, slightly irritated. She hadn't been able to find her engagement ring, and she needed to before she saw Ted again. "I always wear it…usually."

He looked amused. "And have you set a date for your walk down the aisle?"

"Three weeks from this past Saturday," Chloe said, feeling defensive.

Andy winked at her. "Too bad. Nice meeting you." Then he gave her a little salute and walked away.

Chloe frowned at the man's broad back. Too bad? Whatever happened to "good luck"?

ANDY SHEARER WALKED AWAY, fighting the urge to look back for another glimpse of Chloe Parker. When he'd walked into the office and seen her, he'd felt as if he'd been sucker punched. The woman was beautiful, with her big brown eyes, full pink lips and masses of dark wavy hair pulled back with a prim yellow ribbon. And there was something about her....

He shook his head, wondering why someone like her was volunteering for Windfall. He liked to give people the benefit of the doubt, but his gut told him that something wasn't on the up and up here.

Then he sighed. No matter the motivation, a volunteer was a volunteer, so it would be nice to have Chloe around. But he planned to keep an eye on her...a task he was looking forward to, despite the fact that she'd been quick to tell him she was to be married soon.

Because there was something fishy going on with this woman, and he intended to find out what.

CHAPTER
❧ FOUR ❧

C hloe hid a yawn behind her hand, a result of her early morning wake-up, and flipped through the pile of papers in front of her, looking for any mention of a delivery pickup from Melinda's Bridal Shop. "These receipts are from two weeks ago," she announced.

"We're running a little behind," Terri said, "but working at a good pace. See these account numbers listed at the bottom of the receipts? Each one represents an agency that received a parcel of the clothes or items on that receipt. In other words, all of the things listed on this receipt have already been distributed. We just have to make sure the paperwork accurately reflects what was taken and what was sent out or retained."

"Retained?"

"That means it couldn't be shipped out for some reason—maybe it was out of season or in disrepair, a pair of shoes was mismatched, or something like that."

"Wow, you keep a close eye on what comes in and what goes out," Chloe remarked, thinking that even if she found her wedding dress, she'd still have to figure out a way to get it out of there. According to Andy's information, unless the agencies experienced a sudden demand for wedding gowns, she had less than two weeks to find the dress.

But if they were two weeks behind processing paperwork in the office, the dress would be gone by the time the receipt from Melinda's Bridal Shop crossed her desk.

"Our funding depends on good record keeping," Terri said, breaking into Chloe's thoughts. "We'd rather be slow and accurate."

"Are employees and volunteers allowed to take clothes home?"

Terri shook her head. "The donated items are strictly for clients."

"Are they allowed to buy things?"

Again, the woman shook her head. "It's important that no one has the opportunity to profit from the items that are donated to Windfall. We have signed contracts with our agencies that they will provide clothing free of charge to those in need."

It was a simple, effective idea, Chloe acknowledged—matching manufacturer and retailer overstock to agencies through a clearinghouse that ensured the items went where they were most needed. The donors received tax write-offs on products that might otherwise wind up in landfills; the agencies and shelters received much-needed items to satisfy the ever-increasing demand. Even more remarkable, the organization relied solely on private donations and fund-raising events.

"How long have you been working here?" Chloe asked Terri.

"About eight years now. Every year Windfall has grown, and unfortunately, so has the need."

Terri appeared to be one of a handful of full-time employees, and the woman was dedicated to Windfall. It was clear she put in more hours than a standard workweek simply out of love for the organization.

Chloe continued sorting invoices by date. "How long has Andy been here?"

"That's a good question. I'm not sure—he was here when I started, and it seems as if he's always around."

The door to the office opened and Terri said, "Speak of the devil."

Chloe looked up to see the man whose face had plagued her dreams last night. Today he was dressed in jeans and a navy sweatshirt that reflected the blue in his eyes. He gave them a wicked grin. "My ears were burning, so I thought I'd come in to eavesdrop."

Terri laughed and waved him off. "Chloe was asking how long you've been here, and I couldn't tell her."

"Hmm." He looked up to the ceiling. "I guess it's been about ten years now."

Admirable, Chloe conceded, because she knew the man couldn't make much money driving a delivery truck for Windfall. Maybe he was the kind of guy who wanted a flexible, low-pressure job to give him time for other pursuits.

Unlike Ted, who tended to operate at extremes. He put in long workweeks, and on weekends, he preferred a drink in one hand and a TV remote control in the other. He didn't have many interests outside his dental practice and his friends...and Chloe. His career was his top priority, but it would afford them a very comfortable life together.

"How's the first day going?" Andy asked Chloe.

"She's doing great," Terri enthused.

"Just trying to learn my way around," Chloe said.

He nodded, but seemed to study her. Then he threw up his hand and backed toward the door. "Gotta make a delivery. Have a good one, ladies."

When the door closed behind him, Chloe felt Terri's gaze on her.

"Andy's cute," Terri offered.

"I hadn't noticed," she replied.

"And he's single."

"But I'm not," Chloe murmured, hiding her bare left hand. Even though she'd torn her bedroom apart, she still hadn't found her engagement ring.

She excused herself to visit the washroom, which happened to be in the warehouse. Chloe tried to seem casual as she checked for any sign of Andy, but the man wasn't around. Relieved, she took the long way to the washroom, scanning the pallets of clothes for anything that resembled formal wear or dress bags. She smiled at the gloved workers sorting things, and tried to look as if she belonged there.

"Searching for something?"

At the sound of Andy's voice, Chloe froze between two mountains of what looked to be women's pajamas. She turned around and smiled. "Yes—the washroom."

He pointed to the opposite end of the warehouse. "Over there."

She nodded. "Okay...thanks. I thought you were going out on a delivery."

"The truck wasn't loaded yet."

"Oh. Well, thanks." She moved to step past him.

"I see you're still not wearing your engagement ring," he said, nodding to her hand.

Annoyance flashed through her. "It's...being cleaned."

"Gee, it must be a big one if it takes that long."

She gritted her teeth. "It is."

He smiled and gave her his signature salute. "See you later."

Chloe walked away, frustrated. How was she ever going to find her dress with that man seemingly stalking her every move?

Andy watched the lovely Chloe retreat. The plot thickened.

CHLOE SETTLED INTO A routine of working with Terri in the office from seven to nine every morning and sneaking away whenever possible to walk up and down the aisles of donated items. She was feeling a little desperate by the end of the week, when she still hadn't seen any sign of inventory from Melinda's shop. She hoped it was still at the bottom of one of the pallets, waiting to be processed.

She'd been working furiously on the receipts in the office, catching up to only a three-day lag from when the clothes left the warehouse. She continued to ask questions about the process, trying to figure out how she might circumvent the paperwork and find out where the dresses had been stored in the massive warehouse. But as near as she could tell, the receipt she was looking for must be in one of the stacks that the couple of dozen warehouse assistants maintained at their stations. And she couldn't very well go around asking to rifle through them all.

"Would it be all right if I collected receipts from the warehouse assistants?" Chloe asked on Friday morning.

Terri looked up. "They usually just drop them off when they have a pile."

"I know, but I was thinking I might come in tomorrow and try to get caught up."

Terri smiled. "That's not necessary. We've learned to accept that we're always going to be a little behind in the office."

"I'd like to," Chloe pressed.

The woman shrugged. "Okay. You're amazing. I hope you decide to stay around here."

Chloe felt a twinge of guilt, but told herself that her motivation wasn't important—she was doing work that needed to be done. That was what mattered.

Wasn't it?

Meanwhile, she scrupulously avoided Andy Shearer whenever possible, which wasn't easy. The man was everywhere. Anytime he saw her in the warehouse, he approached her and struck up a conversation. Worse, he kept staring at her left hand.

And she still hadn't found her darn ring. Tomorrow after leaving Windfall and running errands, she intended to tear apart her bedroom before her dinner date with Ted. She'd been able to avoid explaining the ring's absence only because they were both so busy getting their affairs in order before leaving for their honeymoon, they'd barely had a chance to talk, much less see each other. If she got lucky, maybe she'd find her dress *and* the ring tomorrow. Then everything would be perfect again.

She entered the warehouse and began going around to the assistants to collect receipts. "Just trying to get a jump on the paperwork," she explained to each one. "By the way, a friend of mine who runs a bridal shop donates to Windfall—do you remember any wedding dresses coming in lately?"

The warehouse assistants spent the entire day on their feet, moving between the loading docks, instructing forklift operators where to drop their load, and continually trying to stay on top of all the sorting, plus packing outgoing pallets to meet the various agencies' requirements. Despite the harried environment, each of them took the time to greet her and respond kindly to her not-so-innocent question, once again dredging up guilty feelings in Chloe for imposing on their time. She'd already spoken to half of them, but no one remembered logging in a shipment of wedding gowns.

"Looks like you could use a hand."

Chloe closed her eyes and swallowed a bad word. Then she turned and smiled brightly at Andy. "No, thanks."

Ignoring her response, he took the armload of papers from her and proceeded to follow her around as she collected receipts from other assistants, his big ears effectively thwarting her attempt to ask questions.

"You must be getting caught up in the office," he commented. "Terri can't say enough about how wonderful your work is."

"She's just glad to have an extra set of hands," Chloe said, feeling her blood pressure rise at his proximity. Why did the man have to be so...observant?

"Speaking of hands—I'm dying to see this gigantic engagement ring of yours. Are you saving it for a special occasion?"

Chloe frowned. "Don't you have something to do?"

He grinned. "Nothing more interesting."

She turned her back and collected a sheaf of papers from the next assistant. "I'm not that interesting."

"I disagree," he said smoothly.

Chloe glanced at her watch. "Oh, look at the time. I have to go."

"Planning any good parties today?" he asked, following her back toward the office.

"As a matter of fact, I am—my bridal brunch is on Sunday," she said pointedly.

"Sounds like a blast. Are all your friends as high-society as you?"

Chloe stopped and looked up at him, thinking he'd be surprised to know that she came from very modest means, that her entrée into high society had been recent and by way of Ted and her fledgling business. Andy's arrogance infuriated her.

"You don't know me," she said, her chest rising and falling. "You don't know anything about me."

"But I'd like to."

His words sent a warm tickle to her stomach. The thought *I'd like to get to know you, too,* floated through her head until she realized the insanity of the notion. Exasperated at her response to him, she said, "Are you deaf? I'm getting married in two weeks."

"Don't you have any room in your life for another friend?"

Chloe considered the man before her and tamped down the confusing emotions churning within her. He was maddening. And the way her pulse picked up when he was nearby eliminated the possibility that they could ever just be friends. Besides, she didn't plan to be at Windfall any longer than necessary.

She reached out and took the papers he was carrying, adding them to her considerable stack. "I have all the friends I need," she said, and walked back into the office.

Terri glanced up at her. "Is everything okay between you and Andy?"

"Fine," Chloe said, putting down the receipts she planned to tackle tomorrow, and picking up her purse. "Have a good day."

CHAPTER
❧ FIVE ❧

C hloe was eager to get to Windfall the next morning, eager to ask the rest of the warehouse assistants if they were aware of a wedding-gown shipment, and then go through all the receipts she'd collected the previous day. A slow drip of panic had begun to remind her that she had only two weeks left to find her wedding gown. She simply couldn't fathom walking down the aisle wearing anything else.

Terri wasn't coming in today, so upon arriving, Chloe sat in the quiet office and sifted through the receipts, her heart pounding. When she reached the last one, she heaved a sigh of relief. No receipt from the bridal shop with outgoing agency codes meant that chances were good the wedding gown was still somewhere in the warehouse.

The place was abuzz with activity this morning as more volunteers arrived. Which allowed her to mingle and move among the mounds of clothing without drawing too much attention to the fact that she was checking every section like a dog on the hunt.

"I didn't expect to see you here today."

Chloe stopped and swallowed a groan. Then she turned to face her handsome tormentor. "Likewise."

Andy smiled widely, as if he knew that he got on her nerves, and enjoyed it. "I see you've left the office to lend a hand out here."

"Just trying to learn more about the organization," she said breezily.

"Really? Would you like to see what happens to all these things?"

"What do you mean?"

He jerked his thumb toward a loading dock where a truck sat. "I'm getting ready to make a delivery. Why don't you come with me?"

Alone with him in close quarters? "I don't know," she hedged.

"Come on, I could use an extra hand." His eyes were warm and hopeful.

How was it possible that someone so maddening could be so irresistible? "Okay," she heard herself say, even though she felt as if she were entering a hazardous zone.

He grinned. "Great. Let's go."

She followed him to the truck self-consciously and allowed him to help her climb into the seat. His big hands felt warm and capable on her arm and waist. A jolt of awareness warmed her all over. He smiled and winked before closing the door, then walked around and bounded into his own seat.

"Buckle up."

She pulled the seat belt over her shoulder. "Where are we going?"

"To a community center to give out toys. Vaccinations are being administered, and the kids are generally more willing to come if they can take home something to play with."

Chloe nodded and concentrated on the passing streetscape. "So you come in on Saturdays, too?"

"Most of the time. I thought Saturdays would be busy for you, with parties and all."

"I've cut back a little to have time to get ready for my wedding," she said, mentioning it as much as a reminder for herself as for him.

"Oh, right—the wedding. Is it going to be a big to-do?" Then he laughed. "Since you're a party planner, I guess so, huh?"

"I suppose. It's something I've always dreamed of."

He grinned. "That's where men and women are different."

"You don't want to get married?" she asked dryly.

"Oh, sure, someday," he said, surprising her with his enthusiasm. "I guess I've always dreamed about the bride though, instead of the ceremony."

Chloe hesitated a moment, then said, "So tell me about your bride."

He shrugged. "I guess she's more of an idea than a face, but if I had to describe her, I'd say pretty, of course, with a great smile."

He threw Chloe a meaningful glance and she smiled in spite of herself.

"Kind and generous," he continued, "and flexible."

She frowned. "That's a little pervy."

He laughed out loud, a pleasing rumbling sound. "I meant flexible in terms of her attitude—willing to adapt."

Chloe squirmed, wondering if he was going down his checklist of desirable traits in a woman for her benefit, implying that she wasn't "flexible." Not that it mattered. Then she frowned. Did Ted have a checklist? Did she?

"And you'll know this woman when you see her?" Chloe asked.

He nodded confidently. "I have good instincts when it comes to sizing up people."

There was that look again, as if he could peer directly into her dishonest heart and see the reason she had volunteered at Windfall. Chloe opened her mouth to confess, but realized suddenly that she didn't want this man to think poorly of her.

"What does your fiancé do?" he asked.

Safer ground. "He's a dentist."

He grinned. "I'll bet he has perfect teeth."

Chloe shifted in her seat. How could he make something positive sound so frivolous, as if that were Ted's best quality?

"Here we are," he said, wheeling into a parking lot and driving to a far corner to bring the truck to a halt.

Chloe jumped down from the seat before he could come around to help her. She didn't like the way she was starting to feel toward Andy, or the way he was making her feel about herself and her upcoming wedding. The man had a propensity to turning things on end.

He unhooked the back door of the truck and lifted it, causing the muscles in his arms to bunch in a most desirable way. Chloe looked away and chastised herself. She shouldn't have come.

"I'm glad you came," he said, as if he could read her mind. "The kids always react better when there's a woman around." He winked. "Me, too."

She couldn't help but laugh as he handed down net bags of toys and stuffed animals. She felt a little like Santa when they walked into the community center. The waiting room was crammed with small children, many of them sitting on their mothers' laps or clinging to their knees. It was clear that most of them knew today's visit involved some kind of needle, and they were under duress. Chloe's heart squeezed for them.

But their expressions changed when they realized they could choose a toy from the many bags Chloe and Andy brought in. When Chloe extended a small doll to a shy little girl wearing a clean but shabby dress, a repressed memory slid into her head. She'd been a little girl much like this one, sitting on her mother's lap, waiting to see the doctor. And someone had given her a toy— a colorful windmill on a stick that spun when she blew on it.

Chloe straightened and blinked back tears. Until this moment, she hadn't realized the toy was charity; she only remembered how much better it had made her feel. She and her mother had benefited from an organization much like Windfall....

"Hey, are you okay?" Andy asked, looking suddenly concerned.

"I'm fine," she said, hastily wiping her eyes.

"You're crying."

"I said I'm fine," she repeated, more vehemently than she'd planned.

Andy's expression gentled. He pulled a tissue from a box sitting on a nearby counter and handed it to her, then smiled at the next waiting child. Chloe took the tissue and dabbed at the corners of her eyes, watching Andy interact with the little ones. His comment about kids responding better to women didn't seem to be true where he was concerned. Despite his large size, the children gravitated to him and squealed in delight as he pretended to steal noses with his thumb, and wiggled his ears for them. Chloe felt her heart lurch sideways. Whenever Andy found the woman he'd been dreaming of, he would make a wonderful father. And he was the kind of man a woman would want to have babies with. He just seemed so genuine and full of life.

She steered her runaway thoughts back to Ted. They hadn't resolved to have children, but hadn't ruled it out, either. Both of them were just so busy in their careers, they had decided to postpone the matter until later, when they'd settled into married life. In retrospect, Chloe realized the decision had been somewhat clinical. Why didn't looking at Ted make her think of freckle-faced children?

She arranged her face in a smile, but troubling thoughts pecked at her as she and Andy finished passing out the toys. To his credit, he didn't ask her any more about the sudden tears, didn't tease her again about her impending wedding. When they returned to the warehouse, he was friendly, but seemed more cautious around her.

"Thanks for asking me to go with you," she ventured.

"Thank you for going."

"I...enjoyed it." Despite the turmoil that the experience had stirred up, it was humbling to be reminded that in a country where most people had what they wanted, there were so many who needed a helping hand or simply a kind gesture. Those children at the community center were a far cry from the ones for whom she planned elaborate birthday parties, kids who were raised to expect entertainment and celebrity guests and even live animals. It seemed so excessive, so wasteful.

Like her own wedding?

"Are you sticking around?" Andy asked.

Chloe checked her watch. She needed time to look for her ring before Ted arrived to pick her up for dinner. "No, I need to go."

"Okay. Well, have fun at your brunch tomorrow," he said, his voice and eyes sincere.

"Thanks," she murmured, surprised that he'd remembered.

"See you later." He gave her a little salute and walked through the busy warehouse.

Chloe drove home, feeling restless and bewildered by her reaction to Andy and to the other folks at the community center. It felt good helping people, making them smile—without getting paid for it. Andy's easygoing attitude made him a perfect fit for his truck-driving job. She wondered about his background, but then reminded herself that Andy Shearer's upbringing was none of her concern. She had so many other things on her plate to deal with.

At her apartment she stood in the doorway of her bedroom and set her jaw. Her engagement ring had to be in this room somewhere. She began to systematically check every square inch, moving clutter and shifting furniture, covering the same ground she'd covered before, with the same result. As the time for her date with Ted drew closer, her anxiety ratcheted higher. When the doorbell rang, her mind whirled for a solution.

From a drawer she removed a flexible cast that fit like a fingerless glove. She'd needed it the time she'd sprained her wrist. Now she slid it onto her left hand and went to answer the door, worried that she might feel different about Ted in the wake of her unwelcome attraction to Andy.

But when she swung open the door and Ted stood there holding a dozen roses, her heart grew buoyant once again.

This thing with Andy was as fleeting as her stint with Windfall. She had a wedding dress to find.

CHAPTER
❧— SIX —❧

"Chloe, I know it's a lot to ask," Terri said Monday morning, "but our annual golf tournament, our biggest fund-raiser of the year, is coming up later this week, and I wondered if you would mind helping there versus here in the office."

Chloe hesitated. She needed to be near the warehouse, looking for her dress, not off-site working a golf tournament. But Terri had been so kind, and Chloe had begun to feel worse about her deception....

"When is it?"

"Friday. But you wouldn't have to be there all day. Morning, afternoon, any time that you have."

"I have an event that morning, but I could get there for the afternoon. What would I be doing?"

"Directing people, taking tickets, that kind of thing." Terri smiled. "It's more fun than hanging out here in the office."

"Okay, sure," she said, nodding. "I wouldn't mind doing something different." Besides, she intended to find her dress between now and then anyway. "As a matter of fact, I was wondering if I could help out in the warehouse this week, just for a change of pace."

Terri shrugged. "I don't mind, but it might not be good for your hand."

Chloe guiltily rubbed the elastic cast she was still wearing. "It'll be fine."

The weekend with Ted and yesterday's shower brunch had been a success, reminding her of all the reasons she was marrying him, all the reasons she was planning a big ceremony. People liked to celebrate important moments in their lives with extravagant parties—there was no crime in that. Andy himself had said it must be nice to make people happy, and it was. So she was looking forward to her supersized wedding; that didn't make her a bad person. But she was less than two weeks from getting married, and still missing a wedding gown. She seriously needed to get out into the warehouse and start poking around.

"I'm sure they could use an extra hand out there today," Terri said, "since a lot of volunteers are already at the golf tournament site, getting things ready." The telephone rang and she reached for it. "The receipts can wait," Terri added, eyeing the stack of paper in front of Chloe. "Anyone can tell you where to pitch in."

Chloe nodded and headed for the warehouse, nervously glancing around for Andy. To her relief, he was nowhere in sight. She asked more assistants about a wedding-dress shipment, but they shook their heads. One admitted that it was impossible to remember everything that came in. She noticed that assistants spotted each other off, changing stations as necessary, and some of them worked only part-time, so they wouldn't have knowledge of every incoming shipment. She walked quickly up and down the aisles, scanning for a glimpse of white, feeling a little desperate.

"I could use a hand over here," someone yelled, and Chloe turned to help. An enormous box of travel-size toiletries donated by a hotel sat on a pallet. A sturdy woman gestured to the box. "A shelter is receiving an influx of refugees this afternoon and they need sets of toiletries individually bagged to pass out."

"How many?" Chloe asked.

"As many as we can give them."

Chloe reached for a bag and began filling it with one of each kind of toiletry. Her two hours evaporated, but there was still so much more to be done that she stayed an extra hour. All the time she kept looking over her shoulder for Andy. It wasn't as if she missed him or anything; she was just so accustomed to seeing him around. But he must have had pickups or deliveries to make.

When she left to keep an appointment with a caterer to taste-test sushi for an upcoming luncheon, she felt good about all the toiletries she'd bundled, but realized another morning had expired and she was no closer to finding her dress.

And so it went all week. Every morning she began looking for her gown and was pulled away by something that needed immediate attention. By Friday she still had no dress and no engagement ring. At her apartment she had resorted to emptying her bedroom of everything she could move. Only the large pieces of furniture remained, and she was considering renting a metal detector.

And strangely, she hadn't seen Andy all week. She mentioned his absence to Terri in passing, but when the woman seemed interested in why she'd noticed, Chloe changed the subject.

On the drive to the golf tournament Friday afternoon, she felt panic licking at her. She was getting married a week from tomorrow and she still hadn't found her dress, not to mention her ring. So why was she wasting her time volunteering at a fund-raising event when she should be back at the warehouse, digging through mountains of sweaters? Tomorrow she had three birthday parties back-to-back, so going to Windfall over the weekend was out of the question.

She sighed and came to a decision: on Monday she would come clean with Terri and ask for her help. And once she had her dress, she would leave with her tail between her legs.

When she found Terri at the entrance to the golf course, she considered telling her the truth and getting it over with. Dread billowed inside her.

"Thank you for coming!" Terri said, giving her a hug that made the words she'd been contemplating stick in her throat. The woman's cheeks were pink with sun and excitement. "The weather is perfect, lucky us. We need someone at the seventeenth tee to collect money for the hole-in-one contest. Are you up for it?"

"Sure," Chloe said, glad for the diversion. Monday would come soon enough. She didn't want to do anything to spoil the mood or the day.

Terri handed her a map and a blue sun visor imprinted with the Windfall logo, then pointed her in the right direction.

It was a beautiful spring day, sunny with a nip in the air. The golf course itself was lovely and green, dotted with mature trees and manicured bushes. As she walked through the crowds, inhaling the sun-scented air, she began to relax. People had come out for a good cause and spirits were high. From the turnout she surmised that the event was well-established, and although things looked to be running smoothly, the event planner in her made mental notes on small details that could be improved upon.

Not that she would be around next year to offer input.

She noted signs for corporate sponsors at each of the tees and silently vowed to patronize the companies whenever possible. When she approached the seventeenth tee, there were additional signs for the hole-in-one contest. On this par three hole, golfers paid five dollars for the chance to hit their ball into the cup in one shot. If they made a hole-in-one, an electronics company called One World would give the winner ten thousand dollars on the spot.

Chloe stepped up to another Windfall volunteer who was taking money and asked how she could help. It was a popular event, so she was instantly busy, handling cash and passing out forms. Less than an hour later a commotion arose on the tee, followed by cheers and high fives and backslapping.

"Oh, my goodness," said the woman Chloe was helping, "somebody won!"

The crowd buzzed with excitement as walkie-talkies emerged and greensmen appeared to be verifying the shot. When a thumbs-up was given, the gallery erupted again and the man who'd made the hole-in-one gave a victory dance. From the sidelines a tall man in a sport coat and slacks emerged, grinning and holding an oversize check for ten thousand dollars. Something about him…

Chloe squinted. *Andy?*

She continued clapping and leaned over to the other volunteer. "Is that Andy Shearer?"

The woman nodded. "He owns One World Electronics. He's one of Windfall's biggest supporters. Rich, handsome *and* good-hearted…I'd like to know what a girl would have to do to catch *his* eye."

Wonder curled through Chloe's chest. So Andy was the owner of a hugely successful company and he moonlighted as a truck driver for Windfall in his free time? He'd never even hinted that he was more than he appeared.

But then again, she'd never asked.

She was still clapping when Andy looked up and caught her gaze. He seemed surprised to see her, then gave her a nod and turned back to shake the hand of the winner and to pose for photographs.

Chloe tried not to watch him, tried to get her mind back on the task at hand. In the wake of a winner, players flooded to the tee to take their chance at the big money. Chloe took cash and handed out forms as fast as she could. Yet she was aware of Andy walking around the tee, giving encouraging pats, gesturing to other over-size checks waiting in the wings to be passed out to future winners.

And then he was making his way toward her.

Her heart beat wildly as he approached. She took money from the last people in her line and thanked them. The sight of Andy in business attire restricted her breathing, and the smile she was preparing felt shaky when he stopped in front of her.

"I didn't expect to see you here," he said.

"You're full of surprises yourself," she said, gesturing to his clothing.

He grinned. "I would've told you about One World sooner if I thought it would've made a difference."

Chloe squirmed. It wouldn't have…would it? Was she that materialistic? "How did you begin driving a truck for Windfall?"

He shrugged those big shoulders. "There was a time when I drove my own delivery truck for my business. Once my company reached a certain level of success, I felt strongly about giving back to the community. When I heard that Windfall needed trucks, I gave them one and volunteered to drive it in my spare time. Then it just became a habit."

"I'm impressed," she said, and meant it.

His blue eyes danced. "Enough to let me buy you a hotdog?"

Chloe hesitated, tempted.

"It's for a good cause," he cajoled.

She smiled and relented, telling herself it was only a concession snack, not a date.

But the hotdog lunch turned into a relaxed afternoon of strolling around the golf course, cheering on the players and pitching in wherever they were needed. Chloe asked about his business and he shared a few highlights, although she sensed he was holding back, uncomfortable with what might seem like bragging. She felt drawn to him, like those children at the community center who recognized warmth and sincerity. It was a goodness that she wanted for herself, yet she didn't think her heart was that big. When she thought of why she had volunteered for Windfall, she burned with shame.

Dusk was settling in when he walked her back to her van. Apprehensive about her burgeoning attraction to this man, Chloe pulled out her keys, ready to vault into the driver's seat.

"Did you hurt your hand?" he asked, pointing to the flexible cast.

"Er, it's just a sprain." What was another lie?

He nodded, his eyes alight with amusement. "If I were your fiancé, I might be nervous if you weren't wearing your ring—what? A week before the wedding."

"A week from tomorrow." Chloe fidgeted and looked away. "It's not what you think."

He put his hand under her chin and lifted her face until she met his gaze. "I think I'd like to kiss you right now," he said.

Chloe labored to breathe as his lips closed in on hers. "I don't... I shouldn't..."

But she did. She opened her mouth to meet his and moaned softly as they came together. His tongue gently probed hers and she responded in kind as thrilling sensations flooded her body. She wanted the fervent kiss to go on and on, but when his hand brushed her lower back, reason returned with a crash.

Chloe pulled away abruptly, covering her mouth. "I can't do this."

"You can if you want to," he said, his eyes hooded. "Chloe, I feel something between us...something special."

She shook her head. "No. I'm not the person you think I am."

"You're beautiful and smart and kind—"

"I'm not kind," she blurted, flailing her arms. "The only reason I volunteered at Windfall was to find my lost wedding gown."

He frowned. "What?"

"My fiancé…called off the wedding and I returned my wedding gown to the bridal shop. Then we got back together and when I went to get the dress—"

"It had been donated to Windfall," he said, his voice thick.

She nodded miserably.

"The bridal shop on Queen Street?"

She nodded again.

One side of his mouth quirked back in a wry smile. "I made that pickup myself." He looked up as if searching for answers, then back to her. "So you went undercover as a volunteer just to find this dress?"

"I was desperate."

"It must be some dress."

"It's the wedding gown I've dreamed of since I was a little girl. I have to get it back."

"It's that important to you?" He gave a little laugh and jammed his hands on his hips. "This one beats everything I've ever heard or seen."

"I'm sorry," she whispered. "I didn't think anyone would get hurt."

STEPHANIE BOND

Andy pressed his lips together as if he sorely regretted the kiss. "Don't worry. The rest of us will be fine, Chloe." Then he turned and strode away from her.

Chloe blinked back tears. It was a horrible realization for a person to learn the depths of her own selfishness. And worse— she didn't think she could change.

CHAPTER
~SEVEN~

C hloe couldn't remember a more wretched weekend. How ironic that of all the Windfall drivers, Andy had been the person to collect her dress...on the day she'd noticed him in traffic with the flat tire.

The look on his face when she'd told him the truth about the gown haunted her, and the words he'd said kept playing in her head.

The rest of us will be fine, Chloe.

In other words, of everyone affected by her selfish actions, she was the person who would suffer the most.

And the kiss...

The kiss that they'd shared had been burned into her brain and onto her lips. Forgotten nuances came to her at unguarded moments—the woodsy scent of his aftershave in her lungs, the scrape of his five-o'clock shadow against her cheek, the slide of his tongue over hers.

And to make the weekend exponentially worse, a thorough search of her bedroom had not turned up her engagement ring. She'd spent hours on her knees, combing through the carpet, searching her bed linens, the floor vents, even the hem of her curtains. She knew that Ted had the ring insured, but she dreaded telling him that she'd lost a ring that had cost more than her van. In her bedroom. It didn't make sense, which only made her more crazy.

And when she woke up Monday morning, she conceded glumly that time was running out on both the ring and the dress.

She drove to Windfall with a white-knuckled grip on the steering wheel. Terri was a wonderful person, who had shown her nothing but kindness, and deserved to hear the truth from her, even if Andy had already informed her of Chloe's deception.

When she arrived, she remembered the trepidation she'd felt that first morning, how she had convinced herself that donating her time to the organization somehow made up for the fact that she was volunteering under false pretenses.

But it didn't.

With her heart in her throat, she dragged herself out of the van and into the office.

Terri looked up with her usual friendly smile. "Good morning!"

"Good morning," Chloe managed to reply, fidgeting as she did so. "Terri, I came by to say that I won't be able to come in this week."

"That's okay, but you didn't have to stop by. You could've just called."

"Actually—"

"Chloe."

She looked up and blanched to see Andy standing in the door leading to the warehouse. His face was less animated than usual, but friendly nonetheless. "Can I see you for a minute?"

She fought the urge to turn and flee, but nodded and made her heavy feet move toward him.

She stepped out into the din of the warehouse, which was already buzzing with activity, voices raised in camaraderie. After the door closed behind them, she tentatively met Andy's gaze, her pulse clicking away. "Yes?"

He tore off a sheet of paper from a small notepad he held. "I tracked down that shipment I picked up from the bridal shop on Queen. The dresses were all delivered Saturday to the Helping Hand shelter—it houses families after natural disasters. They've been busy lately with all the flooding north of here. If you hurry, you can probably be there when they open. Ask for Joanie. She'll help you find what you're looking for."

Deeply touched, Chloe took the paper with a shaking hand. "I don't know how to thank you, Andy."

He gave her a rueful smile. "You can thank me by having a happy life." Then he angled his head toward Terri in the office. "She doesn't need to know about any of this."

Chloe nodded gratefully and watched him walk away for the last time.

Swallowing a lump of emotion, she returned to the office and manufactured a smile. "I was saying that I won't be able to come in this week because I'm getting married Saturday."

Terri smiled back. "Congratulations!" Then her forehead creased in a frown. "Why didn't you say something?"

Chloe shrugged. "There was just so much going on."

"That's the way it always is around here," she said with a laugh, reaching for the ringing phone. "I hope we'll see you in future, though."

Chloe nodded, but she wasn't sure she could face the people at Windfall again, knowing how she had used them.

She walked back to her van, holding the piece of notepaper in her fist. She unfolded it when she got behind the steering wheel, reading the address written in Andy's neat, masculine handwriting. What an amazing man to help her after what she'd done, and to maintain her privacy.

And right or wrong, she had to admit that she was giddy at the thought of getting her magical dress back. She was sure it would help to set her heart right again and would dispel the indefinable pangs she felt when she thought about Andy.

With traffic and a couple of missed turns, she arrived at the Helping Hand shelter about fifteen minutes after it had opened, and found it already busy. Most of the people looked sad and worried as they picked through racks, reminding Chloe once again how frivolous her quest was compared to true misfortune. She asked for Joanie, and the woman was nice enough to direct her to the small section where the formal wear hung. To her immense relief, amid the long gowns were several telltale bags from Melinda's Bridal Shop, with clear plastic windows for a glimpse of the dress inside. Chloe's heart lifted in her chest—then fell to her shoes when she saw her fairy-tale dress…

On another woman.

The young redhead stood in front of a mirror, beaming at her reflection. The magical gown fit her like a dream, sparkling and shimmering like a mirage. Chloe met her gaze in the mirror, swallowed her own bitter disappointment and smiled.

"You look beautiful," she declared.

The young woman blushed and smiled in return. "Isn't it the most magnificent dress you've ever seen?"

Chloe nodded and stepped forward. "Let me help you with the zipper."

"It seems to be stuck."

"I got it," she said, working the zipper past the rough spot she'd created when she'd ripped off the dress in anger. "There."

"Thank you," the woman said, her voice full of wonder.

"Are you getting married?" Chloe asked.

The redhead nodded shyly. "In just a couple of weeks. But my parents' house was flooded and my dress was ruined, along with practically everything else we owned." Her eyes glistened with tears. "This gown is so much more beautiful, though. I love my David so much, and I know this dress will be a blessing on our marriage."

Chloe swallowed hard and nodded. Then she reached into the dress bag. "Look, a veil—and shoes, too. Can you wear a size seven?"

The woman nodded excitedly.

Chloe opened the box and removed the first crystal-studded silk mule and handed it to the young woman.

"Oh, my," she breathed.

"Yes, they're gorgeous," Chloe said, caressing the mate. Something rolled out of the shoe into her hand, and when she looked down, she gasped. Her engagement ring winked back at her.

Luckily, the girl hadn't noticed, so Chloe slipped the ring into her pocket, then handed over the other shoe. "You're going to be a lovely bride."

"Thank you," the young woman said, her face aglow. "I can't wait to be married."

And it hit Chloe—she didn't feel the same way about Ted as this woman did about the man she was going to marry.

Reluctantly, and with no small amount of shame, she admitted to herself that she was more excited about the wedding than about being married to Ted. Her heart didn't flutter when he walked into a room, not the way it did when Andy was around. Ted said he loved her, but he wasn't affectionate toward her. He didn't tease her and tell her she had a great smile, or make her feel as if he'd rather eat a hotdog with her than do anything else.

"Are you okay?" the other woman asked with a little frown.

Chloe nodded. "I will be. Good luck to you."

She returned to the van and sat looking at her engagement ring with a bittersweet pang. She was infinitely relieved to have found the ring. It would be easier to tell Ted she couldn't marry him now that she could actually give it back.

TED LOOKED INCREDULOUS. "What?"

"I can't marry you," Chloe repeated, then placed the engagement ring in his hand.

"If this is some kind of payback for me breaking off the wedding earlier—"

"It isn't," she said. "In fact, I want to thank you, because your hesitation was a symptom of something that we both should have paid attention to."

"But we're good together," he protested.

"That's the problem," Chloe said. "Neither one of us should settle for 'good.' Personally, I want 'great,' and I think you do, too."

His face flushed in a way that told her he'd been having the same thoughts. From the recesses of her brain came a question about the timing of his apology—after Mindy Shale's bridal shower. She'd noticed the chemistry between them, but Ted had denied any interest in his sister's friend. Chloe closed her eyes briefly. Why did love have to be so complicated? If his sudden bout of cold feet was indeed an indication of his feelings for Mindy, she dearly hoped he made his move before the woman married someone else.

"Can I change your mind?" he asked hopefully.

Chloe shook her head. "I'm not blaming you, Ted. I've changed. I have a new perspective on life and what's important to me."

"There's no going back after this, Chloe."

"I know," she said softly. "I'll take care of undoing everything. I'll make sure everyone knows it wasn't your fault."

His smile was rueful, then he angled his head. "I don't know what it is, but you do seem different."

She released a pent-up breath. "I feel different... I feel good." Except when she thought about Andy and the fact that she'd blown any chance she'd had with him.

Andy had spoken the truth—her deception had wound up hurting her more than anyone else.

CHAPTER EIGHT

T he blare of a horn jarred Andy from his musing—but did nothing to improve his sour mood. Why he should be so upset on the day that Chloe Parker married another man made no rational sense. The woman had told him from the beginning that she was engaged, had never encouraged his unexplainable attraction to her, had, in fact, avoided him at every turn.

Plus, his initial instincts that something fishy was going on had proved to be true—in the worst possible way. The fact that she'd used Windfall for her own selfish purposes was unbelievable. The only rationalization that mitigated her deceit was that she must truly love the man.

Which didn't make Andy feel warm and fuzzy inside.

He wheeled the truck into the Windfall parking lot, backing up to an available loading dock. He was glad to be volunteering today. Spending a few hours at Windfall always cured what ailed him, always made him realize that his problems were small, even luxurious, in the grand scheme of things.

When he walked into the warehouse, he greeted a fellow volunteer, then went to get a cup of coffee at the refreshment station. He tried to ignore the nagging sensation behind his breast-bone. There was no use lamenting a never-was relationship with a woman he hadn't really known.

So much for those good instincts of his when it came to sizing up people.

You knew something wasn't right, his mind whispered, *but you overlooked it because you were falling for her.*

Oh, well, he thought as he took a swig of strong coffee, it wasn't meant to be.

He turned toward a group of people who were unloading a truck that had just arrived. His heart warmed to see volunteers pulling together, especially on a sunny Saturday when they could have been doing so many other things.

Then his steps slowed and he zoned in on one volunteer in particular.

Other things such as getting married.

Chloe Parker was one of the people who'd formed a human conveyer belt, passing bundles and boxes from the truck to the floor of the warehouse. Her cheeks were pink from exertion and a few strands of dark hair had come loose from the prim yellow ribbon of her ponytail. He'd never seen a more beautiful sight, and his heart lifted even though he told himself he had no reason to get his hopes up.

Andy joined the chain, hefting the heavier boxes. Chloe didn't notice him until they were finished. She was wiping her forehead with a bandanna when she caught his gaze. She looked away, but when she looked back, he was encouraged, and made his way over to her.

"Hi," he ventured.

"Hello."

Andy drew his hand over his mouth. "I thought today was the big day."

She nodded. "It was...supposed to be."

His heart took flight. "What happened?"

Chloe shook her head. "We canceled the wedding."

Andy reached for her hand and pulled her away from the group. "Didn't you find your dress?"

"I found it," she said, nodding. "But when I did, I realized that being married isn't about the perfect dress."

He smiled and squeezed her hand. "It isn't?"

"No," she said, squeezing back. "It's about the perfect groom."

Oblivious and uncaring of their growing audience, Andy took her into his arms. "How can I feel this way about you when we hardly know each other?"

"I don't know," she murmured, her eyes smiling. "But I feel the same way."

Happiness flooded his chest. "So…how do we go about getting to know each other?"

She thought for a few seconds, then brightened. "How do you feel about Hawaii?"

The planned honeymoon, he realized. "Hawaii sounds amazing."

Then Chloe's expression sobered. "Thank you, Andy."

"For what?"

"For reminding me what's important, for teaching me about this wonderful organization and for showing by example."

He grinned. "Does that mean I'll be seeing more of you here, too?"

She looped her arms around his neck. "Absolutely. In fact, you'll probably be heartily sick of me."

"Never," he murmured, then lowered his mouth to hers for a searing kiss.

Cheers and applause surrounded them. When they looked up, everyone was smiling and clapping with approval.

"Life is good," Chloe said in his ear.

And he agreed.

* * * * *

Dear Reader,

I can't tell you how delighted I am to be part of this edition of the *More Than Words* collection. I'm touched by Harlequin's efforts to recognize and reward organizations that make a difference in this world every single day by touching people's lives.

I have to confess, however, that when I was asked to participate by writing a novella inspired by the amazing work of Windfall Clothing Service in Toronto, I was concerned that my humorous writing style might downplay the seriousness of their achievements. In short, I didn't want to make light of the far-reaching work of the founders, Joan Clayton and Ina Andre, or the volunteers. But editor Marsha Zinberg put my fears to rest—she trusted me to put an amusing spin on a story that would highlight the smart, compassionate work of Windfall. I hope you agree! I had so much fun writing the story of Chloe Parker, imminent bride-to-be on the hunt for a misplaced fairy-tale wedding gown, as she discovers that "It's Not About the Dress."

Most of us, me included, take so many things for granted. I can honestly say my life has been enriched after researching and writing about Windfall Clothing Service. My thanks to Joan and Ina and the volunteers at Windfall for creating a legacy of personal commitment. My thanks to Marsha Zinberg for inviting me to be a part of this charitable collaboration. And my thanks to you, the reader, for supporting our collective efforts to improve the lives of others…one volume of *More Than Words* at a time! Please remember this title when you purchase gifts for friends. And don't forget to visit www.windfallclothing.ca for ideas on how you can help! Together we can make a difference.

Much love and laughter,

Stephanie Bond

NANCY SANDER

↶ Allergy & Asthma Network ↷
Mothers of Asthmatics

Nancy Sander, founder and president of the Allergy & Asthma Network Mothers of Asthmatics in Fairfax, Virginia, is trying to run out the door, take two telephone calls at once and, juggling it all, drops her calendar book and a set of files as she goes.

"I'm a mess," she says brightly. "I'm probably going to be senile before my time. Multitaskers tend to do too much."

The world needs more multitaskers like Nancy, though. Since she launched the grassroots nonprofit organization back in 1985 in response to her daughter's battle with severe asthma and allergies, the AANMA has grown into an international network of families determined to overcome asthma and allergies rather than simply cope with them. Thirteen staff members and seventy outreach service coordinator volunteers offer support and practical strategies in twenty states, while publishing monthly award-winning newsletters, magazines, books and other educational material. Above all, Nancy and the AANMA give hope to parents who thought they would have to struggle with their children's illness alone.

Nancy knows how important it is to feel supported.

For the first six years of her life, Nancy's daughter, Brooke, fought every day to live like other kids her age. She wanted to ride a bike, play basketball with her brothers, sleep through the night— and breathe. Brooke was born with life-threatening asthma and food allergies that routinely landed her in the emergency department and hospital, and out of school. Back in the early eighties, asthma wasn't well understood, and Brooke's doctors warned the family that the little girl would struggle all her life. Nancy believed them and structured her life around her daughter's asthma attacks.

"I did the best I knew how to do, but my daughter's symptoms didn't improve," she says now.

Nancy had no idea where to turn, and remembers clearly the time she stood in church, tears falling, as she tried to sing with the congregation the hymn, "It Is Well with My Soul."

"And I just said to God, 'No, this is not well with my soul. Why is Brooke so sick? I'm exhausted. I don't have the strength to do this. I don't know *how* to do this,'" she recalls. "But the strength I developed during those dark days still powers the work I do today."

It seems her plea for help was heard. When Brooke was accepted into a pharmaceutical clinical trial at Georgetown University Hospital, testing new methods of controlling asthma, life suddenly took a turn. Nancy and Brooke learned how to use a daily symptom diary and a peak flow meter, and Brooke started taking medication regularly, instead of waiting until she had an asthma attack. The regime worked, and after fourteen months, the family's dynamic changed. For the first time, Nancy could leave Brooke with a sitter for longer than an hour and cheer her sons on at their basketball games. For the first time, Nancy was out in the world again.

It was at these events that Nancy would overhear other parents complaining about their children's asthma symptoms.

"I'd listen to their descriptions and think, *This is a cakewalk. They're just not getting good care,*" she says.

Knowing she had to do something to spread the word about proper asthma and allergy control, Nancy fell back on her old skills as a freelance writer and started producing a short, four-page newsletter to be left in her doctor's office. Next thing she knew, a local reporter wrote about Nancy's story.

The article ran on the day of Brooke's seventh birthday. As a houseful of kids ripped through the house wearing high heels, dress-up clothes and jewelry, mothers, seniors, asthma sufferers and professionals from across the country started calling. They haven't stopped.

Nancy admits she never intended to start a nonprofit organization, and if she'd known how much work would be involved, she might have been too intimidated to try. Luckily, ignorance is bliss, and Nancy has found hers in helping make a difference. Of course, most small miracles the organization accomplishes involve individual families, but sometimes Nancy thinks bigger. Much bigger.

Take the Asthmatic Schoolchildren's Treatment and Health Management Act of 2004, one of the last bills President George Bush signed before being reelected. Some would say Nancy gave him no choice. AANMA called every day to remind his office how important the bill was. Finally, as he was thousands of feet in the air on Air Force One, he signed it. The bill protects the rights of children who must carry lifesaving asthma and allergy medication at school.

When Nancy heard that schoolchildren were suffering and others had died because their meds were locked away in school nurses' offices, she realized it was exactly the kind of fight the AANMA needed to tackle.

It was a period of her life she'll never forget, she says.

"Whatever comes into your life, no matter how negative or insurmountable it may seem at the time, it can have a positive impact," she claims.

Nancy, AANMA staff and dedicated supporters are still fighting seemingly insurmountable challenges to end suffering and death due to asthma, allergies and anaphylaxis. She wants to see the day when people who are diagnosed with asthma are treated the same way as those diagnosed with cardiac or brain concerns. Lungs are just as vital, she says, and everyone should have access to specialized care and appropriate medication. She's undaunted by the size and scope of this goal.

"There are very few impossible things," she says.

Meanwhile, Brooke is now a beautiful, accomplished woman of twenty-nine, and Nancy couldn't be more proud of her. Because of her daughter, Nancy and AANMA are moving forward and lending a helping hand to millions of people diagnosed with asthma and allergies.

"I just get such a joy knowing that we can reach people with the information they need, knowing the impact it has on people every day," Nancy says. "I've been blessed."

For more information, visit www.aanma.org or write Allergy & Asthma Network Mothers of Asthmatics, 2751 Prosperity Ave., Suite 150, Fairfax, VA 22031.

BRENDA JACKSON
⌘ WHISPERS OF THE HEART ⌘

☙—BRENDA JACKSON—❧

Brenda Jackson is a die "heart" romantic who married her childhood sweetheart and still proudly wears the "going steady" ring he gave her when she was fifteen. Because Brenda believes in the power of love, her stories always have happy endings. In her real-life love story, Brenda and her husband of thirty-six years live in Jacksonville, Florida, and have two sons.

A *New York Times* and *USA Today* bestselling author of more than fifty romance titles, Brenda is a retiree who worked thirty-seven years in management at a major insurance company. She divides her time between family, writing and traveling with Gerald. You may write Brenda at P.O. Box 28267, Jacksonville, Florida, 32226; her e-mail address at WriterBJackson@aol.com, or visit her Web site at www.brendajackson.net.

CHAPTER
~ONE~

"Dad, the caterer's here. She's coming up the walkway."

Paul Castlewood glanced up from the computer screen in his home office and looked into his daughter's smiling face, so like his own. Her slanted dark eyes were the only feature she had inherited from his ex-wife.

He closed the document file and began shutting down his computer. "Thanks, honey. Please show Ms. Chapman in."

Heather turned to leave. "And she's not bad looking either, Dad," she added. "Real pretty."

Paul shook his head. It wouldn't be the first time his daughter had tried to get him interested in a woman. He always found it amusing, because most literature he'd read said that when it came to single fathers, daughters were notorious for being territorial. Not true for his kid. She would marry him off in a heartbeat if she could.

But that wasn't going to happen.

He'd been married once and it had left a bad taste in his mouth. Heather had been barely five when Emma decided she no longer wanted a husband or a child and had packed up her things and left. Her actions should have come as no surprise. She hadn't wanted a baby and had blamed him for her pregnancy.

Heather, who was now a few weeks shy of sixteen, had seen her mother only twice since she'd left, and sadly, the occasions had been the funerals of her maternal grandparents. Even eleven years later, Paul still couldn't understand how a woman could turn her back on a man who loved her and a daughter who needed her.

It had taken him long enough to stop trying to figure Emma out, and to just accept things as they were and move on. It hadn't been easy when juggling his job as a marketing analyst and that of a single father, but raising Heather on his own had been rewarding. His parents had helped out some in the early years, but since retiring six years ago they had become missionaries and spent most of their time in other countries.

He could hear the door open and the sound of his daughter's voice as she greeted their visitor. Michelle Chapman had come highly recommended as the best caterer in Lake Falls, and he was eager to have her take on Heather's birthday party.

He and Heather had moved from Atlanta to the quiet historical Georgia town six months ago when the company he'd worked for had downsized, and he had accepted a nice buyout settlement. Only a skip and a hop from Savannah, Lake Falls was everything he wanted. Even Heather hadn't complained about the move from the big city to a small town. She had quickly made new friends and had remarked a number of times that what she enjoyed the most was that he was around more often now that he'd set up his own Web site design company at home.

He stood and crossed the room to glance out the window. Moss-draped oak trees lined the pretty cobblestone-paved street. He had stumbled across Lake Falls, a town many referred to as "Little Savannah," a couple of years ago when he had taken a detour off Interstate 95 during road construction. Like Savannah, the small, historic Southern town was the site of many famous Revolutionary and Civil War battles, and Lake Falls could also boast it was once the summer residence of noted novelist Louisa May Alcott.

The town was a step back into time. The old brick and stone homes had retained a lot of their original beauty and charm, and the local residents were so passionate about preserving these resplendent old buildings that an ordinance had been passed requiring city council approval for any new home construction in this section of town.

The house Paul had purchased, like the other homes on the street, had been built in the eighteenth century, with a wraparound porch and stately columns. He had fallen in love with it the moment the Realtor had shown it to him, and Paul considered it as one of the best investments he'd ever made.

As he walked out of the office, he could hear his daughter chatting excitedly with Ms. Chapman, something that didn't surprise him given the purpose of the woman's visit. Heather's sweet-sixteen party would be held here in their home with some of her friends from school and church. Deciding it was time to rescue the caterer before his daughter talked her to death, he hurried toward the living room.

When he rounded the corner to the foyer, he stopped dead in his tracks. Heather had been right. Michelle Chapman was a looker and he had definitely taken notice.

"Ms. Chapman, this is my dad."

Michelle turned and met the eyes of the man who was leaning against the doorjamb and staring straight at her. She caught her breath when she felt a surge of something she hadn't felt in a long time. Physical attraction.

He was absolutely stunning. Tall—probably at least six foot two—and lean, with dark impressive eyes and caramel-colored skin, he was more handsome than any man had a right to be. He looked comfortable and at home in his bare feet, jeans and a T-shirt that accentuated his muscular physique.

She had heard through the grapevine that Paul Castlewood was absolutely gorgeous, but she had refused to believe the wild tales. Seeing was believing. The new guy in town was definitely hot. Michelle figured he must be in his later thirties, and as far as she was concerned, he was the epitome of male perfection.

"Dad, this is Ms. Chapman."

Heather's voice intruded on Michelle's thoughts and reality came crashing back. She was here because he needed a caterer for his daughter's upcoming birthday party. He was a client and therefore off-limits.

Putting on her professional face and wiping any inappropriate thoughts from her mind, she smiled and crossed the entryway as he shoved away from the door frame. She extended her hand. "Mr. Castlewood."

"Ms. Chapman. And I prefer that you call me Paul."

"And I'm Michelle."

"Got it."

He regarded her silently for a moment, not letting go of her hand. That gave her time to decide that the gold-rimmed glasses framing his dark eyes made him look ultrasexy versus brainy.

"We can meet in my office, Michelle," he said, finally releasing his grip.

"All right."

"Do you need my input?" Heather asked, smiling sweetly at her father and reminding them both that she was still there.

Paul rolled his eyes heavenward and then said, "Definitely not. I want to stay within the budget I've established. The menu is something Michelle and I can decide on, but I'll make sure you have the final okay."

"Fine by me, but if you change your mind..."

"I won't."

"But if you do," Heather said, grinning. "I'll be in the kitchen working on my biology project." She turned and sashayed toward the back of the house.

Michelle glanced up at Paul and he smiled. "Sometimes I wonder why I keep her around," he said jokingly.

"Because you love her," Michelle said easily. That's how things had been between her and her own dad. They'd had a special relationship. In Michelle's eyes, Prentiss Chapman had been everything a girl could want and need in a father, and even now, six months after he'd passed away, she was still trying to get over her loss.

"Yes, that I do," Paul responded, directing her down a long hall. "She's a good kid. She works hard, makes good grades in school and is respectful. However," he added as they entered his office and he turned to face her, "on the downside, she will talk your ear off if you let her."

Michelle couldn't help but laugh. "Have you lived in Lake Falls long?" he asked, offering her a chair. She glanced around. The office, like the rest of the house that she'd seen so far, was tidy and neat. There was no clutter anywhere.

"All my life, except for the time I moved away to attend college, then worked in Memphis for a few years. In fact, I grew up in a house right around the corner from here."

"Your parents still live there?"

"No. My mom died eight years ago while I was away at college, and my father died six months ago."

"I'm sorry for your loss."

"Thanks." She felt there was no need to go into any details about why she had turned down the promotion of a lifetime at the corporation in Memphis where she'd worked, to return home to take care of her ailing father. How could she explain that those two years together had been both uplifting and sad?

"I didn't expect you to be so young."

At his appraising glance, she felt a warm rush of blood through her veins. She was attracted to him and that wasn't good. She found herself struggling to remember that this was a business meeting. "I'm here to break the myth that only older women know how to cook these days."

"So, who taught you how to cook?"

"My grandparents. They owned a restaurant in town for years and I worked for them. That's where I learned to peel my first potato."

"Do you mind if I asked how old you are?" he asked.

She wondered why he wanted to know but answered anyway. "Twenty-eight." Deciding they needed to begin talking business, she said, "I have a couple of suggestions for your daughter's party."

"Okay, what are they?"

Opening the folder she was carrying, she placed several colorful documents on his desk and pointed at one. "This popular treat is called a pizza porcupine and will serve as part of the main course. The number of teens you're inviting and whether the majority are boys or girls will determine how many I need to make. Guys tend to have bigger appetites."

"I wouldn't doubt that," Paul agreed. He had meant to go over a guest list with Heather last week. However, she had been a little under the weather after coming down with a slight cold. She was feeling better now but was trying to play catch-up with that science project.

"I'll double-check with Heather to determine the number of friends coming. It'll be less than twenty, I would think."

Michelle nodded. "Here are some other choices I'd suggest, because they're usually big hits. Hamburgers and hot dogs are always popular with teens, and chips are a favorite with practically any kind of dip."

"Everything looks good," Paul said as he scanned the papers.

"My job is to make sure it tastes good as well. Once you give me the go-ahead, I'll come up with a menu that I think will work, and present it to you by the end of the week. And I suggest you do run it by Heather. She'll know what her friends like."

"That sounds wonderful. I've hired Ravine Stokes as party planner. She'll be responsible for working out the music and games."

Michelle smiled. "Ravine is a high-school friend of mine and she and I have worked together on a number of projects. By the time they finish all the activities she'll have lined up for them, they'll be ready to eat. And I'll make sure they have lots of snack foods when they first arrive. I'd like to drop off some sample treats tomorrow."

"You don't have to do that. You came highly recommended by both Ravine Stokes and Amy Poole. And I understand Ms. Amy's word is gospel in this town."

Michelle chuckled as she stood. In a way, she was grateful the meeting with Paul was coming to an end. She found it hard sharing the same space with him. "It is. Ms. Amy has been around forever and has made herself a spokesperson for the town's welcoming committee."

He was about to open his mouth and say something when his brows drew together in a worried frown and he quickly got to his feet. "Heather! Baby, what's wrong?"

Michelle turned in time to see his daughter stumble into the room, gasping for breath. Michelle immediately recognized the signs of an asthma attack, since she had suffered from a number of them throughout her childhood. She rushed out of her seat and made it to Heather's side the same time her dad did.

"Get her inhaler," she ordered, starting to loosen Heather's blouse.

"What?" Paul asked in a frantic voice as he helped his daughter to the sofa. "She doesn't have an inhaler. She hasn't had an asthma attack in years, not since she was around five. She outgrew her asthma."

Michelle glanced up at him. It was obvious he didn't know that a person didn't outgrow asthma. "Grab my purse." She pointed to the chair where she'd been sitting. "We can use my inhaler."

For a split second she could sense Paul Castlewood's hesitation, and then, as if he'd decided to trust her with his daughter's life, he did as she asked. Michelle continued to hold the young woman, who was still fighting for breath.

"Everything is going to be fine, Heather," she said softly. This attack was relatively mild compared to others she'd seen. Her own, when she did have them, tended to be more severe. But Michelle knew mild attacks could quickly become life threatening, and was taking no chances.

"Here." Paul thrust her purse into her hands. She pulled out her inhaler and immediately sprayed four puffs into the air. It was now primed and ready to deliver a full dose. "Relax, Heather. Try breathing out gently. We need to empty your lungs as much as possible."

Luckily, the teen was calm enough to follow orders.

"That's right," Michelle said, putting the inhaler in place. "Now I want you to start breathing in slowly and as deeply as you can."

"I don't understand," Paul said. "Heather doesn't have asthma. Why is she having an attack?"

It wasn't until then that Michelle realized just how close he was standing beside her. She turned her head and looked directly into his eyes. "It's quite obvious, Paul. She does have asthma."

His expression was one of disbelief. "But that's not possible. Like I said before, she had asthma as a child but over the years she's outgrown it."

Michelle shook her head. "You never outgrow asthma. It stays with you for life. Symptoms may go away for long periods of time and then come back when something triggers it again, like right now."

"Something like what?"

Michelle quickly assessed Heather. The girl was breathing more deeply now, though she still looked frightened. Michelle gave her shoulder a reassuring squeeze before turning back to Paul.

"Several things. Pollution, changes in the weather, allergies, colds or flulike symptoms, and—"

"She had a cold last week. But she's had them in the past and this has never happened. That doesn't make sense."

Michelle wished she could explain to him that nothing about asthma really made sense. It was a condition that affected more than fifteen million people in North America, and was the primary reason for most hospital stays. One good thing was that it could usually be controlled enough that a person could live a normal and active life…as she was trying to do.

"I know it might not make sense, but the effects of asthma are real. Heather's symptoms could have been much more serious if not treated early. Ordinarily I would never share my inhaler, but this was an emergency."

Paul lifted a brow. "How long have you had asthma?"

Michelle shook her head. "I don't recall a time that I didn't have it. And because I know how serious asthma can be, I'm a member of AANMA, Allergy & Asthma Network Mothers of Asthmatics. It's a national organization, and I'm part of their network and I volunteer as an outreach service coordinator. In fact, I'm taking a truckload of materials to various elementary schools in town."

Heather made a move to stand up and Paul and Michelle backed away a little. Michelle almost stumbled and he automatically reached out and grabbed her around the waist. Again she felt a rush of warmth at his touch. "Thanks."

"Don't mention it."

She glanced up at him, fully aware that his arm was still around her waist.

"Sorry, Dad."

Paul dropped his arm from Michelle and slipped it around his daughter. "There's nothing for you to apologize for, honey. How do you feel?"

A shaky smile touched Heather's features. "Better. It was scary. One moment I was coughing and the next I felt like I couldn't breathe."

Paul glanced at Michelle before turning his attention back to his daughter.

"That hasn't happened in years," Heather said. "I probably just got overworked doing that project. And the smell of those markers I was using almost took my breath away. That's probably what did it. I don't think it had anything to do with asthma."

Michelle shook her head. "Paul, I suggest that you take Heather to a doctor tomorrow just for a checkup. There are a number of medications for the treatment of asthma and they can—"

He didn't let her finish. "Thanks for the advice, and I appreciate all your help, but I think I can take things from here."

It was obvious to Michelle that he wanted her to leave and wasn't open to anything she had to say regarding his daughter. "All right. I'll contact you about the party menu."

She glanced down at Heather and smiled. "I'm glad you're doing okay now."

The girl returned her smile. "Thanks for being here, Ms. Chapman."

"You're welcome." She turned to Paul, but he was looking at his daughter. "I know my way out."

MICHELLE HAD MADE IT to the front door when Paul called her name. She wanted to keep walking, but then remembered he was a new client and she needed the business. "Yes?" she said, swinging around to watch him approach. Once again a tingling sensation swept through her. Once again she thought that he was a very good-looking man. "Was there something else you wanted?" she asked when he came to a stop in front of her.

"You can't go anywhere without these," he said, holding up her car keys.

"You're right, I can't." She reached out to take them from him.

He handed them over easily and then seemed to hesitate. "About what happened in there…"

"Yes?"

"I appreciate you coming to Heather's aid, and I know you believe you're absolutely sure about this asthma thing, and her not outgrowing it. But I beg to differ. You heard her yourself. She probably got a whiff of those markers she's been working with, and it got to her. I'm thinking it was probably nothing more than an allergic reaction."

Michelle was convinced otherwise but knew it was best not to argue with him. "Just do me a favor and take her to the doctor for a checkup to be on the safe side. She really needs her own inhaler.

He leaned against the doorjamb. "So now in addition to being a caterer, you're also a social worker who gives family advice, as well?"

"No, I'm only a caterer," she said, again hearing a sting in his tone. "One who has asthma. Goodbye, Paul."

She opened the door and walked out.

CHAPTER
~TWO~

"So what do you think of Mr. Castlewood?"

Michelle closed the oven door and glanced up at the elderly woman who was sitting at her kitchen table sipping a cup of tea. Amy Poole had turned eighty-two her last birthday, and years ago the mayor had declared May first of every year as Amy Poole Day in Lake Falls. It was an appropriate honor for a woman whose ancestors had been among the town's founders.

"He's okay, I guess," she responded in a nonchalant manner.

"Just okay? You mean, he didn't make your heart go pitter-pat?"

Michelle smiled, deciding she would definitely not admit the man had done a little more than that. It had taken a trip to the grocery store, as well as a couple of hours of working outside in her yard yesterday, to get her heart rate back to normal. The man had rattled her in more ways than one.

"Yes, just okay. He's definitely a person who doesn't like anyone getting into his business."

Ms. Amy's brow wrinkled. "Why do you say that?"

Michelle decided to tell her about the incident involving Heather.

"My word," Ms. Amy said in alarm. "That child doesn't have an asthma management plan?"

Michelle smiled sadly. "No. And I honestly think he believes a person can outgrow asthma. It's like he's determined to block anything I say regarding the matter out of his mind. But I'm hoping that he takes her in to see the doctor for a checkup like I suggested. I would hate for her to be caught unawares again."

"So other than disagreeing on his daughter's condition, everything is fine between the two of you?"

Michelle raised an eyebrow. Ms. Amy was talking as if they were a couple. "If you're asking if I was hired to be the caterer for his daughter's birthday party, then the answer is yes. Thanks to you and Ravine I got the job."

Michelle placed another tray of cookies in the oven.

"But you do think he's good looking?" her visitor asked.

Michelle's heart jolted in her chest at the thought of just how good-looking Paul Castlewood was. But by the end of their conversation yesterday, she had dismissed the image from her mind and replaced it with one of a grouch.

"Yes, he's handsome but you know what they say. Beauty is only skin deep."

"Yes, that's true, but I had the privilege of holding conversations in church with Mr. Castlewood, and found him to be a very nice man."

Michelle laughed as she joined Ms. Amy at the table. "He would be nice to you, since you're old enough to be his grandmother."

"And you, young lady, are young enough to drum up some interest where he's concerned."

Michelle frowned. It sounded as if Ms. Amy was trying to play matchmaker. She certainly hoped not, but just in case, figured she should set the record straight. "I'm a woman with good eyesight, so there's no way I'm going to sit here and pretend I didn't notice how attractive Paul Castlewood is. However…"

"Hmm, sounds like a big *however.*"

"It is. However, the man rubbed me the wrong way yesterday."

"Is that why you baked all these treats for him today?"

She'd wondered how long it would take Ms. Amy to mention that. "I only baked them because I wanted him to have a sample of what I can do."

"I told him what you could do. He doesn't need any samples. What the man needs is a good woman to mend his broken heart."

Michelle had been up since the crack of dawn and it was nearing noon. She didn't have the strength to argue. Besides, it wouldn't do any good. Amy Poole was convinced that what she was saying was true. "In that case you should have sent Wanda Shaw his way." Wanda worked at the local post office. "She's looking for a husband."

Ms. Amy released a snort. "Wanda is looking for someone to take care of her so she won't have to work again. She and Mr. Castlewood aren't right for each other."

"But you think that he and I are?"

"Yes."

With a heavy sigh, Michelle got up from the table. In her heart she knew that Ms. Amy wanted what was best for her, but she just couldn't figure out why the older woman thought she would be interested in Paul Castlewood or vice versa. "I didn't bake these just for him, you know."

"You didn't?"

"No. I plan to stop by the children's hospital and drop a few batches off there."

"That's kind of you."

Michelle smiled. "I'm a kind person."

Ms. Amy chuckled. "Yes, you are, which is why I think you and Mr. Castlewood would get along nicely."

PAUL PARKED HIS CAR under a moss-draped oak tree and studied Michelle Chapman's business card. He had thought about calling her, but knew that wasn't good enough, especially after the way he'd treated her yesterday. She deserved a personal visit.

After Heather had taken a nap, she had been her old self. Convinced his daughter had had a possible allergic reaction instead of an asthma attack, he had thrown out those color markers she had been using and gone to the store to purchase the unscented kind.

He had waited until after lunch today to drive over to Michelle's. He glanced around now as he strolled up the brick-paved walkway. Michelle had an older house with a large veranda. He was immediately taken by her picturesque flower garden, as well as her home's stately entranceway. The neighborhood, like his, oozed Southern beauty and charm.

When he reached her door, a part of him wondered why he was really paying her a visit. She had indicated that she would be contacting him to provide him with a sampling of her cooking. He could have waited to have this conversation with her then. Why was he determined to see her now?

He would be the first to admit that although he had gotten a bit annoyed with her yesterday, he had appreciated that she was a good-looking woman. And each time their gazes had connected he had felt his pulse rate go up. Her face, the color of chocolate, was a perfect round shape, and her dark brown hair fell like soft waves around her shoulders, giving her a radiant look. Still, he couldn't help wondering how one woman could have piqued his interest so easily.

He heard the sound of footsteps within seconds after ringing the doorbell, and saw the surprise on her face when she opened the door to find him standing there.

"Paul? Is something wrong? How's Heather?"

"She's fine. May I come in?"

"Sure," she said, stepping aside. "Is there anything I can get you to drink?"

He shook his head. "No, I don't plan to be here long. I just wanted to thank you for yesterday."

"You've thanked me already."

"Yes, but I also felt I was a little abrupt at the end. My only excuse is that I was shaken by what happened and wasn't open to any suggestions or comments about what might have been wrong with my daughter."

She nodded. "I understand," she said softly.

"So, will you accept my apology?"

She smiled. "Yes, apology accepted."

Feeling better about things, Paul glanced around the living room. He liked her taste in furniture and decorating, and took the time to tell her so.

She seemed pleased. "Thanks. Are you sure you don't want anything to drink?"

"I'm sure. Besides, I don't want to take you from your work."

She waved off his words as she led him toward the kitchen. "You won't be. In fact, you arrived at the right time. I was just taking some nutty cheese bars out of the oven."

He chuckled. "Mmm, smells good."

She glanced over her shoulder at him. "I'm glad you think so, since it's one of the options for Heather's party."

"Is that a fact?"

She couldn't help but smile. "Yes, it is a fact."

When they reached the large kitchen, Paul was surprised at how well used it was, but still neat. His kitchen had a tendency to look like a war zone by the time dinner was served.

"Your kitchen is huge, but welcoming," he said, taking a seat at the table while she walked over to a double oven.

"Thanks. Now this is my final offer. Are you sure you don't want even a coffee? I brew a mean cup."

He lifted a brow. "How mean?"

"My dad swore it could grow hair on his chest."

Paul laughed. "In that case, I think I'll try one."

Michelle went about preparing coffee, trying not to notice that today, just like yesterday, he had that at-home look. The only difference was that he was in her house and not his. But still, there was something about him in well-worn jeans, a T-shirt and a pair of Nikes that would probably make him look relaxed and at home wherever he was.

"So how long have you had your catering business?"

She shifted sideways and noticed that he was watching her. She was glad she looked fairly decent this morning in a tailored blouse and Capris, although her hair was up in a ponytail.

"I've had it a few months. When I lived in Memphis, I worked as a manager for an accounting firm."

"What happened?" he asked. "You get zapped with corporate burnout?"

She smiled sadly. "No. When I left Memphis, I chose the profession of caretaker."

At the curious look that flashed in his eyes she explained. "The doctor gave my father less than a year to live and I wanted to be with him for every single second that he had left. So I turned in my resignation, packed all my belongings, leased out my home and headed here. Like you, my father was a single dad. But unlike you he was a widower instead of a divorcé."

"And how do you know I'm a divorcé? I don't believe my marital status ever came up in any of our prior conversations."

Michelle swallowed, hoping she hadn't put her foot in her mouth. But she figured she would be honest with him. "You're new to our town, so most of us know everything about you...at least everything you told Ms. Amy."

He looked incredulous. "You mean, she was pumping me for information?"

"Afraid so." Although Michelle smiled, she couldn't help but feel bad for him at the moment. He honestly hadn't had a clue, and probably thought Ms. Amy had been conversing with him because she was a friendly old woman. Of course, that was true, but everyone in Lake Falls knew Amy Poole, who had been married to her childhood sweetheart for over sixty years before he'd passed away a few years ago, was a romantic at heart and enjoyed playing Cupid.

Michelle just hoped their conversations earlier that morning had made the older woman put away her bow and arrow because she had no intention of getting struck. Just like any other woman, Michelle wanted to meet a nice guy and get married, but now was not a good time. She needed to put all her energy into getting her business off the ground rather than investing in a relationship that might not go anywhere. She'd done that before with Lonnie Fields. They had met at a business workshop, and after dating her for two years, he'd decided to leave her behind without looking back when his company transferred him to the West Coast. The only reason she hadn't succumbed to a broken heart was because she had begun to have doubts anyway.

Upon seeing the guarded look on Paul's face she said. "Hey, don't take it personally. In fact, she genuinely likes you and wanted to get to know you. However, at the same time she was sizing you up to see which of the single ladies in Lake Falls was best suited to meet your needs."

He didn't say anything for a moment and then asked, "So, who is this unlucky lady?"

As Michelle poured the coffee, she thought about lying and saying she had no idea. But the truth of the matter was that she did, since Ms. Amy had practically come out and told her. And since

Michelle felt sure nothing would ever come of the older woman's shenanigans, he had a right to know.

She placed the cup of coffee in front of him, met his gaze and said, "Yours truly." At the lifting of his dark brows she added, "I'm the unlucky lady."

CHAPTER
∾ THREE ∾

P aul hoped he had heard her wrong. But staring into Michelle's face and seeing her apologetic expression, he knew he had not. He also knew that she was an unwilling victim of Amy Poole's mischief as much as he was. He couldn't help but recall the last time he had been targeted in an older woman's matchmaking scheme. His grand-aunt Zelda had decided he should remarry when Heather had turned ten, saying his daughter needed a female influence in her life.

Aunt Zelda had given a dinner party, the likes of which he would never forget. She evidently had erroneously put out the word that her divorced and well-off nephew was up for grabs. That night women at the party had flocked around him as if he was the last man on earth. Some had openly flirted, while others had decided to go straight into seduction, regardless of the fact they had an audience. He had sworn he would never let another person place him in such a situation again.

He studied Michelle's features. She was evidently waiting for him to say something. Give some sort of indication that he'd heard and understood what she'd said.

"So, you're looking for a husband?" he asked.

The expression that appeared on her face told him her answer before she opened her mouth. "No."

The fierceness of her tone confirmed it. He believed her, but just to set the record straight, he said, "Good, because the last thing I'm interested in is a wife."

He saw how relieved she looked and automatically lowered his guard. It was just as he'd suspected. She was no more interested in marriage than he was. He knew his reasons, and couldn't help wondering about hers, but was too much of a gentleman to ask. Besides, it really wasn't any of his business.

He took a sip of his coffee as she went back to the oven to take care of whatever she was baking. Moments later she slid one of the pastries onto a plate and then walked back again. It smelled tantalizing and he almost licked his lips as he picked up the fork and took his first bite, after waiting for a moment for it to cool.

His reaction wasn't slow in coming. The nutty cheese bar was the most delicious pastry he'd ever eaten. He quickly told her so and was rewarded with her smile. And that smile, which seemed to stretch from one corner of her mouth to the other, did something to his insides.

"Thanks," she said, going back over to the sink. "I figured on making a number of these as part of the menu. Now as for the cake, since you mentioned Heather likes strawberries, I've decided to bake one with a strawberry filling."

"She's going to love that," he said, taking another bite of the pastry. "And I have her working on that list of invitees so we'll know how many are coming."

He watched as Michelle kept herself busy at the counter, and couldn't help wondering if it was intentional. "Won't you stop a moment and join me in a cup of coffee?"

He could tell his question surprised her, and she took a few moments before responding. Then, tossing aside a dish towel, she said, "Yes, I think I will. You can tell me what the doctor said about Heather."

Paul felt himself getting annoyed again, just as he had yesterday. He was grateful that Michelle was concerned about his daughter's welfare, and he'd appreciated her timely intervention, as well as the information about the asthma organization she volunteered for. But Heather was his responsibility and no one else's. Besides, she was due for a routine physical next month and he would mention to the doctor what had happened then.

He glanced at his watch. "You know, I hadn't realized it had gotten so late. I need to leave." He rose to his feet.

"But what about those treats I baked for you to sample? If you wait a minute I'll pack them up for you and Heather."

It was the least he could do after she had taken the time to do all that baking. "Okay, I'll wait."

MICHELLE PACKED UP a sampling of her baking and watched Paul out of the corner of her eye. He was standing at her kitchen window, staring out. It was plain to see that he was agitated about something. Asking what the doctor had said about Heather had hit a nerve with him for some reason. She had picked up the same attitude yesterday. She could only assume that although he had dropped by to apologize for his abruptness the day before, he still didn't like her butting her nose into his family's business.

"Here you are," she said, handing him the container of baked goods. "I hope you and Heather enjoy them."

He moved away from the window and crossed the kitchen floor. "I'm sure we will."

"And I still plan to have a menu ready for you at the end of the week. If you approve it, then we can go ahead and finalize numbers."

"That will be fine."

Something pushed her to say more, and she hoped her words would smooth the waters between them. "Contrary to what you might think, Paul, I'm not a busybody. My concern for Heather is genuine. I like her. It would be hard not to. She's a wonderful girl. You've done a fantastic job raising her."

She could tell her statement caught him off guard, and for a while he said nothing. At last he replied, "I appreciate you saying that."

"Well, it's true. I'll see you out now."

He walked beside her as they headed for the front door. When they reached it, he said, "Thanks for everything. I'll call you later this week with the exact number of kids who will be attending the party. The RSVPs should all be in by Thursday."

Michelle merely nodded and opened the door. He gave her a slight smile before walking out of the house, and she silently closed the door behind him.

WHEN MICHELLE HEARD THE sound of Paul's car pulling out of her driveway, she leaned against the closed door and squeezed her eyes shut, thinking she liked him a whole lot more than she really should. When it came to his daughter he was overprotective, but hadn't her own father been the same way?

She had practically never spent a night away from home when she was growing up because her father had been afraid she would have an asthma attack while he wasn't there. When she was sixteen, he'd finally relented and allowed her to attend Misty Edwards's sleepover party, only because Ms. Amy had pleaded with him to do so.

Michelle's thoughts shifted back to Paul. Regardless of whether either of them wanted to admit it or not, from the moment they had met there had been an attraction. And although they had agreed today that neither was interested in marriage, that hadn't stopped a heated desire from working its way through her body. And just now, when she'd walked him to the door, she'd had a feeling he wanted to kiss her.

As she headed back toward the kitchen, she was glad he hadn't. All she and Paul shared was a business relationship, and it would be wise for her to remember that.

HE HAD WANTED TO kiss her.

And the very thought of doing so was flooding his senses to the point he couldn't think straight. When she had walked him to the door, he had stood there, breathing in her scent, taking in her beauty and appreciating her caring nature. Although she wasn't interested in marriage any more than he was, she would make some man an exceptional wife.

The words she had spoken about his part in Heather's upbringing had touched him. He had recognized early on that being a single father wouldn't be easy, and if his in-laws had had their way he never would have gotten the opportunity to try. For some reason they'd felt it was their right to raise Heather after Emma had walked out, and that he couldn't go it alone. He had proved them wrong.

He didn't want to dwell on the past, but remembering those times made him appreciate how things were now.

As Paul parked in front of his house, he could see Heather on the porch, leaning against a column and talking to a boy named Jason. Paul couldn't help noticing that Jason had begun hanging around a lot lately. Heather claimed they were just friends, but Paul was beginning to wonder.

His daughter's face lit up in a smile when she turned and saw him; however, Jason was ready to crawl under the porch. The kid always seemed nervous around him, and Paul smiled, thinking that was a good thing.

"Dad, got anything for me?" Heather asked, leaving Jason standing on the porch as she raced over to him.

Paul chuckled. Nothing had changed. She'd been asking him that since the time she was able to talk.

"I stopped by Michelle's house and she sent some baking for us to sample," he answered.

"Wow! That's cool!"

He glanced at the youth. "Hello, Jason."

The young man smiled hesitantly and waved his hand. "Hello, Mr. Castlewood."

"And how are you?"

"Just fine, sir."

"And your parents?"

"They're fine, too. Do you need help getting anything out of your car?"

"No. But thanks for asking." Paul hated admitting it but Jason wasn't such a bad kid. He had good manners, was respectful and didn't have any tattoos or piercings…at least not in plain sight.

"So, you saw Ms. Chapman again?" Heather's excitement couldn't be missed.

"Yes, I saw her."

"That's good." She was almost beaming.

"And why is that good?"

"Because I think she's nice. I like her."

He chuckled again. "You just met her yesterday."

"It doesn't matter."

He studied his daughter, wondering just what she meant.

Both Heather and Jason dived into Michelle's baking as if it were the last food they would eat. They sang her praises while gobbling down a huge portion of the treats, along with tall glasses of milk. A few hours later, before Jason left, he drummed up enough courage to ask if Heather could go to the movies with him the weekend following her sixteenth birthday.

Paul didn't have a good reason to turn him down, especially since he'd told Heather she could begin dating once she turned sixteen. He realized his little girl was growing up, and one day he wouldn't be the most special man in her life, which meant he really needed to start getting a life of his own. His position on marriage hadn't changed, but there was nothing wrong with having a female friend, someone to date on occasion, who wasn't clingy. He'd dated a few clingy women in the past. They'd thought they could storm into his life and become the center of his world, replacing Heather and his common sense. He had proved time and time again that wasn't possible. He couldn't ever see himself letting go and losing control with any woman.

Except possibly Michelle.

There was something about her that had caught his attention from the first. And the remarkable thing was that she hadn't been trying. He could understand why Heather had immediately liked her. The thought of her giving up her career to care for a dying parent touched him.

As Paul slid between the covers that night, visions of Michelle danced in his head, and he wasn't sure whether or not that was a good thing.

CHAPTER
∽FOUR∽

Michelle smiled when she looked through the peephole and recognized her visitor. She opened the door immediately. "Heather? This is a pleasant surprise."

She stood aside as the young girl entered, her smile a replica of her father's. "Hello, Ms. Chapman. Dad gave me your business card and asked that I call you with the information about the number of people attending my party. But when I saw you were only a short walk from school, I decided to drop by instead. I hope you don't mind."

"Of course not. How is school going?"

"Fine. I figured moving to a new town would be hard, meeting a bunch of new friends and all. But everyone here in Lake Falls is nice. I can't imagine living anywhere else now."

Michelle chuckled. "Yes, the town kind of grows on you, doesn't it? By the way, how's your dad?"

"Dad's doing fine. He's busy building Web pages for his clients."

"Sounds interesting," Michelle said, leading Heather toward the kitchen.

"It is. I've watched him do it a few times and he seems to enjoy it. One day he's going to show me how it's done."

"You like working with computers?"

"Not as much as Dad, but they're okay."

When they reached the kitchen, Michelle offered Heather a chair at the table. "I was about to fix a snack. Would you like to join me?"

Her guest beamed. "Sure. Do you have any more of those nutty cheese bars? They were delicious."

Michelle laughed. "Yes, I'm sure I have some more around here. They're one of my most popular treats. People call and request them all the time, and I make a batch every day for Lilly's Café.

Michelle studied Heather. The last time she had seen her had been right after her asthma attack, an attack Paul still hadn't acknowledged. In fact, he had quickly left the other day when she had asked him what the doctor had said about Heather's condition. Michelle was quite sure he hadn't taken her to the doctor for a follow-up appointment. Unfortunately, some of the parents she came in contact with through her work with the AANMA didn't believe asthma was a permanent or a dangerous condition. Too late, they discovered it was something they should have taken seriously, and their child should have been on a management plan.

"And how have you been, Heather?" Michelle asked her softly.

"Oh, I've been fine. I'm looking forward to the party. Turning sixteen is going to be super. Jason has already asked Dad if he can take me to the movies the weekend following my birthday."

"Who's Jason?" she asked.

Heather's smile practically told it all. "Jason Sullivan is a guy I know from church and school. He's seventeen and a junior this year. He's supernice."

Michelle chuckled. "I know Jason. His aunt Carrie is a close friend of mine. We went to school together. I know his parents, as well. Connie and Anthony were older and graduated from school before Carrie and me. And you're right, Jason's supernice. The entire Sullivan family is."

"I think Dad likes Jason," Heather said as Michelle placed a plate of goodies along with a glass of milk on the table. "He lets Jason walk me home, but he just can't take me out yet. And on the weekends, he comes over and we watch movies together. Sometimes Dad joins us, but usually he stays in his office to work."

Heather tilted her head as Michelle sat down at the table. "You can come over if you like and watch movies with us, Ms.

Chapman. We can make it a foursome. Me and Jason and you and my dad."

Michelle was stunned by the invitation and at first was speechless. "Thanks," she said at last, "but I'm not sure how your father would feel about that."

Heather waved off her words. "Dad won't mind."

Michelle had to disagree, considering how quickly he'd taken off yesterday.

"These are so good," Heather said, practically licking her lips as she tried a chocolate-studded cookie. "And before I forget the reason I dropped by. I've invited twenty people to my party. Twelve girls and eight boys."

Michelle nodded. "Twenty is a good number, and I already know it's going to be some party."

"I hope so. You only turn sixteen once."

"That's true. I'm going to do everything I can to make it special, and I have just the menu for you. I spoke with Ravine Stokes earlier today and I think you're going to enjoy all the group activities she's come up with. I'll be getting together with your father to present the menu to him, and I'm hoping we'll finalize everything then. Now that I know how many are coming, I can calculate just how much food to prepare."

Heather smiled at her. "Thanks, Ms. Chapman. Dad made a smart move when he hired you. I'm glad he didn't take Ms. Beaumont up on her offer to help."

Michelle pretended not to hear what Heather had said. Ms. Amy had told her that Latisha Beaumont had set her sights on Paul the moment he'd moved to town. Thoughts of the woman being so aggressive should not bother her. After all Latisha had put out the word a couple of years ago that she was in the market for husband number three. And Paul was definitely a man any woman would be interested in. As Michelle studied Heather's list, she wondered what else Latisha had volunteered to do for Paul, and found it extremely annoying that she even cared.

"I talked to my grandmother last night and told her how well you can bake."

Michelle smiled. "Are your grandparents flying in for the party?"

"No, they're doing missionary work in Africa, but they'll be coming for a visit this summer and we'll celebrate then."

Michelle really liked Heather, and a part of her wanted to ask whether her father had taken her to the doctor, but knowing how Paul felt, she would be out of line to do so. She had asked earlier how Heather was doing and she'd said fine. And she looked fine. But Michelle knew an asthma attack could happen at any moment regardless of how well you looked. And that worried her.

PAUL TOSSED THE PAPERS he'd been reading aside, finding it hard to concentrate. For some reason Michelle Chapman was on his mind and had been since she'd dropped by the other day to finalize the menu.

He would have no other contact with her until the party, when she arrived to set things up, and that was a full eight days from now. Why did the thought of not seeing her again until then bother him? He sighed as he leaned back in his chair after staring at his calendar for a moment longer than necessary.

"Hey, Dad."

He glanced up. Heather was standing in the doorway. "Hello, sweetheart. School's out already?"

"Yes. Today is one of those early dismissal days, where we get out at noon. I mentioned it this morning."

She probably had. His mind evidently had been on other things. Or, more specifically, on someone. Sighing deeply, he picked up the document he'd been trying all morning to read.

"I had planned to stop by Ms. Chapman's house on my way home from school," Heather said.

He swung his head up and stared at her. "Why?" He'd known that she had stopped by Michelle's house last week to tell her the number of people coming to her party.

"Because we still have her container—the one she sent those treats in last week. I wanted to get it back to her in case she needed it for another order or something."

He had forgotten all about the container. He could have easily given it to Michelle the other day when she was here. This was the excuse he needed to see her again. "You're right, she might need it. I'll take it over to her now."

"Thanks, Dad."

"No problem."

After Heather left the room, he quickly shut down his computer and moved from behind his desk. A surge of something he hadn't felt in a long time rushed through his veins. There had to be a reason why he was in such a high-wire mood at the chance to see Michelle again. There had to be a reason why he thought of her constantly. And he was determined to find out what it was. Today.

"COMING!"

Michelle made her way out of her bedroom, entering the hall while putting in an earring. She had finished all the baking she needed to do that day and had decided to get out of the house and treat herself to lunch. Since there weren't too many places where she could go in Lake Falls if she wanted a meal alone, she decided to take the drive into Savannah and dine at one of her favorite restaurants.

She had taken a leisurely bath and slipped on a sundress she had purchased last month when she had gone to visit friends in Memphis. She felt good today. Her Realtor had called that morning and said the couple leasing her condo were interested in buying it. She had no qualms about selling, which meant she had made up her mind as to where she wanted to live permanently. A lot of people would think she was nuts for giving up the fun and excitement of Memphis, but she knew what was best for her. Lake Falls was her home. She hadn't known how much she missed living here until she had returned.

She glanced out the peephole in her door and caught her breath. Paul was standing on the other side. What was he doing here? There was nothing left for them to discuss. And besides, it still bothered her that he refused to acknowledge Heather's condition. A part of her wanted to approach him about it again. But first, she needed to know why he was on her front porch. She inhaled deeply, knowing the only way to find that out was to open the door and ask.

"PAUL, THIS IS A PLEASANT surprise. I hope everything is all right."

Paul blinked and then for the next couple of seconds just stood there staring, allowing his gaze to roam all over Michelle, starting at the top of her head to the sandals she was wearing. Her hair was pinned up, with a few wispy curls framing her face, the style complimenting her softly rounded features. And then there was her dress, a buttercup-yellow that highlighted her smooth brown skin. She had on very little makeup, which gave her a fresh and wholesome look. A downright sexy look.

"Paul?"

He blinked a second time, realizing she'd said his name again, waiting for him to answer. "No, there's nothing wrong. I'm just returning this."

She glanced down at the container in his hand. "Oh, I'd almost forgotten about it. Come in."

She stepped aside and he entered. "It seems I came at a bad time," he said when she closed the door behind him. "You're about to go out."

She smiled, taking the container from him. "You're fine. I decided to drive to Savannah today and treat myself to lunch. Excuse me while I put this in the kitchen."

He watched her walk off, and wondered what there was about her that attracted him so fiercely. She was a looker, but there was something else, too. It had to be her calm and soothing nature. That had been evident during Heather's reaction to those markers. Or maybe it was because Michelle was one of the few single women in Lake Falls who hadn't deliberately put herself in his path at every opportune moment. If Latisha Beaumont came up with another excuse to call him, he was seriously thinking about having a talk with her. No man liked being harassed, and he was beginning to feel that's exactly what she was doing.

"You really didn't have to come make a special trip to bring that to me," Michelle was saying as she returned to the room. "I have plenty of them."

"No problem. Today is a slow day for me, anyway." There was no reason to tell her that he had lots of work to do, but couldn't get in the right frame of mind to do it. "And you're off to Savannah for lunch?"

"Yes, just for a change of pace. I'm going to one of my favorite restaurants."

He nodded. "Are you planning to meet someone there?"

She shook her head and smiled. "No, I'll be dining alone."

Not one to miss an opportunity, Paul asked, "Mind if I join you? I haven't had lunch yet myself, and a good meal in Savannah sounds nice."

He could tell she was surprised by his question, but her smile didn't waver as she said, "Sure. You can join me if you really want to."

He met her gaze. "I do really want to. We can take my car."

CHAPTER
✧—FIVE—✧

Michelle didn't want to think of having lunch with Paul as a date. But what else would you call it when, after leaving Rocco's, they strolled hand in hand around Savannah's historic district? It had been a while since she had enjoyed male company, and found that Paul was a likable guy.

She was surprised when he shared a lot about himself, telling her of his parents' missionary work and his eighty-five-year-old grand-aunt Zelda, whom he was very fond of. He didn't say much about his divorce, only that his wife had never wanted kids and could only hang in as a parent for the first five years of Heather's life before splitting. He was quite sure that Heather probably wouldn't know her mother if they were to pass on the street. The disgust in his voice let Michelle know that he was not carrying a torch for his ex.

She also discovered that he was a guy who liked a lot of the same things she did. They enjoyed eating seafood, loved chocolate, preferred watching basketball to football, and were members of the same political party. The only thing they differed dramatically on was their taste in movies. She liked watching romantic comedy, whereas he preferred blood, guts and gore.

By the time the scenic walk they had taken was over, it was late afternoon, and he suggested they remain in Savannah for dinner and try out a steak house one of the tour guides had recommended. Once at the restaurant, he called Heather on his cell phone to let her know not to expect him until late. He'd told her where he was, but omitted mentioning that the two of them were together.

When he ended the call, Michelle seized the opportunity to ask him about Heather's health. She could immediately tell from his expression that he didn't appreciate her concern.

She leaned back in her chair. If he thought he had a reason to be irritated with her, then she felt she had a reason to be irritated with him. "Why do you get so uptight whenever I ask about Heather?"

He frowned. "I don't get uptight. I just don't know why you're assuming that something is wrong with my daughter."

Michelle sighed. "I'm not assuming anything, Paul. One asthma attack can be followed by another, which could be dangerous, especially if you don't know the reason for it. I can't help but be concerned. Heather needs to be on an asthma management plan. If you don't feel comfortable taking her to the doctor, at least call the Allergy & Asthma Net—"

"You saw her last week. Did she look ill?" he interrupted tersely.

"No."

"Okay then."

A part of Michelle knew it wasn't okay, but that she would be wasting her time trying to convince him of that. When it came to Heather's asthma he was determined to keep his head in the sand.

They didn't talk much on the drive back to Lake Falls, the tension between them was as obvious as the reason for it. There were certain aspects of his life that he was determined to keep to himself. She knew he had that right. After all, there was really nothing going on between them. But she had truly enjoyed spending time with him today and couldn't help but be bothered by his attitude.

By the time they arrived back in Lake Falls it was dark. He parked in front of her home and turned off the engine. "I upset you."

She glanced over at him and shook her head. "No, you didn't."

"Yes, I did and I want to apologize."

She met his gaze, expecting him to say more, something that

might explain why he was so stubborn when it came to Heather's condition.

"I enjoyed your company," he said, pulling her thoughts back to the two of them and the fact they were sitting in a parked car in front of her house.

From now on, Michelle decided, she wouldn't bring up anything related to Heather's asthma episode. Even when she couldn't contain her own worry, she would keep it to herself and not share her concern with Paul.

"And I enjoyed your company, as well," she said, and meant it. She refused to let her annoyance with him over Heather ruin what she felt had been a beautiful day.

"How would you like to join me for a cup of coffee and one of my new pastries?" she offered.

He smiled over at her. "I'd love to."

When they began walking together up to the house, he reached out and took her hand in his, just as he'd done most of the day. He released it only when she had to pull her key out of her purse to open the door. He stepped inside behind her and closed the door.

The lights in the entire house were turned off, and when she switched on the lamp next to the sofa, it cast the room in a soft glow. She turned quickly to find Paul standing right in front of her.

"Sorry, I didn't mean to startle you," he said in a husky tone.

"You didn't."

Her insides were quivering, but not because he'd surprised her. It was because he was so close. He had stood next to her several times that day, but for some reason this was different. She probably could blame the soft lighting in the room, which gave it a sort of romantic setting, or possibly the way he was looking at her. His eyes were deep, dark, intense.

"I guess now is a good time to thank you for today," she said. "But I hadn't meant for you to pay for both my meals."

He smiled. "No need to thank me. I enjoyed your company, and I appreciate you letting me tag along."

"You can tag along anytime. I enjoyed your company, as well."

"Mmm, anytime?" he said in a low, husky tone. "I might take you up on your offer."

Michelle parted her lips, but whatever she was about to say was forgotten when he leaned in close, placed his hands around her waist and kissed the words right off her lips. Desire, fueled by need, made her moan when he deepened the kiss. As if sensing her response, he pulled her closer into his arms, molding her soft curves against his hard muscles and stirring a degree of urgency within her that she hadn't felt in a long time. Of their own accord, her arms reached up and wrapped around his neck, and she kissed him back.

Wow! PAUL SLOWLY PULLED his mouth away and leaned back, his arms still wrapped around Michelle's waist. He felt her tremble, and at the same time acknowledged the way his own heart was pounding in his chest. Had passion been bottled up inside of him for so long that, once uncapped, it had unleashed emotions he'd forgotten he could feel? Emotions that were now eating away at him, making him long for something he'd thought he could do without.

He watched as Michelle raised her hand and touched the lips that he'd just kissed. "I don't know if that was a good idea," she said softly.

He leaned closer, coming within mere inches of her mouth and breathed. "That, Michelle, was the best idea I've had in a long time."

Then he kissed her again, glorying in her automatic response and not allowing either of them to deny what they were feeling. Skyrocketing passion. An overload of desire. He had wanted to seduce her with his mouth, and found she was seducing him with hers, instead.

He pulled back slowly, reluctantly, but knowing that he had to. One part of his mind screamed that they were moving too fast. But another taunted they weren't moving fast enough. The attraction had been there from the first and they were finally acting on it.

"I think I better go," he said softly, taking a step back and releasing his hands from around her waist.

"But what about your treat?"

He smiled. "I just enjoyed it, and it was well worth the wait."

LATER THAT NIGHT, AFTER Michelle had gotten into bed, she took the time to reflect on just how her day with Paul had gone.

He had said that he would see her tomorrow, and she believed him. She just wasn't sure where all this would lead. A few days ago she hadn't been the least bit interested in becoming involved with a man, but being around Paul today had reminded her what it was like to share a special relationship with someone.

But then, she couldn't forget that Paul was deliberately keeping her at bay when it came to Heather's health. Each time she brought up the subject, he closed her out.

She cuddled under the covers, not wanting to think about the time and energy she'd devoted to her last relationship with a man. All the hours she had spent trying to make Lonnie happy, to make him appreciate her. Did she really want to go through that again? Especially now, when growing her business should be her top priority?

But then all she had to do was remember how much she had enjoyed herself today, how special being with Paul had been. A part of her was convinced that having Paul Castlewood in her life wouldn't be all bad.

THE NEXT MORNING PAUL found Heather in the kitchen, sitting at the table, eating breakfast before school. She'd been in bed by the time he got home the previous night. She glanced over at him now and smiled. "Hi, Dad. Did you enjoy yourself in Savannah yesterday?"

He crossed the room, heading straight for the coffeepot. "What makes you think I was in Savannah having fun?" He'd made absolutely certain not to mention anything on the phone about Michelle being with him.

"Come on, Dad, I know that you and Ms. Chapman were together. By now I'm sure the entire town knows."

He frowned. "What do you mean, the entire town?"

"Eli Sessions's mom saw the two of you while she was in Savannah, shopping. She couldn't wait to get back to town and tell Lois Dunlap."

"I see," he said, sitting down at the table with his cup of coffee. And he did see. It was called small-town gossip.

"I think it's cool."

He smiled as he took a sip of coffee. "You would. But don't get your hopes up. There was nothing much to it. We just had lunch together."

"And dinner."

Paul grinned. "Okay, we had lunch *and* dinner." He checked the clock on the stove. "Shouldn't you be leaving for school about now?"

Heather smiled. "Yes. I will in a moment. I just want to know one thing."

He lifted a brow. "What?"

"Will you take her out again? Are the two of you an item?"

"You said you wanted to know just one thing," Paul teased. "Choose which one."

"Okay. Are the two of you an item?"

"Depends on what you mean by 'an item.'"

"Dad!"

He set his coffee cup down. "All right. All right. To answer your question, the answer is maybe. That was our first date."

"So you would call it a date?"

"That's what I'd call it, but I'm sure your generation probably has another name for it."

Heather rolled her eyes. "It's still called dating, Dad."

"I'm glad to hear that." He stared at his daughter for a long moment. "So what do you think?"

"About you seeing Ms. Chapman?"

"Yes."

A huge grin covered Heather's face. "I told you what I thought. I like her. I think it's cool."

He grinned back, thinking just how much he loved his kid. "Yes, I think it's cool, too."

MICHELLE HUNG UP THE phone. If another person called to congratulate her on reeling in Paul, she was going to scream. She'd all but snapped at Lori Coffee, telling her in no uncertain terms that Paul Castlewood was not a fish, he was a man. Men didn't get reeled in. She sighed in disgust. That was the one thing she could do without in a small town—everyone wanting to know your business. She and Paul had shared lunch and dinner, not made plans for a lifetime commitment. Why did everyone assume they had?

The phone rang again and Michelle was about to ignore it when she glanced at the caller ID. It was her friend Brittany Howard, who worked at the headquarters of AANMA. They'd met in college, and Brittany was the person who'd been instrumental in bringing Michelle on board as a volunteer outreach service coordinator. Both she and Brittany suffered from asthma. Giving each other support during their college days had made the condition a lot easier to cope with.

What Michelle enjoyed the most about her volunteer work was the part she played in giving the public a greater understanding of asthma. AANMA was growing by leaps and bounds, spreading the word through a number of national events and other outreach programs.

She quickly picked up the phone. "Britt? How are you?"

"Fine. I'm just calling to make sure you got enough supplies for the school nurses."

Brittany's question made Michelle recall the incident with Heather. Paul still hadn't acknowledged that she had had an asthma attack.

"Plenty, thanks," Michelle told Brittany.

They talked for a few minutes, and Michelle had just hung up when she heard a loud knock at her door. From where she was standing she couldn't tell who was there, but she could see the car parked in front.

Paul.

She thought of the number of calls she'd received that morning, and figured he'd gotten wind that the whole town was talking about them. Was he upset? Was that the reason he was at her house before ten in the morning?

Michelle sighed as she headed toward the door. There was only one way to find out.

CHAPTER
❧ SIX ❧

During the drive over to Michelle's house Paul kept asking himself what he was doing. Why on earth would he want to become seriously involved with a woman after all these years? A woman he'd known less than a month.

The answer was blatantly obvious the moment she opened the door. He experienced a storm of emotions that only she could stir up inside of him. Was she worth all the craziness of waking up in the wee hours of the night just to recall a smile that he couldn't forget?

Yes, she was worth it.

He sighed deeply, and when she gave him the smile that had been his downfall from the first, he couldn't help but return it.

"Good morning. I hate bothering you so early, but we need to talk." Paul knew what he had to do, what he had to say.

Michelle nodded and stepped aside, closing the door behind him when he entered. "I know why you're here," she said.

He placed his hands in the pockets of his jeans. "Do you?"

"Yes." She moved away from the door to stand in front of him. "My phone hasn't stopped ringing all morning, and I apologize for that."

He lifted a brow. Evidently there was something he was missing. "Your phone has been ringing all morning and you want to apologize to *me* for it?"

"Yes."

"You want to tell me why?"

She went over to the sofa and sat down. "Someone has spread a rumor that the two of us are seeing each other."

"And?"

She frowned. "And that's not true."

He moved to sit in the chair across from her. "We did spend the better part of yesterday together in Savannah."

"Yes, but it wasn't what everyone assumes."

"Maybe not. However, we did share a kiss."

He could see the blush that appeared on her face. "I know but—"

He held up his hand, stopping what she was about to say. "Does it bother you that people are thinking that way about us?"

She shrugged. "No, but this is a small town and people will quickly assume what you might not want them to assume. I'm catering your daughter's birthday party, which means we're involved in a business relationship. I don't want to jeopardize that. And I'm beginning to think of you as more than a friend and don't want to jeopardize that, either."

He took a deep breath. She still wasn't getting the point he was trying to make. He eased out of his chair and walked over to where she was sitting. "Scoot over for a second."

He saw the surprised look on her face, but she did as he asked, and he sat down beside her. "Now, then, let me explain something to you." He smiled, and for the first time in a long time felt he was doing something right.

"I like you," he said bluntly, taking her hand in his. He remembered walking around and holding hands with her yesterday. It had seemed like the most natural thing to do. "I mean, I genuinely like you, Michelle, and I'd like to get to know you better. I propose that we become involved."

She blinked. "Involved?"

"Yes, involved. You know, you, me, doing things together like we did yesterday. Sharing lunch and dinner, an occasional movie, walking in the park, holding hands." He raised their joined hands. "I like holding hands with you."

He leaned back against the sofa and studied her expression. "So, what do you think about that?"

MICHELLE REALLY DIDN'T know what to think about it. She would be the first to admit that she had enjoyed their time together yesterday. And hadn't she reached the conclusion that he was a very likable guy? When he'd brought her home last night and kissed her, it was a kiss destined to become embedded in her brain cells forever. And hadn't she decided that having Paul in her life wasn't such a bad idea?

Or *was* it? There was still one thing that bothered her, namely his willful blindness to Heather's condition.

But should Michelle let that one thing stand in the way? If she kept working on him to acknowledge his daughter's asthma, would he eventually come around, or continue to close her out? He wanted them to become involved, so at least that was a start, but still, she refused to rush into anything. He had pretty much defined just what "involved" meant to him, and it all sounded great, but she couldn't help remembering Lonnie and all the time and effort she'd put into making things between them work, only to find out she'd wanted more out of their relationship than he had.

She gently pulled her hand from Paul's and rose to her feet. She stared down at him. "It's been a while since I've been involved with anyone. Maybe I tend to expect more out of relationships than I should." She might as well be honest. "The last guy I dated, I ended up living with for a while when I thought things between us were pretty tight. Then he got a promotion at work that made it imperative for him to move to another state. But he didn't think I was important enough to move with him." She paused for a moment and then added, "I came home from work one day and he was packing."

She saw Paul's jaw stiffen and knew he was angry on her behalf even before he said anything. "It was his loss. Any man who would walk away and leave you behind can't have been in his right mind."

His words touched her in a way that was hard to explain. All she knew was that she suddenly wanted to be held by him, so she eased back down beside him.

As if he knew what she needed, he pulled her into his arms and kissed her. It seemed he was trying to wipe away her hurt, and she appreciated the effort.

When he ended the kiss, he still held her close. "So, do we become involved, Michelle?" he asked in a deep, husky tone.

She looked up at him. "Yes, but do you have any objections to holding off until after Heather's party?"

"No," he said quietly. "I don't have any objections as long as there's a good reason you want us to."

She shrugged. "This is a small town and I want to stay focused on giving Heather the best birthday party possible. I want the attention to be on her next week, and not on us. We owe her that."

Paul threw his head back and laughed. "No wonder Heather likes you so much."

Michelle lifted an eyebrow. "She does?"

"I told you that."

She nodded. "You said she liked me—but a lot?"

"She likes you a whole lot. Now, I'll go along with what you want. We'll wait until after Heather's party, but then we begin acting like a normal couple."

Michelle wasn't sure such a thing was possible in Lake Falls, especially when he was considered such a hot prospect. But before she could say anything else, Paul was kissing her again.

CHAPTER
～SEVEN～

"Nice party. And these are for you, by the way."

Michelle smiled up at Paul before accepting the beautiful bouquet of fresh flowers. She lowered her head to inhale their fragrance. They smelled simply divine. "Thank you. What are they for?"

"This." He indicated the room. "Like I said, it's a nice party and it wouldn't have happened without you."

Although she felt he was giving her far more credit than she rightly deserved, she knew what he meant. Ravine Stokes, the party planner, had come down with the flu a few days before the event and Michelle had stepped in to take her place.

"Thanks," she said, following his gaze around the room. The main thing was that Heather was pleased with her party.

"Well, it's almost over. Now we can concentrate on other things."

Paul's words made her shiver. There was no way to stop the anticipation flowing through her.

"Do you think everyone is enjoying the food?" she asked as a way of changing the subject. His grin indicated he had caught on.

"I don't know why they wouldn't be, since you did an outstanding job. If Brian Frazier eats another one of those lemon squares, he's going to leave here with puckered lips."

Michelle grinned. Paul was right. The teen had gobbled up a number of the treats already.

"I have to make a drive to Brunswick on Thursday. Do you want to come along for the ride?"

She looked at him. "Brunswick?"

"Yes. I'm meeting with a potential client there. I thought that afterward you and I could do lunch."

What he proposed sounded like fun. "Okay. I'd like that."

He checked his watch. "Time to make our rounds. That Summers girl is missing again."

Michelle nodded and walked beside him as he moved around the room. Earlier, the two of them had watched as Rachel Summers tried coaxing Brad Parker to go outside with her.

When Rachel was nowhere to be found, Michelle followed Paul into the kitchen and stepped outside—just in time to interrupt a kiss.

"The party is inside," Paul said, startling the two teens.

Rachel, who was only fifteen but acted older, smiled over at them. "You're right, but we thought we would get some fresh air."

Paul didn't smile back. "Not tonight. I guess you'll just have to settle for the stuffy air inside until your mother comes for you."

Brad didn't say anything, but nodded before following Rachel back inside.

"The Summerses need to keep a closer eye on that girl," Paul said when the pair was no longer within hearing range.

"I agree." Michelle had been around Paul and Heather enough that week to know he took parenting seriously. Although it was obvious Heather had a crush on Jason, she always behaved in a respectful way.

The remainder of the party went well, and by midnight, all the kids had left and the food had been eaten. Heather offered to help with the cleanup but Paul and Michelle convinced her they could handle things and that she should go on to bed and rest after such a busy day.

"You're lucky, you know," Michelle said to Paul while they were taking down the streamers and balloons. "Heather is such a wonderful girl, and I'm not just saying that because she's your daughter. Rachel Summers could learn a few things from her."

Paul nodded. "I hope you're right."

Michelle hoped that she was right as well. Having a friend like Rachel had to be a challenge for Heather. Although Rachel had been with Brad outside, Michelle had noticed the girl making a play at one time or another for all the guys at the party. "Would you and Heather like to come over for dinner tomorrow?"

Paul couldn't help but smile as he pulled Michelle into his arms. "Is that going to be our official way of announcing to everyone that we're involved?"

She tilted up her head and smiled back at him. "Yes, I think that would be a perfect way."

IT WAS CLOSE TO TWO in the morning when Michelle arrived home. Paul had insisted on following behind her to make sure she got there safely. She had waved him goodbye and then on impulse had blown him a kiss before going inside. She was tired, but in a good way, and was glad the party had been such a huge success.

Before getting into bed, Michelle glanced over at her flowers. They were beautiful and filled her bedroom with their fragrance. The bouquet had been a nice gesture on Paul's part and she appreciated his thoughtfulness. Over the past week she'd discovered that she and Paul were so at ease with each other. She'd been busy putting the final touches on the party and he had been busy meeting a deadline for one of his clients' Web sites. But they had managed to talk on the phone late at night, when most of Lake Falls was asleep.

And now they had decided to make everything public.

As she got into bed and snuggled under the covers, she was again reminded of the kisses they had shared. She had enjoyed each and every one of them. She had made a number of mistakes with Lonnie, mistakes she didn't intend to repeat. But she had a feeling that Paul was genuine in his affection and would never do anything to lead her on. Now that the party was over they could turn up the heat a bit, and she could hardly wait.

CHAPTER
~⚬ EIGHT ⚬~

A week later as Michelle sat across the table from Paul, she couldn't help but reflect on the amount of time they'd spent together. He had joined her for dinner on Sunday with Heather. On Tuesday night, Paul and Michelle had gone to the movies. They'd had breakfast together on Wednesday morning, shared dinner in Brunswick on Thursday and here it was Saturday and they were dining together again. This was their first public dinner date in Lake Falls.

"How is your meat?"

Her smile widened. "Wonderful. They may be a mom-and-pop operation, but Wilson's Steakhouse serves the best steaks on the East Coast."

Paul chuckled. "I have to agree." He leaned back in his chair. "So, do you have a busy week ahead?"

She met his gaze. "No more than usual. The Foyers are celebrating their fiftieth wedding anniversary and I'm meeting with their daughter to plan a menu. The guest list, I understand, will be well over a hundred people."

"That's a lot of food."

"Yes, but I'm going to enjoy doing it." She took a sip of her iced tea. "And by the way, I'm having several young people over next Saturday. All of them have had an asthma attack at some point. As part of AANMA's awareness drive, we're having a guest speaker who is going to show us how to use a peak flow meter and holding chamber, and discuss the benefits of a written asthma management plan."

He lifted a brow. "And?"

"And I wanted your permission to invite Heather."

She could tell by his expression that he had a problem giving it. His next words confirmed her observation. "We've been over this before, Michelle, and I don't understand why you feel Heather needs a management plan. What happened to her a few weeks ago—"

"Could happen again, Paul," she interjected. "Why is it so hard for you to understand that, or better yet, why are you refusing to do so?"

He frowned. "Mainly because I don't think Heather's condition is as serious as you tend to make it."

Michelle sighed. And that was the problem. Most people underestimated the seriousness of asthma symptoms until it was too late. "A few weeks ago, you said you wanted us to build a relationship, yet even now you refuse to take seriously something that I know and feel very strongly about."

"It's not that I don't take it seriously. It's just I don't think it applies to Heather. Do you really think I'd jeopardize my daughter's health?"

"No, I don't think that, Paul."

"Then what, exactly, do you think?"

They were doing nothing but going around in circles, as far as she was concerned. "Let's just drop it."

She felt him closing her out again. How could they pursue a serious relationship when he constantly did that.

She was not surprised when he refused her invitation to join her for coffee and a snack at her place, saying he had a big project to work on. She knew he was intentionally putting distance between them.

That was fine, she would deal with it...or maybe she wouldn't. She had hoped his attitude would change once they began seeing each other, but it hadn't.

There was more to building a relationship than the occasional dinner together, some heated kisses. There was also that shared sense of connection, the feeling that your thoughts and deepest convictions were taken seriously. And that's what disturbed her the most, knowing that even after all this time, that she and Paul were no closer to resolving their differences about Heather's condition than they had been before.

Ms. Amy was staring at her.

"What is it?" Michelle asked.

"You look rather sad," the older woman said with concern in her eyes.

Michelle drew in a deep breath and then slowly exhaled. Ms. Amy had dropped by for lunch and they were sitting in the kitchen, eating chicken-salad sandwiches and enjoying cold glasses of lemonade. They had been talking about the weather, when Michelle's mind had wandered and she began thinking about Paul. The last time she had seen him was almost a week ago. He had called once or twice to say he was tied up with a major client, but part of her felt he was deliberately putting distance between them.

"Do I?" she asked now, deciding not to pretend for the older woman. It wouldn't do any good, anyway. She was sure Ms. Amy was fully aware things had cooled between them.

"Do you want to talk about it, Michelle?"

Michelle took another sip of her lemonade, knowing it wouldn't help to talk about it. Things were as they were, and wishing wouldn't change that.

Suddenly, an emotion she thought she would never feel again

ripped through her, making her tremble so much that she had to place the glass she was holding on the table.

"Michelle? Are you okay?"

She glanced over at Ms. Amy and swallowed. How could she explain that she'd just realized she had fallen in love with Paul?

She was spared from having to explain anything when her phone rang. "Excuse me." She got up from the table to answer it.

She recognized Paul's voice immediately, and another shiver ran up her spine. Regardless of how things were between them, she missed him. But the pleasure she'd felt at hearing his voice suddenly died. "When?" she asked as she tried to calm her racing heart.

At his response, she nodded. "All right, I'm on my way."

She quickly hung up and glanced over at Ms. Amy. "That was Paul. He was calling from the hospital. Heather was taken there from school after suffering another asthma attack."

MICHELLE ARRIVED AT THE hospital and went straight to the E.R. Paul was sitting in the waiting room but rushed over when he saw her. He pulled her into his arms and clung to her tightly.

When he drew back moments later, she saw the haggard look on his face. "I should have listened to you," he said brokenly. "How many times did you suggest that I check into Heather's condition? I should have taken her to the doctor! Then this wouldn't have happened. She's on a ventilator now and I can't even see her."

Michelle led him back to the chair. "What did the doctor say?"

"She had another asthma attack. I spoke with the school principal and *she* said she knew it was an asthma attack because of the in-service class you taught a few weeks ago. She followed the instructions in the materials supplied by your organization. Otherwise they don't know what they would have done."

He sighed deeply and then said in a shaken voice, "Twice now you've saved my daughter's life, and I want to thank you and that organization you volunteer for."

Michelle didn't say anything as Paul continued to grip her hand. She could imagine what he was going through. By the time she'd reached her sixteenth birthday she had been hospitalized for the condition at least five times. That was one of the reasons she volunteered for AANMA. There were so many people who assumed that asthma was a way of life, and had no idea it was also a way of death if not treated properly.

"I should have taken her to the doctor," Paul said again.

Michelle knew she didn't have to tell him he should have. He wasn't the first and, unfortunately, he wouldn't be the last who would make that mistake. The important thing now was for Heather to get better.

"Have you seen her at all?" she asked him.

"I saw her briefly when I first got here. She was gasping for breath, could barely breathe. The doctor asked me to step out while they connected her to a ventilator. That was over an hour ago. What's happening to her? What is the asthma doing to her?"

That, at least, was something Michelle could explain. "When asthma occurs, usually three things happen. The lining of the airway swells. Cells overproduce mucus, which starts clogging the passageways, and the surrounding muscles tighten."

"What do you think brought it on?" he asked.

She inhaled deeply. "It could have been caused by a number of things. The doctor should be able to give you more specifics when you talk to him."

Paul glanced around nervously. "Why is it taking so long? When will they give me an update about how she's doing?"

Michelle understood his frustration. "I'm sure they will soon. For now, let's just give them time to do what's needed."

Paul nodded and squeezed her hand again. "Thanks for being here with me, Michelle."

"Under the circumstances, I wouldn't want to be anywhere else."

And she meant it. Paul and Heather had become part of her life. She looked forward to Heather's after-school visits, and when the teen had mentioned she would love to learn how to bake, they had discussed the possibility of Michelle starting a cooking class on Saturday mornings for some of the young women in the community.

"Mr. Castlewood?" It was Heather's doctor, Paul quickly told her.

Paul quickly got to his feet, pulling Michelle with him. "How is she?" he asked, sounding on the verge of panic.

"Heather will be okay. We've sedated her and she's resting comfortably now. We're not sure what brought on this attack but we're doing a series of tests to pinpoint the cause."

"I thought she had outgrown her asthma," Paul said, sounding defeated.

The doctor nodded in understanding. "A lot of parents think that, especially if an attack hasn't taken place in a while. Asthma attacks can be separated by years. That doesn't mean the condition is gone. You and Heather are new to this area. The attacks could be caused by her body getting used to the air she's now breathing. There are a number of paper mills down the road in Brunswick."

"I'll do whatever I have to. Even move away if that will make my daughter better."

"I don't think you have to go that far," the doctor said wryly. "We just need to establish Heather on a solid asthma management plan. Pretty soon she'll be leaving for college. You'll want her to be able to live a fulfilling life anywhere in the country she wants to go, not someplace that's dictated by her condition."

Paul nodded. "When can I see my daughter?"

"You can see her now, but you need to know what to expect. She's sedated, of course, and on a ventilator to help her breathe, and there are a lot of tubes connecting her to the machine. If her condition continues to improve we'll be able to remove the ventilator so she can breathe on her own by tomorrow."

Moments later, walking hand in hand, Paul and Michelle followed a nurse through the E.R. doors to the Intensive Care unit. Michelle felt Paul's fingers tighten on hers the moment he saw his daughter, and standing so close to him, she could feel his body tremble.

"Remember what the doctor said, Paul. Heather is going to be okay."

Instead of answering, he pulled her into his arms, as if he needed whatever strength she had to pass on to him.

"I let my little girl down," he said moments later when he released her and glanced over at the bed.

"No, you didn't," Michelle said softly. "You didn't fully know or understand her condition. But you do now, and organizations like AANMA can help out. The important thing is for us to get Heather well and to keep her that way."

Paul lifted Michelle's hand up to his lips and kissed her knuckles. "Us," he said softly, meeting her gaze.

She smiled, not wanting to read more into the word, not exactly certain what he was implying. But for the moment, she wanted to reassure him. "Yes. Us."

NOT WANTING TO LEAVE Heather alone, they both remained at the hospital for the rest of the day. In the wee hours of the night, they rotated watch duty so each of them could go home to shower and change clothes.

Jason visited the next morning and Michelle could tell how shaken up he was about what had happened to Heather. She was appreciative when Paul took Jason downstairs to talk to him, to reassure the young man that Heather would be okay. She knew Paul's respect and admiration for Jason had gone up another notch.

The doctors decided that, since Heather was breathing comfortably on her own, they would remove the ventilator. However, it would be a few hours before the sedation wore off and she opened her eyes to acknowledge their presence.

Michelle and Paul were in the room when she came to, and she smiled at them before quickly dozing off again. Paul, overjoyed at seeing that his daughter was doing a lot better, pulled Michelle into his arms and kissed her, letting her feel all the happiness that was a part of him at that very moment.

"Wow! I liked that," Michelle said, smiling up at him when he ended the kiss.

He chuckled. "Glad to hear it, because I happen to like you."

A few moments later, when a nurse came in to take Heather's vital signs, they decided to go downstairs to the coffee shop. They were about to get on the elevator when Rachel Summers stepped off.

"Hey, Rachel." When Michelle saw the stricken look on the young girl's face, she quickly asked, "Are you okay?"

"I wanted to see how Heather is doing. I wasn't at school yesterday, and when I got there today, everyone was saying she was in a bad way and they had to call an ambulance."

"Yes, but she's doing better now," Paul said reassuringly.

"Do you think I can see her? Heather has been a good friend to me." Rachel wiped away her tears.

"Well, I'm sure she'd be glad to see you," Michelle said, placing a comforting hand on her shoulder. "But you'll have to check with the nurse. I think visitors are limited in Intensive Care."

Rachel's features brightened. "I'll go find out. Thanks."

Paul and Michelle watched as the girl quickly walked away, and then Paul punched the elevator button again. "Do you know what I think?" he asked Michelle when Rachel was no longer in sight.

"No, what do you think?"

"I think that somehow Heather has been a positive influence in Rachel's life."

Michelle smiled. "Yes, I think you're right."

"I HOPE I NEVER HAVE TO go through anything like that again," Heather was saying as she sat up in bed in her hospital room. Paul and Michelle had returned to find that Rachel was there and Jason had returned. Heather was anxiously awaiting her first meal in over twenty-four hours.

"Michelle and I are going to make sure you don't," Paul said, pulling Michelle to his side and placing his arm around her shoulders. "There's this asthma network that Michelle is affiliated with and they're going to help us set up an asthma management plan for you. We spoke with your doctor earlier and he will be working with the team on it."

"Cool. And do you know what would be even cooler, Dad?"

"No, what?"

"If you and Ms. Chapman could get a little serious."

Paul looked confused. "About what?"

"Each other."

He couldn't help but laugh out loud at his daughter's candidness. "Michelle and I *are* serious about each other. We're just taking things one day at a time and getting to know each other better. When we think the time is right to make any kind of commitment, you'll be the first to know."

"Promise?"

Paul took Michelle's hand in his and held it up for his daughter to see. He smiled at Michelle before turning back to Heather. "Yes, we promise. But the most important thing is for you to get well so we can get out of here and back home."

HEATHER, DRIVEN BY THE belief that her father's happiness hinged on her good health, worked hard at recovering. On the fourth day she was overjoyed that the doctor released her from the hospital. Once back home, she was her old self again.

"Not so fast, young lady," Paul had to say when she immediately wanted to get on the phone to call all of her friends. "The first thing you're going to do is subscribe to that *Allergy and Asthma Today* magazine. I borrowed a copy from Michelle and it's very informative reading."

Heather rolled her eyes. "I'm taking your word for it, Dad."

Later that day, Paul went over to Michelle's place. She was busy taking a batch of chocolate chip squares out of the oven, and invited Paul to eat a couple with a glass of milk.

"Thanks," he said, sliding into a chair at the table. "But first..." Reaching out, he snagged her elbow and pulled her down into his lap.

She grinned at him. "Is there a reason you're keeping me from my work?"

He smiled. "Yes. This."

And then he captured her mouth with his, kissing her thoroughly. She moaned, aware of the intense desire that consumed them both. When Paul finally ended the kiss, he pressed his forehead against hers and sighed deeply.

His heart was pounding rapidly in his chest and he knew now was the time. She had been there for him. And for Heather. He enjoyed her company, but most importantly, he loved her. This strong emotion he was feeling, that he had been feeling for quite a while, just had to be love.

"I need to explain something to you."

She looked at him. "What?"

"The reason I didn't want to accept that Heather hadn't outgrown her asthma."

"Okay, what's the reason?"

"Emma, my ex-wife. She never wanted children, and Heather was not planned... She never let me forget it. She tried convincing me that we weren't ready for a baby and she should get an abortion. I was totally against it. The day Heather was born, Emma looked at her and had the nerve to say that she would be nothing but trouble for us. And each time Heather got sick for any reason, I always got an "I told you so" glare from her mom. It wasn't that Heather was a sickly child. She had the normal childhood illnesses, but Emma would use any reason to try and make her point. And after our daughter's first asthma attack, Emma left. She walked out of my life and Heather's."

He sighed. "I've been protective of Heather since then, probably overprotective. And when you kept bringing up the possibility that she had this condition that could come back, instead of taking your warning in a positive way, I took it as a negative."

Michelle nodded as understanding dawned. "The last thing you needed was another woman dwelling on the issue of your daughter's health."

"Yes. And that's why I always went on the defensive about it. I was wrong in doing that and I apologize. You have been the best thing to come into our lives. We love you. I love you."

He took her hand in his. "Marry me," he whispered, feeling the words coming straight from his heart. "If you want we can have a long engagement, but I want to know you are promised to me and one day our futures will be entwined. Will you marry me?"

Tears clouded Michelle's eyes. She didn't need any additional time to think about it. When Paul had told her about his ex and that she hadn't loved the child they had made together, Michelle's heart had gone out to both Paul and Heather. She knew that she was willing to step in and be the woman they needed in their lives, and to love them unconditionally.

"Yes, I'll marry you," she said, her voice quavering with all the emotions she felt. "And it doesn't matter what the state of Heather's health is. I will always love her. I promise."

And then she leaned in and gave him a kiss that sealed their love and the promise she had just made. He was everything she could want in a man, and Heather was all that she wanted in a daughter. Her life was filled with more happiness than she thought possible. And she was ready to move toward the next stage of her life. With Paul.

~EPILOGUE~

"**D**addy, please tell me a story."

Paul smiled as his three-year-old daughter crawled onto his lap. He glanced out the window to see his parents and Michelle busy decorating the yard for Heather's coming-home party. It was hard to believe his oldest daughter had completed college at the University of Georgia, earning a degree in business, and was coming home for the summer to help Michelle with her catering business before taking a job in the fall with a corporation in Boston.

"Daddy?"

He glanced down at the bundle of joy in his lap. "Yes, Amy?"

"A story."

He chuckled. Amy had been born two years after their wedding. Life was better than good. He had two beautiful daughters and a wife he loved more each day.

Heather hadn't had another asthma attack, but remained on a management plan. Like Michelle, she was now an outreach service coordinator with AANMA.

"What story do you want to hear?" he asked his daughter, who'd been named after Ms. Amy Poole, the town matriarch, who'd been instrumental in getting him and Michelle together.

"The one about the three bears."

Paul smiled. "All right."

He was about to begin his narration when he looked up to see Michelle walk in. "I thought I'd come inside and check on you two," she said, leaning down and placing a kiss on his lips.

"We're fine. Amy wants to hear the story about the three bears."

Michelle grinned and said in a low voice, "No need. Look."

Paul followed Michelle's gaze to see Amy had fallen asleep in his arms. "Oh, well."

Michelle smiled. "Yes, oh, well."

Once they'd tucked Amy into bed, they stood in the doorway of her room and smiled at the sight of her sleeping peacefully. Michelle turned to her husband. "Life has been good."

Paul nodded as he drew her closer. His mouth curved into a smile. "Yes, it has. Thanks for loving me."

She leaned closer. "It has been my pleasure." And she stood on tiptoe, captured his mouth with hers and demonstrated to him just how much.

* * * * *

Dear Reader,

I was honored to be asked to be one of the contributing authors for this year's *More Than Words*.

From the moment I was introduced to Allergy & Asthma Network Mothers of Asthmatics (AANMA), I was inspired to write a very special love story. And talking to Nancy Sander, the organization's founder, was like putting the icing on the cake. I learned so much information and gained valuable insight as to the severity of asthma, as well as the support AANMA provides.

Then in the midst of writing this story, I encountered my own near tragedy when my cousin was rushed to the emergency room, where he spent the next five days fighting for his life after having a severe asthma attack. I was able to share what I'd learned from my research about asthma with family members and friends. And I saw firsthand the importance of having an organization like AANMA.

Paul and Michelle's story is a very special one and I hope it moves you to help raise awareness and much-needed funds for organizations as admirable as this one. Please visit www.aanma.org to learn more about AANMA.

Happy reading!

Brenda Jackson

SANDRA RAMOS
∾ Strengthen Our Sisters ∾

To put it simply, Sandra Ramos knows how to get things done. At once charming and determined, energetic and blunt, the New Jersey woman—who founded North America's first shelter for battered women in the seventies—is brilliant at pinpointing a crisis and then moving heaven and earth to make things right.

"When there's a truck on your foot, you don't go to the library to find out how much it weighs. You get it off," she says simply.

There's no denying that Sandra is the real deal. For almost forty years, she has done whatever it takes to help beaten, bruised and broken women find dignity, grace and safety away from their abusers. Her grassroots, community-based nonprofit organization called Strengthen Our Sisters is now a high-quality, 177-bed program with seven shelters, a computer school where women can upgrade their skills, two thrift stores, a day-care center and a car donation program. She no longer receives a salary, but volunteers about sixty hours a week.

Though she says she feels optimistic—probably helped by her daily walks and meditation—Sandra's work, sadly, seems never to be done. With one woman physically assaulted in her home every fifteen seconds in the United States and nearly six million women battered in a single year, Strengthen Our Sisters has its work cut out for it. Yet thousands of women have found, and continue to find, not only a sanctuary of safety, but also a place to rebuild self-esteem when they enter the doors.

It seems Sandra's doors have always been open for people who need her. Not long after her divorce, in 1970, a nurse she knew landed on Sandra's doorstep in the middle of the night. The woman was clutching three children and three cats and needed refuge from the husband who beat her. Sandra quickly set up bunkbeds, her own three children making room for the newcomers.

Soon word got around about Sandra's open-door policy to those in need, and more women and children arrived. And then more. Soon her Hackensack, New Jersey, home was filled to the rafters with twenty-one moms and kids, including Sandra's own brood. Not everyone was thrilled with the arrangement. One woman told Sandra that she didn't want abused women living in the neighborhood. To which Sandra replied that they already were, and it was simply a question of them living in peace with support, dignity and respect, or living with hatred, violence and dysfunction. Still neighbors complained, and the building inspector came.

"How many people do you have here?" he asked her.

Sandra says she could have lied, but decided it was time to deal with the situation head-on. She told the truth.

"Twenty-one," she said. At that exact moment, a young woman pushing a toddler in a stroller wandered into the room. "Make that twenty-three," said Sandra.

Although she was threatened with jail time for infractions from overcrowdedness to running a business without a license and allowing more than three unrelated people to reside together, Sandra refused the throw the families out of her home. For the next ten years she marched, staged sit-ins and defied court orders, to protect women and children from abuse.

Then came the moment she could milk for every dramatic purpose she could fathom. When local freeholders denied funding to a battered women's shelter, but awarded $500,000 to fund an animal shelter, Sandra attended the meeting with a woman who had been battered—and her dog. If the council could build a shelter for the woman's dog, would the shelter be willing to take in the woman, too?

Sandra got her funding to open the first official safe haven for battered women and children in the nation, Shelter Our Sisters.

Not bad for a woman born Sandra Blumberg, a Brooklyn-born, only child of Jewish parents, who ran away from home at eleven. (She eventually made her way back home after two weeks, at which time she was promptly sent off to a boarding school for delinquent children in Westchester.) She now has a master's degree in applied urban anthropology and has taught at several colleges and universities.

In 1986, Sandra left Shelter Our Sisters and moved to Passaic County, the rural area where she planned to retire. She wanted to hike, swim, dance, meditate and write a book. But her reputation as a passionate advocate for women followed her, and soon people were asking for Sandra's help again.

When she discovered that the underserved rural area was without a battered women's shelter, she and other dedicated supporters launched Strengthen Our Sisters Inc. Slowly the group acquired housing in the area, turning apartments and houses into safe homes. Finally, in 1990, the organization expanded its programs and services and bought a 4.5-acre site complete with a farmhouse in need of repair, a cottage and ten motel units. A few years later Strengthen Our Sisters bought a day-care center so women could learn job skills without worrying about who would take care of their kids. More buildings have been snatched up since and more programs added.

At the core of all this frenetic energy is Sandra. She still comes to work most days, and on Thursdays runs her battered women's support group. At sixty-seven years old, and abiding by her philosophy Dare To Struggle, Dare To Win, Sandra exudes an energy that seems unlimited to people even half her age.

Yet it's the women she meets each day, the battered, molested and abused women in the process of dusting themselves off and finding the help they need to live full and fearless lives, who continue to inspire Sandra.

"When women blossom and grow, they're saying, 'I am not afraid anymore. I can survive. I can stand up. I deserve more,'" she says.

Sandra has no immediate plans to slow down. She can't. There's still so much work to do to create a humane, just society where women flourish and grow without fear. And if she can find a shortcut in the meantime, she'll grab it.

"I want to enhance my magical powers so I can just wiggle my nose and batterers will go poof!" she says, laughing. "That's what I want. And I'm working on it."

For more information, visit www.strengthenoursisters.org or write to Strengthen Our Sisters, P.O. Box U, Hewitt, NJ, 07421.

TARA TAYLOR QUINN
❧ THE MECHANICS OF LOVE ❧

ഏ─TARA TAYLOR QUINN─ഏ

With more than forty-five original novels, published in more than twenty languages, Tara Taylor Quinn is a *USA TODAY* bestselling author. She is known for delivering deeply emotional and psychologically astute novels. Ms. Quinn is a three-time finalist for the RWA RITA® Award, a multiple finalist for the National Reader's Choice Award, the Reviewer's Choice Award, the Bookseller's Best Award and the Holt Medallion. Ms. Quinn recently married her college sweetheart, and the couple currently lives in Ohio with their two very demanding and spoiled bosses: four-pound Taylor Marie and fifteen-pound rescue mutt/cockapoo Jerry. When she's not writing for Harlequin and MIRA Books or fulfilling speaking engagements, Ms. Quinn loves to travel with her husband, stopping wherever the spirit takes them. They've been spotted in casinos and quaint little antique shops all across the country.

CHAPTER
⚛— ONE —⚛

"What do you see?" Hands on the hips of her faded, ripped-on-one-thigh and skin-hugging jeans, 105-pound Tina Randolph glanced from the computer screen to the 200-pound, tattooed nineteen-year-old at her side.

"A bent camshaft."

"Excellent." Of course, reading the computer diagnostic wasn't the tough part of the job, but it was a start. A very good start.

"The camshaft operates the valves. You have two intake and two exhaust valves per cylinder..." Tina said, walking around the opened hood of the seven-year-old sedan, her rubber-soled black work boots making hardly a sound on the cement floor of the

Cincinnati, Ohio, garage. She spent the next ten minutes explaining the intricacies of gas moving through cylinders. Things she had learned growing up in her father's garage. "So, the upshot is, we have to replace the camshaft. And in order to do that, we have to get this thing out of here." She pointed to the engine.

"The first thing we're going to do is remove the motor mounts," she continued, ratchet and socket wrench in hand as she bent over the engine. They'd already disconnected hoses, the gas line and wiring.

Justin Jones moved in closer behind her. She gave the ratchet a twist. And ended in a brief full-body contact with her newest student.

It took Tina one second to sidestep and spin. "Watch it, buddy," she said, hands on hips, facing him.

He stared her down. For all of two seconds. And then his head bowed. "Sorry."

She could barely hear him. "Excuse me?"

Glancing up, he met her gaze. "I said I'm sorry."

She let him stand there long enough to make him good and uncomfortable as she studied him. After twenty years of practice reading the male species, though, she'd determined almost immediately that his apology was sincere.

"It happens again and you're out of here."

"It won't."

Holding his gaze a bit longer, Tina eventually turned back to the job at hand, removing the motor mounts, attaching the hoist, lifting the engine from the car. All without saying a word.

All without help.

"Am I fired?"

She hooked up the engine hoist. "You haven't been hired yet." With some hearty cranks, she raised the engine.

"I thought…Scott said I had the job."

"No Tina Randolph certification, no job," she said easily, her back to him.

"You aren't going to pass me."

"You asking or telling?"

"Asking, I guess."

Stopping, Tina stared at the young man. "You guess?"

"Okay, I'm asking, already. I screwed up. I'm sorry. I really need this job."

"But do you want it?"

"Yes."

"Then get a wrench and get to work. And if you ever so much as look at me again, or touch any woman without her express invitation and I hear about it, you'll wish you'd never been born."

"Yes, ma'am."

She meant to leave it at that. Should have left it at that if she were ever going to be as professional as her starch-shirted partner, Scott Harbor.

"Didn't you learn anything during your stays at the shelter?" she asked instead. Scott said Justin had volunteered, doing handyman work, at the battered women's establishment in Denver where he'd spent some of his youth.

Justin didn't look up.

"What about your mama?" Tina prodded, against her better judgment. "Think about her the next time you touch a woman disrespectfully. Remember the bruises."

"Holy heck, ma'am—" The brute-sized kid spun, staring at her. "There wasn't nothing disrespectful there."

"What would you call it?"

"I...you're beautiful, okay? You might cut that blond hair short, but you can't change what God gave you, you know? I got a little close, yeah, but I wasn't forcing anything. As soon as you said no, I stopped. I always stop."

He looked as if he wanted to say more. Tina was pretty sure she didn't want to hear what it was.

"I'm eleven years older than you," she told him with more bravado than she felt, not that he was to know that.

"You're single and gorgeous. When a guy meets a single woman who attracts him, the next step is to see if the feeling is mutual."

"You could ask."

He shook his head. "Too embarrassing. For her as much as me."

"I'm your boss."

"I made a mistake there."

At least they'd established that much.

"Just make certain it's the only one you make and you might pass."

"Yes, ma'am."

With some detailed instructions on how to proceed, Tina wiped her hands on one of the cloths that were always close by, and turned away from their newest potential employee on Jiffy Jobs's 700-member national team.

If her instincts were correct, Justin was going to be good.

If her instincts were correct, she'd just overreacted. Again.

Which was one of the reasons why Tina Randolph's closest relationships were with engines.

And books. Always books.

CHAPTER
∽ TWO ∼

"Tina?"

Rolling out from beneath a vintage blue Camaro, Tina ignored the young man still working on replacing the camshaft in the stall next to her, and answered her receptionist. "Yeah?"

"You might want to come here."

"I'm in the middle of changing a starter." What was Amy thinking?

"I think you need to come here. Quickly." The twenty-five-year-old single mother came closer, her gaze darting to the doorway between the garage and the front office.

Scott's secretary, Jean, was in the office, as well as three other women who helped oversee the paperwork involved in running the fixed-priced, full-service Jiffy Jobs chain. Why couldn't any of them help Amy?

Frowning, muttering silently about a girl never getting any peace to enjoy the day's work, Tina dropped her box wrench in the tray and stood up to take the towel Amy held out to her.

"Where's Scott?"

"He left already for lunch with the mayor, remember? We're getting another award."

Right. He'd told her that. A commendation from the city for Jiffy Jobs's civic-minded hiring of the less fortunate. Or some such garbage.

"Can't it wait until he gets back?" She was a mechanic, not a businesswoman. Or a people person.

Amy glanced again at the door, the worry lines on her face more pronounced than usual, and shook her head. "Hurry."

Wondering how the young woman could walk in those high heels—or why she'd chosen to wear them with the jeans and Jiffy Jobs pullover that was standard uniform for all employees—Tina followed the receptionist past Justin.

"Good work," she said, noticing the orderly line of bolts and parts that would simplify the putting-back-together process.

"Thanks." The youth didn't look up.

Expecting to see bruises on Scott's secretary again, or a flood in the bathroom, Tina was surprised when Amy headed straight for the front foyer. Problems outside their door weren't their problems.

Not that that stopped anyone at Jiffy Jobs from trying to help if they could. It's what they did, this group of misfits from battered women's shelters across the country—helped each other.

They all, to the very last paycheck, knew what it was like to be down. In need of help.

Every one of them had fought in the battle to survive. And won. So far.

A baby's cry interrupted Tina's thoughts. Had Maria's babysitter skipped out on her again?

With a quick glance, Tina took in the outer office. Everything seemed perfectly fine. Orderly. Except...

The cry came again. From just outside the opened door. All four of their full-time office employees, Maria and Jean included, were out there, huddled together. Amy joined them.

"What's going on?" Tina asked, coming up behind them.

As they parted, allowing her entrance to the inner circle, Tina stopped. And stared at the red face—all that could be seen from within the blanketed baby carrier—of the squalling infant she'd heard. A large diaper bag was hooked around the edge of the makeshift bed.

"Whose is that?" she asked with her usual finesse.

Jean handed her an envelope.

"Scott Harbor" was printed on the otherwise blank surface. No address. No postage or other marking. She turned it over.

No return address.

Shaking inside, something no one but perhaps the man whose name was shining starkly from that paper missive would ever guess, Tina focused on the baby as a way to avoid the circle of eyes pinned on her.

She needed privacy.

And quiet.

"Jean, would you please see what you can do about quieting that thing?" she asked Scott's secretary. "The rest of you, go back to whatever you were doing. I'll take it from here."

"It" meaning the baby? Or the problem? She wasn't sure.

As the other women, with concerned and curious glances at the infant in the carrier, turned to leave, Tina watched Jean untangle the baby from the mass of pink blankets and noted the pink and white flowered sleeper.

"It's March—fifty degrees, not twenty," Tina said aloud while panic tried to take her over. "What kind of person doesn't know that it's not good to keep a child too warm?"

Who was trying to cause trouble for Scott? And how was Tina going to make this problem go away?

Jean cradled the unwrapped baby in the crook of her arm, supporting a head that lolled uncontrollably. The facial bruises from the last time Jean's husband had hit her were fading. Finally.

"She's so tiny," the secretary said softly, reverently.

"Can't be more than a few weeks old." Tina forced every bit of emotion out of her tone, the unopened envelope burning her fingers.

The baby continued to cry, making far too much noise, alerting anyone and everyone of her presence. Telling everyone that Scott might be in trouble.

"Here, let me take her." Tina settled the baby up against her shoulder, plopping her head in the crook of her neck like the sack of potatoes she'd always likened the little ones to. Lord knew she'd carried enough of them.

Cared for enough of them.

With a father who had kept her mother pregnant, and beaten up, until the day he'd died drunk behind the wheel of his truck, it had been up to Tina, the oldest, to make certain that her siblings made it out of childhood alive.

Books had kept *her* alive.

The baby quieted almost instantly. Thank God.

"Grab the carrier and bag, would you?" she asked Jean, heading back to Scott's office, when what she wanted to do was to slide back under the Camaro awaiting her out in the garage and have the good day she'd planned.

Twenty minutes later, having heated and dispensed the formula they'd found in the bag, Tina dismissed Jean, settled into Scott's impressively high-backed and comfortable leather office chair, and laid the sleeping infant faceup across her lap. Her gaze kept trying to return to the cherubic little cheeks, the impossibly long lashes and mostly bald head.

What's your name, little one?

She didn't want to know. Anything. At all. She wanted this baby to be a nightmare from which she could awake. An aberration she and Scott would laugh about some night after she'd had her third or fourth beer and started talking too much and told him about this craziness.

Yeah, that's how it could go.

Except that an envelope lay on the desk. Taunting her.

She could have left it there. Might have left it there, taking the baby, with carrier, out to the garage to let her sleep off her morning while Tina worked, but for the fact that Scott would be returning. And Tina wanted a plan before that happened.

The only way to survive life was to take control. Stay in control. Control everyone and everything around you.

Even when you couldn't.

She opened the envelope. Pulled out the single sheet of halfway decent stationery, impressed that it didn't smell like perfume or have any lipstick kiss marks.

The handwriting was definitely feminine, but not flowery.

Dear Mr. Harbor,

You don't know me.

Tina dropped the letter. Thank God. Scott didn't know her. This problem wasn't theirs.

The kid hiccuped in her sleep. Tina figured she ought to know her name. And picked the letter back up.

My name is Claire Reese. This is Kennedy Ann. She's three weeks old and she's your daughter.

Tina jerked so hard the baby's head bounced. The infant opened her eyes, but as Tina rubbed the top of her head—a motion that soothed Tina as much as anything—the kid settled back to sleep.

His daughter? But she didn't know him? Come on. Tina knew Scott had casual affairs, but this was a bit of a stretch.

Wasn't it?

Please tell her it was.

I don't have time to go into it here, but I found out who you were from a breach of confidentiality at the fertility clinic...

She named a place that Tina had never heard of.

...I never intended to use the information, but I am desperate. My life is in danger and Kennedy is at risk as long as she is with me. I don't know where else to turn. I read about you, about your work with women's shelters and I know it's too much to ask, but I need you to keep Kennedy for me, just until I can sort this all out.

If I go to the state, they will take her from me. I made one bad choice that continues to haunt me. I'm a good woman, with a college degree and the ability to care for my child. I'm a good mother. All I have ever wanted was to have a child of my own. A family filled with security and love. Please, please, Mr. Harbor, I'm begging you, take Kennedy for me. Keep her safe. I'm hoping to be able to return by this evening, but am leaving her with you just in case it takes longer.

Please do not call the authorities. I could lose her for abandonment or something—and she could lose her only chance to be raised by her birth mother. She'd become part of a system that may or may not do well by her. And who knows if they'd give her back to me when I return.

She is your child. DNA will prove that to you.

This letter is to serve as my permission to you to have full custody of our child in the event that I cannot care for her.

I love this baby more than life, Mr. Harbor. I will give up my life for her if I have to. She makes the twenty-seven years of hell I've spent on this earth worth every difficult moment. I promise I will not let her—or you—down.

P.S. I am not in trouble with the law, nor am I involving you in anything illegal.

Illegal or not, Tina felt like puking.

CHAPTER THREE

K ennedy Ann was a wise child. She slept on, in spite of the clanking and grinding and buzzing of electric tools in the two-stall garage, allowing Tina to roll back under the Camaro and complete at least one thing on her agenda for the day.

Engines did what she told them to do. They didn't talk back.

The whole communing process with non-breathing, motorized objects worked better if she didn't also have to wheel herself out every five seconds to check on the carrier she'd placed close enough to grab in case of an emergency, but out of bounds of anything that could possibly fall on top of it.

"It's probably loud in here for her," Justin said, eyeing the sleeping infant.

Sitting on the floor, forearms resting on her knees, Tina studied the topic at hand. "Doesn't seem to be bothering her any."

"Might hurt her hearing or something."

Tina didn't think so. Sleeping in the playpen she'd set up in her father's garage hadn't seemed to hurt her siblings.

She'd read a lot of medical books, especially during her teens, when she couldn't come up with money to get regular checkups for all the kids, and not once had she come across anything that said garages were bad for ears.

"I could take an early lunch and hold her or something."

Jean had offered, too. Tina gave the young man the same answer she'd delivered to Scott's secretary: "You've got work to do."

This was their problem—hers and Scott's. She'd handle it.

SHE GAVE SCOTT TWO SECONDS in his office before she descended upon him.

"What's that?" he asked, glancing briefly at the plastic carrier looped over Tina's arm, before returning his attention to the pile of papers Jean had left in the middle of his desk.

Typical Scott, he hadn't even taken a seat before getting to work.

"A baby." She tried to keep the accusation out of her voice. Obviously this…child was a mistake. Scott had casual affairs; he didn't make babies. Though, in that suit, he looked good enough to get takers if he wanted to.

"I see that," he said, calm as usual. "Whose baby?"

Drawing a deep breath to hold back the pithy comment that wanted to slip out, Tina reminded herself that he wasn't at fault here—wasn't to be blamed for the interruption in her day, or the weakness of her stomach. "That's the six-million-dollar question."

"I don't have six million dollars. Whose baby is it?"

"The note says she's yours." And she was going to be waking up any minute. Needing more formula heated—and delivered to her mouth. She'd need a diaper change, too.

Scott's hands froze on the envelope he'd been opening, his eyes wide as he stared at Tina. "Mine?"

"That's what the note says," she clarified. Didn't make it true. *Please, God, don't let it be true.*

Scott was a good one. A rare breed. He sat on the local school board, spent holidays cooking at the homeless shelter, fought injustice with time and energy as much as money. Fought for the small guy. He didn't deserve some gold digger trying to take them for their money.

Money they didn't have in any liquid form, with ten new stores opening in the next year. Jiffy Jobs was already a two-hundred-store national chain with its head office and training center right here.

"Tina?"

He was still standing behind his desk.

"Yeah?"

"Where's the note?"

Pulling it out of her back pocket, Tina hesitated before handing it over. Maybe if she read it to him, the impact would be less alarming. Maybe if she fed it to the shredder, the whole problem would go away.

Kennedy jerked, rocking the carrier on Tina's arm. The baby's eyes opened. And shut again.

Tina gave Scott the letter.

"WHAT DO YOU THINK?" Tina asked a full minute later. She'd waited as long as she could.

He continued to gaze at the paper in his hand, as though not sure it was real. Or that he'd read it correctly. Or maybe he still hadn't finished reading. Or needed to read it again for everything to sink in.

"I don't know what to think."

"It's a hoax," Tina said. "She's going to sue you for support."

"I don't think so."

Tina's chest tightened. "There can't be any truth in what she says. I mean, maybe, if she was one of your flings. But look, she says she got your sperm from that center. You didn't donate sperm. And all that about DNA...I don't know what she's hoping to prove, but—"

"I donated sperm."

This time, Tina jerked the carrier. "What?"

"I've gone to the center a few times."

"Why? Did we need the money? Why didn't you tell me?"

"I don't tell you everything."

Maybe not. But just about. "You tell me the important things."

"I've been donating sperm since college," Scott said, his gaze darting from her to the baby she held. Tina had to resist the urge to snatch the carrier away from his sight.

His reach.

She wanted to set the damn thing down and be done with it.

"I'd have loaned you cash," she said. She'd had her dad's garage by then. It wasn't much, nothing like the business Scott had built for them over the past six years, but it had been enough.

"I didn't do it for the money."

"Why then?"

"So that women who want children don't have to be beholden to a man to have them. So that they don't feel forced into getting married—settling for men who aren't right for them—to have their families."

Okay. They had a problem.

Why in hell did he have to be so...so...Scott?

Kennedy moved again, her little arms stretching, poking fists above her head as her legs, encased in a pink, one-piece sleeper, scrunched up to her belly.

"You better look at her, then," Tina said, doing nothing to facilitate the action.

Scott didn't move.

She gave him another couple of minutes, and then she did. Walking over, she turned so that his gaze would fall directly on the baby's face.

Kennedy's eyes popped open again. She blinked against the fluorescent light in the office ceiling. Squinted at the six-foot-tall, dark-haired man staring helplessly down at her.

And started to cry.

Tina wanted to join her.

IT TOOK TINA ONLY a couple of minutes to change the baby's diaper and get a nipple in her mouth, and then peace fell over the office again.

Enough quiet so they could talk.

"You're good at that."

She barely looked at the child in her lap as she sat across from him. "I've had practice."

Scott nodded. He knew all about her adolescence. He knew everything about her.

Sitting behind his desk, watching her every move, he looked lost.

"It'll be fine." Tina told him what she most wanted to hear, whether she believed it or not. "We'll watch her for a few hours, her mother will return and the two of them will ride off into the sunset."

"She's my daughter."

"Biologically. Heck, at the rate you've been going, there could be a hundred of them. Or ten, at least."

"But they don't know about me."

"You don't know that. If there was one breach, there could have been more."

"I haven't seen them."

"Scott, you don't have any rights to this child," Tina said, her voice growing stronger as the panic that had been pushing at her doors slipped through a crack. Someone was going to get hurt here. "Or any obligations."

He didn't owe the world. Didn't have to sacrifice himself every single time. Wiping up drooled milk from the side of Kennedy's face, Tina continued to feed the newborn, glad to see that she ate well.

Now if only the kid would quit looking up at her with those big blue eyes...

"What if her mother doesn't come back?"

Leave it to Scott to put her worries right out there.

"She'll be back. You heard her. She loves the kid."

"What if she doesn't make it back tonight?"

Tina was ahead of him there. "We'll leave a note on the door with my cell number, and I'll take her home with me. My hot date with the *Textbook of Transpersonal Psychiatry* is a little more flexible than your school-board meeting."

It'd only be for one night. She could handle it. For Scott.

"It's not as if I haven't cared for a baby before," she reminded him. "For the next few weeks all she's going to do is eat, poop and sleep. I can pretty much facilitate all three in my sleep."

"Tina."

She hated it when he got that tone of voice. Raising her chin, she stared him down.

"Yeah?"

"We have to call the police."

"Not yet we don't."

"We can't just walk off with a baby."

"We aren't walking anywhere. We're babysitting until her mother returns to get her. I called information and she's not listed. There's no way we're going to find her tonight, so we should give her a chance to return. Come on, Scott, you know what happens to kids in the system."

"Sometimes they're placed in wonderful homes, get adopted by great parents and have happy lives."

"How many times?"

"A lot."

"Fifty percent?"

"Seventy-five. At least."

"I'll give you sixty and that's pushing it. Which leaves a forty percent chance that this kid'll get lost in the bureaucratic shuffle. You want to take those odds?"

What in the hell was she doing? Trying to shackle Scott with a kid? He didn't need this. Didn't deserve it. She didn't need it, either.

And Kennedy did?

"Her mother's obviously in some kind of trouble," Scott said. "She might need help."

"How well did the cops do for your mom?" Tina lifted the baby to her shoulder, gently patting her back.

"They couldn't do anything without her cooperation. Couldn't prove anything." Which was why he'd spent his teenaged years in and out of battered women's shelters. His mother would run for help when the bruises scared her enough. But, in the end, she'd always protected Scott's dad. She'd always gone back.

Was still living with the man—in a retirement community in Florida.

Kennedy let out an unladylike burp that Tina figured fit right in with her lifestyle. "Exactly," she said aloud. "And the little one's mother said not to call the authorities. It doesn't sound like she'd cooperate, either."

Scott studied them for a full minute before replying. "Okay, but only for tonight."

She'd won this round.

Whatever happened tomorrow happened tomorrow.

CHAPTER
~❧ FOUR ❧~

Having a baby around again wasn't the worst thing that had ever happened. Anything was better than having a man around, Tina thought as, at a little after nine that evening, she put the infant down in the bed she'd made out of a sofa cushion, a dresser drawer and a cut up and hastily sewn sheet.

She'd done that a time or two before. And all had survived.

With her cell hooked to her hip as she waited for a call to come through from the as-yet-unheard-from Claire Reese, Tina cleaned up the sink from the bath she'd just administered, wiping the trial-size bottle of tear-free baby shampoo that had been one of the many supplies in Kennedy's pink-hearts-and-teddy-bear bag.

There'd been lotion there, too. And powder. And diaper-rash

ointment, though there was no sign of a rash or blemish of any kind anywhere on the baby's soft white skin. Kennedy had come with enough formula for several days. Disposable diapers. Clothes and stuffed cloth rattles.

She'd come with everything but a mom.

At ten after nine there was a rap on her door. A familiar, three-beat sound.

What was he doing here? Tina tried to be surprised. To pretend that she hadn't been expecting him.

Certainly she hadn't needed him.

"Hey," she said, opening her door to her business partner and best friend—the only male who'd ever stepped foot inside the door of her ancient and adored cement home in an older but well-kept burb just outside of Cincinnati. "How'd your meeting go?"

"It's budget time," he said, as if that explained everything. "With state funding cutbacks, we're either going to have to pass an emergency levy or next year's athletes are going to have to pay to play."

Walking down the hall, he glanced at the living room off to the right, peeked into the kitchen, and ended up where she always ended up, the family room at the back of the small house. It had a full wall of windows looking out at an acre of wooded backyard that, at this time of night, was visible due to the landscape lighting she'd installed around the grounds.

The room also had another full wall of books. More textbooks than she'd ever have been assigned had she gone to college. All read.

"She's in the bedroom."

Scott didn't say a word as he headed for Tina's room—the only sleeping room on the ground floor—with Tina right behind him. Nor did he speak as he stood over the baby's temporary crib, positioned in the middle of Tina's king-size mattress, safe from the drafty floor.

She waited until he was ready, and then followed him back out to the family room, after a quick detour to the kitchen. Unscrewing the top of a bottle of beer, she handed it to him before settling into the corner of her favorite chair, while he took his usual spot on the couch, the beer bottle resting against his thigh.

"She's had a bath, so I'm hoping she's out until at least midnight," Tina said.

"We're going to have to do something."

"I think we're doing it." Tina told him about all of the things she'd found in the baby's bag. "There's even a list of the shots she'll need. She's due for a one-month checkup next week, though, of course, no information as to who's already seen her. Still, Claire Reese is a good mother. She obviously loves her kid."

His look was piercing. "She left a newborn baby at a garage with a man she'd never met."

"She left her at the home office of a national chain of mechanic shops that is making news, with the kid's father, who is always in the news. My God, Scott, you're a saint. Big Brothers named you Man of the Year. Who wouldn't want to leave their kid with you? Besides, if what she says is true, she chose the lesser of two evils. Leave the kid someplace she thought Kennedy would be safe, or keep her with her and put her life in danger."

His lack of response didn't surprise her.

"The woman's obviously desperate, Scott. Something we both understand. My guess is she's fully aware of our work with battered women's shelters. She knows that Kennedy will be looked after, if not by us, then by those we know. Hell, at this point, the whole country knows we have contacts. Can't much miss a commendation from the First Lady. And look at all the applications for work we get."

More than seventy-five percent of their hirees came from shelters.

His expression lightened. "The shelter."

"What about it?"

"I'll bet Tonya knows Claire Reese. If Ms. Reese is half the mother you say she is, she'd have checked up on us there."

"It'd be easy enough to do."

"If she came asking, she'd have been referred immediately to Tonya."

"Who would have given glowing recommendations with complete confidentiality." You didn't keep women safe without learning how to keep—and when to tell—secrets.

He stood, leaving the full beer on the side table. "I'm calling her."

"It's Wednesday," Tina reminded him. The one night a week the private shelter owner went down to Kentucky to the little shack on the river to spend the night with the eighty-year-old woman who insisted on living alone in the home she'd shared for almost sixty years with Tonya's father, the love of her life.

The one night a week she left her cell phone behind and refilled an emotional well that gave freely to all who needed sustenance the other six days of the week.

Tonya was one of the lucky ones, raised and nurtured in unconditional love.

"I'll get her in the morning then," Scott said, pacing the seventy-year-old hardwood floor.

Tina nodded, wished he'd sit down.

And when he did, when she saw the troubled look in his eyes, she almost wished he hadn't.

CHAPTER ✦ FIVE ✦

"**I**'m not going to be able to walk away from this."

She'd known that.

"If we don't find her…"

"We will."

"And if we don't, I'm not going to be able to just turn away."

"You don't owe anyone anything here, Scott. You chose to provide a means for someone else to make a choice, to have a child when a biological father was not available. You didn't choose to *be* a father."

Elbows on his knees, he looked over at her. "There's a little person in the other room who is my flesh and blood," he said, his voice muddled with emotion. "You and I both know, far too well, how it feels to grow up unwanted. You can't think, for one second, I'd ever knowingly inflict that fate on someone."

Tina wanted to argue. Needed to argue. But she couldn't. Not about a child's right to belong.

Anything else—rules, regulations, obligations, responsibilities, men—she'd take him on. And win.

But not here.

He knew her too well.

"What are you thinking?" she asked instead.

"The first thing we have to do is find Claire Reese. Who is she? What does she do? Where did she come from? Where does she live? Who does she know?"

"If we're lucky, Tonya will have most if not all of those answers."

"Right. And then, I'm thinking, we go from there."

"Okay."

Some people would be at peace with the plan.

But this was Scott.

"I can't take them in," he said.

"Them?"

"If Claire shows up. I can't take them in."

"Has she asked you to?"

He shot her a look. But she knew he got her point.

"I can't take the baby, Tina. I can't have her in my home."

She had some things to say about that. But had learned a long time ago to pick her times—and her words—with Scott Harbor. Sometimes he was a little slow to learn.

"You're jumping the gun there a bit, cowboy," she said instead. "She has a mother who has no intention of giving her up."

"The same woman who said she'd be back in a matter of hours."

His glance was piercing again. Nothing Tina wasn't used to. "Maybe. She didn't say for sure."

"She said she's in danger. Something could have happened to her. And we're just sitting here."

Tina had thought about that.

"Police don't take missing-person's reports on adults for twenty-four hours," she said. "Especially not one who left of her own accord and indicated she might not be right back. We'll call Tonya in the morning and go from there."

Picking up his beer, Scott drank. And drank again.

He stared out into the dimly lit yard. Ran a hand through hair cut far too short, in Tina's opinion. Loosened his tie. And buttoned and unbuttoned his suit coat.

Tina let him stew—she knew he would regardless—and poked her finger in and out of the rip in her jeans. She really needed to get a new pair or two. But then she'd just have to go through the trouble of wearing them in. Jeans weren't jeans without rips.

And enough washings to make them soft.

"I have a daughter."

"Mmm, hmm."

"I'm not having kids."

"That's what you've always said."

"What do I do now?"

"I figure the first step is you wait around until she wakes up and then you actually touch her. Pick her up. Hold her."

She wouldn't challenge him to feed her. Not yet. She wasn't out to push him over the edge.

"I'm not taking her home with me."

"No one's suggesting you should." Although he should.

"Don't give me that look," he said now, resembling his daughter, with the bottle hanging around his lips. "You think I should just ignore the lessons of my youth, pretend like everything's rosy, and move an entire clan into my home."

"Do I?"

"You think I'm scared."

"Are you?"

"Cut the crap, Tina." His voice was rougher than usual, which made it one notch above soft. "This isn't counseling. And I'm not one of your textbook cases. We've both had enough of that to last us a lifetime."

"It doesn't seem to have helped you much." She hadn't meant to say the words aloud. But he was killing himself.

And she couldn't just sit and watch it happen. Not to him. It hurt too much.

"I am my father's son. No amount of pretty words are going to change that fact."

"You're also your mother's son. And beyond that, there's nothing that says your father's broken synapse has any basis in genetics."

"I know that there's no scientific proof that a tendency to violent outbursts is in any way based in genetics. I wouldn't have donated sperm if I thought there was. But I also know, as you do, that there's a ton of factual evidence pointing to environment as a cause. You know, if he didn't love my mom, then maybe I'd see things differently. If he wasn't truly sorry each and every time he raised his fists in anger, then okay, he's just a jerk. But that's not the case here."

"He has anger issues, Scott. You know that as well as I do."

"And I've been exposed to them since birth."

"Yes, you have. But you don't have irrational mood swings, Scott. You don't experience aggressive actions or outbursts that are out of proportion to the situation."

If he wasn't careful, she was going to start spouting from *Transpersonal Psychiatry*. She'd gotten a full chapter in already that night—in spite of infant interruptus.

"No, but then, I live alone," he argued. "I'm not challenged in my most personal space. Every night I have the opportunity to regroup, to vegetate—to be moodless. I have an emotional escape."

"So did your dad, every time you all came to the shelter. For weeks, even months that one time. His anger didn't stop."

"Maybe because we always went back home."

"Scott, you know as well as I do that there is no scientific basis in your fears. You're a nurturer. A caregiver. Look at the business. It's not there to make us rich—though you've done such a great job we aren't hurting. But your prime goal is to offer things to other people that will make their lives better. You're a lover. And you spend all of your life giving to the masses. You need someone in your home, in your heart of hearts, someone personal, intimate, to give all that love and caring to."

"What I know is that I am my father's son. I could have his bad side in me. I could have some kind of environmentally bred emotional deficiency that just hasn't had the right circumstances to make itself known. There's no guarantee that, if given the right stimulation, I wouldn't raise my hand to a woman I loved."

"There isn't a violent bone in your body."

"You don't know that."

"I've been your best friend since you were fifteen. That makes, what, fifteen years? I've seen you sick drunk, in tears over your mother's broken bones and black eyes. I've seen you fight eviction because of a cat, I've seen you late and tense behind a slow driver. I've seen you get taken by credit card companies, lose your shirt in a casino and watch your sister marry a man who is not much better to her than your father is to your mother. I think I'd know if you were the violent type."

"But the one thing you've never seen—and never will see—is me deeply, personally in love. As long as I can keep a distance between my emotions and the people I'm around, I'm good. You don't see my father beating up on his secretary. Or his boss. Or shooting some guy in a fit of road rage."

"I've heard him let fly with some pretty colorful words over a messed-up pizza order."

"But he didn't throw the pizza."

"Scott..."

"I know what I'm talking about, Tina. I don't experience violent anger because I don't expose myself to any intense emotions. If I were to open up to the depths of love that you're talking about, I'd be opening up to the possibility of its shadow side—and that's a chance I just can't take. Period." His voice was still soft. Calm. And now, also implacable. She'd made him hit his wall.

So she'd shut up for now. But she wouldn't give up. Scott Harbor would kill himself before he'd ever inflict pain on someone else. Somehow she had to find a way to convince him of that fact.

If not now, for Kennedy, then for Scott—and the rest of his life.

He was thirty years old.

And it was time for him to stop running.

CHAPTER
↜ SIX ↝

S cott didn't stay for the midnight feeding. Which was just
as well, because the little patoot didn't wake up until
two—and that was only because Tina shook her slightly
just to make certain that everything was okay.

Kennedy didn't seem to understand what the fuss was about,
but apparently she didn't mind, either, as she happily sucked her
bottle dry, burped twice and fell back to sleep.

Life wasn't as simple for Tina, who hardly slept at all.

But she didn't let it show as she sat in Scott's office the next
morning, after Kennedy's ten-o'clock feeding, listening on the
speakerphone as her partner called the fertility clinic, only to find
that they wouldn't give him any information at all—even when

he told them the woman might be in danger. They suggested he call the police.

Scott's second call was to the woman who'd been part-time mother to both of them during some pretty important years.

"Well, you know I don't give out information about anyone who walks through my door, but because she asked about you, and because it's you, I'll tell you that she was here," Tonya said, speaking to them from her cell phone in her home office. Tonya had people who worked for her who handled the daily operation of the thirty-bed shelter—though she still spent most of her days there, working on fund-raising. "About a month ago."

Claire Reese would have been very obviously pregnant a month ago.

"We need to find her," Scott said, delivering the understatement of the year. He still hadn't even so much as touched his daughter's fingers.

Because he knew if he did, if he had any contact at all, he'd fall irrevocably in love?

Before Tonya could answer, Tina chimed in, giving their housemother-turned-friend the details behind the morning's call—most importantly, the fact that the woman hadn't been in touch and could very well be in danger.

Tonya's reply was instant. "She filled out a form. We might be able to get an accurate address from that."

Of course, you never knew, when you were dealing with frightened and desperate women on the run.

But Tina homed in on something else. "She filled out a form? Was she there as a client?"

"I assumed so. She was obviously nervous, kept looking over her shoulder as though she expected someone to come barging in at any minute."

"What did she say about Scott?"

"She just asked about him as she was leaving—said she'd read the Man of the Year article about him last year, in which he'd mentioned the shelter. She wanted to know if he was really as decent as he'd sounded."

Scott's expression impassive, he said, "And you told her I was hardheaded and stubborn, right?"

"I told her you were my hero." Tonya's comeback was matter-of-fact. "Meet me at the clinic and we'll see what we can find on her. And bring that little one with you," she added. "I want to meet the daughter of the most decent man alive."

To which Scott rolled his eyes.

TONYA'S INFORMATION WAS scant. An apartment building, whose manager was certain he'd had no tenants named Claire—nor had any tenants who recently had a baby.

Which was about the only description they had on the missing woman.

She'd left no phone number.

"I'm calling the police," Scott said as the two of them, with Kennedy strapped into her baby carrier in the backseat of his Lexus, drove back to Jiffy Jobs just before noon. "I have a note saying that I'm the baby's father. That ought to get us the right to hold on to her for a few days—until we can get this all sorted out."

Us. Did that mean Tina?

Or had Scott suddenly been cured of his aversion to caring for the child he still hadn't touched?

"Or they could take her...."

"Only until a paternity test is done."

Studying him as he drove, Tina wished she could erase the pinched lines from his mouth, his eyes.

Wished she could remove the clamps from his heart.

"And then what?"

He glanced her way and then back to the road. "I don't know."

"Say you call the cops and they leave her with you. You taking her home?"

"No."

Uh-huh.

"Who is?"

He looked over at her again.

"Amy?" His secretary, Jean, was out, since her abusive husband was still in the picture.

"Tina."

"What?"

"You know you aren't going to ditch me here. We both know that."

"You could still ask."

"Like you asked me to take on your dad's garage, your dream of owning a nationwide chain of affordable mechanic shops, and make it reality?"

He had her there. "I helped."

"Helped! You're the majority of the business, we both know that. You work harder than anyone I know. That's not the point."

"What is the point?"

"You didn't ask for my help. You just knew you had it. You always have. And you always will."

It wasn't something to sneeze at. Or play around with.

"We'll need to get some kind of bassinet," she said, sharing the number one item on the list already prepared in her back pocket. "Something with wheels that we can move from room to room."

No more babies in her life were going to grow up in drawers, as though there wasn't really a place for them in the world.

"Fine."

"And I want baby washcloths—mine are too rough on her skin."

"Okay."

She rattled off another five gotta haves, including a bath that would fit in the kitchen sink.

"Done."

"You're footing the bill," she told him as they pulled into the lot behind Jiffy Jobs, in spite of the fact that they both knew she'd give him the shirt off her back if he needed it.

"I wouldn't have it any other way."

SCOTT MIGHT THINK HE had it made, foisting off his kid on her, but the minute she heard the police officer ask him if he wanted to keep the child while they located her mother, and heard him answer in the affirmative, she knew she had him.

The baby might be an inconvenience. She might even be the cause of a bad week. But Tina also now saw that little Kennedy was going to be the reason for Scott's crash into real life. The catalyst that forced him over the edge of nonentity into the land of the living.

She didn't need one of her psychology texts to tell her that.

Kennedy Ann, all seven pounds of her, was going to push her daddy on to love and off Tina's to-do list.

A few sleepless nights were worth getting that worry off her chest.

Which was why she was feeling so cheerful as she and Scott, with Kennedy in tow, set off for the baby-supply store at quitting time on Thursday afternoon.

And why she couldn't seem to work up much irritation when the little rat decided to wake up in the middle of the venture and cried for the next hour straight—through checkout, the drive home and what should have been dinnertime, but who could eat?

"Maybe we should take her to emergency," Scott said, pacing in her family room again, watching as Tina rocked the distressed baby.

"Don't be ridiculous," Tina retorted, laying Kennedy down and rubbing her tummy as another wave of vigorous wails ensued. "She doesn't have a temperature. She's been eating fine. And she hasn't had a dirty diaper since she's been here. She's constipated. My guess is her mother breast-fed her and the sudden switch to formula is playing havoc with her system."

Scott grabbed his keys off the mantel.

"Where you going?" If he thought he was going to leave her alone with this, he was sadly mistaken. This was his lesson. His chance to get cured from the ramifications of watching his old man use his mother for a punching bag.

"To get some prune juice," he said. "We can dilute it to half-strength with water and give it to her slowly. I remember my mother using it on my sister."

Or Tina could just rub the baby's stomach enough to help stimulate the natural flow that would eventually take place. But stop Scott from actively loving his daughter, even from afar? Not on her life.

CHAPTER
∽SEVEN∽

"**A**re you going to call your mother? Let her know that she has a granddaughter?"

It was late. After midnight. Kennedy, asleep in her new bassinet, should be waking up soon. She'd been out a couple of hours. Tina had been reluctant to give the baby prune juice, but hadn't wanted to hurt Scott's feelings. Luckily, the tummy rubbing had produced the desired results—in impressive quantities—before he'd returned from the store.

"Not yet." Wearing an expression that was half frown, half speculation, Scott lay back against the corner of the couch, one leg on the floor. He'd lost the suit coat, but still had on his belt and wing-tip shoes. "Why get her all worked up until I know what's going on? She'll just worry. Or get her hopes up."

"She'd give you support as you figure out what to do."

"I know what to do."

Sure he did. That's why he looked so disturbed and lost.

"What's that?"

"Find the child's mother and give her back. And then make certain that the two of them stay safe and have all the money they need."

Uh-huh. Okay. For now.

"Are you going to ask for a paternity test?" Tina had changed into black-and-white-checked flannel pants and her favorite T-shirt—black with white lettering proclaiming that she lived in her own little world, but that was okay because she liked it there.

"Makes sense to do so, wouldn't you say?"

"Yeah. If Claire is gone for good, you're going to have to prove paternity to get custody. And if the mother does return, it makes sense, before you shell out a bunch of money, to make sure she's your kid. I mean, we're rich and all, but even you can't afford to support every fatherless kid in the city, you know?"

He looked over at her. "Do you think she's mine?"

There was that damned vulnerable look again. It had hooked her fifteen years ago. And every time she'd seen it since. "How do I know?"

"Gut reaction, Tina," he said. "You're on, ninety percent of the time."

"She's here, isn't she?"

"Are you mad at me?"

"Why would I be mad? I offered to keep her. It's not like this is all new to me. I told you I could take care of her in my sleep."

"I meant for donating sperm."

The tacos he'd brought home with the prune juice were in danger of repeating on her. Or that's what she was going to call the sudden tightness in her chest.

"It's absolutely none of my business what you do with your sperm."

"You think it was a dumb idea."

"Did I say that?"

"You didn't say anything and that usually means you don't agree."

Or it meant that she was not going there.

"I'm not mad."

"But you think it was dumb."

"No." And then, because she knew him well enough to know when he wasn't going to let go, she added, "It's never dumb to try and make something better."

"Yeah, well, I think it was stupid as hell," he said. "I was so busy thinking about saving women from abusive men, providing them with a way to fill the very natural drive to procreate, without making them beholden to any man—so that they wouldn't feel pressured to marry and maybe make a dangerous choice—that I didn't think about the other side."

"What other side?"

"Filling the world with kids without dads, kids with mothers who aren't able to take care of them."

"Most women who can afford in vitro fertilization and who make the decision to have children as single parents are in a position to be able to take care of the children. Seems like most women who would go through that alone would have to really want those children to willingly put themselves through all the difficulties, financial and otherwise."

"What about you?"

His gaze was too close. Too personal. The lights were low. His legs long and lean and...

This was Scott. He wasn't a guy. He was just Scott.

"What about me?"

"You're great with kids, Tina. Look at you tonight. You knew exactly what to do with that baby. It's clear that you're a natural mother."

Whoa. Nope. Not going there. "Knowing how to do something because you were forced to learn how in no way makes you a natural at it."

"That tough exterior works with everyone else—" Scott's voice was soft, far too tender "—but it doesn't fool me. You've got a huge heart, my friend. And an affinity for children."

"I have an affinity for cars. And books."

"What are you afraid of? You'll never be your mother. Or mine. You've already proved that."

"I'm not afraid of anything."

"Your dad was a mean, angry bully. You were the oldest and took the brunt of his brutality, but…"

"My mother took the brunt of it. The man only hit me once." But she and Scott both knew how many times Walt Randolph's anger had erupted around Tina, how many times she'd had to protect herself and her siblings from flying materials—flying anything within the jerk's reach when he was in a rage. In the olden days, Tina used to talk to Scott about such things.

Nowadays she just forgot about them.

"What about Ronald? How many times did he get away with roughing you up?"

"Once." When she was eighteen, she'd agreed to marry him. He'd agreed to let the little ones live with him. She'd thought she'd loved him. He'd changed her mind. End of story.

"Exactly."

"What?"

"You aren't going to put up with abuse."

"I know that. I told you, I'm not afraid."

"Then why are you alone?"

"Because I like it."

"I don't believe that. I watched you growing up, remember? You were in your element when someone needed you. I'd forgotten that look you used to get on your face when you were caring for one of the little ones. Until tonight."

"You're imagining a look." She was certain about that. "I spent my youth being a mother, Scott. From the time I was old enough to have a coherent thought of my own I was taking care of people—my mother included. I did it because I had to—and, yes, because I love them. But it wasn't because I wanted to. Or had some nurturing talent that drove me. If I didn't look out for them, we'd have all ended up dead.

"Do you have any idea how good it feels now to be able to come home and just be? I can actually listen to the thoughts in my own head. Eat what and when I want to eat. Or not eat if I don't want to. I can take a bath without anyone pounding on the door. Or read and not have to repeat the page six times before I get what it says. Mostly, I don't have to be alert, on edge, every single second that I'm home."

Well, she did sort of, with Kennedy around, but that was different. Probably because it was only for a few days.

"For the first eighteen years of my life I didn't even know what it meant to relax. I crave peace, Scott. I thought you, of all people, would understand that."

"Of course I understand that. And everything else you're saying. But sharing your life with someone and living without the residual effects of abusive outbursts aren't exactly mutually exclusive."

"Yeah, so why are *you* still alone?"

That stopped him. Something had to.

"Living responsibly with a possible built-in time bomb is far different from letting an abusive past rob you of your future."

"My future stretches before me, oh, wise one. Just because it's not colored with your crayon doesn't mean it doesn't exist."

"Yeah, like your own little world?" he asked, nodding toward her shirt. "You think I don't know that you wear that to shut people out? Because you're afraid to let them in?"

"I wear it because I like my world, even though it's not the same as everyone else's, and I don't feel like I have to apologize for that."

"Are you happy, Tina?" How such tired eyes could suddenly appear so alert, she had no idea. And she didn't like it. His piercing looks, his trespassing into emotional places that hadn't been shared with him in years were making her uncomfortable. "Or are you just content to settle?"

"If I'm content, what does it matter?"

"If you aren't being honest with yourself, it matters a lot. Your life, which you pride yourself on being so stable, might just be based on lies and perched on sinking sand instead of the rock you claim."

Okay, he'd crossed a line there. "Where do you get off talking to me like that? At least I *am* content. You're so busy staying busy just so you don't have time to see how unhappy you really are."

"I'm not unhappy."

"Oh, no?"

"No." He looked her straight in the eye. And almost convinced her.

"Then what are you?"

"Truthfully?"

This was her chance to check out. To return their relationship to the conveyer-belt steadiness that had somehow come to define them.

But Tina was not—had never been—a runner.

CHAPTER
~EIGHT~

"**Y**eah. I want to know the truth."

"Truthfully, I'm running in that sinking sand you're perched on."

"Because no matter what, you aren't going to be able to walk away from Kennedy? Assuming she's your daughter."

"Partially."

"There's more?"

She'd never seen that look in his eye. She didn't want to see it now. It was wrong. Threatening.

And she couldn't look away.

"I…it felt…right, watching you with that baby tonight. Relying on you to care for my daughter. I knew you could. And more, I knew you would."

She could handle that. "Thank you."

"It gave me a view of you I've never seen as an adult before."

"Get off it, Harbor, you've seen a kid on my hip from the first day you met me." That long-ago time it had been her six-month-old sister. Who was now sixteen and living with Tina's mom and another woman in San Francisco. She had three brothers out there, as well. And another sister...someplace. She heard from all of them whenever they were short on money. Or needed advice.

Tina had been cursed from birth with some kind of natural emotional intelligence. Or maybe her family members were all just naturally emotionally stupid.

"You aren't making this easy." Scott studied her. If their status quo was going to change, life was not good. "I'm...hell, Tina, I'm losing it here. I look at you and suddenly I...feel things. Things I shouldn't be feeling. What we've got going—it's great. I don't want to blow that."

"Then don't."

"Tell that to my emotions."

A peculiar restlessness descended on her groin area.

Oh, God. Please. No.

"Don't go getting all squirrelly on me, Scott. It's late. The day's been weird. This whole situation's weird. You're in shock. And I'm safe. That's all. What you think you're feeling, it's not real. It'll be gone in the morning. You'll see."

"How do you know?"

"I just do. This is us, Scott. If there was going to be some flaring attraction between us, it would've happened when we were sixteen or seventeen and driven by pubescent hormones."

He shook his head. "You never had time for puberty," he reminded her. "You were too busy being a mother to five younger siblings, keeping them, and yourself, out of your father's path. And working almost full-time in his garage, too."

"Okay, but it's not me who's supposedly having these feelings now, either."

"You sure about that?"

"Completely."

"So why are you shredding the fringe on that afghan your mother made for you?"

Looking down, Tina saw the pile of yarn fuzzies she'd created. And stopped. "Because this is strange, that's why."

"Why won't you look me in the eye?"

"I don't like what I see there?"

"Why not?"

She glanced up, getting mad again. Which was good. Anger kept every other feeling at bay. "I want my friend back. Not this...this...guy sitting there looking at me like I'm, I don't know..."

"Desirable?"

"Scott, stop!" Glancing at the bassinet again, she marveled at the baby's ability to sleep through ruckus. But then, Kennedy had had practice in the garage for the past two days.

And what about the first three weeks of her life? Her mother was in danger. Had there been violence in her home? In spite of Scott's attempt to provide women with the opportunity to have children without having to resort to men who didn't treat them well?

"You aren't the settling kind," she reminded him, diverting the conversation before something irrevocable took place. "We have a business together. And a friendship that I value more than anything else in my life. Don't mess that up."

Sitting forward, his elbows on his knees, Scott grew more serious—and more in control.

"That's what I'm talking about," he told her. "Our friendship *is* the rock on which my life is built."

The words sent a bolt to her heart. He'd never told her that outright.

"And now I'm suddenly seeing it in danger—threatened by feelings I don't want, but can't seem to make go away."

"You said they'd only been there since tonight," Tina reminded him.

"I only recognized them tonight."

"How long have they been there?"

"I don't know."

When she scoffed, he continued. "I mean it. I really don't know. It's something that's been coming gradually, I guess."

No way.

"And you're right. I'm not ever going to settle down to a committed one-on-one relationship, or marry. And anything casual between us would ruin everything that matters most between us."

At least he had that much right.

"Then let's just stop this talk. Right now."

"I'd love to," he said, shaking his head. "But one thing I know about sexual desire is that it's most dangerous when ignored. It hangs there, insidiously waiting to creep up on you. If you don't meet it head-on, it'll make some surprise attack, catching you at your lowest moment and explode all over you."

"Meaning we'll get drunk some night and end up in bed." She couldn't believe she'd said that. Not to Scott.

"Possibly."

Waiting for the fear, the revulsion to calm the butterflies in her belly, to stop the flow of feeling to private places, Tina thought hard about what he was saying. Tried harder to chase him away. And the more she focused, the more the heat within her continued to spread.

"We won't," she finally said, because it was the only thing she could say.

"I'd believe that if you could convince me that you have not one iota of desire for me."

"I don't."

"I'm not convinced."

"What am I supposed to do, Scott?" Tina asked, too agitated to choose her words carefully. "Kiss you and burst out laughing?"

"Come sit next to me."

"No."

"Why?"

"I never sit next to you."

"Now you're scared."

"No, I'm smart."

"Then come over here. Sit next to me."

"Scott, stop this."

"I'm making a point here, Tina. This is me. Scott. Your best friend. We've shared every bad memory we've ever had—and most of the good ones, too. We even share a bank account. But you're afraid to sit next to me. You know I won't hurt you, so you have to be afraid of something else. Something that might happen if you get too close. And it's that that's got me worried. It's that kind of thing that makes us a walking time bomb around each other."

"Scott!" With another quick glance at the bassinet, Tina lowered her voice one more time. "What's the matter with you? You're going to mess up the only great thing either of us has going."

"Or maybe we're already messing it up." The continued seriousness in his tone slowed her down. And panicked her at the same time.

"What if there's more here, Tina, and we're both so scarred we aren't seeing it?"

"There isn't more."

"Are you sure?"

She tried to hold his gaze. She tried really hard. She didn't want to do this. Didn't want to open hearts and get all messy. She was here to help him take his heart elsewhere.

"Come, sit next to me. Just sit. Tell me that you don't feel anything from my nearness and I'll be convinced that I'm just in shock. And you're safe. Because mark my words, Tina, if there's some kind of latent force here working on us, and we ignore it and some night, as you say, end up in bed together, then our friendship really will be ruined. Our entire relationship will be ruined. Because I will never ever be able to do right by you."

She couldn't afford to hear the sense in his words. She was tired. Overwrought. Who knew what crazy things she might feel tonight. She had a baby in her home. His baby.

"I'm not coming over there. Not tonight. It's late. You need to get home. We have to work in the morning."

"I'm not leaving."

He was pushing too hard.

"Yes, you are. This is my home and I say you're leaving."

"And that's my daughter—at least we think it is—and she's had a rough evening, and if she's going to keep you awake all night, or worse, need medical care, I'm going to be here to help you."

Tina wanted to remind him that he didn't have a toothbrush or anything to sleep in, but he did. He'd stayed over before, in the spare room, when she'd had the flu. And the night they'd done the *Godfather* trilogy.

And on Christmas Eve a few times.

And...

"Come," he said. "Sit. That's all."

She couldn't.

But she wanted to.

And that scared Tina most of all.

CHAPTER
❧ NINE ❧

She barely slept. And her lack of rest had very little to do with the baby sleeping soundly in the bassinet next to her bed. Kennedy woke her every three hours. Tina's racing thoughts kept her up most of the rest of the long night. She'd told Scott that she wouldn't try his little experiment that particular night. But she'd agreed that she would sit with him the next night after work, just to prove her point and get him to shut up and quit worrying about things that weren't there, and to get things back to normal with them so they could deal with the baby.

Between Kennedy's eight- and ten-o'clock feedings—if they still had the baby—they were going to watch a movie, her choice. And sit together on her couch.

The whole thing was stupid. Asinine.

But he did have a point. If she felt nothing for Scott in "that" way, why was she having such a hard time sitting next to him?

The fact that he'd brought the discrepancy to her attention didn't endear him to her.

Hell, she should be able to sit on his lap without any reaction. Right?

And she probably could. They were making a big deal out of nothing. She was letting him psyche her out.

She'd probably fall asleep during the movie.

She'd have a better chance of it if she could keep herself awake the rest of the night.

The sheet beneath Kennedy rustled. The baby was waking. Tina had her up and changed, with a nipple in her mouth, before the infant ever made a sound. No point in risking another encounter with Scott that night.

Tomorrow would be soon enough.

SHE AVOIDED HIM AT WORK on Friday—mostly because he was out, at another meeting with the investors who were trying to get them to take Jiffy Jobs public. Something they weren't going to do.

And Tina was in the garage, being harder on Justin than he deserved, dismantling a '72 Ford F-150 and feeding the infant, who was never more than five feet away from her in spite of Jean's continued offers to take the baby off Tina's hands.

The kid was Scott's problem. And hers. Not the employees'.

But far too soon, and in spite of Tina's efforts to keep the tiny girl awake that night, she found herself moving in slow motion as she slid a DVD into the player. He'd said it was her choice.

She'd chosen *The Truman Show*. An oldie but goodie. It was all about independence. Following your own course even if it meant going against every single person you'd ever known. And it was a comedy.

Not intimate. Not romantic. Not intense.

"Good afternoon, good evening and good night." The movie's best-known and oft-repeated line ran through her mind.

Where would she be, a couple of hours from now, when Jim Carrey issued that climaxing line for the last time?

"Quit stalling, Randolph, and get over here. Let's just get this done."

He'd changed into jeans. A lot less yielding than the fabric business slacks were made of. And a blue corduroy shirt that was buttoned all the way to his throat.

She'd left her Jiffy Job shirt on. With her oldest pair of jeans. Hopefully she smelled like grease.

She wasn't going to feel anything for Scott, that was a given, but it didn't hurt to take out insurance.

Nor did she ask him if his ailment of the night before was still present. She'd just assume any attraction he'd thought he felt for her had faded.

This little experiment was merely a safeguard—convincing both of them, once and for all, that they had nothing to worry about on that score.

"You want something to drink?"

Scott held up the bottle of water he'd brought in from the dinner table. They'd had seven-layer salad. Only because she had to use up the red onion in her refrigerator. And because she could use garlic.

When she caught herself ready to wring her hands together, Tina went to get a bottle of water. And thought about putting a shot of Scotch in it. She probably would have if there'd been no baby to see to in a couple of hours.

"Sit." Scott's command came as soon as she reentered the room. He patted the spot on the couch next to him with a touch of impatience.

And that's when she really understood that this was every bit as hard on him as it was on her.

Tina sat.

"GOOD AFTERNOON, GOOD evening and good night." She'd made it to the first delivery of the famous line. Which meant they were through the opening credits, and the scene where Jim Carrey, Truman, talked to himself in the bathroom mirror while he was getting ready in the morning.

Making a fool of himself.

Which she was not going to do.

"How you doing?" Scott's voice was a little too physical. Only because she wasn't used to it being so close.

"Fine."

Of course her nerves would be on edge. She'd worked herself up. Over nothing.

She'd ask him on the next break how he was doing. Maybe.

"Good afternoon. Good evening. And good night." Another day for Truman.

The same night for her. Scott moved and she tensed, ready to bolt. He'd uncapped his water. Was taking a sip.

That was okay.

"Good afternoon. Good evening. And good night." How many times did Truman actually say that line before the final time? She hadn't remembered it being this many. Or the movie being so long.

And why had she thought the story was funny? It was sad…horrible what they were doing to such a nice guy. Every single person he knew was playing with him. Playing him.

People instilled fears just to control and manipulate him.

They pretended to love him.

She'd never pretended to care for Scott. Her affection for him had been real from the very beginning. The first day they'd met,

at the Chrysalis Center, there'd been something about him standing there—so male and yet so real. Hurting. A victim just like
her. And tough, too, as his mother had checked them in.

He'd watched his mother like a hawk. As if he'd kill anyone
who got anywhere near her. Or the bruises covering her slim,
well-dressed body.

"You okay?"

Tina jumped. Tried to figure out where they were in the
movie. "Yeah. Fine." She'd make everything that way. It's what she
did.

"Tina, the whole point of this exercise is to find out, honestly,
where we stand. What we're facing. What dangers lurk that we
need to confront."

"I know that."

"Denial is not welcome here."

She wanted to argue. Opened her mouth to argue. And saw
what denial was doing to Truman. And, in another way, to the
man sitting next to her. If he didn't come out of his own denial,
thinking he could never have a family of his own, he could very
well lose the daughter that was here to save him.

If admitting a thing or two would help him—things that they
were going to deal with, not give in to; things that weren't anything *to* give in to—then that's what she had to do.

She was Tina Randolph. She'd handled challenges much worse
than this one. With aplomb. Always with aplomb.

"I'm just feeling a bit jumpy, is all," she told him. "This is weird, sitting so close to you."

"I've seen you sit this close to your brothers."

"I changed their diapers."

"Not in the last ten years. Not since they became young men."

This wasn't working. "What about you?" she asked, taking a chance that he'd noticed her lack of allure. "You seem to be completely unaffected by all of this and since you were the one we were most concerned about…"

He grabbed her hand, put it over his racing heart. "Guess again."

Face flaming, she stared at the tips of the tennis shoes she changed into every night at the garage after work, wishing she could wipe away every ounce of feeling at the moment.

Needing to obliterate the flood of answering sensation inside her.

Scott's heart was beating fast and hard. For her.

Something was happening on the television set. Rushing water. Or white noise. Or maybe that sound was from inside her…

"Tell me you feel nothing." His voice sounded strangled.

"I…I…" She tried. She really, really tried. "Can't."

CHAPTER
～ TEN ～

"Okay." Tina was sitting on the opposite end of the couch, facing Scott. Truman had just tried to leave the island by boat. Because he'd been asked to do so. By people who knew that he couldn't.

They were showing him his weakness.

Because he'd dared to defy them. To ask questions. He'd dared to refuse to live by the status quo just because.

They were taking away his power so he'd remain in theirs.

She knew because she heard part of the scene. She wasn't looking at it. Her gaze was on a best friend gone man.

"Okay, what?" Scott didn't look any happier than she felt.

"It's just proximity," she said. "Because of the baby and all." A baby who could wake up anytime, as far as Tina was concerned. But who wasn't due to eat for another hour at least. "We're thrown together in an intense situation where we're acting like parents. Sharing the responsibility of caring for a child. Of course we'd naturally turn to each other."

"For a hug, maybe. Or reassurance. But an attraction?"

He was right. Maybe more right than he knew.

"So maybe it is just an attraction."

His eyes narrowed. "Meaning?"

"How long's it been since you've, you know, done anything with a woman?"

"Six months. Maybe a little more."

Before Christmas. Long before they'd spent the best Christmas Eve of her life here, at her house, just the two of them.

"And for me, well, we both know the answer to that—"

"No, we both don't," Scott interrupted. "I know about Ronald, but that was twelve years ago. Since then you've been remarkably discreet."

Would the indignities of this night never end?

"I've been remarkably celibate," she said dryly, finding no sense in playing coy at this point.

He shifted. Leaned forward, looking briefly back at her over his shoulder. And then seemed inordinately interested in his hands. "You're trying to tell me that Ronald's the only man you've ever slept with?"

"I'm not trying. I *am* telling you." And then, before he could make her feel like even more of a freak by making a big deal of her announcement, she added, "Which is why I think this is only some kind of weird attraction that's just going to go away. We've been together a lot. This whole baby thing has us both kind of freaked out. All of our emotions are out of whack. We're adults with adult…you know, and neither of us has been involved for a while. Who could blame us for going a little haywire?"

He seemed to be pondering that. Truman's dead dad had come back to life on the show now. He'd returned as a homeless man on a bus.

Or had the maker brought him back to further confuse Truman?

"If we go with this theory, if we accept that it's just proximity and a lack of involvement with anyone else, what do we do about it?"

"Ignore it until it goes away."

He shifted. She couldn't look at him, afraid of what she'd see.

"Do you think you can?" he asked.

Not at the moment. But give her time. She could do most things she put her mind to.

"Because let me tell you, I don't think I can. You're all I've thought about all day. First thing in the morning. After working out. Sitting fully dressed at the kitchen table, eating peanut butter and jelly sandwiches."

Tina gulped. "You got any ideas what to do about it?" She tried to handle this with calm. Strength. And was shocked to hear the squeaky tone to her voice.

Tina was not a squeaky woman. Ever.

Hell, she was sitting there in ripped jeans and a greasy-smelling garage shirt. She'd have left the grease under her fingernails if not for the baby she had to feed and change.

Because Kennedy's father had yet to touch his daughter.

"I think we should be together and just get it over with and out of our systems." Scott's pronouncement shocked the thought right out of her.

"It's not like we can stay away from each other," he continued, sounding so damned in control when she was jumping out of her skin. "Not only is there the current situation to consider, but we're business partners. And we have season tickets to the Reds games."

Oh, right. There was that. She couldn't see either of them giving up their Reds tickets. Crazy as it seemed, the thought was reassuring somehow.

"If we ignore this, let it go, chances are it's going to come back and bite us."

"Probably after a Reds game," she had to agree, "a win." She expanded on the idea. "We would have had too much beer..."

"Right."

"And then we'd be out of control and would hate ourselves in the morning."

"But if we do it now," he stated, "we're in control. We decide when, and we stay in control, and when it's done, we go on with our lives."

"Because nothing would have changed, really," she said. "We both know the score. We're doing each other a favor. That's all."

"A favor. I like that."

She did, too. When she wasn't panicking. Or anticipating.

"In all honesty," he said, leaning back as though not in a hurry now that they'd decided to tackle their problem head-on, "have you ever thought about me in that way?"

"That's not a question a gentleman asks a lady."

"Then I guess it's good this is just me and you—no gentlemen or ladies present."

Thank God. He was still Scott.

"In all honesty, of course I have," she said. And every single time, she'd chastised herself and moved on.

Usually underneath a car. To things she could control. Things she could make do what she wanted them to do. Things she could succeed at.

Chances were she was going to disappoint him in the bedroom. He had a lot of experience—with women who knew the score.

Which was a good thing. As quickly as it had begun, this phase of their relationship would fizzle out and they could get on with the business of being best friends for life.

"So we just decided to have a one-time physical fling."

"Yep."

"Tonight."

"Seems as good a time as any."

"I think so, too."

He didn't move.

Neither did she.

"Good afternoon. Good evening. And good night."

The movie had ended.

And Kennedy started to cry.

CHAPTER
❧ ELEVEN ❧

W hile Tina changed Kennedy's diaper and resnapped the footed onesie, thinking all the while about seeing the infant's daddy naked, Scott heated the baby's formula.

"Check it," he said as he brought it into the family room, where she sat with the newborn. She did. The temperature was perfect, as was the amount. Just as she'd known it would be.

Just as he would be. And she wasn't.

She handed the bottle back to him.

"What's this for?"

"You're going to feed your daughter."

Scott set the bottle on the table beside her. "Not tonight I'm not," he said. "I will tomorrow." He sounded just a tad impatient.

And was staring at her. Hard.

Tomorrow, he'd said. After he'd seen Tina without clothes on. Touched her privately. "You promise?"

Not once, in the fifteen years they'd been friends, had Scott ever broken a promise to her.

"Scott?"

"All right, I promise." He didn't sound happy about it.

Tina didn't particularly care.

SHE TRIED TO LET Kennedy take all the time she needed. Tried not to imagine what it was going to feel like to be with Scott. Tried not to be nervous. Or worry that she might get hurt.

She tried not to want him. Or to think about how much she might like being with him.

And when Kennedy started to doze off before her bottle was empty—something she'd done during every other nighttime feeding, always to wake up again in a matter of seconds—Tina nudged the baby, keeping her awake so they could finish the business at hand and get the little girl back in bed.

It wasn't that she couldn't wait to go lie down with Scott. It was just that she wanted to get this whole ordeal over with. Put it behind them.

Move on with living their lives.

Right up until Scott's daughter was fast asleep in her bassinet and Tina was leading the way down the hall to her bedroom. Then she felt like a sacrificial virgin.

She stopped just short of the door, turning around. "Are you sure—"

"Tina, unless you're having second thoughts about the advisability of this, get in there and let's get this done."

Well, when he put it like that, like they were doing a chore, the coming activity sounded a whole lot better. More manageable.

In her room, she wasn't so sure. Did she just get undressed? Get in her bed and wait?

"Do you have protection?" Seemed like the thing any modern, reasonable woman would ask. She sure didn't have birth control.

He pulled out his wallet. "Never travel without one," he said.

She'd turned on one light—figuring the dim glow would hide important things.

Like the fact that her upper arm muscles were too big. And her legs too skinny and short. She had freckles on her tummy. And...

"Let me help you." Scott was there, his hands on the bottom of the shirt she'd been holding on to for dear life.

Tina stumbled. Turned away. "I need to shower." Suddenly, greasy didn't seem as great a hygiene choice as it had earlier in the evening.

"Me, too." He was right behind her.

That wasn't a good idea. At all. Showering together was so…personal.

But if he didn't join her, he might stand outside the glass shower door in the bathroom adjoining her bedroom and watch her.

She turned on the water. Just like every other time she'd showered in the past five years. Grabbed a towel from the linen closet and tossed it to him.

And stood there. How did you shower with a guy you'd never even kissed?

For that matter, how did you shower with a guy, anyway? Certain things would get in the way. Like the view.

Scott was wearing a T-shirt.

She should have known. Scott always wore T-shirts. Even in the middle of summer. To catch the sweat. And in the winter to insulate. They'd had a discussion about it once, while at a Reds game, when the guy with the ticket in the seat next to her showed up with wet stains under his arms.

Scott had switched seats with her.

The last time she'd seen Scott's chest, he'd been about sixteen. They'd gone swimming at a public pool as part of a Chrysalis Center Memorial Day outing.

He'd looked sixteen then. He didn't now.

Tina had no idea what to do about that. Except stare.

The piece of art was coming closer, close enough to touch. Close enough to touch her. He was warm against her, making her hot. Until she started moving. And couldn't stop. Rubbing her nose, her lips, against his chest, Tina made no decision to start kissing. She just did it.

On some level she knew the water was running. That the hot water was going to run out.

She wasn't sure why that mattered.

And then, when she was settling in, happy to remain with her face traveling her best friend's chest for the rest of her days, he pulled her chin up, giving her a brief glimpse of an unfamiliar blaze in his eyes before he lowered his mouth to hers.

TINA THOUGHT SHE WAS in complete control until she ended up back in the bedoom with no clear idea how she got there. She'd never taken a shower, though the water was no longer running.

"God, Tina, you are far more than I ever imagined."

"I haven't done anything yet." But she was going to, wasn't she?

"Oh, sweetie, just kissing you is amazing. It's like I recognize you."

That sounded serious. And this was just a chore. Something that had to be done so they could move on. She remembered that very clearly.

"You kiss good, too."

And as he took her in his arms, standing there almost fully clothed, the blinders came off and she knew that everything she was, everything she would ever be, had always been his.

CHAPTER
~TWELVE~

They had to talk. Staring at Kennedy's baby cheeks, trying to decipher the thoughts behind those big blue eyes, Tina felt the prick of tears in her own.

She couldn't remember the last time she'd cried. Maybe when her father died and she knew that the legacy of his pain would be with her forever. But she hadn't shed any tears at his funeral. Or for him.

She wouldn't give him that much of herself. He'd already stolen far more than he'd ever had the right to have.

And now she'd given everything she'd had left, all of the heart and soul she'd managed to keep alive in spite of her father's abuse, to a man who would never ever love her back.

Who was she kidding? Scott had had her all along. She'd just managed to fool herself into thinking that she was alone by choice. Her choice.

"Hey, baby, what's going on?"

His voice, coming out of the darkness, shamed her. This wasn't what he'd signed on for—a weak idiot who'd broken her word, who'd fallen for him.

Head down, she knew she had to get ahold of herself. They'd done it. An hour ago. It was over now.

She couldn't entangle him. She'd lose him.

And he'd lose himself.

She heard him moving now, from the door to the couch, where she sat, feeding his daughter.

"Tina? What's going on, sweetie?" His words made it nearly impossible to be strong. And when he knelt on the floor beside her, the tears came with even more force.

"Don't call me that." She sounded like a shrew. A wet one.

He sat back. "Why? What's going on?"

"I'm not your sweetie. I'm me. Tina."

"I know who you are."

Realizing there was no point in trying to hide the obvious, Tina glanced up at him, his eyes more shadowed than clear in the soft light from the one lamp she'd turned on. "I don't think you do know," she said, strengthened by the clear and confident tone in her voice.

At least that was hers.

"You're regretting what we did."

"Darn straight I am."

He stood, and she knew he was going to leave her, in spite of the fact that it was his daughter, not hers, clutching her robe as she suckled robustly from the bottle in her mouth.

Part of Tina, the sane, survivor part, wanted him to leave.

He sat down beside her.

"I'm not regretting it," he said, with a note of defiance that might have been comical. If they'd been sixteen. "At least, not yet."

Of course he wasn't. He'd gotten what he came for. Was cured. Could go on. While she was facing an honesty she could have done without. Funny, all along she'd thought she'd been in control—choosing her life, making it what she wanted it to be, rather than allowing it to be taken from her, as her father had done to all of them. Instead, she'd been burying her head in the sand just as her mother had done all those years. She'd been in denial about what was really going on.

She was her mother's daughter, after all.

The thought made her sick.

Kennedy released her grip on the nipple. Lifting the infant to her shoulder, Tina patted the tiny back as despair raged through her.

Here she'd thought she was free, with an entire life of possibility stretched before her, when in truth, she was more trapped than she'd ever been. In her youth the traps had been mostly physical, circumstantial, surface—a matter of money and responsibility. Tonight she knew her spirit was trapped in a love that had no beginning. No end. But no in between, either.

He was watching her. Trying to figure her out. He might as well give up. He wasn't going to get this one.

"Talk to me."

"I can't."

"Tina, this is just what we were trying to avoid. Okay, so maybe the experiment didn't work for you. That's fine. But let's talk about it. Don't let it ruin us."

"Did it work for you?" Was she out of his system? His desire for her gone as if it had never been?

God, where had this…this *woman* come from? She'd gone from nationally known mechanic to simpering, needy, insecure wench in the space of an hour.

Far too high a price to pay.

"Not if it gets me this, a best friend who won't even look at me."

But otherwise he was cured?

Kennedy still had half a bottle to go, and after a burp that was bigger than she was, accepted the nipple greedily.

Tina fed her. Because that's what Tina did. She took care of others. Lord knew, she didn't need anything for herself. Never had.

Needing meant disappointment.

Who wanted to live with that?

"Tell me why you were crying."

Driven by anger, at herself mostly, Tina said, "I'm not feminine."

"You're kidding, right?"

She gave him a quick—derisive, she hoped—glance. "Do I look like I'm kidding?"

"My gosh, Tina, you're more woman than any two females put together. You've got it all. Strength. Intelligence. Humor. Compassion. You nurture like Mother Teresa and still manage to look sexy as heck."

Just what she always wanted. To look sexy.

But beggars couldn't be choosers, could they? That's what her mother had always told her.

"Did it ever occur to you, Scott, that I might not always want to be so darned strong? That I might actually have a heart capable of falling in love? That I might want to be loved?" Of course it hadn't. How could it? It had never occurred to her, either. "I was thinking a while ago about the first time I saw you," she continued without giving him a chance to answer. "You stood there with your mother, just a kid, and yet all grown-up, too, a man protecting a woman that he cared a great deal about. There she was, with a body swollen and covered with bruises, and for a second there, watching you, I wanted to be her. Crazy, isn't it?" Once started, she couldn't seem to stop. "Just once, I'd like to be a woman that raises those protective instincts in a man. In you. Just you. But I'm not, you know? I've never been that type of woman. No, I'm the give-it-to-Tina-she'll-handle-it type. Even as a little girl. Did my father ever once, just once, watch out for me? Protect me? No. I was there to do his bidding. To push around. To be on the other end of his fist. Well, you know what?"

Tina stood up.

"I'm not going to be pushed around anymore. Here." She plopped the daughter he'd never touched in his lap, bottle and all. "She's yours. You feed her."

Before she could stop herself, go back and grab up the baby who'd already found a place in a life Tina felt she was only visiting, or worse, see Scott with his daughter in his arms for the first time, she marched out of the room, down the hall into her office, and locked the door.

She didn't come out for the rest of the night. Not when Scott knocked. Or begged. Not when Kennedy started to cry—though Tina listened for the sound to stop, and might have relented had that not happened. She didn't come out until Scott told her at seven the next morning that the police had called.

They'd found Kennedy's mother.

CHAPTER
∾ THIRTEEN ∾

Claire Reese had made a deal with the devil. Or rather, she'd fallen in love with him—a rich senator from her home state. She'd married him before she'd really gotten to know him. And had left him after the third time he'd beaten her, in spite of his threats. She'd gone straight to Strengthen Our Sisters, a New Jersey women's shelter, founded by Sandra Ramos back in the '80s.

Tina and Scott were both familiar with Sandra, having heard of her work from Tonya, who'd taken classes from her. Sandra had grown Strengthen Our Sisters to a 177-bed, seven-shelter organization complete with two thrift stores, a computer school, a day care and any number of other ventures.

With help from Sandra's people, Claire had found her own inner strength and sense of self-worth. Leaving most of her worldly goods behind with her ex-husband, she'd taken the small nest egg she'd managed to stash away a little at a time during her marriage and moved to Cincinnati, where she'd started a new life. A good life, culminating with Kennedy's conception, for which she'd spent most of her savings, according to the women the police had questioned. Though she'd only been in her late twenties, after her time with the senator, she was certain she didn't ever want to marry again. But she had wanted a family.

To stay under the radar, she'd taken a job at a day care that had benefits and free babysitting, and she'd lived very simply.

And then, shortly before the baby was born, the senator found her. Her pregnancy enraged him, because the baby wasn't his. He threatened her life. The baby's life. Her livelihood. His only offer for some kind of peace was if she went back to him.

To keep herself safe until she could give birth, Claire had agreed to move back, but not until after the baby was born. She planned to talk to him, to appeal to the good, caring man she knew resided beneath his anger issues. To the man she'd once loved.

She would agree to marry him again if he'd go through counseling, sign a prenuptial agreement that gave her every dime of his estate if he ever left counseling without doctor's orders.

And she wasn't taking Kennedy until she knew for certain that the baby would be safe.

She'd met the senator as agreed at her place on Wednesday. He'd come to collect her and Kennedy. And flown into a rage when she hadn't produced the baby. Another man's baby. There'd been a witness, a neighbor who'd heard the fight, but then had seen Claire get willingly into a Lincoln Town car with a very affluent-looking man.

Her body was found in the trunk of the senator's car, which had just been pulled from the Ohio River—with his body still at the wheel.

Claire had no next of kin. A couple of her friends, one in New Jersey and one in Ohio, offered to take Kennedy—at least until the state sorted out where the little girl was to go.

Scott, with his letter from Claire Reese granting him full custody, refused to part with Kennedy.

He hadn't put the baby down, except to change her and buckle her in her car seat while he drove, ever since Tina had come out of her office in the very early hours of the morning. Probably even before then, if she had to guess.

He looked good in baby.

Great, as a matter of fact.

Kennedy didn't seem too worse for wear, either, other than the unbalanced bulge where a smooth and puffy diaper should have been. But she was dry. Tina had checked.

"We need to talk," Scott told her as they left the police station just after nine on Saturday morning.

"The baby's stuff is at my place," she said, hunched in her leather jacket as they crossed the street to his car. "I can cook us some breakfast."

Was it only the night before that they'd eaten salads there together? And then done other things?

Seemed like years ago.

As did their easy camaraderie.

Scott frowned silently all the way out to her place. And barely spoke, except in gentle tones to Kennedy, through the baby's feeding and the breakfast that followed.

Tina sat across the table from him.

His silence was driving her crazy. "I thought you wanted to talk."

"I do," he said, his glance more uncertain than confident. "I'm just not sure where to start—or even what I think at the moment."

"That's understandable. We've just found out a woman we've never met is tragically dead. Her baby could very well be yours, a part of your life for the rest of your life. Your life might have just changed drastically. Irrevocably. I'm not sure what I think, either."

"Do me a favor?" he asked.

Of course she would. Anytime. Always. "What?"

"Hang out in limbo with me for a few days, a week tops, while we figure all this out?"

"Sure." And then, remembering the night before, asked, "What does that mean, exactly?"

"Kennedy stays here for the time being, at least until we know what's going on. I'm…there's no way I can take her to my place, be there alone with her."

Tina told herself not to push.

"Maybe you should have let one of those women take her."

"No. She's my daughter. I'll provide for her."

"How?"

"That's what I have to figure out."

Don't push. "I'll make a deal with you."

"What?"

"You stay here, too, and I'll keep her. But you have to help bathe her, feed her, everything."

The glint in his eye unsettled her all over again.

"And one other thing," she added.

"What?"

"You sleep in the spare bedroom."

He still didn't speak. And though he was watching her, she didn't have a clue what he was thinking.

"Well?"

"Well what?"

"Do we have a deal?"

"Do I have a choice?"

"Sure, you can call the state. Ask them for help. Or take her home. Or call any one of your lady friends, or—"

"We've got a deal, Tina. As if you didn't know that. There's no way I'm taking that baby away from you."

Tina ignored the warmth that flooded through her at his words. She couldn't afford to be warm.

"Fine," she told him. "You've got a week."

Or a year, if that's what he asked. It wasn't like she was going anywhere.

And her job over the next seven days, since she'd accepted it, was to find a way to keep her heart intact so that when Scott Harbor and his daughter moved on, she'd make it without them.

Tina couldn't get in her shower without thinking of Scott. Or in her bed, either. So, against her wishes, she thought about him everywhere she went over the next couple of days. And she went a lot. To the grocery store. The mall, which she hated. To work on Sunday afternoon. And to the gym—though she hadn't been in weeks.

As much as she could manage, she got out of the house. Away from the family that was using her space, but was not hers. The family that she loved as though it was her own.

Because she loved Scott Harbor. If there'd been any doubt Friday night when she'd lain in his arms, it was obliterated as she cooked with him, ate with him, watched his fingers fumble with diapers and a slippery little body lathered with soap, watched those fingers gently massage a tiny head, watched a pair of big blue eyes gaze up at him with innocent awe and trust.

Had Tina ever looked at her father that way?

She didn't think so. Walt Randolph wouldn't have been around at bath time. He might actually have to wash his hands. To do something besides bellow.

"She's a good baby," Tina said Monday night when the infant, freshly bathed and fed and smelling like a baby, gave one last shudder as she settled to sleep in her bassinet. They rolled it into Scott's room at night now. During the evening, though, they still kept it in the family room, kept the baby close.

"Unbelievably," Scott agreed.

"I've heard that a baby's demeanor is often attributed to the mother's emotions during pregnancy," Tina said, dropping sideways into her chair. "Claire Reese must have been feeling pretty peaceful. Happy even."

Over the past forty-eight hours Tina had thought of the woman a lot. Pretty much anytime she hadn't been thinking about Scott. Or Kennedy.

Settling back into a corner of the couch, his tie loosened and his jacket off, Scott laid his head back and stared up at the ceiling. "It was a pretty remarkable thing she did."

"Which one?" Tina asked. "Having the courage to leave someone who was threatening her? Daring to live her life, to reach for happiness by following through on her desire to have a baby? Trusting enough to open herself to friendships in spite of what she'd been through?"

"All of the above. But you know what's most remarkable?" Scott looked at her as he issued the challenge.

"Of course I do," she told him. "The woman was willing to give up the heart of her heart, to sacrifice everything for the safety of the child she loved."

Something neither of their mothers had been able to do.

"That little girl is going to grow up without her biological mother, and I don't make light of that," Scott said. "She'll always have a vital piece of herself missing. But she's also going to grow up knowing that she was completely, unconditionally loved. How many of us can say that?"

"And what, more than that, does any kid need?" Tina agreed. "I've been wishing for the past two days that I could have met her. You know, if only I'd been out front a few minutes earlier, seen her come up the walk…"

"She might not have left the baby if she'd been seen."

True. Very true.

As true as Tina's love for the man who'd given Kennedy's mother a chance at happiness.

CHAPTER
❧ FOURTEEN ❧

C laire's body was being shipped back to New Jersey, where a group of friends were holding a small service for her. The belongings she'd managed to accrue over the past year would be sold to pay for her burial. The little bit of savings she had left would go into a trust for Kennedy—that and a long letter they found in her diary for the little girl she'd brought into the world just a few short weeks before.

After consultation between state officials, and confirmation of his parentage from the fertility clinic, Scott was being awarded full custody of the baby. It was only Wednesday. Three days short of the week Tina had given him to figure out what he was going to do next.

And every single time she saw him, walking through her house, his hands on the steering wheel of the car as he drove them to work, changing the baby, or dozing on the couch, she loved him more. Wanted him more. One time in his arms had done nothing but open her eyes to a truth she'd long been denying, and given her a hunger that she feared would never be satisfied. At this rate she wasn't going to make it until Saturday without blowing a gasket.

But she knew better than to push him.

Taking Kennedy into his office on Wednesday afternoon, to greet him as he came in from a business lunch, Tina couldn't even meet Scott's eyes. His long legs made her want to lie with him. Seeing his eyes would have her confessing an undying love that would ruin everything between them.

As he took the baby from her, his arm brushed her breast. He didn't appear to notice. She felt the residual tingles all the way down to her groin. Kennedy, who'd just eaten and not yet fallen back to sleep, gazed up at him.

Tina couldn't take much more of that.

He has three more days, she reminded herself. *A little less than seventy-two hours.*

"Have you decided what you're going to do about her?" she asked on the heels of the reminder. *Don't push, Randolph.* "I mean, you're going to keep her, that seems pretty obvious."

Scott studied her over the baby's head. She'd pushed. Darn.

"Yeah, I guess I am."

"So you're ready to move home with her then? We could do it tonight. With both cars, it'd only take one trip."

"I didn't realize you were so eager to get rid of us."

The very real hurt in his tone had her backtracking and on another path before she could come up with a coherent thought. "Of course not! Never. Ever." She followed with, "Scott, you're the most important person in the world to me, you know that. And now Kennedy's right up there, too. Look at her. How could she not be? My home is always open to you. You know it."

"You mean that?"

Shocked by the doubt she read in his eyes, Tina stepped forward, regardless of the grease on her boots and the carpet on his office floor. "Of course."

"Even after Friday night?"

That damned night again. So much for them controlling the force before it controlled them.

"Yes."

"Then have a seat. I have a proposal to make to you."

He wanted her to keep Kennedy for him. That had to be it. And she'd have to say no. Because to do so would be enabling him to hide for the rest of his life.

Though, considering her own recent coming out, she wasn't sure that hiding was such a bad thing. Not if it allowed one to live life contentedly. Peacefully.

She sat. Slouched down with her hands across her stomach. Whatever was to come, she could take it.

With his sleeping daughter in his arms, Scott leaned back against his desk.

"I think we should get married."

Ha-ha. Good one, Randolph, she told herself as she heard her mind play a little joke on her. She watched Scott, hoping he was going to repeat whatever it was he'd just said and she'd missed.

"Say something."

Those couldn't be the words she'd missed.

"I don't know what to say."

"That's fair. I know this is completely out of the blue. All I'm asking is that you'll think about it. You, by your own admission, don't ever intend to have a relationship with anyone else."

"Because I want to live alone." Obviously her mind hadn't been playing tricks with her. Did he get that married meant family? Togetherness?

"And I…well, I…"

He what?

"You don't trust yourself to live with anyone else," she finished for him. "So how do you propose to be married and raise a daughter?"

The lost look in his eyes tore at her. But she couldn't make this one better for him. It was something he had to do for himself.

"I've got this crazy thought that we can make it legal for

Kennedy's sake and then continue on like we've done these past few days—at least for a while. A kind of trial period. See how it goes."

Now there was a proposal for you.

"We're already financially tied," he said. Which was true, though they had their own accounts, as well. "We both love this baby."

She wanted to be able to argue that—to tell him he could take his daughter and go.

She just wasn't sure how well she'd survive without the little girl—or hide the truth from him when he came to work.

"If anything happens to me, I want Kennedy to go to you and our marriage would ensure that."

So there was a fraction of sound reasoning in all of this.

"I'd keep my condo," he said. "Just in case."

"In case what?" In case he found a woman he wanted for a night?

"In case I screw up."

Eyes narrowed, she stared at him. "Screw up how?"

"In case, in the midst of all the togetherness, I forget myself and do something I'll regret."

He still didn't trust himself. And maybe he never would. Maybe that was the legacy his father had left him.

But she trusted him. And it occurred to Tina, in that moment, that loving wasn't about safety and security. It wasn't about peace. It was about being there—no matter what. It was about taking up the slack when those you loved couldn't do it for themselves.

Just as Scott had done for her when she'd been losing her father's business and couldn't imagine any other life but being in charge of her own garage. It hadn't been about the cars. Or about the money. It had been about being in control, about spending her days doing something that she loved and was good at, about not having to be beholden to any man ever again as long as she lived.

"I have enough trust for the both of us," she said aloud, only just understanding this for herself. Scott might not fall in love with her. When her trust in him gave him the ability to trust himself, he might leave her. He might open up to the possibility of finding the woman of his dreams and just do it, too.

But loving wasn't about saving yourself. It was about giving of self. With the understanding that you would be loved, too. Somehow. Some way. By someone.

"I would never have had a child, or contemplated marriage, on my own," he said.

He would have. Eventually. Because she wasn't willing to watch him while his life away. But they could get to that later. Ten years later, if it had to be.

No matter what, he'd still be her friend then. She knew that now.

"But neither can I walk away from this child."

"I know."

"So what do you say? Will you take a chance on me?"

"On one condition."

"What's that?"

"That you tell me, honestly, why me. It's because you know that I'm tough. That I can handle the abuse, right? Because I'm not vulnerable like other women. You know I wouldn't let it happen a second time. I'd take Kennedy and leave."

Laying the baby in the carrier Tina had brought in with her, Scott knelt at her feet.

"You asked for honesty," he said, taking her hand in his.

With what she knew was a nonchalant look on her face, Tina braced herself. "I did."

"Then prepare yourself."

"I have."

"I don't think so."

Get on with it already, she wanted to scream. Instead, determined to prove to him that she was tough, she continued to look him straight in the eye and not flinch. Or shake.

"Last Friday night was more than just an experiment," he said. "It was self-revelation, atonement, answer and relief all wrapped in one."

"I'm not following."

"My whole life, I've known that I had to protect the female sex against me," he said. "I was never, ever going to put myself in a position like my father is in, where I was too angry to control myself, and too weak to walk away. My dad is so in love with Mom he can't bear to leave her, even to protect her from himself."

"Your dad is a selfish man, Scott. You're nothing like him."

"You're prejudiced because you see the best in me, just like my mother does with my father."

Tina shook her head. "Your father has never made any sacrifices in his life, from everything I've seen. He's truly a weak man. His comforts, his security come first. With you it's just the opposite. Only when you're certain everyone else is satisfied do you look to satisfy yourself."

Scott slid onto the chair next to her, still holding her hand.

"You see," he finally said, "I didn't realize until Friday night quite how much my determination to protect womankind from me had me locked up."

So it was working. Thank God.

"The truth is, I'm in love with you, Tina. Head over heels, irrevocably in love with you. And I have been since I was a kid. That's why I could never feel anything but passing interest in other women, why I hunted Ronald down and would have killed him if he hadn't already been in jail...."

He had?

"It's why I've spent my life by your side, and kept my distance at the same time. Then, seeing you with Kennedy, nurturing my baby as you'd nurtured your brothers and sisters while we were growing up—it brought the feelings I'd hidden from myself so clearly into focus that I could no longer deny them. Or at least, while my mind was a little slow to catch on, my body recognized you."

He was talking jibberish. Nothing but jibberish.

"Scott." She had to stop him. "It's okay. You've obviously figured out I'm in love with you, but don't worry about it. I'll be fine. I always am. And I'll take care of Kennedy, marry you even, if you're sure that's what you want. Just don't lie to me about your feelings. It might seem kind now, but in the long run, honesty is always better. And you're right," she added while she had his attention, "I am tough and I would take Kennedy and go if you ever raised a hand to us, but I know you won't. Not because I'm blind. Or in love. But because I know you."

"What do you mean, I'm right?" he asked. The grin on his face unnerved her. She didn't like it. Or understand it, either, for that matter. "I'm not the one who said you were tough and would walk away. You said it for me. I don't believe for a second you'd walk away. You'd protect Kennedy, but you'd never be able to turn your back on me. Just like you didn't skip out on your parents when you had the chance."

Tonya had found a scholarship for Tina that would have allowed her to go to a fancy establishment back east for high school. A boarding school. Her—a mechanic. She'd have never fit in.

"I have another condition," she said now, all of his words playing tag with each other in her brain.

"What's that?" He still looked half-amused. She still didn't like it.

"If we're getting married, you're giving up the condo. I can't do this if you have one foot out the door."

"As long as you promise to leave the house until I get to a doctor if I ever get violent."

"That's a given."

He watched her for a long minute. "I don't like it, but I'll do it. But I have a condition, too."

How could he? She was the one sacrificing here. The one doing the favor.

"What?"

"I move out of the spare bedroom."

"Fine." There was always the couch.

"And into your bed. Starting tonight."

Tina's heart was pounding so hard it interrupted her breathing.

"And another thing," he added, as though he hadn't just started thunder rolling in the room. "From now on, I at least get a shot at doing my thinking for myself. And when I tell you that you're wrong about something, you take a shot at believing me."

"I'm too pushy."

"You care. You make things happen. It's one of the things I love most about you."

Staring at him, Tina was starting to fear that she was going to make a total fool of herself again.

"Yes," he said, his whole demeanor softening as he leaned toward her. "I do love you, my sweet best friend. So much I ache with it. These past few days, living in that house with you, not only showed me that I could possibly make this work, it also drove me crazy. I think I slept about two hours a night. The rest of the time I spent tossing and turning and listening for you to come open my door."

"Scott…" Tears welled in her eyes. Darn it, she couldn't do this.

"It's okay, babe," he said, and before she knew what was happening she was on his lap, cradled in his arms as he held her close, rocking her softly. "It's okay to have expectations. To ask for things for yourself. It's okay to cry."

"This whole love thing, it's not what it's cracked up to be if I'm going to be a walking rain shower from now on."

"Ah, Tina, I do love you."

"I don't know why."

"Because you're the other half of me, don't you get that?"

She did. But she hadn't thought he did. Or ever would.

"The one promise I can make you, other than the obvious ones of love and fidelity, is that I will try, for the rest of our days, to give you what you ask for anytime you ask for it."

Pulling back, trying to find some semblance of herself in the room, Tina said, "You'd better be careful there, buddy. That's a pretty serious commitment. One I'm sure most everyone in this world would tell you is a stupid one to make."

"That's because they don't know you," he said. "But I do. And what I know is that even after you learn to ask, you aren't going to ask if you don't really need. Besides, I figure you're due, after a lifetime of asking for nothing."

"Hey, Scott?"

"Yeah?"

"We're the bosses around here."

"Yeah."

"So we can give ourselves permission to pack up our kid and split."

"Yeah."

"Then, sir, I respectfully request that you take me home and love me until I don't have an ounce of energy left."

If all of her requests were granted as speedily and voraciously as that one was, Tina figured she was going to have the best life ever known to woman.

* * * * *

Dear Reader,

The preceding story, while fiction, is based on a lot of facts. The fact is, women are abused in America every single day. And the fact is, there are many thousands of men and women who work every day to help those who are abused. One such woman is Sandra Ramos. This is a woman who wanted to change the world. And so she did. There was no drama. No fanfare. She just acted. And her actions produced amazing results. As a single mother she shared her house with another woman from her church, because the woman needed a place to stay, Sandra had the room, and they could help each other out with child care. In less than two years she had twenty-one people living in that three-bedroom house. The state tried to evict Sandra. She was ordered to kick people out immediately. Instead, she went to court and, after many battles, ended up with a shelter for all her housemates. She had created the first shelter in North America for victims of domestic violence. Today, more than thirty-seven years later, Strengthen Our Sisters, the organization Sandra eventually founded, incorporates seven shelters, 177 beds, a day-care center, two thrift shops, a computer learning center, a computer repair shop and a car donation program. In her spare time, this sixty-seven-year-old woman teaches a college-accredited course at two universities, a course she designed, on the dynamics of domestic violence.

Please visit www.strengthenoursisters.org to learn more about Sandra and her remarkable work.

The fact is, women are abused every day. But many, many women do not seek help. Many don't know that help is available to them, or don't realize how accessible that help is in America today.

The fact is, thanks to Sandra Ramos and hundreds like her, there is help available, 24/7. There are answers. There is hope.

The fact is, there is someone who cares.

Elaine Taylor